Bitter Ground

The epic journey of a banished people

D.A. Galloway

Bitter Ground

Frontier Traveler Series - Book 3

First published by Continuous MILE 2023

To Rebecca and Rachel

It does not require many words to speak the truth.

~ Chief Joseph

Contents

Foreword

This is a story of indigenous tribes who resist giving up their ancestral lands. Unfortunately, it is one of many such events in the nineteenth century as European Americans moved westward and settled lands inhabited by natives for thousands of years. What makes this story remarkable is the resiliency and skill of a few hundred Nez Perce warriors as they shepherded families (and more than a thousand horses) across nearly twelve hundred miles of Idaho, Wyoming, and Montana territories. They did this while fending off the superior force of the army, which was charged with capturing these renegade tribes and forcing them onto a reservation.

Historians have documented this struggle for freedom based on first-hand accounts, letters, and government papers. I relied on these sources for writing this story. I commend the books and articles in the *Notes* to readers who would like to learn more about this conflict.

Bitter Ground is historical fiction. It describes a clash of cultures fueled by mistrust, language barriers, and the political realities of the post-Civil War era. This novel is also a love story: the love that people have for the land and for each other; the love of a way of life; the love between Graham and Makawee.

This is the third book in the Frontier Traveler series. In this saga, Graham and his Crow wife travel with the fleeing Nez Perce from June through October, 1877. While Graham and Makawee's family are fictional, *every other character in the story is based on a historical figure*. I depict events through the eyes of the protagonist and key leaders.

The illustration on the following page shows the flight of the Nez Perce. It also displays the routes taken by the battalions that engaged with the non-treaty tribes as they moved toward the British territories in present-day Canada. The refugees hoped to be granted asylum and settle in the same area as Sitting Bull's followers. The reader may find this map useful to track the combatants' location as the story unfolds.

Enjoy!

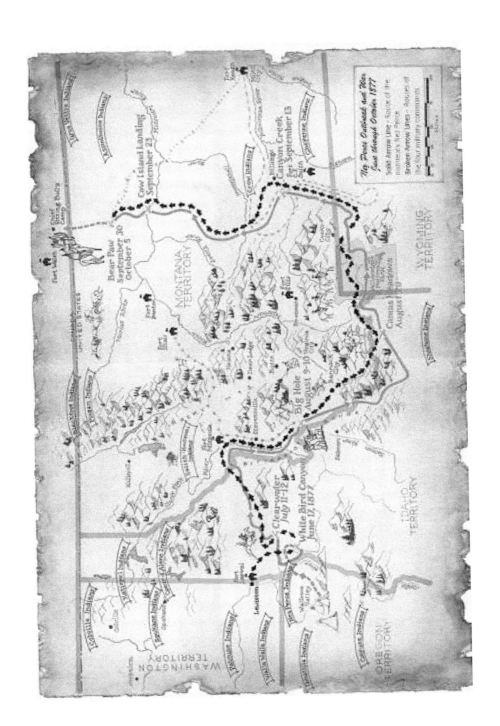

Prologue

3 July, 1863

Cannon smoke hung like a blanket on the fields west of Cemetery Ridge. General Winfield Scott Hancock stood behind a low rock wall and waited for the haze to dissipate. He trained his field glasses on the Confederate forces assembled several thousand yards away. Artillery from both sides had been pounding at the opposition for over an hour. It only recently stopped.

The sultry mid-afternoon air was silent except for the moans of wounded soldiers in hospital tents erected behind the Union line and the whimpers of injured horses. This was the calm before the storm of men preparing to advance across the field. But where would the enemy concentrate their forces?

Hancock removed his slouch hat. He wiped the sweat from his brow before placing it back on his head and looking to his left. Thousands of men in blue were tucked behind rock parapets or nestled in rifle pits, their muskets trained on the open field to the west. Near the end of the line on a small rise called Little Round Top, Sedgwick's VI Corps was waiting in reserve.

Scanning in the opposite direction, he saw a row of men snaking along the ridgeline. The line of soldiers gradually curved to the right several hundred yards away to form a line that guarded the north. He could see the backs of the men in the Eleventh Corp under General Howard as they faced the small town of Gettysburg.

"Lieutenant," Hancock said, turning to his adjutant.

"Yes, sir."

"Tell General Howard I wish to speak with him. Take my horse. And be quick about it. Those Rebs are itchin' for another fight."

"Yes, sir."

As the junior officer turned away, Hancock added another order.

"And tell Colonel Smyth to have someone put that animal out of its misery," the general said, pointing to a wheezing horse. "Lord knows we don't need a dying horse as a constant reminder of our casualties."

The lieutenant saluted and mounted the gray mare of his commanding officer. He stopped briefly to relay the message to Smyth before galloping north. A short time later, he returned with Oliver Otis Howard. The general dismounted. He walked to a cluster of trees, where Hancock was peering at the rebel brigades in the distant woods.

There was tension in the air, and it wasn't only because of the impending battle. Two days ago, Howard assumed command when General Reynolds was killed. Later that day, Hancock arrived at the battlefield with verbal orders from General Meade to take command, even though Howard was the senior officer. Howard and Hancock argued for hours until Meade showed up that night. He promptly pronounced Hancock commanding officer at Gettysburg.

Howard saluted with his left hand. His right arm was amputated a year earlier when he was wounded at the Battle of Fair Oaks. He insisted on returning to service and prided himself on being able to handle a field command with no limitations.

"You wanted to see me?"

"Yes. The Rebs are assembling for another assault. I'd like your opinion on where you believe they will hit us," he said, handing the binoculars to Howard.

Hancock knew his fellow officer was still chafing from his field demotion. He extended an olive branch by seeking the older man's counsel. Importantly, he needed Howard's men to hold their position. When the Rebel surge came, he didn't want to be flanked by a group skirting the ridge.

Howard raised the field glasses and scanned the enemy line. Thousands of gray and butternut-clad men cloistered in the trees. Some were casually drinking coffee. Some were smoking. Others appeared to be writing letters. Most were nervously rubbing the barrels of their muzzle-loaders. He looked behind him. Hundreds of small craters pocked the soft earth. Clods of dirt clung to scores of broken caissons and dead horses.

"They shelled the middle of our line. I'd say they tried to soften this position," Howard said, handing the field glasses back.

"I agree," Hancock said. He tilted his head back and looked at the canopy of several oak trees overhead. "If I were them, I'd tell my boys to meet at this copse. Everybody can see these tall trees, regardless of how much smoke is in the air."

"If I were leading those men, I'd tell them to pray. Most won't see the sun set tonight."

Hancock stroked his goatee. "You're right," he said pensively. "My dear friend Lew Armistead is down there. We haven't seen one another since we were in

2

California before the start of the war. I hope..." His voice trailed off as he bowed his head and stared at his boots.

Howard shifted his feet and struggled for something to say. He empathized with Hancock's mixed emotions about the pending battle. Most of their fellow officers knew someone who fought for the Confederacy. There were rumors Howard's West Point classmate from North Carolina, Dorsey Pender, had been severely wounded during yesterday's attack. No man wanted to kill his friend. Yet, that was a possibility with every engagement.

"You're a religious man. Much more so than I," Hancock said, looking into the older man's eyes. "A lot of men on both sides will lose their lives in the next few hours. Does your god have any words for a moment like this?"

"I have something in mind. Give me a minute."

Howard reached into the breast pocket of his coat and extracted a palm-sized copy of *The Soldier's Prayer Book*. He opened the worn brown cover and thumbed through the pages, stopping on a selection from Psalm 46. He cleared his throat before reading the first three verses aloud.

God is our refuge and strength, an ever-present help in trouble. Therefore we will not fear, though the earth give way and the mountains fall into the heart of the sea, though its waters roar and foam and the mountains quake with their surging.

"General, the Lord is with us," Howard said, closing the book and looking up.

"You don't think those boys in gray worship the same god?" Hancock asked, nodding toward the enemy.

"Of course. I meant ours is a just cause and..."

Hancock held up his hand. Prayer time was over. He returned to a fighting frame of mind. The commander peered through his field glasses at the enemy again.

"Will the Eleventh be able to stand against anything that comes your way?"

Howard flinched at this question. Two months ago, Howard's men were routed at Chancellorsville. Many of the Germans in the XI Corps fled when a large force under Stonewall Jackson flanked them. Instead of retreating in an orderly fashion, most men turned and fled. When word reached the newspapers about the humiliating defeat, the German-speaking immigrants were assigned the moniker "Flying Dutchmen."

"May I remind you, sir, that we held our own yesterday against Early's troops?" Howard said through clenched teeth.

Hancock lowered the binoculars but kept his gaze fixed on the enemy.

"If it looks like our line might break, I'm counting on you and Sedgwick to fill in the gaps. I'll send word if we need reinforcements. Dismissed."

Howard returned the *Prayer Book* to his breast pocket, saluted, and mounted his horse for the short ride back to his command. As his horse trotted along the ridge behind a line of blue, he heard a series of muffled sounds in the distance. He stopped and looked down the slope at the open field. Confederate brigade commanders were barking orders. Soldiers lined up at the edge of the woods at the base of Seminary Ridge nearly a mile away. A moment later, a series of parallel gray lines appeared from the shadows of the trees, muskets glinting in the hot afternoon sun.

The Confederate troops advanced into the fields and marched toward the Emmitsburg Road.

Boom! Boom!

Union batteries immediately opened fire. Solid shot and percussion from Napoleon guns whistled through the air, the munitions exploding on contact and hurling hundreds of pieces of shrapnel in all directions. The artillery was deafening.

General Howard urged his horse forward, following the rock wall through a small wooded area to Cemetery Hill. His aide-de-camp and younger brother, Major Charles Henry Howard, greeted him and took the reins of his horse.

"They're coming, Charles!" he shouted. "God only knows why Lee is sending his men up that hill. They will be slaughtered. The middle of the ridge will take the brunt of the attack. We need to hold our position and not allow the enemy to flank us. I'm going to stay mounted, so I have a view of the battlefield to our left. Tell Steinwehr to hold fire until the enemy is at a skirmish distance."

The major saluted and hurried down the line, seeking the German army officer.

Boom! Boom!

Howard's XI Corps started receiving sporadic musket fire from the rebel brigade on the outskirts of town. But Jubal Early's troops were not advancing. Their objective was to keep the Union forces on Cemetery Hill occupied while the major thrust came from the west. Confident that Steinwehr's troops would not be overrun, the one-armed general turned his attention to the confederate brigades as they advanced up the hill. They slowed momentarily to dismantle the rail fence bordering Emmitsburg Road and were partially hidden when they marched into a swale. When they emerged, they were staring straight into rifles and cannons aimed at their chests.

Thousands of men and boys walked in unison toward the crest of the hill, their heads held high. With muskets on their shoulders and regimental flags hanging limp in the humid air, they marched onward. It was an impressive sight of grandeur, discipline, and courage. And almost certain death.

The cannons on Little Round Top opened up and enfiladed large swaths of soldiers, who fell like wheat before the blade of a scythe. The gaps in the front lines were rapidly closed by those on either side or from men in the second row.

Boom! Boom!

The Union cannoneers switched from solid shot to canister. Thousands of pieces of shrapnel filled the air with each burst, mowing down entire sections of men. The constant roar of the artillery drowned the screams of the wounded. Smoke hugged the hillside and obscured the advancing enemy.

The men in blue crouched behind the rock wall didn't need to see their targets. They just aimed down the slope and fired, confident they would hit someone.

When the graycoats were within a hundred yards of the summit, someone let out a rebel yell. A thousand men unleashed a primal scream and ran uphill, their rage and fear fueled by adrenaline.

Boom! Boom!

Double canister shot decimated the lines. Arms, legs, and heads spiraled into the air. Most amputees were dead before they hit the ground. If they did not die from a severed limb, shrapnel riddled their torsos.

Miraculously, several hundred men made it to the copse of trees. A small wave of desperate humanity scrambled over the rock wall and engaged in furious hand-to-hand fighting. Both sides used pistols and sabers as they fought in close quarters in a small sector of Cemetery Ridge. For a moment, the impenetrable Union line was breached. But there were too many men in blue — too many reinforcements. In less than ten minutes, the Union troops killed or captured all who scaled the wall.

The surviving Confederate soldiers realized the attack failed. Slowly at first, then rapidly, they retreated down the slope. Many tripped over dropped weapons and bodies. Stopping only long enough to assist fallen comrades who cried for help, they made their way across the road and back into the safety of the trees.

A raucous cheer erupted from Hancock's men as they watched the enemy retreat. Everyone on the battlefield knew this was a significant victory for the Union — and a devastating defeat for Lee's forces.

Howard checked with Steinwehr and Smyth, who reported less than one hundred casualties among their men. The one-armed general ignored the sound of jubilant Union troops, some of whom were singing *Battle Hymn of the Republic.*

He sought a place to gather his thoughts alone. Sitting on a stone wall, he scanned the macabre scene. The acrid smell of gunpowder permeated the late afternoon air. Bodies were scattered across the fields as far as the eye could see, their limbs twisted at odd angles.

Working in pairs, stretcher bearers responded to moans and cries for help, then hurriedly carried the wounded to the field hospital. Unburied corpses from the previous two days of fighting lay bloated in the sun. Overhead, a kettle of vultures circled. The avian scavengers were waiting for the men with guns to leave so they could pick the flesh of the hapless victims.

Removing his hat and setting it on the wall, Howard placed his left hand inside his coat breast pocket and gripped the *Prayer Book*. He closed his eyes, tilted his head back, and thanked the Lord for protecting him. He petitioned God to care for the wounded and provide comfort to the families of the deceased — regardless of the color of their uniforms.

Perhaps this dreadful war will end soon, he thought.

Upon learning of the outcome of the battle, millions of Americans weary of incessant fighting became hopeful their loved ones would be home by the end of the year. But the war would rage for another twenty-one months, taking tens of thousands more lives.

A continent away, the ink had barely dried on an 1863 treaty between settlers and Nez Perce tribes in the Oregon and Idaho Territories. Its purpose was to prevent conflict between the groups by establishing clear boundaries. Instead, the controversial agreement was a harbinger of bloodshed in the northwest American territories fourteen years after the Battle of Gettysburg.

General Oliver Otis Howard would be the central military figure in this epic event where hundreds would suffer and die.

Tuekakas sat by the fire with his arms crossed. Old Chief Joseph, as the whites called the Nez Perce chief, returned to his ancestral home in the Wallowa Valley. His dark eyes reflected the flickering flames. Anger filled his chest as he recalled the conditions of the most recent treaty.

Government representatives met with Nez Perce tribal leaders at a council called by the governor of Washington Territory. The treaty proposed that all Nez Perce move to a reservation near Lapwai in north central Idaho. In exchange for moving to this location, each family would receive a small allotment of land and become farmers like most of their white neighbors. The payment for their land would be individual plots near Lapwai.

Tuekakas and several Nez Perce leaders strenuously objected to this agreement. Their grievances were ignored, largely because the officials incorrectly identified one man as the head chief and spokesperson of all Nez Perce.

Many called *Hallalhotsoot* "Chief Lawyer" because of his eloquence in speaking English. He was a young teen when Lewis and Clark's Corps of Discovery team visited his village on the Clearwater River in 1805. His tribe assisted the starving and nearly frozen explorers, almost certainly saving them from death. Since that first encounter with whites, he became deeply interested in their culture. He converted to Christianity when H.H. Spalding established a mission in Lapwai in 1849.

Chief Lawyer favored the terms of the treaty, perhaps because his tribe's allotment was on land where his people already lived. The government officials welcomed negotiating with a man who not only spoke and understood their language, but was also agreeable. Hallalhotsoot was the first man to sign the document, which designated him as "Head Chief Nez Perce Nation." When he encouraged those attending to sign, the majority complied. One by one, they formed a line and came forward.

Other than Chief Lawyer, none of the Nez Perce present at the signing ceremony could read or write English. The recording secretary asked each person to state his name as he approached the table. The official recorded what he heard phonetically. Then he handed the quill to the man, who placed an "X" after his name.

UTE-SIN-MALE-E-CUM (X)
HA-HARCH-TUESTA (X)
TIP-ULANIA-TIMECCA (X)
ES-COATUM (X)
IP-SHE-NE-WISH-KIN (X)

WEPTAS-JUMP-KI (X)

...

The ceremony continued until fifty-one men signed the treaty.

A small group who had not joined the queue huddled in the back of the room after everyone took a seat. Tuekakas was speaking in a low voice to his sons and four other tribal chiefs.

"Excuse me, gentlemen," Superintendent of Indian Affairs Calvin Hale said to the loitering men, "Won't you come forward and join your brothers in fixing your seals to our treaty?"

The interpreter repeated Hale's question.

Tuekakas turned to face the front of the room. His eyes narrowed as he pointed at the officials seated behind the table. He spoke in his native tongue interspersed with Chinook jargon phrases.

"You are asking us to give up our *illahie* [land] and be paid for our loss with a portion you have stolen. You cannot purchase what is not for sale. It belongs to our ancestors."

"But Chief Lawyer has signed the treaty along with fifty Nez Perce leaders. Almost all your people see the wisdom of this arrangement."

"Hallalhotsoot does not have the authority to speak for all Nez Perce. We are independent tribes with our own leaders. Each tribe decides what is best for its people. *Wake mahkook* [No deal]."

Calvin Hale shrugged his shoulders.

"Well, this is unfortunate. We have a binding agreement between the US government and the Nez Perce Nation," he said, holding up the document. "Perhaps you will reconsider your decision and come back tomorrow to sign."

"It is a treaty that steals from others."

Everyone in the room heard the bitterness in Old Joseph's voice. Before the interpreter could finish translating, the chief and his sons exited the clapboard building with the others. The dissidents quickly mounted their horses and galloped away.

Hale turned to the military officers seated behind him and sighed.

"Unfortunately, we have two groups — those who signed, and a few tribes of non-treaty Nez Perce. Let's hope the army doesn't have to enforce this agreement. It could get ugly."

Days later, the injustice of the treaty lingered in the mind of Tuekakas. It seeped into his consciousness like the smell of smoke penetrated a blanket. He slept fitfully since the council at Lapwai. The more he thought about what the white men orchestrated in this treaty, the angrier he became. The chief looked at his sons sitting by the fire and wondered what their world would be like when he passed away.

Heinmot Tooyalakekt, or Young Joseph, was his eldest son. At twenty-three, he was tall and had a round face. He resembled his mother and shared her disposition. Joseph was bright, thoughtful, and patient. These qualities would bode well for him when he became chief of this Nez Perce band.

His brother *Ollokot* was four years younger. He was handsome and featured an angular face. He was more compulsive and assertive than his older sibling. Ollokot was also charismatic. Even as a teen, older men were attracted to him. They often invited him to join their hunting parties.

"I have given the treaty much thought," Tuekakas said. "You were in the room during the council. We cannot allow the white man to steal the land of our ancestors. That is why I and a few others did not sign. They cannot trick us into signing a legal agreement that sells the souls of our loved ones and forces the *Niimíipuu* into a sedentary lifestyle."

The chief looked at his sons, who listened intently to their father.

"Tomorrow, we will place poles in rock pillars along the borders of our land. White men, *soyapu,* are not the only ones who can mark boundaries. If they want to give away land to others, let them choose an area outside of our ancestral ground. We will not yield. We will not move."

Young Joseph and Ollokot nodded.

"Eight years ago, this treaty guaranteed we could remain in the Wallowa Valley," he said, holding a copy of the 1855 treaty in front of him. "Now they pretend this never happened. So be it."

Tuekakas stood. He tore his copy of the previous treaty into strips and tossed it into the fire.

He picked up a small book, ran his fingers over the dark leather cover, and admired the gilt lettering.

"This is *Matthewnim Taaiskt,* The Gospel According to Matthew, given to me by missionary Spalding many years ago. I was going to gift it to Heinmot Tooyalakekt before I entered the spirit world."

He sighed and shook his head. "If this is how Christians treat one another, I do not want my sons to read these words."

Tuekakas opened the book. The chief angrily ripped chunks of yellowing pages from the binding and tossed them into the fire until the book was empty. The flames grew higher, then rapidly diminished after the paper burned. He pitched the leather cover into the fire and watched as it shriveled and charred.

In less than a minute, a good faith treaty and a book of faith were destroyed.

And the nascent resistance movement of non-treaty Nez Perce was forged.

Chapter One
Hell Mend Ye

14 June, 1876

The morning sun was peeking over the mountains as Alexander Findley stood on the porch of his cabin holding a cup of coffee. He pulled the collar of his shirt around his neck to fend off the chilly air. He just finished a hearty breakfast of venison with eggs his wife gathered from the henhouse.

The six Findley children were still sleeping, but he planned to wake the oldest boy to help plant their extensive garden along the Wallowa River. Eleven-year-old Amos assisted his father with many farm chores. Alexander smiled when he thought about the boy who was at the awkward age between boyhood and teenager.

Findley flipped the tin cup upside down and banged it on top of the railing to remove the residual coffee grounds. He opened the door, set the cup on the kitchen table, and donned a coat and hat before stepping back outside. As he walked across the pasture toward the small barn, he sensed something was wrong. Six horses would normally nicker and trot toward him in anticipation of being fed. But this morning, only two greeted him.

He whistled and called out to the missing horses, shielding his eyes from the low rays of the sun as he scanned his property in all directions. The farmer walked the split-rail fence line. He noticed the top rails in one section had slipped out of place. The ends of two rough-hewn logs were stuck in the mud. Findley lifted and placed them into position.

"Alex!" a rider shouted as he approached the fence. "Guid mornin. Are ya' ready to get after the plantin'?"

Wells McNall was one of Findley's neighbors. He staked a claim several miles upstream. The Scottish immigrant lived alone and kept to himself. Findley wasn't sure if this was by choice or whether his irascible nature discouraged others from being neighborly. The two men partnered on seasonal tasks. Farming on the frontier was hard work. Both men recognized the value of having someone they could call on when the need arose.

"Did you see any horses on your way here?" Findley asked.

"Naw. Why?"

"I'm missing four of 'em. Don't know if they got out or something else happened to them."

"Didja gander down by the burn?"

"They're not at the river. I put 'em inside the fence last night."

McNall's eyes narrowed as he looked down from his saddle at Findley. "More 'n likely one of those thievin' red devils stole 'em."

"Now, now, Wells. Let's not get ahead of ourselves. We've been on this land for almost six years. None of Chief Joseph's people would steal from us."

"You give those Indians too much credit. They wander 'round like a bunch that don't know where they belong. How can they raise crops and breed horses if they dinna stay in one place?" McNall spat tobacco juice on the ground, wiped residual brown liquid from his lower lip, and tugged on his salt and pepper beard. "Their young bucks prob'ly took 'em last night."

"Well, regardless, I need to find them. Let me tell the missus we'll be gone for a while. I'm gonna bring Amos along. You can grab a cup of coffee while we saddle up."

Fifteen minutes later, the group headed downstream. They rode for six miles when they came upon a clearing near the river. Ashes from a fire were smoldering. Five deer were hanging in trees by their hind legs. Piles of entrails lay on the ground. A crude wickiup made from deadfall and branches leaned against a large ponderosa pine. The soft earth was pocked with hoofprints.

"Nez Perce hunting camp," Findley said, placing both hands on the pommel.

"They sure 'nuf be usin' your horses to chase deer," McNall said. "Let's wait here 'til they come back. We'll catch 'em red-handed and give 'em a skelping."

Findley sighed and dismounted. He doubted the hunting party had anything to do with his lost horses. But he didn't argue with his neighbor.

"When they return, we'll ask about my horses. Perhaps they've seen them."

"Humph," McNall grunted as he swung his leg over the saddle and stepped down from his horse.

They were in the camp for less than twenty minutes when they heard hoofbeats in the distance. McNall pulled a revolver out of his holster and checked the chamber to make sure it was loaded.

"Wells, take it easy," Findley said.

"They stole your horses. Their cattle been eatin' me grass. It's high time they know we ain't gonna look the other way."

A Nez Perce man rode into the clearing. He was leading a mule fitted with a travois that held the carcass of a mule deer.

"Speak o' the Devil!" McNall said.

"We only need to ask some questions," Findley said, putting a hand on his neighbor's shoulder.

"*Kla-how'-ya!*" Wilhautyah said, raising his hand in greeting before dismounting.

Findley knew the hunter. Wind Blowing, as he was called in English, was a member of Chief Joseph's band. Unlike McNall, Alexander Findley always got along with his Nez Perce neighbors, who set up a seasonal camp across the Wallowa river after spending the winter in the canyons. Findley's family visited the camp of Chief Joseph many times. He found the tribal leader and most of his followers affable and welcoming. Amos befriended Red Feather, Wind Blowing's son. The two boys, who were close in age, played games and practiced bow and arrow shooting skills during the summer months.

Shortly after moving to the valley, some white settlers learned a little of the *Niimíipuu* language spoken by the Nez Perce. Most picked up Chinook Jargon, which used simplified grammar, body language, and sign language to communicate. Chinook Jargon was a *lingua franca*, a unifying language, developed by natives, trappers, and traders in the Pacific Northwest to bridge the communication barrier.

"*Kla-how'-ya!* You remember my son, Amos," Findley said, placing a hand on the skinny boy's shoulder. "And Mr. McNall?"

Wind Blowing nodded.

"I see you've had a successful hunt." Findley observed, using sign language and pointing at the carcasses. "*Kah mowitch?*" ["Where are the deer?"]

Wind Blowing signed his hunting group located a herd a few miles downstream in a thickly wooded area.

"Ask him where's he's hidin' your horses," McNall said in a low voice, leaning close to Findley.

"Stay calm," Findley said, as he flashed a stern look at his neighbor.

"Keep me heid? These sleekit redskins stole yer horses!" McNall said.

Findley ignored his ill-tempered neighbor and turned back to the Nez Perce hunter.

"*Nanitch kiuatan,*" ["Search for horses"] Findley said, signing that he was trying to find four plow horses. Had he seen them?

"*Wake,*" Wind Blowing said, shaking his head.

Findley signed. He asked Wind Blowing to inform him if the lost horses showed up.

"He's a chancer!" McNall said. "Ye can tell by his shifty een. I'm gonna keek aboot."

The surly Scotsman drew his pistol and strode toward one of the deer carcasses hanging from a tree branch. As he walked past Wind Blowing, the Nez Perce man grabbed his wrist. The gun slipped from McNall's grip and fell onto the grass.

"Lemme go, you minger!"

McNall took a swing at the Nez Perce with his free hand. Wind Blowing blocked the fist and pushed the white man backward. McNall charged into the Indian, hitting him in the chest and knocking him down.

The white man outweighed Wind Blowing by twenty pounds, but the warrior was strong and wiry. He flexed his hips and rolled over on top of McNall, pinning him to the ground by his arms.

"Alex!" McNall shouted, "Shoot the fecker!"

The sudden turn of events horrified Findley.

"Amos! Get my rifle!" he said to his son, who was staring wide-eyed at the two men wrestling in the mud. The boy sprinted to his father's horse and yanked the Winchester from its scabbard.

Mammook kopet! ["Stop it!"] Findley yelled at Wind Blowing.

The Nez Perce Indian looked up and released the struggling man's wrists. Wind Blowing stood and backed away.

Anger flushed McNall's face as he scrambled to his feet.

"Wake kapswalla mamook kiuatan," ["I did not steal horses"] Wind Blowing said.

Findley chambered a round and was holding the Winchester in front of him.

"What's he sayin?" NcNall asked his neighbor.

"He doesn't know where my horses are. C'mon, let's keep looking," Findley said, lowering the rifle as he turned away.

"Dinna be telling yer havers!" McNall shouted. He swiped the hat from his head, tossed it on the ground, and drew a knife from his belt. The Scotsman lunged toward the Indian a second time.

Wind Blowing stepped to the side and used the white man's momentum against him, tripping McNall as they both fell to the ground. The men rolled several times before the warrior again ended on top. He squeezed McNall's right wrist and thumped it against the ground until the knife fell from his opponent's grip. Wind Blowing pinned McNall's forearm to the ground with his knee, scooped up the knife, and pushed it toward the aggressor's chest. McNall grabbed the warrior's wrist with his free hand in a desperate attempt to prevent being stabbed.

"Shoot him, noo!" McNall implored.

Findley raised the Winchester and aimed at the back of the Indian's head a few feet away. McNall was squirming underneath Wind Blowing while the Indian tried to plunge the knife into the Scotsman's chest.

"Pa, don't!" Amos said. "He's the father of Red Feather! Please!"

Findley hesitated. What should he do?

"Kill the sleekit bastart!" screamed McNall, his face red from the exertion of trying to defend himself. "I'm feart!"

"No!" Amos pleaded, tugging at his father's arm.

Findley heard his son's plea. He looked at his neighbor writhing under the knife-wielding warrior and made a split-second decision. Closing his eyes, he pulled the trigger.

Bang!

The .44 caliber centerfire cartridge entered the base of the warrior's skull, spraying bits of brain and bone on the face of Wells McNall when it exited. Wind Blowing fell limp on top of the white man.

McNall pushed the dead man away and got to his knees. He was sweating profusely. He inhaled and exhaled in rapid succession, then wiped blood from his face with his coat sleeve. Rising slowly to his feet, the Scotsman stumbled across the wet grass and retrieved his hat and pistol. He slipped the revolver into his holster and walked over to Findley, who was staring at the Winchester that took the life of the Nez Perce warrior.

"What have I done?" Findley asked no one in particular.

Amos placed his hands on his cheeks. Tears welled in his eyes. He was visibly shaken by the brutal murder.

"Pa, why did you... did you shoot him?"

McNall spat on the chest of the dead man and hitched up his trousers.

"Hell mend ye."

This comment snapped Findley out of his state of shock.

"Hell mend ye?" Findley asked incredulously, glaring at his neighbor. "What do you mean, 'It serves you right?'"

"Och aye. I'm gled the sleekit bastart got kilt."

Findley handed the rifle to Amos. He turned to face McNall and punched him with a hard right to the jaw. The Scotsman stumbled backward and nearly fell.

"Shite! Why'd ye wallup me gob?" he yelled, touching his split lower lip.

"You forced me to kill a man because you're an idiot! You provoked this fight. Your temper got us into this mess."

"Get aff ur high hoarse!" McNall said. "Ah dinna pull the trigger. Ye did!"

"Get outta here!" Findley said. He snatched the Winchester from a trembling Amos and pointed the rifle at his neighbor.

"Yer aff yer heid!"

"Go!" Findley ordered.

McNall raised his hands and slowly backed away, keeping any eye on Findley. The Scotsman untied his horse, mounted, and was soon out of sight.

Findley kneeled by the body of Wind Blowing, placed the butt of the rifle on the ground, and gripped the barrel with both hands. He shook his head and closed the eyes of the warrior.

"Amos, come here," he said after a minute.

The boy obliged, wiping tears from his cheeks.

"Yes, Pa?"

"Go home. Tell your mother what happened. Everyone stay inside. Bolt the front door."

"You're not coming?"

"I'm staying here. When the other hunters come back, I'll be here. They deserve to know how Wind Blowing was killed."

"But... but, Pa, what if they...?"

"Go home, Amos. I'll follow you after I talk to our Indian friends," Findley said, standing and hugging his son. "Everything will be fine."

The boy nodded, walked to his horse, and mounted.

Findley forced a smile and waved as his oldest son rode upstream. When Amos disappeared into the woods, Findley sat heavily, propped his elbows on his knees, and placed his head in his hands. Everything happened so quickly. He had no intention of killing a man over allegedly stealing horses. That damned fool McNall caused this tragedy with his hot head and prejudice against the Nez Perce. But the Scotsman was right about one thing. It was Findley who pulled the trigger.

As the farmer sat by the body of Wilhautyah waiting for his companions to return to the camp, he debated whether to flee the scene of the crime. He had second thoughts about how the Nez Perce hunters would react upon seeing their dead friend.

One thing was certain — this would definitely change the relationship between the homesteaders along the Wallowa River and their Nez Perce neighbors. There was an uneasy tension between the white settlers and the Indians for years. There was an unwritten agreement to tolerate one another. This murder would seed mistrust between the groups and possibly lead to retaliatory killings.

Findley hung his head and prayed.

With the death of Wind Blowing, a tiny tempest was brewing in the Wallowa Valley — one that would devolve into the winds of war in less than a year.

"Will the *soyapu* Findley face justice?" Ollokot asked his older brother Chief Joseph.

The two men were sitting by a fire, discussing Wilhautyah's death at the hunting camp three days earlier.

"Time will tell."

"We both know the answer," Ollokot said, looking at his sibling. "Every time something like this happens, the white man is found innocent. But if an Indian does anything against a white man, our people are beaten or imprisoned — regardless of the situation."

Joseph knew his brother was right. He spent hours talking with government and military officials over the past decade, trying to reason with them. He promised his father the *Niimíipuu* would never give up the land of their ancestors. Government officials were taking an increasingly harder stance toward any tribes who would not sign the latest treaty. With each passing year, more settlers were arriving in the Wallowa Valley, staking claims on land they did not have a right to own. More invaders meant a greater potential for disagreements between the homesteaders and the nomadic non-treaty tribes.

The killing of Wilhautyah came as a surprise to no one in Chief Joseph's band. It was only a matter of time before the white man would force his will upon the Nez Perce.

Chief Joseph thought about a drawing at the courthouse in the Grande Ronde Valley. He and Ollokot met with officials at the building the previous year to discuss the unsigned 1863 treaty. When he inquired about the meaning of the blindfolded woman, the court clerk explained the symbolism of Lady Justice. The blindfold over her eyes represented the notion of impartiality. Scales signified the weight of evidence for and against an issue should be weighed before issuing a ruling. The sword represented authority. It meant justice would be administered quickly and in its final manner.

The chief was initially encouraged when he saw Lady Justice. After all, his argument for being able to stay in the Wallowa Valley had always been primarily a legal rather than a moral one. How could the government force him to abide by an agreement that neither he nor his father signed? If Lady Justice was impartial and weighed the evidence, surely a ruling would be made in favor of the Nez Perce who refused to sign.

But the officials and military officers were relentless. At the conclusion of each meeting, it became clear the scales of justice were slowly tipping in favor of the government. The authorities claimed all Nez Perce should accept the government's generous offer to move onto a reservation, where they could be "protected" from the white settlers who had stolen the tribes' ancestral land.

Impartiality? Perhaps in disputes between *soyapu*. But the concept didn't apply to the non-treaty Nez Perce.

Joseph picked up a stick and poked the fire, sending a thin column of embers into the night sky.

"Wilhautyah's widow demands Findley pay a price for taking her husband's life," he said. "What do we tell her?"

Ollokot shook his head. If a member of their band or another tribe had murdered Wind Blowing, the answer would be obvious. Vengeance would be swift and certain. The man would either be ostracized or killed. But when a white man was charged with murdering an Indian, the blindfold on Lady Justice only covered one eye.

"We tell the truth. We can do nothing," Ollokot said wistfully.

"Agreed. The government might use our blood brother's death at the hands of a white man as proof that we cannot live with them. It would give them another reason to force our people onto a land with narrow boundaries."

"Some of our young men will want revenge," Ollokot said, staring at the fire.

Joseph nodded. "I will speak to them. We need to remain calm. I will continue to advise peace."

The brothers sat for a moment in silence. Both men were in a pensive mood. Surely there was an alternative path to accepting whatever decisions came from the white man.

"If only the other Nez Perce tribes had not signed the agreement, we would have a united front to resist the government's policies," Ollokot said.

"It would make no difference," Joseph said. "I heard the Sioux are being chased by the army in the buffalo hunting grounds. They have twenty times more warriors than we do. If they are defeated, what hope do we have?"

Ollokot sighed. "Our way of life is slowly disappearing, my brother."

"All the more reason to enjoy the time we have remaining on this land. This could be our final summer in this valley — and our last winter in the canyons."

Ollokot stood and turned to leave. He stopped, drew a knife from his belt, and faced his older brother. Reflections of yellow flames danced on the shiny blade as he extended his arm toward the fire.

"We have tried diplomacy for many years. Perhaps it is time for a different strategy to protect our homeland."

The warrior returned the weapon to its sheath and disappeared into the darkness.

Chapter Two
Volatile Valley

30 October, 1876

G raham reined his horse at the top of the hill and gaped at the bucolic scene below. Makawee, who was leading a mule behind her horse, rode up beside her husband. The couple fitted the pack animal with a travois to carry their meager household belongings from eastern Montana. Nahkash, their four-year-old daughter, scrambled from the pole sledge where she was sitting and ran ahead to her mother.

"*Naha!*" ["Mommy!"] the little girl called out. "Look at the pretty *bilichké!*" [lake!]

Makawee smiled. Her daughter often spoke by combining English and her mother's native Crow tongue. She wasn't concerned. The girl would learn to distinguish between the two languages within a few years.

A long, finger-shaped lake lay at the base of the ridge. The water from the alpine ribbon lake fed a river that wandered north through an immense valley of grass. Seven miles in the distance, the edge of the Wallowa Valley disappeared into a network of deep canyons. On the horizon, snow-capped peaks stood like sentries guarding the pristine prairie.

Makawee slid from her horse and knelt beside Nahkash. She placed her arm around the girl's waist and pointed to a cluster of tepees assembled at the north end of the lake. It was comforting to see a collection of pole lodges after six weeks on a rugged trail. They reached their destination.

"That is our new home," Makawee said, brushing a lock of black hair from her daughter's eyes.

"Are you sure it's the camp of Chief Joseph?" Graham asked. He took field glasses from his saddlebag and scanned the temporary settlement along the lake shore.

Makawee held out her hand, and Graham gave her the binoculars.

"It's a Nez Perce village," she said after a moment. "I can tell by the arrangement of the poles and the markings on the tepees. I do not know if they are followers of Joseph and his brother Ollokot."

"Well, it's a magnificent land. I can understand why people would want to settle here," Graham said, accepting the field glasses from his wife. "Let's keep going. I'd like to get to the village before Dakkoótee wakes."

Graham strapped the nine-month-old boy into a cradleboard which he carried on his back. The orphaned child became a part of their family four months earlier.

Graham and Rides Alone, Makawee's brother, served as army scouts. They discovered the infant after the victorious Sioux and Cheyenne left the valley following the Battle of the Little Bighorn. The baby's Sioux mother was killed during the seventh cavalry's attack on the Indian village. An army officer mistook Rides Alone for an enemy scout and shot Graham's friend while he was rescuing the child. Before he died, the Crow warrior told Graham to take the baby boy. When he returned home and presented the infant to Makawee, she was overjoyed. They agreed to name him Dakkoótee, the Crow word for Sioux.

Makawee picked up Nahkash and hoisted her onto the horse, then mounted behind her daughter.

"You can ride with me," she said, reaching around the girl's waist to retrieve the reins.

Graham nudged his horse down the hill, turning to check on his wife, who led the mule. They were careful to descend the steep slope at an angle so the pack animal could handle the heavy pole sledge. After descending for twenty minutes, they reached the undulating foothills.

As the horses settled into a rhythm toward the distant village, Graham hoped they had found a place to settle down. He considered how a baby boy was the reason his family made this arduous trek to the Wallowa Valley.

Makawee explained to her father, Chief Long Horse, that she and Graham would take care of the orphan until an Indian agent could find a home for the child. She soon changed her mind. When she informed her father they would adopt the child, Long Horse became indignant. He lost both sons, Little Wolf and Rides Alone, to the Sioux, hated enemy of the Crow. The chief forced Makawee into a terrible choice. She must give up the baby — or she and Graham could not live in his village.

Upon hearing this news, Graham moved his family. He intended to settle near Bozeman, but his wife pleaded with him to leave Crow country. Makawee wanted to escape the constant fighting among rival tribes, as well as the war on the plains between the army and non-treaty Indians. She convinced him to move to Idaho Territory, home of the Nez Perce, longtime allies of the Crow. The couple became friends with Ollokot, the younger brother of Chief Joseph, during a meeting inside Yellowstone Park several years earlier. Makawee was convinced Ollokot, and by extension Joseph, would welcome them.

Now, as they made their way along the lake shore toward the tepee village, Graham was anxious. What if the Nez Perce did not welcome them? Where would they turn? Would they have to stake a claim like the other whites who homesteaded on the traditional lands of the natives? If so, their family members would be part of the growing list of valley invaders.

Looking to his right as they rode toward the village, Graham could see settlers erected barns and log homes along the river that bisected the valley. These permanent structures were visible reminders white men planned to make this valley their home. The buildings stood in stark contrast to the temporary pole lodges used by the Nez Perce for hundreds of years as part of their nomadic lifestyle.

When they approached within several hundred yards of the tepee village, a young boy playing along the lake became startled when he saw the strangers on horseback. He ran toward the camp and shouted. A group of women gathered at the edge of the village. Most were empty-handed, but some held knives, and a few were armed with rifles. Small children peeked from behind their mothers' legs.

"*Ta'c meeywi,*" ["Good morning"] a middle-aged woman said to Graham and Makawee as they reined the horses.

"*Kla-how'-ya!*" Makawee replied, switching to Chinook jargon. She hoped the woman knew basic pidgin trade language. Makawee had limited knowledge of the *Niimíipuu* language.

"*Nah cheechako,*" ["Hello stranger"] the woman replied in jargon.

Graham carefully dismounted so as not to waken the baby on his back. He walked to Makawee, who handed Nahkash to him before sliding from her horse. Makawee talked with the woman in jargon coupled with sign language. She was relieved they could communicate.

The Nez Perce woman introduced herself as Heyoom Yoyikt, the older wife of Chief Joseph. She turned to the knife-wielding woman standing beside her.

"Wetatonmi," she said, touching the woman's shoulder. She signed the woman was Ollokot's wife.

"Ollokot! *Tillikum,*" ["friend"] Makawee said excitedly.

Makawee signed she was part of the Crow tribe and met Ollokot across the Bitterroot Mountains in the land of hot water. They were hoping to stay with Chief Joseph's people for a while. Could she speak with Joseph or Ollokot?

Heyoom Yoyikt explained the men were on a hunting trip. They would return late in the afternoon. She opened her arms, stepped to the side, and invited Makawee's family to visit her home.

Two young boys took the reins of the equines and led them toward an area where a dozen horses were picketed. An immense herd of ponies dotted the grassland between the river and the foothills.

Makawee took Nahkash by the hand. The family walked with their hosts into the village. The other women followed, chatting and pointing to the small child on Graham's back, excited to have visitors from a faraway place.

When the entourage reached the chief's tepee, Wetatonmi opened the flap. After the guests entered, Heyoom Yoykit held out her arm and flicked her wrist at the gawking women. A person need not speak the language to know she was shooing the curious villagers away.

Graham's family sat on blankets and let their eyes adjust to the dim light. A cooking fire was burning near the center, with a pot suspended between two forked branches. The lodge resembled those of the Crow, but with subtle differences. Crow tepees used twenty or more poles built on a four-pole base. These poles were several feet longer than those of other tribes. For this reason, the Crow lodges appeared larger than the tepees of most tribes, since their poles rose several feet higher above the apex. The home of Heyoom Yoyikt used a three-pole tripod as the base against which they laid the others. She leaned sixteen poles on the tripod to make her tilted conical lodge.

Two girls entered the lodge. Heyoom Yoyikt introduced her twelve-year-old daughter, Hophop Onmi. The host cupped one hand behind her ear, placed the other palm down, and let her fingers dangle. By moving her fingers back and forth, she signed the girl's English name was Sound of Running Feet.

The second girl was seated beside Wetatonmi. It surprised Graham and Makawee when the woman spoke broken English.

"This my daughter, Sara. She is eleven."

"Pleased to meet you," Graham said, removing his hat.

Dakkoótee started crying, and Makawee removed the boy from the cradleboard. She held him against her shoulder and patted his back.

"I need to feed him," she said, placing a hand in front of her open mouth.

"Hungry? *Hiyu muckamuck,*" ["Plenty to eat"] Wetatonmi said, pointing to the pot suspended over the fire. She looked at her sister-in-law, who approved with a nod.

The hungry travelers enjoyed the hearty venison stew. Graham whispered to Makawee between bites what a blessing it was to be welcomed in the camp. The girls soon were playing hand games and showing glass beads to Nahkash.

During the meal, a woman in her early twenties entered the lodge. She picked up a bowl, ladled some stew, and sat.

When no one offered to introduce the visitor, Makawee took the initiative. "I am Makawee. This is Graham."

The woman looked up, then said something unintelligible while signing.

Wetatonmi interpreted for the guests. "Her name Springtime. Second wife of Chief Joseph."

Makawee smiled, nodded, and continued to feed Dakkoótee the dark brown broth.

Heyoom Yoyikt, who was in her late forties, slurped stew from a bowl and ignored the younger woman.

Graham was taken aback. He knew it was customary for some tribal leaders to have multiple wives. He told himself not to be judgmental. But he wondered about the family dynamics in a polygamous relationship. There was obvious tension between the two women who shared a husband.

Hophop Onmi and Sara led Nahkash outside after the meal. Dakkoótee fell asleep, and Makawee lay the baby on a blanket. She combined signing and Chinook jargon to talk with the wives of Joseph and Ollokot.

Graham understood parts of their "conversation" but realized he would have to sharpen his language skills. He told Makawee to ask Heyoom Yoyikt for permission to set up the family tent. When the chief's wife nodded, Graham rose and walked to the grassy area where the young boys picketed their horses and mule.

Graham retrieved a canvas tent, wood poles, and a cluster of stakes from the travois. He scouted for a place to pitch the tent and found a suitable location just outside the camp. After setting up the support poles and placing the center ridge pole between these, he pulled the canvas over the poles and worked his way around the base, pushing stakes through loops and pulling the cover taut. As Graham turned to retrieve the rest of their belongings, he was surprised an audience gathered to watch. The women pointed to the canvas structure and whispered to one another.

When Graham walked toward the group to explain what he was doing, they backed away. He could see fear in their eyes but was puzzled. Why were they afraid of a tent?

The sound of hooves pounding the prairie caused the women to turn around. A large group of warriors on horseback approached the camp. The leader reined his horse twenty feet from Graham. His fellow riders stopped behind him and watched as a tall man with braided sidelocks and a pompadour dismounted.

~ *Chief Joseph*

"*Kla-how'-ya, cheechako. Wawa Niimíipuu?*" the leader asked, extending his arms with his palms facing upward.

"*Wake,*" Graham said, nodding his head.

He guessed the man wanted to know if he spoke Nez Perce. Graham wished someone with multilingual skills from the village would show up.

The leader looked behind Graham and lifted his chin, nodding at the white A-frame canvas tent.

"Soldier house?"

It occurred to Graham why the women were afraid.

His tent was a soldier's house — a temporary shelter used by the army. Why would a bearded white man have a tent unless he was a part of the army? The women's reaction was an indicator the relationship between this band of Nez Perce and the government was strained. Graham tried to find the right jargon and sign language to ease their concerns.

"*Wake.* No soldier. *Tillikum!*" Graham said, hoping to convey he was a friend, not an enemy.

A young man urged his horse toward the front of the group and dismounted.

~ *Ollokot*

"*Kla-how'-ya,* Graham Davidson!" the man said, extending his hand.

Graham sighed in relief at the sight of his old friend. "Ollokot! *Kahta maika?*" ["How are you?"] Graham replied, reciting a common jargon phrase he remembered. They grabbed each other by their forearms.

The young Nez Perce warrior turned toward the man who first dismounted and addressed him as *tyee* [chief]. Ollokot introduced his older brother as Heinmot Tooyalakekt, or Joseph.

Makawee pushed her way through the gaggle of spectators. She joined Graham by his side and greeted Ollokot, who was pleased to see his Crow friend. After Makawee acknowledged Joseph, Ollokot spoke with his brother and explained how he came to know the Crow woman and her *soyapu* husband. He recounted the story of meeting Graham and Makawee in the Land of Burning Ground several years earlier. Ollokot reminded his brother the Crow people under Chief Long Horse renewed their commitment to remain allied with the Nez Perce.

Joseph smiled. This was good news, indeed. Few stood beside the non-treaty Nez Perce as they fought for their legal right to remain on ancestral lands. He recognized the political advantage of having the daughter of a Crow chief as a visitor. Joseph assured Makawee her family was welcome in his camp for as long as they wished to stay.

Later that evening, after they shared a meal, Graham pulled a long-stemmed briar pipe from his pocket. He packed the bowl with kinnikinnick and lit the tobacco and willow bark mixture. Graham wanted to show his appreciation to Joseph and Ollokot for welcoming his family into their camp. After taking several puffs to kindle the embers, he handed the pipe to their host.

Joseph drew air through the bowl, inhaled the pungent smoke, and held it a moment before exhaling. He gave a satisfying nod to Graham, then passed the pipe to Ollokot. Others took a turn inhaling smoke as they passed the pipe around the circle. It surprised the chief when Makawee took part in the ritual. She noticed the chief's raised eyebrow and explained through jargon and signing that Crow women were permitted to join a tribe's Tobacco Society.

After everyone smoked the pipe, Joseph announced a messenger sent word of another meeting with white leaders at Lapwai. He unfolded a paper and handed it to Graham. Makawee pressed against her husband's side. They leaned forward in the firelight to read the letter.

A commission comprising David Howell Jerome, esq., of Michigan; Brig. Gen. Oliver Otis Howard, U. S. A.; Maj. Henry Clay Wood, A. A. G., U. S. A.; William Stickney, esq., of Washington, and Amos Chafee Barstow, esq., of Rhode Island, has been appointed by the Secretary of the Interior, to inquire into the status and claims of the so-called non-treaty Nez Percés, and to effect a permanent settlement of the difficulties existing between them and settlers.

You are hereby formally requested to meet with these gentlemen at Fort Lapwai on 8 November to take part in these discussions.

— Regards, John B. Monteith. United States Indian Agent, Nez Percé Indians.

Graham returned the paper to Joseph, who laid it in front of him. The chief signed an interpreter delivered the note several days earlier. The messenger read the words aloud in the *Niimíipuu* language and asked if Joseph understood.

"I understand these words," Joseph said in jargon. "But I am skeptical this will yield anything for our people. It would be helpful to have someone to listen to the words of the white men at this meeting and tell me the words *behind* the words."

Makawee interpreted for Graham.

"Is he asking if we are willing to attend the meeting?" Graham asked.

"Yes. It's the least we can do since he has welcomed us to his village."

"But we just arrived. The meeting is only a week from now."

Makawee repeated this for Joseph, who showed he understood.

"We will go when we are ready, not when the white leaders demand," Joseph said in jargon.

After Makawee interpreted the chief's words, she whispered, "We need to honor this request."

Graham turned to the chief and nodded.

"*Ah-ha*. We will go."

Oliver Otis Howard dipped his hand into the wash basin and splashed cool water on his face. He used a towel to wipe his eyes and dry his beard. The general stared at his reflection in the mirror.

The man looking back at him aged visibly since the end of the war. His wavy hair turned gray, as had most of his beard. Wrinkles formed under his lower eyelids, and Crow's feet creased the outer corners of his blue eyes. He looked older than a man who just celebrated his forty-sixth birthday. What would cause a man to prematurely age?

Perhaps it was the stressful years spent in Washington heading the Freedman's Bureau after the war. Howard enjoyed leading a group that was charged with integrating former slaves into society and politics as part of reconstruction. He set up a system that allowed freed people to work on former plantation land under terms negotiated by the Bureau with white land owners. The Bureau was also responsible for the legal affairs of the freedmen. It was satisfying work. But his political enemies constantly sought to undermine his endeavors.

~ Oliver Howard

His efforts to establish a school of higher learning for blacks took a lot of energy. Howard was among ten members who met in Washington to discuss plans for an educational institution for former slaves. The groups' efforts were rewarded when the school was chartered in 1867. Not only did the Board of Trustees vote to name the university after Howard, they also elected him president of the school. It was a humbling experience, but it added to his responsibilities leading the Freedman's Bureau.

Those years in Washington were a blur of activity. When the Bureau was abolished in 1874, Howard had to find another way to support his growing family.

When he rejoined the active-duty military, they gave him orders to assume command of the Department of the Columbia. This immense area of the frontier included Washington, Oregon, and Idaho Territory. It also included Alaska, which had been purchased from Russia seven years earlier.

The long journey from Washington to the Pacific Northwest was an adventure for Howard's five youngest children who traveled with him. But it was arduous for his wife, Lizzie. The one-armed general worried about his family and what life would be like as they settled into the tiny seaport outpost of Portland.

Now, as Howard stood in the washroom of the rectory next to the Presbyterian Church in Lapwai, he seethed. An esteemed group that included bankers and prominent businessmen awaited his return to the church, where they were discussing the Nez Perce tribes.

John Monteith, Indian Agent for the Nez Perce, assured Howard a messenger delivered his request to parley with Joseph. The five-man negotiating team arrived on November 7. Nearly one week later, Chief Joseph and the other non-treaty invitees were still absent.

Howard always treated Joseph with respect, and considered the chief reasonable in his demands. The general listened to the Nez Perce leader's arguments for keeping his ancestral lands in the Wallowa Valley for the past two years. Joseph and Ollokot made a compelling legal case for being allowed to maintain their nomadic lifestyle.

But the political climate was changing. Washington wanted a resolution to this lingering "Indian problem" in Idaho Territory. The group's mission took on more urgency, as the last of the Sioux had either been rounded up or taken refuge in the British Territories north of the forty-ninth parallel.

It was time to push the remaining tribes onto reservations — for their own protection. How could the United States achieve its full potential if Americans could not settle the west? Howard agreed with prominent politicians that Europeans were preordained to expand across North America. John O'Sullivan coined a phrase for this belief thirty years earlier. The newspaper editor called it *manifest destiny.*

While waiting for Joseph and members of the other non-treaty bands to arrive, the commission members heard from the treaty bands living on the Clearwater River near Lapwai. It was heartening to hear from Christian Nez Perce, who spoke of their life as farmers. Not only had these Indians converted to Christianity, they became educated, were learning to speak English, and wore the modern clothes of the white man.

The conclusion reached by military and government officials was obvious. Those who signed the treaty and accepted a new way of life became 'civilized.' These people were qualified to be called Americans, unlike their brethren who had not signed the 1863 document.

A light rain began as Howard left the pastor's home and made the short walk to the spartan clapboard building that was the Presbyterian church. A short whitewashed picket fence encircled the church, which featured an open bell tower. A simple cross jutted from the apex of the steeple. Several tepees were erected around the perimeter. These temporary lodges were juxtaposed with the rectory and several wooden outbuildings.

Forty Nez Perce who signed the treaty and agreed to live on the reservation were milling about among the wooden pews. The general took a seat at a table on a raised platform at the front of the sanctuary with his fellow commissioners.

The chairman of the group, David Jerome, called the meeting to order.

"We ask Agent Monteith to provide an update on the unfortunate incident in the Wallowa Valley earlier this summer."

John B. Monteith was appointed as Indian Agent for the Nez Perce five years earlier. The slender man in his late thirties had a triangular face, a full beard, and a receding hairline. He removed reading glasses from a vest pocket and slipped them on before consulting his notes.

He reported Alexander Findley, the settler who shot and killed Wind Blowing, spoke with Joseph and displayed contrition. When the chief approached the ranking officer at Fort Lapwai and demanded they arrest Findley, the major deferred to the courts for a decision. Months later, no legal action had been taken against the killer of Wind Blowing. There were no indictments or punishment of the man who admitted pulling the trigger that ended a warrior's life. The non-treaty Indians insisted Findley be tried for the murder of their brother.

"Tell me, Agent Monteith," Howard said, "When you spoke with the non-treaty leaders, did you sense they were prepared to go to war over this issue?"

"No, general. The non-treaties beat drums for several days when no action was taken against Findley. They made a show by stripping to their breechcloths and encircling some settler's cabins on horseback. But they are not seeking vengeance."

"It sure seemed like a provocation to me," Major Henry Wood said. Howard's adjutant crossed his arms on his chest. "Ask any white man who looked out at those painted Indians from a boarded-up window. Those settlers were scared. That's why I sent a detachment to the Wallowa Valley. I wanted a military presence to quell any uprising."

"But they didn't attack anyone," Monteith countered. "They went home after a few days. General, to answer your question, they seek justice. Joseph told me there was no law that permitted murder — whether it is the white man's laws or Indian laws. I believe they want equality with whites."

"If these renegades comply with the legal agreement of 1863 and move onto a reservation, it would be a good faith response," William Stickney said. "That action might yield a more favorable outcome in these kinds of disputes. They do not make a convincing argument."

Monteith pulled another paper from a stack in the front pew.

"These are notes from my meeting with Joseph in late summer. He said something you should hear."

"Go ahead," Howard said, leaning back in his chair.

"Chief Joseph claimed if an Indian killed a white man, an all-white jury would indict the Indian, try him, find him guilty, and hang him. He gave several examples of where this happened over the last decade."

"And?" David Jerome asked. "If they judged the man guilty, the punishment is death by hanging. What's his point?"

The Indian agent cleared his throat before looking at his notes.

"Joseph argued when a white man kills an Indian, the tribe should have the right to try the alleged killer by Indian laws."

A few seconds after the interpreter translated these words, the Nez Perce in the room murmured and whispered to one another. Many nodded in agreement at the words of Chief Joseph.

"Agent Monteith!" Howard said, loud enough to be heard over the din of voices in the room. "A word in private, please."

John Monteith approached the table at the front.

"Yes, sir?"

"Are you purposely trying to undermine our group's work?"

"Why, no. Certainly not. I agree wholeheartedly with the commission's aim of moving the non-treaties onto a reservation for the good of everyone in the region. I was only..."

"You were stirring a pot that should be left alone. If Chief Joseph wants to make an argument, we need to hear directly from him. What we *don't* need is someone planting seeds of doubt among Indians who are contented with their new way of life. Do I make myself clear?"

Monteith glanced at the others at the table on either side of Howard. All were nodding their heads. The agent swallowed hard.

"Yes, sir. You are clear."

"Good. You may be seated."

Jerome asked for quiet in the room.

"Thank you for the report, Mr. Monteith. Does anyone else have something to say?"

"Yes. Mr. Jerome, I'd like to add that everyone knows there can't be two sets of laws, or it ain't a country," Amos Barstow said. "Chief Joseph can't lecture us about the law when he won't abide by a legal agreement. He isn't even willing to talk to us."

The door swung open at the back of the church and a sergeant poked his head inside.

"Excuse me, gentlemen. Joseph and the other Nez Perce have arrived."

Everyone rose and began walking toward the exit.

"Stop! Please sit." Howard said, motioning with his left hand.

The congregants obliged and shuffled back into the pews.

"Chief Joseph has been disrespectful. He made us wait for six days. We will not go out to greet him. Sergeant, take our interpreter with you. Let the chief know his group can join us inside."

Howard was sending a message. The rebellious chief embarrassed Howard with his insolence and cavalier attitude toward this meeting. The general glanced at his fellow commissioners. He could see they approved.

Outside, Joseph and Ollokot led a contingent of sixty people. The brothers reined their horses several hundred feet from the church. They decorated their horses with beads and ribbons. Feathers adorned their long hair. Most wore buckskin jackets, white blouses, bead necklaces, and leggings. Graham and Makawee were near the back of the group. They left Nahkash and Dakkoótee in the care of Hophop Onmi and Sarah.

The sergeant donned a kepi and walked to the chief on horseback. He relayed Howard's message through the interpreter.

Joseph stared at the church for a moment before replying.

"Tell Cut Arm we meet out here."

The interpreter translated.

Everyone in Lapwai — both military and civilian — knew the Nez Perce referred to Oliver Otis Howard as "Cut Arm" since he first arrived in the territory two years earlier. The general didn't take offense to this nickname. Indians commonly had several names, many of which were derived from events or physical attributes. Howard thought it was an appropriate name for a man whose right arm was amputated.

"Chief, it's raining. It would be more comfortable for everyone if we met inside," the sergeant said. The interpreter translated.

Joseph hesitated. He disliked churches for what they represented. They were symbolic of the change the white man was imposing on his people. He told government officials years ago he wanted no churches in the Wallowa Valley because people would end up arguing over which God to worship. There was only one Creator. He had seen Protestants and Catholics get angry discussing deities, as if more than one existed.

"Cut Arm invites you *inside*," the sergeant said, sensing the chief's reticence.

Joseph looked at Ollokot, who nodded. The brothers dismounted, and soon others stepped down from their horses. Everyone filed into the building, their wet shoes squeaking on the wood floor.

The commissioners remained seated on the dais at the front. After the newcomers crowded into the church and stood by the windows along the sides, Howard spoke.

"Please, gentlemen. Have a seat. We're glad you could finally make it." Howard pointed to the first rows of pews.

Joseph looked at the Indians seated in the pews at the front of the church. These Nez Perce sported short hair and dressed in western-style clothing. Some wore suits. All looked the part of Indians who were 'civilized.' The chief motioned for his group to sit in the back.

He was also sending a message. His people would not be integrated with those who signed the treaty.

Makawee and Graham sat in the last pew just inside the door. They hoped not to be noticed.

"Mr. Barstow, now that our guests have arrived, would you lead us in a word of prayer to open the formal part of this meeting? After all, we are in the house of the Lord."

Amos Barstow asked everyone to rise. "Of course. Many of you know The Lord's Prayer. Feel free to say it in your own language."

A cacophonous mixture of English and Nez Perce filled the room as white men and treaty Nez Perce simultaneously recited the familiar passage from the New Testament.

Our Father, which art in heaven, Hallowed be thy Name. Thy Kingdom come. Thy will be done in earth, As it is in heaven. Give us this day our daily bread. And forgive us our trespasses, As we forgive them that trespass against us. And lead us not into temptation, But deliver us from evil. For thine is the kingdom, The power, and the glory, For ever and ever. Amen.

Numin Pist kem in ues eis nuespa. Taz He imene wanikt paraquaneitag uag Pahatauyaitag. Taz He imin Miogatoit painag. Taz He imene nekt patuignaitag kino uetespa. kam kus Einuespa ituigneitanig. Taksain hipt neozenim nuna. kapsisuit nas usunanim. kag kus nun nuaunaisig kakimem inaskapsisuiyutenig. ka wet met nez nikukum kapsisuitg. metu kapsieuitkinig nez nakettem. Nunag kus.

These biblical words triggered a powerful memory within Joseph. Thirteen years earlier, he and Ollokot watched as their father, Tuekakas, shredded a translated copy of the Gospel of Matthew and tossed it into a fire. The old chief felt betrayed when officials asked him to sign the 1863 treaty that gave their ancestral lands to the government. On that evening, Tuekakas renounced his ties to Christianity and vowed to never surrender to the white trespassers.

Now, standing in this Presbyterian church and hearing scriptures for the first time in more than a decade, Young Joseph was reminded of his father's words on his deathbed. He pleaded with his twenty-three year old son to "never sell the bones of your father and mother." These words strengthened Joseph's resolve to keep his homeland even as strangers staked claims and built homes on land they did not own.

"Chief Joseph," David Jerome said when everyone was seated. "You know General Howard. Let me introduce myself and the other members of this commission."

Having done this, Jerome explained the President created the commission. They wished the Nez Perce could live peacefully. The Great Father, Jerome explained, was deeply concerned about the welfare of the Nez Perce. He wanted to improve their lives by placing them under the protection of the US government.

Joseph listened to the interpreter. He was circumspect of this opening statement. Nothing the government did in the last decade supported this goal, in his mind. He remained silent.

"Can you tell us who traveled with you?" Jerome asked.

The chief stood. Most were his followers, he explained. But prominent men from the non-treaty bands of White Bird, Toohoolhoolzote, Husishusis Kute, and Looking Glass had also been asked by their leaders to attend.

"Major Wood, why are the other non-treaty chiefs not present? Did you extend an invitation?" Howard asked his adjutant.

"Yes, sir. It seems they are deferring to Joseph as their spokesperson."

"Hmmm. Well, at least his band is the largest. Perhaps when we convince him to follow the terms of the treaty, the others will follow."

Howard scanned the room and noticed a white man sitting in the back pew. "You, sir," Howard asked, lifting his chin. "What's your name?"

Everyone turned and looked at Graham.

Shit! Graham thought. *It's impossible for a tall bearded white man to remain inconspicuous.* He sighed, squeezed Makawee's hand, and rose to introduce himself.

"I'm Graham Davidson. This is my wife Makawee. We recently moved to the Wallowa Valley. We're here at the request of Chief Joseph to serve as interpreters."

"Are you missionaries?" Barstow asked.

"No. We're just looking for a place to call home."

"Homesteaders?"

"Yes. You could say that."

Wrinkles creased Howard's forehead. He looked skeptical.

Joseph motioned for Makawee and Graham to come forward and sit in the pew with him and Ollokot. Now that the chief introduced the couple as interpreters, they needed to perform that duty.

"Can you communicate with the chief?" Graham whispered to his wife as they edged their way along the pew toward the aisle.

"Using jargon," she said in a low voice. "They have an interpreter. Joseph wants me to make sure they're honest."

"Thank you for the introductions, Chief Joseph," Jerome said. "You have the floor. Please provide your opening remarks."

Joseph patiently laid out his claim that his band — and the other four bands represented in the room — did not sign the 1863 treaty. Therefore, they were not legally obligated to that agreement. He made this same argument many times to many people during the past decade.

Jerome dismissed this assertion. He explained that according to the white man's law, the majority determined the outcome in any dispute. It did not matter that Joseph's father did not sign the document. Those who did not sign were in the minority.

"What would you have our people do?" Joseph asked.

"Why, move onto a reservation, of course. Abandon your roaming lifestyle. Settle down. Learn how to cultivate the earth and take care of yourselves. The government only wants to protect you. This is an excellent arrangement for your people," Jerome said.

When the interpreter repeated these words in the Nez Perce language, Joseph turned and looked at Makawee.

"Yaka kumtux kliminawhit," she whispered.

Graham leaned over and asked his wife what she said to the chief.

"I told him the man is a liar."

Graham gulped. She was right. The Nez Perce, like every other native people, were being compelled to radically change their way of life. They would be forced onto a reservation and stripped of their dignity. Either they could accept the inevitable, or they would be physically relocated to a place where traditions, culture, and language died a slow death over generations. He wished there was an alternative to this bleak future. But history would prove Makawee correct. The government implemented policies to "civilize" the natives and to satisfy the country's desire to settle the west.

Joseph's eyes narrowed.

"Mamook solleks!" ["You make me angry!"]

The chief's voice grew louder as he spoke.

"Do you think we cannot care for ourselves? Do you think we want to settle down and *mamook comb illahee* [plow the land]? Before the white man, there were no boundaries. You cannot divide something that has no boundaries. We have been on this land for thousands of years before the white man came. I will not permit the white man to dig up the earth where my ancestors are buried. We have the right to this land. If you disregard our rights, you should be filled with fear."

Joseph sat and waited for the interpreter to finish. When the chief's last words were translated, Howard's face reddened. He stood so rapidly his chair tipped over behind him.

"Are you threatening the US government?"

Joseph glared at the one-armed general behind the table, but said nothing.

Ollokot, who had been listening to his older brother, realized he needed to do something to de-escalate the fiery rhetoric. He stood and spoke for a minute. The interpreter converted his words to English.

"My brother is upset that our concerns are not being heard. We seek a legal, peaceful solution. We desire an acknowledgement of our rights to the land, which we owned long before the white man arrived. We are tired from our journey and will counsel tonight."

Before Ollokot's words were translated, Chief Joseph rose and walked down the aisle toward the exit. His followers emptied the pews.

"Heinmot Tooyalakekt!" Howard shouted over the noise of moccasins shuffling on the wood floor. The Indian leader's behavior peeved him, so he got Joseph's attention by addressing him by his Nez Perce name. The general used this tactic when he wanted to get one of his children's attention or to scold them. He would call them by their first, middle, and last name.

Joseph stopped at the door and pivoted toward the front of the room. The others stepped aside so their leader could see the commissioners.

"Hear this. You have until tomorrow at noon to decide whether you will accept our generous offer to leave the Wallowa Valley and relocate to the reservation. If we do not hear from you, we will adjourn. And we will have no choice but to recommend the treaty is *enforced.*"

Chief Joseph and General Oliver Otis Howard looked at one another across the sanctuary while the translator repeated these words. In that instant, both men sensed a seismic change in their relationship. They enjoyed congenial meetings and fruitful discussions over the past two years. But this was a seminal moment. They were on a steep slope, sliding from friendship toward enmity.

Howard picked up the fallen chair, sat heavily, and placed his good arm on the table. He waited for a reply that never came.

Joseph clenched his jaw, turned, and walked out the door into a soaking rain. Graham and Makawee joined sixty non-treaty Nez Perce as the group walked in silence to their horses.

It would be a cold, wet ride back to camp.

Chapter Three

Ultimatum

12 May, 1877

Yellow Wolf stepped from the bank and walked to the center of the stream. He stopped and gazed at the night sky. Gray clouds drifted across a waning crescent moon.

"Bring the light closer," he said.

Graham hesitated, then followed the young man into knee-deep water, holding a lantern in front of him. The cold water made him gasp. Smooth rocks on the creek bottom made walking tricky. He gingerly made his way to Yellow Wolf.

"What are we fishing for?" he asked.

"Hesu."

Graham furrowed his brow. "What's the name in English?"

"Eels. Hopefully, they have reached this part of their journey. It is early in the season."

Graham's thoughts drifted to the origin of their nascent friendship. The twenty-one-year-old was the nephew of Chief Joseph. His mother was Chief Joseph's sister, Swan Lighting on Water.

The young man resolved to learn English. Graham spent countless hours during the dark winter months helping his friend learn a new language. Yellow Wolf reciprocated by teaching him *Niimíipuu*. By spring, both could carry a conversation in his friend's language, though they supplemented with Chinook jargon words or phrases.

The more they immersed in the other person's language, the more they learned about one another. Graham talked about the Land of Burning Ground, a place Yellow Wolf visited only once, when he accompanied a hunting group to buffalo country.

~ Yellow Wolf

Yellow Wolf told stories that had been passed along for generations. He spoke of his love for the land and taught Graham about *wey-ya-kin,* or spiritual beings. The Nez Perce believe these spirits are mediators between humans and the invisible world of spiritual power. Yellow Wolf explained how he received a *wey-ya-kin.* When he was twelve, he was mentored by an elder for several months before going to a sacred place known as The Heart of the Monster on a vision quest. After fasting for three days, a pale canine visited and spoke to him. He was known as Yellow Wolf from that day.

"The wolf is a powerful spirit. I am fortunate to have this animal as my guide," he said proudly to Graham.

Graham marveled at the similarity of the Crow beliefs to those of the Nez Perce. The young man's story compelled Graham to share the story of his own vision quest, where he acquired something the Crow call *baaxpée,* or sacred power. He told of his Crow friend who gave him a necklace with a bear claw and an eagle carved from stone. Graham showed Yellow Wolf his necklace and announced he was also known as Eagle Bear.

He talked about his trip to the Dragon's Mouth Spring. He met Makawee at this sacred thermal feature, and she tossed the placenta of Nahkash into the roaring spring. Of course, he omitted the fact he traveled through time on his spiritual journey. Makawee was the only person in the nineteenth century who knew about his time travel.

Their shared vision quest experiences created a strong bond. The Nez Perce warrior received a *wey-ya-kin.* The *soyapu* (white man) acquired *baaxpée.*

"Do you have the basket?" Yellow Wolf asked.

The question snapped Graham back to the present.

"Uh, yes. Right here."

Graham slung a woven basket over his shoulder with a rope. He pulled the reed container over his head and followed Yellow Wolf, who was making his way upstream. They stopped at the base of a small cascade. Water gurgled as it tumbled over rocks, flowing toward the Snake River three miles distant.

"Are these freshwater eels?" Graham asked, handing Yellow Wolf the lantern.

"No. They go to the ocean and return — like salmon."

Yellow Wolf lowered the lantern and bent forward until he was inches from the surface. He squinted into the dark water.

"Ah-ha!" he said, handing the lantern back to Graham, who slipped the wire loop over his wrist and gripped the handles of the basket.

The Indian punched his arm into the cold water. His hand emerged with a slender, brown, foot-long fish. It squirmed and wriggled as Yellow Wolf held it under the light and showed it to his partner.

Graham saw freshwater eels in the creeks of his native Pennsylvania. The creature Yellow Wolf caught looked different. Unlike an eel, this fish had a boneless body and a jawless sucking disc mouth. Although Graham was no expert in ichthyology, he suspected this was a lamprey. He would not call into question what his friend called these ancient fish. They were catching eels.

Yellow Wolf tossed the slender fish into the basket and went back to work. They filled the basket with three dozen eels in less than thirty minutes. Graham handed the lantern to his fishing partner, who was grinning broadly.

"These will make an enjoyable meal. Let's return to camp. I can already taste them!"

Each man took a handle of the basket. They walked a half-mile on a well-worn path, using the lantern to light the way on this cloudy evening. Yellow Wolf told his friend the Nez Perce called the place where Chief Joseph established camp Hesuutin. It translated as "place of the eels."

Heyoom Yoyikt and Wetatonmi greeted the fishermen and peered into their basket. Their eyes glistened as they sorted through the squirming mass of eels, selecting eight of the fattest ones. The women took the slender fish behind the tepee to behead and gut them.

Yellow Wolf and Graham carried the basket from lodge to lodge. They offered four to each resident. Everyone was grateful for the gift. The first eels of the season were always the best tasting.

When the men came back to Chief Joseph's lodge, the eels were cooking over the fire. The women cut the fish into two-inch segments and placed the pieces on flat iron skewers suspended between two rocks. They also cut chunks of beef and placed these on skewers. Tonight they were having surf 'n turf.

Makawee and Nahkash joined Graham by the fire. Dakkoótee fell asleep in the tepee. The family watched the fire spit and sizzle each time a drop of fish oil fell into the embers.

Heyoom Yoyikt used two sticks to place a pot under the fish skewers. She centered it so the kettle caught the drips.

Yellow Wolf explained what his aunt was doing.

"Eel fat is burned in lamps. It is also good medicine. Everyone cooking eels tonight will save the oil for these purposes. It takes many eels to create enough oil to fill a small bottle. We use every part of what the Creator has given us."

Graham appreciated how the Nez Perce valued natural resources more than the white man. It was the same story with bison on the plains. Indians used every part of the animal. White men slaughtered the great bovids by the thousands to harvest a tongue or a skull, then left the carcasses to rot.

After the meal, Ollokot lit and passed a pipe. When it started around the circle a second time, he pulled his knees toward his chest and stared into the fire.

"I have bad news, my brother. We received a message from Cut Arm. He requests all non-treaty leaders meet at Fort Lapwai. The purpose of the meeting is to plan our move onto the reservation."

Chief Joseph paused with the pipe stem at his lips. He expected this news after the events of the past few months. It was still difficult to imagine their way of life would soon disappear.

Following the meeting with Howard in the fall, Joseph received word the Department of the Interior adopted the five-man commission's recommendation to place all Nez Perce on a reservation. This was necessary "to maintain peace and to improve the quality of life for the Indians."

Ollokot met with Agent Monteith in March to appeal to his sense of fairness and equality, but to no avail. The Nez Perce warrior did not give up. General Howard granted him a meeting. The two met at Fort Walla Walla in April. But the general took a hard stance and would not yield. Howard warned the chief's younger brother that a day of reckoning was coming. Today's message was that announcement.

"When are we to meet? Where?" Joseph asked.

"In two days, at Lapwai."

The chief nodded. His camp at Hesuutin was less than ten miles from Fort Lapwai.

"I will not speak for the non-treaty bands this time. My voice is not powerful enough to enter the white man's ears."

"But our band is the largest," Ollokot said. "Howard listened to you for years. Are you sure?"

"I'm not speaking," Joseph said. "Ask the *tooat* from the Pikunan band to be our spokesperson. Perhaps a shaman can find a way into their hearts."

Ollokot sighed. He could see and hear his brother's frustration.

"I will ask Toohoolhoolzote to represent us at these talks."

Joseph drew air through the pipe bowl, held it for a moment, then exhaled. A white cloud of tobacco and willow bark smoke rushed from his lungs into the night air.

"Howard wants us to meet in two days. We will be at Lapwai in three days."

It was one last act of defiance by a man who realized his world was collapsing.

Wetatonmi raised the spade and used two hands to plunge it into the dry soil. She stood on the top of the blade and pushed it deeper, then lowered the handle to lift a chunk of dirt that exposed the plant's root. Her daughter Sara pulled the loosened two-foot high plant from the earth and beat it against a rock to remove the soil. Sara handed the plant to Makawee, who cut off the top and placed the remaining stubby, radish-shaped root in a basket.

The women were harvesting biscuit roots. These plants were ubiquitous on the dry, rocky hill near their camp. Their bright yellow flowers, arranged in small umbrellas of multiple tiny blooms, made them easy to find among the bunch grasses that shared the hillside.

The seasonal task of digging roots was familiar to Makawee. Crow women scoured the land in southern Montana for timpsila, or prairie turnips, for a thousand years. The spindle-shaped tubers were a staple for many Plains Indians. Makawee learned biscuit roots were of similar importance to the Nez Perce diet.

Like Graham, Makawee became fluent in *Niimíipuu*. Her family spent the winter in a canyon where Joseph's people set up camp. She had long conversations with Ollokot's wife as they dried fish, tanned elk hides, wove baskets, and crafted bead necklaces. Sara enjoyed playing with Nahkash and watching Dakkoótee. Makawee and Wetatonmi became close friends.

Now that *wewé·xp* (spring) arrived, the band moved from the canyons to the Wallowa Valley. It was time to harvest the first roots, which the women would grind into a paste and shape into flat loaves.

"I want to gather the roots of another plant before we return to camp," Wetatonmi said, as she looked at the full basket. "It grows near the water."

"Will it take long? I want to check on my children."

"Sound of Running Feet is watching Nahkash and Dakkoótee. I'm sure they are fine. *Mamook hyak* [We will be quick]."

They walked down the slope and into a meadow. A tiny stream saturated the soil. Coneflowers, lupine, and purple loosestrife competed for space along the edge of the water. The women followed the stream as it wandered through the meadow, their moccasins sinking into the soggy soil with each step.

Wetatonmi stopped and pointed to a cluster of wetland plants four feet tall. Their erect stems were speckled with purple spots. The plants had dark green leaves with a toothed margin. Makawee recognized the plant.

"Hemlock? Why do you want roots from this poisonous plant?"

"For medicine."

"But... It is a poison root."

"It is deadly when used in large amounts. Our medicine man adds a tiny drop to a mint tea. He gives it to a woman to help ease pain when it is her time to bleed each month."

Makawee brought her hand to her mouth. Hearing Wetatonmi describe a poisonous substance in an herbal tea triggered a wave of painful emotions. A kaleidoscope of images passed before her eyes. Feeling light-headed, she sat on the wet earth. She drew her knees toward her chest and bowed her head.

Four years earlier, Makawee gave birth prematurely after an evil medicine woman in her tribe gave her mint-flavored pennyroyal tea. The midwife, who knew pennyroyal would cause a fetus to be aborted, claimed this tea was useful in preventing early contractions.

"Makawee! *Sick tumtum?*" ["Are you ill?"]

Wetatonmi kneeled beside the Crow woman and rubbed her back.

Makawee raised her head and wiped tears from her cheeks.

"I'm... I'm just a little tired. My stomach is empty. Perhaps I should eat something when we return to camp."

"We will go right away," Wetatonmi said.

"No, *tillikum*. Gather water hemlock roots. I'll be fine. I will sit and watch."

Wetatonmi nodded. "We won't take long."

True to her word, Ollokot's wife and daughter filled a parfleche with the toxic roots in less than ten minutes and returned to Makawee.

The women harvested thick, fleshy tubers from the bottom of the hemlock stem. Wetatonmi sliced open a root to expose a multi-chambered tuber filled with a straw-colored liquid. The cut root smelled of carrots.

"Are these roots used for something other than medicine?" asked Makawee.

"Hunting."

Makawee raised an eyebrow and cocked her head to one side.

"The *oleman* [old men] in our tribe tell stories about using hemlock to make poison arrows. They claim you can kill an animal by shooting an arrow into any part of the body, not just the heart. The poison causes death in a short time when it enters the blood. We have no need for arrows that are poisoned. Most warriors today have a rifle."

"I have a special bow made from the horns of a ram. It belonged to my brother, Rides Alone. The Sioux killed him last year. I honor him by using this bow for hunting. Can someone help me make poison arrows?"

"White Bird showed me how to make poison arrows. You boil the roots in water until the oily liquid is thick. Then you apply it to the arrowheads and let them dry. I can show you."

Makawee nodded.

"I would like that."

"Now, let's get back to camp. You need some venison stew!"

General Howard clasped his hands behind his back and paced the parade grounds at Fort Lapwai. He expected a large crowd of non-treaty NezPerce. Needing to set the right tone, he decided not to convene the meeting at the Presbyterian church. By inviting the renegade bands to a military post, he was sending a simple message. These talks were not negotiations. This was official government business.

Because no clapboard houses or soldier barracks had rooms large enough to accommodate the visitors, the general ordered two hospital wall tents erected end-to-end. It didn't take long for the sun to heat the poorly ventilated tents. They tied the walls up to let the spring breeze flow through the canvas structures. Howard wanted every leader, shaman, elder, and spokesperson to have a place under the tents. These would be the last talks before he ordered the non-treaties to a reservation. His plan was to let everyone speak, show them the land promised by the government, and set a deadline to relocate their families.

"Agent Monteith!" Howard barked as he passed by the open end of the tents for the twentieth time.

"Yes, general?"

"Where are they? I'm expecting five non-treaty bands. None have showed."

"I don't know, sir. They received your message in ample time to travel here."

"Perhaps the rains delayed them. The rivers are swollen," offered Captain David Perry, the post commander.

"Well, if they don't show themselves by the end of the day, we will round them up like cattle and..."

"Look!" Monteith said, pointing south.

Joseph and Ollokot were leading a column of men on horseback, riding two abreast. The men painted their faces red below their eyes. Some had white stripes across the bridge of their nose. Eagle feathers adorned their braided hair. The women were next in the procession. They wrapped themselves in colorful blankets and were singing songs. The children were last. The mothers dressed even their youngest in beaded clothing.

Graham rode with Yellow Wolf near the front of the column. The bearded white man looked out of place among his Nez Perce friends. He was wearing a cowboy hat, buckskin jacket, and jeans. He had not painted his face.

Howard and the other officers waited for the Nez Perce to dismount when they arrived at the tents. Instead, Joseph kept riding. Sixty people from Joseph's band rode the perimeter of the fort in a slow horse parade. Ten minutes after they entered the fort's grounds, Joseph and Ollokot completed the circuit, dismounted, and greeted their host.

Howard was stoic. He shook the chief and Ollokot's hands, then motioned for them to enter. Graham and Yellow Wolf joined six elders under the tent. The remaining men, women, and children sat outside. The onlookers could view and hear the proceedings through the open sides.

"This is the general we have been hearing about?" asked Yellow Wolf, whispering to Graham.

"Yes."

"He does not look like a *skookum tyee* [powerful leader]. He has only one arm."

"Don't be quick to judge. His words are strong, and he leads a powerful army."

Joseph invited Graham to attend. He felt more confident as an interpreter now that he was conversant in the chief's language. Makawee stayed in camp with their children.

Howard and the other officers sat on camp chairs at one end of the tent. Joseph's people sat cross-legged across from them on the ground. Before the two groups spoke the first words, there was already a divide between them. The tension was higher than the gathering in the church the previous fall. The stakes were higher this time, and everyone knew it.

"We are here to listen," Oliver Otis Howard said. "What do you have to say?"

The military post's interpreter, who was also a missionary, repeated the general's words in Nez Perce. It pleased Graham to hear someone translate. It permitted him to compare his knowledge of the chief's language with those of an experienced translator. He would add words to his *Niimíipuu* vocabulary after these sessions.

"We have much to say," Joseph said. "But I am not the spokesperson. We have asked Toohoolhoolzote to fill that role."

"He is not here. You are. Speak."

Chief Joseph shook his head. "We will wait until all non-treaty chiefs are present."

Howard threw his hands in the air in exasperation.

"Alright. You don't want to speak. But I do. Here is what you can expect over the next few days. Your spokesperson can talk, and I will listen. But after the talking is finished, I will be clear. All white men and all Indians are subject to the laws of the US government. The Interior Department has ordered every Nez Perce onto the reservation. You will choose your land within those boundaries. That is not my decision. That is the law. It is not negotiable."

Joseph stared at the general and saw a different person. The one-armed man in this tent was not the same one who greeted him warmly when he arrived in the region over two years earlier. This was someone with a hardened heart. He became like all the *soyapu* over the past decade with whom he had spoken about keeping his ancestral land. Initially, those officials were compassionate. Inevitably, they bowed to the political pressure of giving white settlers what they desired – his people's land.

"And if we choose to stay in our homeland?" Joseph said. He knew the answer before asking the question.

"Then you will give us no choice. You will be taken to your new home by force."

When the interpreter repeated Howard's words, the Nez Perce sitting inside and outside the tent gasped.

Ollokot jumped up. "Why are we being punished? We have done nothing wrong!"

Before Howard could answer, Joseph stood. He put his hand on his brother's shoulder, looked into his eyes, and shook his head. Joseph turned and exited, with Ollokot and the elders following close behind. Men, women, and children mounted horses in silence.

"You will be back tomorrow?" Monteith said, standing at the entrance to the tent. It was half-statement and half-question.

Joseph looked at the Indian agent.

"We will come when the other non-treaty bands arrive."

"What the devil does that mean?" Howard demanded, shouting from inside the tent. "Tomorrow? The next day? How dare you make us wait!"

Monteith ignored the general's tirade. He knew nothing could be done. The chiefs would come to the fort when they were ready. After what the general said today, who could blame them?

The procession started toward their camp several miles away. The backs of the men and women were not as straight as an hour earlier when they paraded around the fort. Their blankets were not as bright, and their beads appeared to have lost their luster. Over the many years since the unsigned treaty, Joseph always expressed hope the white man would see how his people were being treated unfairly. Today, his followers heard what Howard said.

The words of the general were harsh and unforgiving.

Three days passed before the other non-treaty Nez Perce arrived. They camped several miles from Fort Lapwai. Toohoolhoolzote, Looking Glass, White Bird, and Husishusis Kute counseled with Ollokot and Joseph. After hearing about the unfriendly reception from General Howard, the chiefs agreed their only hope was a united front. They reconfirmed Toohoolhoolzote as the person to represent them.

Each band invited elders and followers to attend the meeting. Over two hundred people comprised the combined entourage that arrived at the military post on May 6. Two dozen elders joined the chiefs under the double tent. The other attendees encircled the canvas structure to observe the proceedings.

General Howard opened the meeting by speaking to Toohoolhoolzote. The sixty-year-old was thin with graying, shoulder-length hair and a prominent aquiline nose.

"I am told that you will speak for the non-treaty Nez Perce."

Toohoolhoolzote stood and tossed a blanket over his shoulder.

"My brothers appointed me."

"You have something to say on behalf of those present?"

"Joseph has spoken many times about our people's desire for equality. That has not changed. I do not know the law. I am a medicine man and a prophet. My words come from someone who sees the natural world. We belong to the same land you wish to take from us. The Earth is our mother. Can you understand why a man would not want to be separated from his mother?"

Howard rolled his eyes and sighed. This was going to be a fruitless discussion. He was espousing the typical Dreamer argument, the belief that Indians should shun white culture, especially farming, and live as their ancestors lived. If they did this, the Creator would reward them by bringing dead Indians back to life and ridding Indian lands of white people.

"I do not intend to meddle with your convictions. But there is only one government in the land where you live. And that government has one set of laws. Everyone must answer to these laws — regardless of that person's skin color. The law says you are required to live on a reservation. That is why we are here. To help you get started with your new life."

"We are not subject to the 1863 treaty. No one here signed it." The prophet swept his hand in a wide arc to emphasize how many people in attendance were not signees.

"As I explained, that does not matter. Today's law says you must leave your land and go to another land where you will be cared for."

"We do not need a government to care for us. Our ancestors have taken care of themselves for thousands of years before the white man arrived and stole our land."

Howard filled his cheeks with air and exhaled. This fellow was more unreasonable than Joseph.

"That was in the past. This is now. The government has divided the land so the Nez Perce and the whites can live peaceably together."

"But the Earth is part of my body. She is my mother. You cannot cut up part of my body and give it to someone else. Who gave you that right?"

Howard's face flushed. "The President of the United States! My orders are to get all of you onto a reservation — and that's what I'm going to do. You can either do this the easy way, with our help, or the hard way, where I provide soldiers as escorts."

Toohoolhoolzote's voice grew more forceful.

"I have *simiakia!* I am a man and will not go! My home is where I will stay. And neither will any of our people go!"

Graham leaned over to Yellow Wolf and asked the meaning of *simiakia*.

"It's the pride of being an Indian," his friend responded.

Howard saw the spokesperson for the non-treaty Nez Perce as a troublemaker. He needed to end this argument and let everyone know who was in charge.

"It's unfortunate the other chiefs allowed you to speak for them, because you are advising them to sign up for trouble. The whites will keep coming. They will continue to settle on the land. And they can do this legally. In the end, your stubbornness will cost your people their wealth. They will have to give up all their horses. All their cattle. If the Earth is your mother, she gave birth to a man with a bad heart."

"I am not afraid. You cannot tell me what to do or where to do it!"

"Captain Perry!" Howard said.

"Yes, sir."

"Arrest this man."

Perry signaled to a burly sergeant, who grabbed Toohoolhoolzote by his upper arm and pulled him toward the exit. The crowd gasped at the sight of a respected leader being manhandled. A second soldier grabbed the Indian's other arm. The two men dragged the old man away. Toohoolhoolzote's boisterous objections echoed against the wood buildings. The prisoner's voice gradually faded as they pushed him toward the stables, where an enclosed horse stall served as a temporary jail.

General Howard leaned over to Captain Perry and said something. The post commander nodded, turned and gave an order to his lieutenant, Edward Theller.

The lieutenant rose and shouted, "Company, assume positions!"

Twenty-four cavalrymen moved to the perimeter of the parade grounds. They distributed themselves around the tent and those sitting in the grass, their carbines at the ready.

Howard collected himself, straightened his frock coat, and cleared his throat.

"Now, let's resume to the business at hand, correct? We've been speaking about the reservation, but some of you may not have seen it. Let's take a few days and ride around the beautiful place you will call home. The land along the Clearwater is some of the finest in the region."

"We need to counsel," Joseph said.

Howard nodded. "We will wait."

Joseph motioned for the chiefs and elders to gather outside the tent. Most were still stunned at the way they treated Toohoolhoolzote.

"Why did Cut Arm *show the rifle*? There was no need!" said Ollokot.

"The general has changed. He uses threats instead of words of peace. This is a dangerous time for our people. I will ask each of you. Should we move to the reservation, or stand and fight?"

Joseph looked at Husishusis Kute.

"Chief of the Palouse River band, what say you?"

"Our people do not want war. We only want to be left alone. We will move."

"Chief of the Lamtáama band, what say you?"

"I do not want my people to suffer. Although it pains my heart, we will move," White Bird said.

"Chief of the Alpowai band, what say you?"

Looking Glass spoke with sad eyes.

~ *Looking Glass*

"We do not have to move. Our people are already on reservation land. I am only here because no one from our village signed the treaty. All of you are welcome to be our neighbors. But you will not be able to keep your large herds of horses and cattle on the land. There is not enough grass for everyone."

"What about Toohoolhoolzote's people?" Ollokot asked. "We cannot decide without him."

"Who is the ranking elder of the Pikunan band on the Salmon River?" asked Joseph.

A man with a hunched back, wrinkled face, and dark brown eyes hobbled from the edge of the tent to the circle of chiefs.

"I am the most senior member of our council," he said.

"They took away Toohoolhoolzote. We need someone to speak for his people. Have you heard the question?"

"Yes."

"What say you?"

"Our prophet's words upset the bluecoat today. We want peace, not war. No one can win against such a powerful enemy. We will move."

Joseph nodded.

"I agree. Let us save our people and some of our dignity by riding with the soldiers and choose the land we will call home."

The Indian leaders ducked under the open walls of the tent. Chief Joseph spoke to General Howard.

"When do we make the journey?"

"Excellent decision! We ride first thing in the morning. Captain, put together an escort for our visit to the reservation."

"Yes, sir," Perry said, saluting.

"Oh, one more thing," Howard said, addressing the chiefs. "You have thirty days to pack your things. If you have not left your home territories by June 15, you will be removed by force."

As the translator relayed the general's closing comments to the Nez Perce, a loud murmur arose from the crowd. How could they pack everything in four weeks? How could they round up all the horses and cattle? What about the roots and foods they would normally spend all summer preparing and preserving for the winter months?

The chiefs and elders hung their heads and shuffled from the tent. As the visitors filed by the soldiers to their horses, a pall hung in the air. It reminded Graham of the funeral processions he experienced as a child. Indeed, there was a collective death in the Nez Perce that day. This was the first stage of mourning.

In thirty days, the way of life for the non-treaty Nez Perce would be buried with their ancestors.

Chapter Four

Retribution

13 June, 1877

Warriors whooped as they circled the camp on horseback. Each one took turns shouting to the older men gathered by a bonfire. Young boys pounded on drums in a rhythmic cadence that amplified emotions. The riders boasted of killing enemies or stealing horses. These fighting-age men from White Bird's band relished the opportunity to display their manhood.

Nez Perce tribesmen had staged a *tel-lik-leen* ceremony for hundreds of years. This summer's ritual was especially poignant. The one-armed general ordered the band onto a reservation, and the deadline for them to comply was only days away. It was an opportunity to vent frustrations and reassure themselves they were warriors at heart, even though the government forced them from their ancestral land.

Five non-treaty bands camped by a lake six miles west of Grangeville. As White Bird's warriors paraded around the perimeter of the camp, the sound of the drums drew in warriors from other bands, who joined the endless procession. The circle widened to accommodate additional riders. After an hour of riding, shrieking, and chanting, the warriors dismounted and gathered at the fire.

The shirtless young men sat behind the older men, sweat on their bare chests glistening in the dim light. They bragged to one another about who was the bravest and most noble.

An elder in White Bird's band raised his hand. *Hahkauts Ilpilp* was in his late seventies. Red Grizzly Bear, as he was known in English, needed a walking stick for support and was blind in one eye. He claimed he lost the eye as a young man during a fight with a Flathead warrior. Others say an arrow accidentally pierced his eye while playing Indian games as a boy. Regardless, his empty eye socket seemed fitting for someone with a prickly personality. As a respected elder, when he asked for silence, everyone listened. After the noise around the fire dissipated, he spoke.

"I heard voices of boasting warriors. Many can hold your head high. You have honored our ancestors with your deeds. But some are not worthy of being called a warrior. You have shamed your families."

The ritual participants looked at one another, wondering to whom the old man was referring.

"Shore Crossing!" Red Grizzly Bear said, raising his chin and pointing to a young man on the other side of the fire. "The *soyapu* Lawrence Ott murdered your father, Eagle Robe, three years ago. A true warrior would not have hesitated to avenge his death. The white man should have lost his life at your hands!"

Everyone turned their attention to Shore Crossing, who bowed his head so the others would not see his face in the firelight.

It was a cruel accusation. Even as Eagle Robe lay bleeding from a mortal wound to his chest, he pleaded with his son not to retaliate against the settler. Every Nez Perce man knew any retribution on a white man, regardless if it was justified, would end with the Indian's execution. He simply honored his father's wishes.

"Red Feather!" the old man said, looking to his right with one eye. "How can you show up for a *tel-lik-leen*? You are a member of the Wallowa tribe. I know Joseph and Ollokot are not here tonight. But listen to my words. I would say these things even if they were sitting here. You are a weak man. A white man also killed your father. Wind Blowing and I were good friends. Why have you done nothing? Have you no shame?"

Red Feather blinked. The elder's words shocked him. The memory of his father's death came flooding back.

Why was this old man confronting him? Chief Joseph and Ollokot pursued justice through the courts, but no one charged Wind Blowing's killer. Why was he to blame for a failure of the white man's law? He stood, mounted his horse, and galloped away.

"I have another name who does not deserve... ," Red Grizzly Bear said.

"*Talkiza!*" shouted White Bird, interrupting him.

The chief was also frustrated at the recurring acts of violence by white men against Indians that went unpunished. But he was a pragmatist. If his small band fought their oppression, the government would crush them. He needed to guide his people toward the reservation. It was their only chance to remain unharmed.

~ White Bird

"We respect and appreciate your words, *Hahkauts Ilpilp*. But tonight we remember past victories and take pride in our heritage. It is not about shaming others. The ceremony is finished. Everyone go and rest. Prepare for tomorrow."

Men and boys rose and retired to their pole lodges. But Shore Crossing stayed seated by the fire. The words of Red Grizzly Bear rang in his ears. He was a prominent warrior. No one accused him of failing to avenge his father's death. After hearing Red Grizzly Bear's words, would his fellow tribesmen believe he was a coward?

As the shamed warrior stewed in his thoughts, Red Moccasin Tops and Swan Necklace returned and joined him by the fire. The trio sat cross-legged in silence for a moment.

"I am not a coward," Shore Crossing said, hoping that saying it aloud would make it true.

"Do not let the old man's words affect you. He does not know your heart," Swan Necklace said.

"You are a warrior. *We* are warriors," Red Moccasin Tops said, nodding his head. He had been close to Shore Crossing since they were boys. He had no doubts in his friend's courage.

Shore Crossing turned toward his friend. His eyes were filled with rage — not at the old man, but himself. "Red Grizzly Bear is right. We parade on horses and boast about past victories. But we do not fight back against an enemy that steals our land and kills us without consequence. I am a warrior in my heart. But I am not a warrior in the eyes of my people. Not after tonight."

"What can we do?" Swan Necklace asked.

"We can take revenge. We can show the white men we will not be treated like animals," Shore Crossing said, his eyes narrowing.

"Do you plan to...?"

"Yes. Our *kapsis* [evil] enemies will pay the price for their wickedness with their lives. Who is with me?"

Red Moccasin Tops and Swan Necklace glanced at each other in the light of the fading fire.

"We will go," Red Moccasin Tops said. "At the next *tel-lik-leen* ceremony, we will tell others of the night three warriors struck fear into the hearts of the white settlers."

"Paint your faces. Prepare for battle," Shore Crossing said. "Bring a rifle and your knife. Meet here in thirty minutes. We will ride to the Salmon River."

As they stood, Swan Necklace said, "Should we ask Red Feather to join us? Like you, he has yet to avenge his father's death."

The veins in Shore Crossing's neck bulged. His adrenaline was already flowing in anticipation of a deadly raid on Ott's homestead.

"Did he stay after hearing Red Grizzly Bear's words? No. He rode back to his camp. Joseph's men are trained to talk, not fight. What did years of talking with the white man yield? Life on a small piece of land where we are expected to grow crops!"

The two friends nodded at Shore Crossing's impassioned reply. If Red Feather wanted to regain his dignity and seek retribution, he was on his own.

General Howard laid his bible on a chair and peered out the window of his stateroom on the *Spokane*. The mountains reminded him of the Hudson River Valley, where he attended West Point Military Academy in the early 1850s.

Steamer Spokane

The shallow-draft steamer took two days to navigate up the Snake River from Wallula, it's tall stack belching black smoke as the paddlewheel churned the waters and pushed against the current. The boat would soon dock at Lewiston, where he was expecting Captain David Perry to meet and escort him to Fort Lapwai.

The Christian general was pleased at the series of telegrams he received. The non-treaties packed their possessions, rounded up their horses and cattle, and were currently camped within a day's ride of the reservation. He was looking forward to seeing Joseph's people and the other bands settled on their new land.

This news from the Wallowa Valley validated his strategy of taking a strong stance and setting a deadline for compliance. He always believed the non-treaty Nez Perce would come around. These people were not fighters — not like the Apache in Arizona. Cochise was a warrior. Yet Howard was able to negotiate a peace with the Apache five years earlier. He was confident he could do the same with Chief Joseph.

Howard sat back and removed his reading glasses. He considered the strategy that led to his diplomatic triumph. It wasn't only the threat of military intervention that convinced the non-treaties to comply with relocating to the reservation. A few days after the chiefs left Lapwai, they petitioned the army to release Toohoolhoolzote from prison. Howard consented. This magnanimous gesture let them know he was not unreasonable. If they followed the law, he was willing to overlook the old chief's petulant behavior and set him free.

His achievement was especially gratifying because it helped fulfill a purpose. He had a personal mission to introduce people to Christianity. By ordering the non-treaty Nez Perce to a reservation, he provided the opportunity for missionaries to educate these people. They could abandon nomadic lifestyles and live more comfortably by raising and selling crops. The non-treaties may not see it right now, but one day they would be grateful. By having a designated land, they would be freed from potential conflicts with white settlers. His bold actions would save them from themselves.

The *Spokane* nudged against the dock at Lewiston, shaking Howard from his thoughts. The general donned his slouch hat and walked to the port side of the first deck. When he reached the gangway, he spotted Captain Perry and Agent Monteith ashore.

"Permission to come aboard!" Perry shouted to the captain in the wheelhouse.

"Permission granted," the captain said. The two men walked up the narrow plank and met General Howard on deck.

Perry saluted. "General, the ship will be docked for a few hours. Agent Monteith and I would like to speak with you about recent events. Can we use a room aboard the ship to talk?"

Howard furrowed his brow. "What's the news?"

"Well, sir, it's about the non-treaty bands," Perry said evasively. "I'll have one of my men take care of your luggage."

The three men walked aft and climbed a set of stairs to the second deck. They sat at a table in the open area near the stern. Howard leaned back in his chair and propped his feet on the table, crossing them at the ankles. He removed his hat and placed it on his thighs.

"It's been a long trip from Portland. I'm eager to hear about the non-treaties. Today is the deadline for them to be on the reservation. I plan to visit after they are settled and thank Chief Joseph for cooperating."

Perry glanced at Monteith, then cleared his throat.

"I'm afraid I have bad news."

"Out with it!" Howard said.

"Two nights ago, the non-treaties held a *tel-lik-leen* ceremony and..."

"A what?"

"It's a ritual where fighting-age men parade in a circle and commemorate past battles against their enemies," Monteith said.

Howard nodded. "Understood. Please continue."

"A few treaty Nez Perce attended this celebration. We received an account of what happened that night. Three young men left after the ceremony and rode to the Salmon River. That's where the killing started."

Howard dropped his feet to the deck, sat up in his chair, and leaned across the table.

"Killing? What killing?"

"The warriors killed four men and badly wounded another."

The general shook his head in disbelief.

"Were they randomly chosen? Why these men?"

"No one knows for sure. But the neighbors believe all the victims treated the Nez Perce badly over the years and were not punished — at least in the eyes of the Nez Perce."

This is horrible news, Howard thought. *I need to put a stop to this violence before it spreads.*

"What have you done in response to these four murders?"

"Well, sir, those are not the only casualties. When the killers returned to camp, they incited others to join in more raids. More than a dozen Nez Perce went on a rampage, looking for more settlers to kill. Several other ranchers and their families were murdered. As you would expect, the settlers near Grangeville banded together. They attacked several Indians. I believe at least one was killed. And then..."

"Captain! Enough!" Howard said. "Innocent civilians have been murdered. You have not answered my question. What have you done in response?"

"Yes, sir. Allow me to explain. We expected the non-treaties at the reservation today. When they did not arrive, I sent a detachment to the non-treaty camps to determine the reason. They returned to the fort several hours ago with this news. Before I left to meet you, a courier delivered a message from settlers who blockaded themselves inside a building in Mount Idaho. They pleaded for help."

Howard stood and paced the deck. He considered what he heard. His efforts to bring peace through negotiations were quickly unraveling.

His mind switched to developing a strategy to deal with this crisis. The citizens needed immediate assistance. There were only two companies stationed at Fort Lapwai. He required additional troops, but they were hundreds of miles away in Walla Walla. He needed to wire a message to Portland for more soldiers. He had to get word to the cavalry company in the Wallowa Valley, one hundred miles to the south. Division headquarters in San Francisco would want to know what was happening...

"Monteith, go to my stateroom and fetch a quill, ink, and paper."

The Indian agent scurried down the steps to retrieve the requested supplies.

"Captain, have your men pack my things. I need two men to serve as couriers. We will leave for Lapwai as soon as I write these notes. There is no time to waste."

"Yes, sir," Perry said, hurrying toward the gangplank.

Howard walked to the stern and gazed at the paddlewheel. It was slowly turning, providing just enough energy to keep the steamer pinned against the dock. The wooden blades slapped the surface and created ripples in the river.

This news was stomach-churning. It meant he needed to change from diplomat to commander. He resolved to quell the violence and bring the miscreants to justice.

Makawee and Graham stood in front of their wall tent at dawn and observed a flurry of activity in the camp. Women peeled buffalo hides off pole lodges. They stacked kettles, utensils, blankets, baskets, and clothing on travois. Men and boys herded horses while dogs barked and ran among the skeleton frames of the tepees. The Indians were breaking camp with urgency. Everyone knew they needed to move quickly.

"What do we do?" Makawee asked, watching Nahkash entertain her little brother with glass beads. Her children were oblivious to everyone's haste.

"We've done nothing wrong," Graham said, comforting his wife by putting an arm around her. "Let's wait for Joseph to return. His band is not packing."

Joseph and Ollokot had taken a small group to slaughter cattle in their sizable herd. They were expected back in camp later with beef-laden packhorses.

The women finished removing the animal skins of their homes and started disassembling the tepees. Anxious voices blended with a chorus of clacking sounds that echoed across the prairie as they stacked lodge poles.

Red Moccasin Tops arrived in camp the previous evening and announced a successful raid. He reported the trio of warriors led by Shore Crossing killed four white men and wounded several others. The young man expected congratulations for this feat. Instead, the elders of the bands in camp were horrified. White Bird chastised the messenger for impulsive behavior that put everyone in great danger.

The warrior was not deterred by the chief's scathing remarks. He was emboldened. Raising a rifle above his head, he shouted for others to join Swan Necklace, Shore Crossing and him for a second set of raids on homes of *kapsis* (evil) white men. Sixteen young men emerged from the shadows of the campfires and yelled their approval. Within minutes, additional fighters were galloping across the prairie toward the Salmon River, eager to prove their bravery.

The chiefs and elders held council after the young men left. They agreed their people would be in imminent danger from the army when news reached Fort Lapwai. Their only choice was to move to a safer place first thing in the morning.

The band led by Looking Glass struck out across the prairie an hour after sunrise. The chief told the other leaders his people had a safe haven. Their land was within the reservation boundaries. They would ride north and wait there until the violence subsided.

Thirty minutes later, the Nez Perce led by White Bird, Toohoolhoolzote, and Husishusis Kute rode west out of camp. Their destination was Lahmotta, or as the white men called it, White Bird Canyon. Everyone in Joseph's band gathered at the edge of camp and watched as the procession slowly disappeared into the canyon several miles distant.

"Aah!" a voice called from inside a tepee.

Wetatonmi ducked inside. She emerged a moment later and announced Joseph's second wife, Springtime, was in labor.

"She started having pains last evening. The baby will come soon. Who will help me deliver the child?"

"I will boil water. Nothing more," Heyoom Yoyikt said. She picked up a bucket and walked toward a stream several hundred feet from the southern edge of camp. Joseph's first wife made it abundantly clear she was not going to help his second wife give birth.

"I can help," Makawee said, glancing at Graham.

"Are you sure? You don't have training as a midwife," he said, whispering in her ear.

"I am not a midwife. But I know what should *not* be done to harm a child or the mother."

Graham nodded. She was victimized by Among the Grass, an evil Crow midwife who caused Makawee's second child to be aborted. He could see in his wife's eyes she wanted to assist in this delivery. Perhaps it would be cathartic.

"Go ahead. I'll watch the children."

After the other bands departed, the routine in camp seemed normal. Young men tended to the horses. Children romped and played hide-and-seek in an endless carpet of blue camas, which had just begun flowering. Women pounded biscuitroots on rocks, forming starchy pita-shaped breads they laid in the sun to dry. The sounds of children laughing, dogs barking, and women pounding were interrupted periodically by the shrieks of Springtime as her contractions increased in frequency and intensity.

Joseph, Ollokot, and three others rode into camp in the early afternoon leading two packhorses. Heyoom Yoyikt greeted her husband with the news of his second wife's imminent delivery. She asked her nephew Yellow Wolf to brief the brothers on the unwelcome news of the past two days.

Yellow Wolf told the story of the brazen young warriors and their deadly raid on white settlements. He spoke of how others joined in the violence, vowing to bring death to ranchers and honor to themselves. Finally, he shared the plans of the other chiefs, each having decided to find a safe place to avoid the army, who would certainly hunt them down.

When Yellow Wolf finished speaking, Joseph became pensive. He feared something like this would happen. The non-treaty bands had been days from living in the protected area of the reservation. He did not want to move, but ceased to resist because his people would face a formidable enemy. Joseph asked a few elders and Ollokot to a council. They walked to the stream that meandered through the prairie.

"The others have fled, but we should stay," Joseph said. "Let the army come. We will explain the actions of a few brash young men should not reflect on everyone. Perhaps we can negotiate an end to this temporary violence."

"Negotiate?" Ollokot asked. "My brother, that time has passed. Did you not hear Cut Arm one month ago?"

"What would you have us do?"

"Howard does not care who killed those settlers. We are all the same to him. He will punish our people. I will not be humiliated again."

"Are you saying...?"

"*Miogat!*" ["Chief!"] a voice called out from the village.

A young man on horseback galloped to the group and dismounted. After catching his breath, the messenger said he was sent by White Bird to share the latest news. There were reports of more killing along the Salmon River. The victims were not only white men. Women and children were murdered. In retaliation, the whites ambushed a group of three Nez Perce, killing one. Skirmishes were happening all over the river valley. White Bird requested all the bands come together and defend themselves. There was strength in numbers.

Joseph looked down and placed a hand on his forehead. This escalation changed everything. There would be no negotiations — only fighting.

"We will move to Lahmotta," Joseph said.

As Joseph led the group back to camp, they heard the wail of a newborn. The women gathered by the tepee where the new mother gave birth. Wetatonmi stepped outside, holding an infant wrapped in a blanket. Makawee followed, wiping her hands on a damp cloth. Both women were smiling broadly.

"Springtime has given you a daughter!" she announced, handing the bundle to Chief Joseph. The women in the village clapped and shrieked with joy.

Joseph turned to Ollokot and the elders. He spoke in a low voice.

"Wait a few minutes before you tell everyone our plan. We will soon face hardship. Let them share in the happiness of this moment."

The women followed Joseph as he walked toward his tepee to greet the mother of his child. They danced and sang an ancient song that praised the Creator for new life. When he reached his home, he turned toward the joyous crowd and lifted his hand for silence.

The women stopped singing and dancing. A light northwesterly breeze carried faint sounds of gunfire across the prairie. Another skirmish between Nez Perce and whites erupted. After a brief silence, they could hear more rifles being fired. Everyone knew these were the sounds of war.

"Gather your things. We leave for Lahmotta in one hour. Hurry," he said.

Everyone dispersed and set to work breaking camp.

Joseph stared at his newborn daughter, her face slightly swollen from the trauma of birth. A tear trickled down his cheek and dropped onto the blanket. This child represented what was good in the world, but she was born in troubled times.

Shifting his gaze from the infant in his arms to the sky, he closed his eyes and petitioned the Creator to guide his people.

"Oh, Great Spirit, guide us to a place where we can live in peace."

Chief Joseph could not have imagined his quest for a safe haven would require a journey of twelve hundred miles.

Chapter Five
Chaotic Canyon

17 June, 1877

G raham woke at sunrise. He pursed his lips and exhaled, watching the water vapor from his breath dissipate in the frosty air. He debated whether to stay under the blankets a while longer or start a fire.

Five more minutes. Then I'll get up, he thought.

As he lay in the tent, he could hear Makawee softly snoring. For a moment, he was tempted to roll onto his side and put his arm over his wife. He would love to feel the warmth of her body and caress her soft shoulders, but he didn't want to disturb her. She needed rest because she had been up several times during the night when Dakkoótee became fussy. He propped himself on one elbow and squinted in the dim light. Nahkash was sleeping under a blanket, her black hair askew across her face.

Graham lay down and considered what happened when word about the fighting reached Joseph's camp four days earlier. The people led by White Bird and Toohoolhoolzote joined Chief Joseph's band in traveling to Lahmotta. The non-treaty bands camped along White Bird Creek, a mile from where it flowed into the Salmon River. It was a place the Nez Perce knew well.

The chiefs needed time to discuss their options before the army tracked them down. White Bird deployed several scouts to ride northeast toward Grangeville with orders to report any sighting of the bluecoats.

Graham sighed and slid from beneath the blankets. He tugged on his jeans, slipped on his boots without lacing them up, donned a buckskin jacket, and stepped out of the tent. As he stretched his arms skyward and arched his back, he noticed a cooking fire in front of a neighboring lodge. He ambled over to borrow a burning stick.

Yellow Wolf emerged from behind the lodge with an armload of dry pine branches.

"*Ta 'c meeywi,*" ["Good morning"] he said, dropping the sticks.

"*Alliksa,*" ["Light a fire"] Graham said, imitating the motion of scraping flint shavings. "May I borrow some coals or a burning piece of wood?"

The young warrior waved his hand over the fire, indicating his friend should help himself. Graham picked up the unburnt end of a chunk of wood and pulled it from the flames.

A series of short howls and staccato yips echoed against the buttes.

"Coyote?" Graham asked.

"Scout. He has spotted the enemy. I will inform Joseph and Ollokot."

Graham tossed the stick in the fire, causing red embers to scurry skyward. He hurried to his tent, pushed the flaps aside, and whispered to Makawee.

"The army is coming. Take the children. Follow the creek south for a few miles and stay there. I'll come get you when it's safe to return."

"No."

"Makawee! Don't argue with me!"

"What about the other women? Will they leave? I will not flee at the first sign of a fight."

Graham was exasperated. There wasn't time for a debate.

"How will you defend yourself?"

Makawee snatched her sheephorn bow leaning against the sidewall of the tent, whipped an arrow from the quiver, nocked it, and raised the weapon into a firing position.

"*Naha?*" ["Mommy?"] Nahkash said, sitting up and rubbing her sleepy eyes. "I'm hungry. Will you make me something to eat?"

"Yes. Go back to sleep for a few minutes. We will eat soon," Makawee said, lowering the bow and releasing the tension on the arrow.

The little girl lay back down and pulled the blanket under her chin.

Graham forgot how proficient his wife was in handling the bow. Still, the ancient weapon seemed woefully inadequate compared to a firearm.

"Will you at least take this?" Graham asked.

He pulled the Colt Cobra from his belt and handed it to her. He brought the snub-nosed gun with him from the future.

Makawee nodded. She laid down the bow and grabbed the pistol.

Graham breathed a sigh of relief. He laced his boots, then retrieved his Spencer carbine. He stepped toward the entrance to the tent. Before leaving, he turned and looked at his wife.

"We will be fine. Go," she whispered, smoothing her sleeping daughter's hair with one hand and clutching the Colt with the other.

Ollokot and Joseph were at the cooking fire when Graham returned. Chief Joseph stood behind his brother. He folded his arms across his chest and watched as men gathered from all parts of the camp.

The two leaders of the Wallowa band knew their strengths. Joseph had always been the diplomat. He used his ample powers of persuasion and debate to forestall the inevitable conflict that was unfolding. He would have a secondary role within the band in the months ahead.

Although he was four years younger, Ollokot was a charismatic and more experienced fighter. He was the band's war chief.

Soon, sixty-five warriors assembled in the center of camp, awaiting orders.

"Where is everyone? We have over one hundred warriors among our three bands," White Bird said.

Wounded Head, an older man from White Bird's band, spoke.

"The barrels of spirits we stole from the wagons and homes are almost empty. Many are still asleep."

Ollokot gave a disgusted look.

"We need as many fighting men as we can get, and we need to protect our herds."

White Bird nodded.

"Anyone who can walk should tend to the horses and make sure they do not scatter," he instructed Wounded Head.

The man hurried off to find men sober enough to handle the horses.

"Perhaps we can negotiate a truce," Joseph said.

"We are done talking. Did you forget they put me in jail?" Toohoolhoolzote said in an embittered tone.

"My brother has a point," Ollokot said. "It would be helpful to learn their intentions. Let's send a group ahead to see if they will talk."

"I agree," White Bird said. We should send two men from each band in a gesture of goodwill.

Toohoolhoolzote reluctantly agreed.

"I will meet the soldiers," Shore Crossing said. "I'm afraid of no one."

"No! You have only fighting on your mind. Chief Joseph has agreed to lead a dozen warriors in guarding the camp. Stay here with him," White Bird said.

Shore Crossing pursed his lips, but stayed silent. His actions started the fighting, and he knew better than to question the chief's decision.

"I can go," Graham said, stepping forward.

"No white man will speak for us. Stay here and help defend the camp," Ollokot said. "Yellow Wolf and Two Moons will represent our band."

"Prepare for battle. Meet back here in ten minutes. If the soldiers desire a fight, we will ride to meet them," White Bird said.

The warriors dispersed to their lodges. They sang songs while stripping to breechcloths and leggings.

A few minutes later, Yellow Wolf exited from his lodge holding a musket. Three beaded necklaces lay against his bare, sinewy chest. He tied his hair back with an elk-hide cord. The young man approached Graham and handed his friend a metal container.

When Graham opened the tin, he saw a black paste.

"Eagle Bear, paint," the young warrior said, touching his forehead.

Graham noted Yellow Wolf addressed him by his Indian name. It was an honor to paint a warrior's face for war. As he looked around for something to apply the substance, Yellow Wolf held up his index finger.

Graham nodded, dipped his finger into the tin, and smeared the charcoal mixture onto his friend's forehead. Yellow Wolf directed Graham to apply additional black paint on his temples and in front of his ears.

When Graham finished, Yellow Wolf opened a second tin of ochre clay and withdrew a pinch of the red pigment. It crumbled when he rubbed his finger and thumb together. He spat into the tin and mixed his saliva with the clay. Testing it a second time, he nodded, then handed the tin to Graham. Yellow Wolf motioned to apply the red pigment beneath his eyes and across the bridge of his nose.

As he looked into his friend's glassy black eyes, Graham saw excitement. Yellow Wolf was eager to prove himself against a formidable foe.

"You look ready," Graham said, as he stepped back to admire his handiwork.

"Should I prepare Eagle Bear for battle?" Yellow Wolf asked as he dipped his index finger into the ochre clay and held it up.

Graham was taken aback. He was reminded Rides Alone did the same thing in preparing for a fight in the Little Bighorn Valley last summer. Graham would defend his family to the death. But it seemed presumptuous to adopt this warrior custom. He was a white man. No amount of paint would change the color of his skin.

"I, uh, have my own way of preparing," Graham said. He pulled the eagle-bear claw necklace from beneath his shirt and kissed the eagle pendant suspended on the elk-hide cord. "My *baaxpée* will protect me."

Yellow Wolf nodded as he placed the lid on the tin container.

"You don't have the best weapon for a fight. Let's trade," Graham said.

He held out his Spencer carbine and motioned for Yellow Wolf to surrender his old muzzleloader.

Yellow Wolf shook his head. "I will kill a soldier and take his rifle." He hurried to meet those chosen to greet the soldiers.

Graham nodded. His friend's confidence and courage were inspiring. He would only have one chance to retrieve a rifle. He would not have time to reload. If he missed...

"Remember, we prefer to talk," Ollokot said, as he tied a white cloth on the end of his nephew's long barreled musket. "If they choose not to listen, we will speak with arrows and bullets."

Yellow Wolf and five others galloped north a few minutes later. They ascended the rolling buttes lining the canyon, seeking mounted bluecoats.

The chiefs positioned their warriors behind the knolls east and west of the campground. If the soldiers rode toward the tepee village along the creek, the Indian fighters would shoot at them from both directions. They lay flat and waited. While the Indian leaders desired a peaceful resolution, every man lying prone in the grassy foothills hoped for a fight.

Graham walked to his tent to see how his family was doing. When he lifted the flap, Makawee picked up the Colt and aimed in his direction.

"Whoa! It's just me!"

She laid the revolver on a blanket and returned to breaking up biscuit root bread and placing the pieces in a bowl with berries. Nahkash and Dakkoótee were picking up the bread and fruit with their fingers. Dakkoótee had a blue circle around his mouth. Berry juice was running down his chin. He giggled and slapped his chubby hands against his thighs between each bite.

"Are you hungry?"

"Yeah, but I'm gonna wait. We'll know soon whether the soldiers want to fight or talk."

"May we enter?" a voice called from outside the tent.

Graham lifted the flap to see Shore Crossing. Like the other warriors, he painted his face, using red and yellow to represent his spiritual guide. Vertical, alternating stripes on his cheekbones highlighted his narrow jaw. Random orange streaks appeared where he blended the two pigments. He applied the paint without looking into a mirror.

"I do not want to leave my wife alone. Can she stay with Makawee?" he asked, nodding behind him.

Graham looked over the shoulder of Shore Crossing. His sixteen-year-old wife, Lautiss, was seven months pregnant. She was resting both hands on top of her belly, which bulged under a tight-fitting elk-hide dress.

Makawee befriended Lautiss after she became pregnant. This did not surprise Graham. Ever since Makawee lost her only son in a premature birth, she was on a mission to help women give birth to healthy babies. Graham was uncomfortable with his wife becoming close to Lautiss. Her husband sparked the conflict with his lethal raids on white settlements. Makawee reminded Graham he should not judge Lautiss for her husband's behavior.

Graham resolved to keep Shore Crossing at arm's length. Makawee may wish to have Lautiss as a friend, but that didn't mean he had to do the same with her husband. He stood to one side and motioned for them to enter.

"Do you mind if someone joins you?" Graham said.

Makawee glanced up and saw her visitors.

"Not at all! Please, sit down."

Lautiss eased her way onto a blanket.

"*Qe'ci'yew'yew,*" ["Thank you"] she said.

"You are getting bigger each day! We need to enlarge that dress. Let's work on that together."

Crack!

A shot echoed in the distance.

Graham and Shore Crossing scooted out of the tent and looked north. Silhouettes of tribesmen lay in the short grass atop the knolls. From the valley floor, the men and horses were hidden among the distant undulating hills.

Another shot rang out, then another.

Shore Crossing dashed toward a waiting horse, his long hair bouncing on his bare shoulders.

Graham could see Yellow Wolf and the rest of the advance Nez Perce group charging back to camp. Fifty yards behind them, a line of cavalry was in hot pursuit.

Here they come, thought Graham, as he poked his head into the tent.

"The fighting has started," he said to Makawee, grabbing his binoculars. "Stay here. Shoot anyone you don't recognize."

Graham sprinted to a ridge overlooking the camp a few hundred feet to the west. He sat and laid the carbine beside him. Placing his elbows on his knees, he trained the field glasses downstream. The higher position allowed him to see the battle while ensuring no soldiers threatened the tepee village.

Canyon Creek

The cavalry formed two lines spaced two hundred feet apart. One hundred bluecoats were riding toward camp at a fast trot. A group of twenty men dressed in civilian clothing took a position alongside the cavalry on the higher ground. Thankfully, none of the soldiers or volunteers advanced within shooting distance of the camp.

He watched in amazement as a group of warriors emerged from willow trees along White Bird Creek. They charged up the knoll where the volunteers dismounted. The Indians stopped less than fifty yards from the enemy's position. They fired at the attackers and wounded two men within a minute. The civilians retreated, galloping north in the canyon, leaving the left flank of the cavalry exposed.

Nicely done! Graham thought. He swung the field glasses to his left and used the thumb wheel to refocus.

Thirty Nez Perce, including the six men who approached the soldiers under a flag of truce, rode forward to meet the assault head-on. Ollokot was in the lead. He raised a Winchester and fired into the front of the column. The warriors behind him opened fire or shot arrows.

Confronted with this counterattack, the column halted. The soldiers fired back, but no one hit their target. Horses reared and threw riders, then galloped away and mixed with the ponies of the Nez Perce. A cloud of dust and smoke settled over the valley, obscuring parts of the battlefield. Troops scrambled up the knolls, dismounted, and formed a skirmish line. Every fourth man held the horses so their fellow soldiers could shoot.

The tide of the battle turned when warriors on both sides of the canyon rose from their positions and fired. The soldiers were caught in a crossfire. Panic ensued.

A bugle call rose above the chaotic gunfire and sounds of dying horses. It was a signal for the troops to engage in an orderly retreat. Graham trained his glasses on the bugler. A moment later, the trumpeter was shot through the heart. The cavalry commander lost his primary way of communicating to the troops.

Frightened horses kicked and lunged. A quarter of the horses yanked free of their holders and scattered, seeking to escape the noise of the battlefield.

With no bugle call to coordinate the soldiers and Indians firing from all sides, it became every man for himself. The rout was on.

The troopers broke formation. Those who had a horse mounted and galloped north. A few men without horses hitched a ride with other soldiers. Those left in the field without a mount scampered after their comrades on foot, hoping the enemy would not follow. Their hopes were not realized.

The Nez Perce on the knolls mounted and chased the troopers on foot, shooting them in the back or piercing them with arrows. A thick cloud of gun smoke obscured the battle that raged a mile away. The noise faded into muffled sounds of distant gunfire.

Graham lowered his field glasses and exhaled. Unless there was an unexpected counterattack, this was a surprising victory for the non-treaty Nez Perce. He picked up his carbine and ambled down the hill to check on his family.

By the time he reached the village, most warriors returned from the canyon. Riders fired into the air, yelling and whooping in celebration. Women joined in, waving their hands in the air and banging pots with wooden spoons.

Graham pushed through the crowd. He passed Lautiss, who was making her way to meet her husband. Shore Crossing was grinning, pleased his Nez Perce brothers fought back against their oppressors.

Makawee was standing in front of their tent, holding Dakkoótee, Colt in hand. Graham kissed her on the cheek and picked up Nahkash.

The three Nez Perce war chiefs remained on horseback so they could be seen and heard. The men gathered close together. Women and children stood behind the men. When the celebratory noises stopped, White Bird spoke.

"We have won a glorious victory for our people today. There is much to be thankful for, but we have work to do. The men will round up all horses, including those left behind by the bluecoats."

Toohoolhoolzote spoke next, his deep guttural voice rumbling in the morning air.

"We will treat our enemy as I was treated at Lapwai. We will take their dignity. The women will strip the dead. Leave nothing behind but a naked body for the coyotes and crows."

Shrieks of approval erupted from the crowd. Ollokot raised his hand and waited for silence.

"Make no mistake. This fight is not over. The army will return with more soldiers. Enjoy tonight. Tomorrow we move."

The crowd dispersed. Men chased after frightened horses. Women walked up the canyon, collecting valuables from the dead soldiers and placing the items in baskets like they were harvesting camas roots.

How long can these people hold out against the army? Graham thought. The government would succeed in forcing them onto a reservation. He wished he knew about the history of the Nez Perce. It wasn't something he learned in history class.

Graham turned to Makawee, who was balancing Dakkoótee on her hip.

"You were never in any danger. I saw the fighting unfold from up there," he said, pointing to the knoll on the west side of the canyon.

"I was not worried."

She handed the revolver to Graham.

"Maybe you should keep it. You never know if..."

Makawee pushed the side of the revolver into Graham's stomach, forcing him to take the weapon.

"I don't need it. I have the sheephorn bow."

"Daddy, can I play with Sara?" Nahkash asked, interrupting their conversation. "She is right there."

"Uh, sure. Go ahead."

Graham put the little girl down. He watched her run to the daughter of Wetatonmi.

"You heard the chiefs. We are moving again tomorrow," Graham said. He paused, trying to think of the best way to share his thoughts. "I was thinking this would be a good time for us to part ways with Joseph's people."

Makawee turned to face her husband, with Dakkoótee still perched on her hip. "Why?"

"This battle is the beginning of a long conflict. And it's not our fight."

"Not our fight? Graham, these people welcomed us into their homes. This is our family."

"You are Crow. I am a *soyapu*, a *baaschiile* — a white man. We are not Nez Perce."

Makawee stepped to the side and hitched Dakkoótee further up on her hip. She walked in a small circle with her chin on her chest, then looked up at Graham.

"Do you see how Nahkash enjoys playing with Sara and Sound of Running Feet? Do you know how close I've become to Wetatonmi?

"Yes, but..."

"You and Yellow Wolf are close. You haven't had a friend like him since Rides Alone."

She was appealing to their relationships within the tribe. Everything she said was true, but he held his ground.

"Look, I don't know *exactly* what will happen. But it will not end well for the Nez Perce. I don't want our family to be in harm's way. Let's go to a place where there's less violence. Portland, perhaps."

"These people are family. Are you willing to fight for your family? Or will you run away?"

That's not fair, Graham thought. *She knows I'd do anything to protect our family.*

"Well, you ran away from your family," he retorted.

As soon as the words left his mouth, he regretted saying them.

"That's not the same, and you know it!" she yelled, her eyes welling with tears.

Dakkoótee cried at the sound of his mother's angry voice. Makawee ducked into the tent.

Graham's emotions were a mixture of remorse, frustration, and anger. He wasn't angry at his wife. He was angry at allowing his emotions to get the best of him. It was inappropriate for him to bring up Makawee's relationship with Long Horse. The situations were not the same. Long Horse refused to admit Makawee into his lodge because he would not accept her adopted Sioux child. She was not running away from her family, she was standing up for her principles.

I really screwed up, he thought.

Graham could hear Makawee soothing Dakkoótee by whispering to him. He rested the carbine against the tent wall and ambled toward the creek. He needed to think things through and create a more convincing argument to persuade Makawee to leave Joseph's band.

Graham was distressed when he and Makawee argued. The words of his father echoed in his brain. "Son, there's an old saying I've found very helpful. 'Never go to bed angry at one another.' It's one of the reasons your mother and I have stayed married for all these years."

It was only mid-morning. He had almost an entire day to devise an apology.

"*Wéeptes Xáxaac!*" ["Eagle Bear!"]

Graham looked up and saw Yellow Wolf riding toward him. The young warrior slid off his mount and hugged Graham, catching him by surprise.

"*Qe'ci'yew'yew*" ["Thank you"] he said, after releasing Graham and stepping back.

"Thanks? For what?"

"My *wey-ya-kin* was powerful today. I was like grass in the wind. My body moved back and forth, and the bullets missed me. I sliced off a man's ear with my knife before I shot him. I stole his rifle. See?"

Yellow Wolf held up a Winchester.

"What did I do to deserve your thanks?"

"You painted my war face! My spirit guide knew where I was at all times. That's why I was safe in battle."

"I'm... I'm glad I could help."

"When I prepare for the next battle, will you paint my face?"

Graham studied the young Nez Perce warrior standing in front of him. Black charcoal ran down the side of his face and created thin dark lines on his neck. The ochre clay smudged on his cheekbones thinned with sweat, forming red streaks near his mouth. It appeared as though he had been drinking blood. He was a gruesome sight. But he was drunk with the joy of a battlefield victory in which he proved his manhood.

"Yes," Graham heard himself say. "It would be an honor."

Yellow Wolf emitted a scream, leaped on his horse, and galloped toward the village.

Makawee's words rang in his ears.

"*These people are family. Are you willing to fight for your family? Or will you run away?*"

Graham sighed. She was right. These people were family.

General Howard would learn of the cavalry's defeat at White Bird Canyon by the end of the day. Graham prayed he could keep Makawee and their children safe from the fury that was coming.

Chapter Six
Raining Bullets

26 June [17 miles traveled]

The scout galloped to a halt at the entrance to White Bird Canyon, where nearly two hundred men marched from Fort Lapwai on a mission to find the non-treaty Nez Perce.

"Sir, the battlefield is straight ahead. There are no signs of any hostiles."

"Thank you," General Howard said. "Keep a sharp eye and report anything right away."

"Sir, permission to see the surgeon?"

Howard furrowed his eyebrows. "Are you ill?"

"I... I would like something to calm my stomach."

"Captain Perry!"

The Lapwai post commander moved to the front of the column.

"I'm giving this man permission to seek medical attention for an illness. Send another scout forward. Then join me. You will be my guide."

A minute later, the column was on the move. It was soon obvious why the scout reported feeling queasy. The bodies of those killed in action were scattered on the canyon floor, among the foothills, and in the swales. It had been more than a week since the battle. The stench of death filled the air. Soldiers vomited at the sight and smell of bloated and rotting corpses, which became more frequent as the battalion approached the south end of the canyon.

Perry instructed his lieutenant to appoint a two-man burial detail whenever they encountered a victim. He waited for Howard to interrogate him on the details of the battle, but the general remained silent. The officers dismounted when they reached the abandoned Nez Perce camp.

Howard handed his reins to an aid and turned to gaze up the canyon. The intermittent *thunk, thunk* of spades digging into rocky soil blended with the sound of soldiers puking. He had not experienced such a macabre scene since the last day at Gettysburg. He removed his slouch hat and winced at the brilliance of the midday sun.

Men can be brutal toward one another, he thought, bowing his head. *Lord, accept those fallen into your loving arms.*

Those not burying the dead remained on their horses and awaited orders. Many sniffed or wiped tears from their eyes.

"Captain Perry, how many men did we lose?"

"Thirty-four, sir."

"Out of one hundred soldiers?"

"Yes, sir."

"And how many hostiles did we kill?"

Perry cleared his throat before answering.

"We can't be certain. Based on interviews with survivors, the enemy suffered minimal casualties."

Howard nodded.

"We will camp here tonight, Captain. Pass the order and return with Captain Whipple."

"Yes, sir."

Howard donned his hat and walked to a fire ring. He kicked the cold ashes with the toe of his boot, then kneeled and poked his fingers into the charred remains of the fire.

Joseph, you sly fox! the general thought. *Where are you headed?*

Yesterday, scouts spotted the non-treaty Nez Perce on the other side of the Salmon. The army would have to traverse the fast-flowing river. The only question was the best place for the artillery and cavalry companies to do this.

Joseph and his people crossed the river weeks earlier when the water level was higher from the spring snowmelt. A settler from Grangeville observed the river crossing and recalled the exceptional feat.

The Indians made several square rafts from buffalo skins. They loaded families and their possessions onto these crude vessels and tied the corners to horses. Four riders guided each raft across the roiling rapids, emptied their cargo, and returned to repeat the process. Everyone reached the other side safely. It was a different story for livestock. The river swept away a dozen heads of cattle when men herded the bovines across the angry water.

This territory favored the enemy. Joseph and his people knew the land much better, but Howard commanded a superior fighting force. His army had more than enough supplies and ammunition to defeat an enemy that had to protect women, children, and old men. All he needed to do was be strategic about where and how he attacked.

"General, Captains Perry and Whipple reporting."

The voice shook Howard from his thoughts. He looked up to see the officers.

"Chief Joseph tricked us," Howard said as he stood. "I saw him as a diplomat — as a man who wanted to find a peaceful solution to a territory dispute. That was a ruse. It's now clear he always wanted to fight. He planned to lure the army here and ambush our men."

"I agree," Perry said. "If I knew warriors were lying in wait behind the hills, we would have never ridden down the valley."

"We can't do anything to change the past. But we can dictate what happens from now on. News of this battle will quickly spread to other Nez Perce bands. Some tribes may become emboldened if they believe the army is weak. This one victory might tempt them to join Joseph in his revolt. We need to act quickly to suppress any thoughts others may have about resisting the government."

Whipple and Perry nodded. They watched as Howard paced in a circle around the fire ring, stroking his beard with his left hand. Talking aloud was the general's way of working through a problem before deciding on an action.

"Captain Perry, we will head to the Salmon River first thing in the morning. Consider the best way to get our men and equipment safely across. Make sure the men get a good night's rest. We pursue the enemy tomorrow."

"Yes, sir."

"Captain Whipple, do you know where the village of Looking Glass is located?"

"It's across the Camas Prairie, on the middle fork of the Clearwater River."

"That's correct. Your cavalry will ride there tomorrow. Arrest the chief and the tribal elders. Do not negotiate. Shoot anyone who resists."

"But, sir, Looking Glass is on reservation land. He's the only non-treaty chief to abide by the government order."

"We can't risk his people joining Joseph and the non-treaty bands. They won't leave home if their chief is in jail. Besides, we need to send a message to all tribes in the region. If you tangle with the US army, we will crush you."

"Yes, sir."

The officers saluted and hurried toward the camp, where a sergeant was barking orders about sentry duty and setting up lines to picket the horses.

General Howard glanced at the sky. Patchy gray stratocumulus clouds were streaming from the west. The dark honeycomb-like shapes portended a rainy day.

No matter, Howard thought. *Rain softens the earth. It will be easier to find a trail. And when I find you, Joseph, I will show no mercy.*

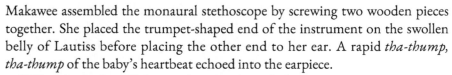

Makawee assembled the monaural stethoscope by screwing two wooden pieces together. She placed the trumpet-shaped end of the instrument on the swollen belly of Lautiss before placing the other end to her ear. A rapid *tha-thump, tha-thump* of the baby's heartbeat echoed into the earpiece.

"What do you hear?" the pregnant woman asked.

Makawee lifted her ear from the wooden tube.

"Your child has a strong heart. Continue to eat berries, camas roots, and meat. If you do this and drink plenty of water, you will have a healthy baby."

"Can you tell if it will be a boy?"

"You are carrying the child low. It's likely you will have a son."

Lautiss smiled and rubbed her belly.

"Shore Crossing will be pleased."

Makawee ducked out of the tepee into the bright mid-July sun. She walked to the wall tent and found Graham inside, cleaning the Colt revolver.

"Where are the children?" she asked.

"Playing with Hophop Onmi and Sara. I see you're practicing to be a midwife again," he said, pointing at the stethoscope with his pistol.

"Well, yes. I'm teaching the women in our village some habits to keep them healthy. I don't have the experience of someone like Among the Grass."

Graham's face darkened. "Don't compare yourself to that bitch."

Just hearing Among the Grass's name made his blood boil. The evil midwife took his only son's life. Long Horse expelled the midwife from his camp when the chief learned of her treachery. Graham squeezed the grip on the Colt. If he could do it over again, he would have shot her in the head.

Makawee sat beside her husband and grabbed his upper arm.

"*Chiaxxapaachí-k.*" ["Calm down"] I'm sorry I mentioned her, but I want to be a healer. I have herbal medicines, but I don't understand how to use many of these things," she said, pointing to a black bag near Graham's feet.

When the Nez Perce women sorted the items stolen during the raids on settler homes and businesses, they tossed the handled bag aside. Makawee recognized the doctor's bag from her visit to the clinic at Fort Parker years earlier. She was soon using the stethoscope, listening to the heart of anyone who sat long enough for the amateur nurse to place the bell-shaped tube on their chest.

Graham placed the revolver on top of the cleaning cloth and pulled the medicine bag closer.

"Well, we haven't taken an inventory. Let's see what we have."

Graham reached into the bag and spread the items on the blanket. Besides the stethoscope, there were three scalpels, a pair of tweezers, pliers, a straight razor, scissors, tourniquets, gauze bandaging, catgut sutures, needles, bent tongs of various lengths, a glass mercury thermometer, and a bottle of whiskey.

"What's in this bottle?" Makawee asked.

She held a light green, flat bottle of 'Laudanum Poison' up to the light.

Graham read the instructions on the label aloud:

```
        Three months old,  2 drops;
          One year old,  4 drops;
        Four years old,  6 drops;
         Ten years old, 14 drops;
      Twenty years old, 25 drops;
              Adults 30 drops.
```

"It's opium mixed in alcohol — a painkiller," he said, setting the glass container on the blanket.

"And this?"

Makawee handed him a clear, round, corked glass bottle containing spherical calomel and opium pills.

"Opium in powder form."

"Do these medicines help?"

"Opium works well to deaden pain." *Almost too well,* he thought, returning the items to the bag. "It's good to know we have surgical tools and medicine."

"I'm going to check on Nahkash and Dakkoótee," she said, jumping up and exiting the tent.

Graham set the physician's bag at the back of the tent and stepped outside. The village was bustling. Women were cooking, pounding cous roots, and hanging fish to dry. Some men were fishing or tending to the enormous herd of horses. Others were butchering a steer for the next meal.

Many things happened in the two weeks since they left camp in White Bird Canyon. They crossed the Salmon River, then recrossed it several days later. While it was an arduous and dangerous task, doubling back had the desired effect on their pursuers. The army struggled to move their equipment and heavily loaded mules across the wide, swift river. Soldiers took three or four days to move from one bank to the other, while the Nez Perce traversed the raging waterway in an afternoon. The army was nowhere in sight.

The camp population swelled considerably when Looking Glass showed up with his band to join Joseph and the other non-treaty bands at the beginning of the month. Captain Whipple's cavalry unit appeared on the outskirts of their village. When the chief sent an emissary to explain they did not want any violence and were inside the reservation boundaries, the officer responded by firing on the village. Looking Glass and his people fled, leaving many of their possessions behind.

Now, a group of nearly seven-hundred-and-fifty people camped at the confluence of Cottonwood Creek and the South Fork of Clearwater River. Graham estimated about two hundred of the villagers were fighting-age men. The government considered these five non-treaty bands renegades. The Nez Perce may have won the initial battle, but the army would be relentless in pursuing these people. Graham didn't know how long they could fight the powerful military. Indeed, he wondered why General Howard's forces had not discovered...

Boom!

An earsplitting sound erupted from a bluff overlooking the camp as a howitzer shell burst high in the air over the valley.

Everyone tried to comprehend what they heard. The villagers looked in the direction of the noise. Was a storm approaching? A few minutes later, they saw a white puff of smoke on a clearing at the crest of the hill.

Boom!

A second blast echoed through the valley when a cannon ball exploded over the horses. The frightened animals squealed and snorted. Boys herded the livestock upstream away from the bluff. Women scurried to gather the children into the tepees.

The enemy had arrived.

Toohoolhoolzote grabbed his front-loading rifle and yelled for his warriors to follow him. Young men hurried to find their weapons. The chief forded the Clearwater River and scrambled up the ravine on the opposite side. Looking Glass and others from his band scurried up the steep slope. Everyone knew they had to stop the soldiers from advancing to the camp.

Graham ran to find Makawee and his children. As he raced to the edge of the village, he saw Yellow Wolf mounting his horse. The young man had stripped to his breechcloth. He was holding a Winchester from the soldier he killed in White Bird Canyon. He looped a cartridge belt over his shoulder. Yellow Wolf saw his friend and galloped to meet him.

"No time for war paint. I hope my *wey-ya-kin* is with me today," he said, turning his horse toward the creek.

"Wait!" Graham shouted. He removed his eagle-bear claw necklace and held it over his head.

Yellow Wolf hesitated, then grabbed the necklace and placed it over his head. He nodded to Graham before reining his horse and splashing across the river.

Graham dashed to the tepee of Wetatonmi. He was relieved to find Makawee inside with Nahkash and Dakkoótee. The women were packing baskets and parfleche pouches with dried food and personal possessions.

"Are you getting ready to leave camp?" he said.

"Joseph instructed the women to bury anything we cannot fit on a horse or travois," Wetatonmi said.

"Good idea. Makawee, we should do the same."

"I will, as soon as I finish helping Wetatonmi."

"But... the soldiers are on the bluffs. They could be here soon!"

"Our warriors will prevent them from entering the village," Wetatonmi said in a calm voice. "We need to pack these things carefully. There is no need to hurry."

Boom!

Graham was incredulous. The village was under attack from men armed with repeating rifles and howitzers. These women wanted to take their time burying household items? Makawee's eyes met his. She shook her head as a signal for him to remain silent.

"I will meet you at our tent," he said, exiting the tepee.

Ollokot, White Bird, and Husishusis Kute positioned men along the river. They challenged the warriors to defend the camp if the soldiers broke through the forward skirmish line of Toohoolhoolzote.

Graham retraced his steps to the tent. He grabbed his Spencer carbine, tossed the Blakeslee cartridge box over his shoulder, and hurried back.

Up on the hill, the warriors engaged Howard's troops. The gunfire was continuous. Bullets zipped down the slope, tattering leaves and plunking into tree trunks. Every few minutes, a blast would erupt from a howitzer. Seconds later, a cannon ball would crash in the village's vicinity. Incredibly, no one in the camp panicked. The women calmly buried household goods and valuables. Old men and boys herded horses and cattle into the canyon while the battle raged on the bluff.

Ollokot walked among the warriors, giving words of encouragement. He stopped when he saw Graham.

"Half our men do not have a rifle. Only bow and arrows. We will get better weapons after we kill soldiers," the war chief said.

"I'm ready to fight. Where do you want me?"

"Are you an excellent shot?"

Graham hesitated. He wanted to answer in the affirmative, but he knew the truth. Every time he fired the Spencer, he was off-target. He gave an honest response. "Only at close range."

"Stay in the village with my brother Joseph. Guard the women."

Graham nodded and headed to the village. He wondered if Ollokot assigned him to protect women and children because he was a poor marksman or because he was a white man. He stuck his thumb under the leather strap of the Blakeslee cartridge box looped across his chest. Something didn't feel right. He had given his eagle-bear claw necklace to Yellow Wolf!

The sacred necklace given to him by Redfield years earlier protected him. He believed in its powers. Without it, he felt naked and vulnerable. Perhaps he was meant to remain behind the front lines. Yellow Wolf certainly needed protection more than he did. Somewhere high on the bluffs, a pitched battle was unfolding. Fifty warriors were fending off an attack by a well-armed and supplied enemy ten times their number.

Clearwater Battlefield

A frightening new sound reverberated from the plateau above the river. It mixed with rifle fire and periodic blasts from the howitzer. It was the unmistakable rapid *bang-bang-bang* of a Gatling gun. A soldier cranked the multiple-barrel firearm and emptied a forty-round box magazine of .45-70 black powder cartridges in less than thirty seconds. Bullets rained on Nez Perce crouched behind improvised rock rifle pits. After reloading, the artillery crew created another deadly hailstorm.

The women dug faster to bury their caches. Some disassembled tepees. Everyone knew it was only a matter of time before Howard's troops would overrun the courageous defenders on the bluff.

Graham awoke with a sudden jerk when his head fell forward. He fell asleep while sitting, his back resting against a pile of firewood and the barrel of his carbine leaning against his shoulder. He rubbed his eyes, then stood and squinted in the gray light of dawn. Donning his hat, he walked to his campsite.

Makawee and the children were asleep beneath a blanket. She draped her arm over Dakkoótee, and Nahkash snuggled next to her brother. Anticipating they would have to move on a moment's notice, Graham packed the tent and most of their belongings. He instructed Makawee to sleep under stars. It surprised him to see most of the tepees in the village were erect. They disassembled only a dozen. Women stripped the buffalo hide coverings from another ten lodges, leaving the conical-shaped timber skeletons standing.

Graham cradled the carbine in his arms and walked to the river. Three sentries stood watch while the others slept. It was eerily silent. The only sounds were the snoring of the men and the soft gurgling of water as it flowed over smooth rocks. Graham peered up the ravine and wondered how the tribesmen at the top of the hill were faring.

The fighting continued until dusk. The gunfire ceased when darkness fell. Women carried buckets of water and food to the exhausted warriors at the crest of the bluff. According to two young men who hurried down the slope after dark, the soldiers took a defensive position. Aside from a few brief charges from both sides, neither side launched an offensive.

"*Ta 'c meeywi*," ["Good morning"] a voice said from behind.

Graham turned to see Ollokot approaching. The warrior blackened his face below his eyes, then painted white chevron stripes on both cheeks.

"Hello," Graham replied. "Do you know if any of our people were hurt yesterday?"

He wondered if the war chief noticed Graham's choice of words — referring to the Nez Perce as *our* people.

"Some injuries. Nothing serious. The real fighting happens today. We must be prepared for Cut Arm when he attacks."

"Will the women take their lodges down?"

"The other chiefs decide what to do with their people. Joseph gives orders for the Wallowa band."

"Don't you think we should be ready to..."

Crack!

A lone rifle shot pierced the early morning air.

Crack! Crack! Boom!

Gunfire and a cannon blast signaled another day's fighting had began.

Ollokot leaped onto his horse. He dug his heels into the flanks of his steed, urging warriors to prepare for battle.

Graham ran to his family. He found Makawee holding the toddler. She was comforting the child from the strange, sharp noises in the distance. Nahkash was sitting by her mother, clinging to her arm.

"Please listen," Graham said as he kneeled. He sat the butt of the carbine on the ground and leaned on the barrel. "You cannot offer help while trying to care for our children. Take them and go into the canyon. Ask Wetatonmi if she will allow Sara to watch them. You can come back and help the other women. Understood?"

"But... why are we leaving now? No one else is..."

"Don't you see? Within the next few hours, an army will march down that hill and overrun this camp. I don't want our children here!"

"But what about Lautiss? Who will...?"

Boom!

Makawee and Graham flinched. A howitzer unleashed another ball that landed sixty yards away. Frightened horses bucked and ran through the camp, knocking over copper kettles and trampling baskets.

Graham removed his hat and looked into his wife's eyes. He said nothing. She could see the determination in his stare.

"I will do as you say."

Graham leaned forward and kissed her, then planted a kiss on the forehead of Nahkash.

"Everything will be okay," he said soothingly to his daughter. "Mommy will take care of you."

He donned his hat, stood, and ran toward the river, the Blakeslee cartridge box banging against his side.

As the sun arced toward its apex and the temperature climbed, the fighting intensified. Those remaining in camp sensed the warriors on the bluff were losing the battle. Three fighters ran down the ravine and stuck their heads in the river's water to slake their thirst. White Bird asked them what was happening on top of the hill. They simply shook their heads and hurried toward camp, looking for their family members. Soon, five more men followed. Then three more.

We've lost the battle. They're coming! Graham thought.

Within minutes, clusters of warriors raced down the hill, struggling to keep their balance as they leaped over fallen logs and dodged willow bushes. A line of men from camp splashed across the river and took up positions on the opposite bank at the base of the ravine. The gunfire came closer as the Nez Perce retreated. Bullets zipped through the trees. The soldiers were close enough to hit horses and puncture holes in lodges.

Chief Joseph mounted his horse and rode through camp, instructing the residents to leave behind anything they had not packed.

"*Koiimze!*" ["Hurry!"] he yelled, pointing toward the mouth of the canyon.

Women and boys assisted the elderly onto horses before mounting themselves. The village emptied as the entourage made their way from the open floor of the valley toward the safety of the steep canyon walls.

Graham lowered his Spencer and fired when he saw bluecoats sheltered behind rocks on the steep slope. They were too far away to be viable targets, but he needed to buy time for the villagers to escape. As he chambered another round, he looked around and saw Makawee bandaging a young man's wound on his arm. He scrambled from the river bank, crouched to avoid zipping bullets, and rushed to her side.

"He's bleeding," she said.

Graham snatched the bandage from her.

"Go! Now! I will take care of him."

"Have you seen Lautiss?"

A bullet pinged a kettle suspended over a nearby firepit. Graham's heart rate quickened.

"She may have left with the others. I'll look for her. Go!"

Makawee tossed a parfleche bag of cloth strips over her shoulder. She mounted and reined her horse to face Graham.

He looked up from the wound he was tying off and emphatically pointed his finger toward the distant parade of families exiting camp. She galloped away to join them.

Graham turned his attention to the wounded warrior.

"*Uselikse?*" ["Stand?"] he asked, lifting his hand with the palm facing up.

The young man struggled to his feet.

"*Sikum?*" ["Horse?"]

He nodded and ran toward the area where the men picketed two dozen horses.

Graham picked up his carbine. He ran to join the defensive line at the river when he heard a familiar woman's voice.

"*Mamook!*" ["Help!"]

Lautiss was struggling to mount her horse. Her husband, Shore Crossing, must still be fighting in the ravine. Or perhaps he had been killed. No one assisted the pregnant woman.

Graham sprinted to Lautiss and grabbed the reins of the horse. After calming the frightened animal, he interlocked his fingers to make a stirrup. He motioned for her to step into the foothold. Before she could oblige, a bullet zipped into the horse's hind quarter, fracturing the fibula. The mare screamed and fell onto its side, nearly collapsing the rope line where the horses were tethered. Blood oozed from the bullet wound as the horse thrashed about in pain.

He pulled the Colt from his belt, shot the poor creature in the head, then motioned for Lautiss to follow him.

They hurried down the picket line to a large stallion. He hoped there were enough rides for everyone. If not, some warriors would have to double up. After hoisting Lautiss aboard, Graham led the nervous horse beside a log. Standing on the fallen tree, Graham slid on behind her. He reined the horse toward the fleeing families. They were easy to find. The mass exodus of people, horses, and cattle created a cloud of dust as they hurried along Cottonwood Creek.

The gunfire faded as they approached the canyon. Graham was thankful his family escaped harm. He wondered about the fate of the retreating warriors and those providing cover fire. He had not seen a bare-chested young man wearing an eagle-bear claw necklace since yesterday.

He hoped Yellow Wolf's *wey-ya-kin* kept him alive.

Chapter Seven
Through Looking Glass
12 July [37 miles traveled]

General Howard sat on his horse and surveyed the abandoned Indian camp. The Nez Perce had spaced tepees in staggered rows at the mouth of Cottonwood Creek and along the Clearwater River. The occupants stripped most lodges of their buffalo skins. Rumpled blankets lay inside the circular floor of some lodges. Pots hung over dormant cooking fires. Opened bags of coffee and flour leaned against piles of firewood. Flies swarmed around a side of beef dangling from a tree. These remnants told a story of people who left in haste.

The enemy was on the run. This was a sweet victory for the army following their humiliating loss at White Bird Canyon.

"General," a scout said, reining his horse to a stop and saluting. "We've identified a trail leading into the canyon."

Howard saluted and dismissed the scout.

"Captain Whipple!"

"Yes, sir," the officer replied, urging his horse forward.

"One of my aides observed Looking Glass fighting on the bluffs this morning. The chief joined forces with Joseph. The enemy's ranks have swollen."

The general was reminding the captain of failing in his mission to arrest Looking Glass earlier. Whipple said nothing.

Howard paused. "At least the non-treaties are all together."

"Should we follow them?" Whipple asked, trying to change the subject.

"No. That's too dangerous. They would lie in wait and ambush our column. After we are supplied and reinforced, we will find the best place to trap and punish the hostiles."

Howard scanned the camp again, noting the excellent location.

To the victors belong the spoils, he thought.

"Tell Captain Perry we will stay here tonight. The men are welcome to anything left behind. Burn the village on our way out tomorrow."

"Yes, sir."

The exhausted soldiers were grateful for an evening of rest. They bivouacked for more than a week while pursuing the non-treaty Nez Perce to the edge of the Camas Prairie. Although the cooks occasionally made flapjacks, the men subsisted on hard tack, raw bacon, and coffee. Now, they enjoyed eating their enemy's food. They dined on beef, potatoes, berries, and camas bread.

Two civilian scouts rode into camp while the men were eating and asked to speak to the commanding officer. A lieutenant escorted them to the general's tent, where Howard was sitting outside, dictating a note to an aide about the day's events.

"General, permission to look for valuables," one of the scouts said.

Howard looked up from his folding chair and squinted at the man with a short salt-and-pepper beard. He was one of the Idaho volunteers who fought at White Bird Canyon. While civilians were helpful, most lacked the discipline and training of a soldier. Howard was circumspect with his reply.

"I believe our men already claimed anything edible or of value."

"Begging your pardon, but there are many items you haven't discovered."

"Oh, how's that?"

"The Indians buried them."

"What kinds of things?"

"Stuff worth diggin' for."

Howard cocked his head to one side. He pondered the stranger's motives.

"What do you want?"

"A detail of six men. I'm confident we'll dig up valuables under our feet... maybe right below where you're sittin'."

The general peered between his legs and stroked his beard.

"What's in it for you?"

"All we want is a fair share of anything we find. You decide what we keep and what the army keeps."

Although he was skeptical, Howard saw no harm in digging. If they found valuable items, he reasoned, the bounty would add to the victory they earned. He turned to his aide.

"Tell Captain Perry to give him some men. Have someone supervise."

Twenty minutes later, the digging crew was busy. They utilized hatchets to sharpen the ends of stout pine branches. The scouts demonstrated to the soldiers how to thrust sticks into the earth and investigate for zones that were softer than the nearby dirt. The men fanned out and prodded their crude stakes into the soil at regular intervals. One scout improvised by using a ramrod from a muzzleloader.

Soldiers bathing in the river and sitting by fires chided those armed with sharpened sticks.

"Hey, fellas! You think those Injuns buried greenbacks?"

"Whatcha lookin' fer with those pig stickers?"

"Ignore 'em," the lieutenant overseeing the operation said. "They're just relieved you're not digging graves for them like we did for those up on the hill."

The Nez Perce killed twelve infantry and artillerymen during the two-day battle. The soldiers buried the victims in a mass grave at the top of the bluff.

"Aha!" a scout shouted as he pulled a stake from the ground. He shoved it into the dirt several more times. "Over here! Bring a spade!"

Curious onlookers watched as two men dug into the soft earth and tossed the dirt onto a pile. A foot below the surface, the iron blade of the shovel hit a buffalo hide. The soldiers dragged the animal skin from the hole and unfolded it. The crude wrapping held jewelry, spoons, beaded shirts, knife sheaths, leggings, moccasins, and shiny pieces of obsidian.

"There's more. I'm sure of it," the scout said. "The Nez Perce camped at this site for decades. They buried anything they couldn't take with them and returned every year to retrieve their stash."

Within minutes, the six-person digging crew tripled. Using bayonets and tent stakes, men poked and prodded the soil along the river. Each man hoped to find a cache of valuables or souvenirs. The massive treasure hunt paid off. By sunset, shallow holes pocked the bottomland where diggers removed canvas bags, reed baskets, and parfleche wraps filled with clothing, tools, and artifacts.

General Howard watched the proceedings with amusement. He smiled as he read the last lines of his communication to General Sherman, extolling the victory he named *Battle of the South Fork of Clearwater River*. He handed the note to an orderly sergeant.

"My aide wrote three copies of this letter. Have a courier deliver one copy to Portland headquarters immediately. I've instructed Major Wood to telegraph it to General Sherman. The courier will take the other copies to *The Oregonian* and *The Oregon Statesman*."

After the sergeant saluted and hurried away, Howard sat and listened to a group of soldiers singing beside a fire. It was nice to hear cheerful tunes befitting the occasion. The general's critics would argue the hostiles were still on the loose, but he saw it differently. This victory was important. It bolstered the confidence of his men.

It also didn't hurt to prime the political pump. That's why he sent copies of his letter to the Portland newspapers. He learned the power of the press could either make or break a military man's career. He wanted to be sure the public knew he could rid the region of these menacing non-treaty Indians.

Howard slipped on his reading glasses and reached for his Bible. He thumbed through the pages and stopped at Psalm 144.

Blessed be the Lord my strength, which teacheth my hands to war, and my fingers to fight. My goodness, and my fortress; my high tower, and my deliverer; my shield, and he in whom I trust; who subdueth my people under me.

God had guided him to a much-needed victory. Surely, the Lord would give him the strength to subdue these heathens.

Shore Crossing and Yellow Wolf were the last warriors to leave Cottonwood Creek as the soldiers advanced down the bluffs into the abandoned camp. Shore Crossing was relieved Lautiss was safe. Makawee noticed Yellow Wolf was bleeding, but the young man insisted it wasn't serious. He promised to let her inspect the wounds when they camped for the night.

The Nez Perce refugees crossed the Clearwater River on buffalo hide rafts at Kamiah. The chiefs assigned a group of warriors to guard the rear of the column. Two dozen remained on the north bank of the river. They were told to fire at any soldiers who approached the swollen river. This strategy was designed to create more distance between the Indians and their pursuers by keeping the army on the opposite bank.

Yellow Wolf rode up beside Graham and Makawee in mid-afternoon. He pointed to a grass-covered mound on the valley floor.

"Heart of the Monster," he said. "I will share the ancient story of that place when we camp."

By evening, the Nez Perce climbed out of the Clearwater Valley onto an expansive plateau called Weippe.

As the men cared for the horses and cattle, women set up shelters using whatever they had time to bring from their camp at the mouth of Cottonwood Creek. Most women barely had the opportunity to roll the hide coverings from their tepees and toss them onto pack horses. Now, they were tasked with cutting small diameter trees for the lodges' infrastructure. They had hatchets and hand axes, but it was a laborious task. Because the group needed to travel light, they would leave most poles behind and cut new ones at each campsite. The camp was a hodgepodge of traditional tepees and improvised low-slung shelters created by draping buffalo hides over short poles.

Yellow Wolf joined Makawee and Graham at their fire after Nahkash and Dakkoótee were asleep.

"Let me look at your wound," Makawee said.

Yellow Wolf tilted his head back. Makawee dabbed a wet cloth under his left eye and removed dried blood under a gash.

Graham pulled a bottle of whiskey from the medical bag, took out the cork, and handed it to Makawee.

"Use this," he said.

She frowned. "I don't think it's wise for someone to drink firewater."

"I don't want him to ingest it," he said. "Give me your cloth."

He tilted the bottle, moistened a corner of the fabric, and gave it back to her. Makawee cleaned the wound again.

"Ow!" Yellow Wolf exclaimed, wincing and pulling his head away.

"I know it stings, but alcohol destroys germs. We don't want that cut to become infected." Graham said.

Makawee and Yellow Wolf looked at him quizzically.

Graham realized few people who lived on the American frontier were aware of germ theory or infections in the 1870s.

"Trust me. It's good medicine. How did you get cut?"

"We built stone rifle pits. The big, noisy cranking gun broke off pieces when it fired. A rock hit me here," Yellow Wolf said, pointing to the nasty slice.

"What about this?" Graham said, as he pulled Yellow Wolf's arm toward him. The tip of a bullet lodged under the skin of the warrior's wrist.

"It doesn't hurt badly," Yellow Wolf said, shrugging.

Graham used tongs and gave a quick jerk. He stared at the extracted slug, amazed it only broke the skin, but avoided bone and blood vessels.

"Keep?" he asked, holding it up for Yellow Wolf to see.

"Yes! This proves the power of my *wey-ya-kin*. They shot me, but I did not bleed."

Graham dropped it into his friend's hand.

"Tell me the Heart of the Monster."

"Ah, yes. It's the sacred place where I went on a vision quest," Yellow Wolf said, rubbing his wrist where Graham removed the bullet.

He looked up at the night sky, closed his eyes for a moment, then told the ancient story his ancestors passed down for thousands of years.

"After the world was made, but before there were people, there was an enormous and fierce monster that would swallow animals alive. The animals held a council to devise a plan to destroy this creature. *Iceye-ye*, or Coyote, was selected to fight the dreaded monster.

"Coyote gathered pitch pine and flint. He approached the sleeping monster and hit him. The monster jerked open his mouth and inhaled Coyote, who started a fire in the beast's belly. He used the flint to stab the monster. The beast groaned and opened its mouth before dying.

"Coyote sliced the monster into pieces and tossed them in many directions. The Blackfeet emerged from the monster's feet. Crows and Flat Heads sprouted from the monster's head. The other tribes came from different body parts. Nothing was left but the heart. The Heart of the Monster is the grassy mound we passed near Kamiah. Coyote washed his hands with the blood of the monster and sprinkled it on the land. The Nez Perce people were created from these drops of blood."

"That's a beautiful creation story," Makawee said, clutching Graham's arm as they sat beside the crackling fire. "I can understand why your spirit guardian is a powerful protector when you completed your vision quest at the birthplace of your people."

"That reminds me. I have something of yours," Yellow Wolf said.

He slipped the eagle-bear claw necklace over his head and handed it to Graham.

"Thank you for loaning your sacred necklace."

Graham pushed Yellow Wolf's arm away.

"Wear it. You will be close to the enemy again. The necklace will provide an extra measure of protection."

"*Qe'ci'yew'yew.*" ["Thank you"]

"You're welcome."

Yellow Wolf stood and tossed some branches onto the fire. Red embers danced into the night.

"This place is also special for white people," he said after sitting with crossed legs.

"Oh?" Graham asked. "How so?"

"Over seventy years ago, William Clark and a small group of fair-skinned men approached our people on this plain. They were tired and hungry. Chief Red Bear gave the strangers food rather than kill them. The white men ate dried salmon and berries and camas."

Graham nodded. He learned about Lewis and Clark's Corps of Discovery expedition in school. The Nez Perce's hospitality enabled the explorers to reach the Pacific Ocean.

Shore Crossing emerged from the darkness and stood in the fire's light.

"Come. We are rounding up cattle in the area. The women are slaughtering them tonight."

Over seven hundred men, women, and children needed to be fed while fleeing from the army. The non-treaty Nez Perce would have to be resourceful to supply food for such a large group. Tonight, they supplemented their herds by stealing livestock from homesteads.

Yellow Wolf stood. He turned to Graham and shared a final thought before leaving.

"We befriended the *soyapu* long ago. Now, the white man repays our friendship by hunting us like animals."

A cow bellowed somewhere in the night, its mournful cry ending abruptly with a gunshot. The butchering had begun.

"Is the baby well?" Lautiss asked.

Makawee lifted her ear from the stethoscope resting on the pregnant woman's stomach. She placed the listening device into the medical bag and sat across from her patient.

"I hear a strong heart," she said in a reassuring tone. "Let others set up your lodge when we make camp. You should not be lifting heavy things."

"I should not rely on others to do my work."

"Graham and I will help you if Shore Crossing is busy with the herds or guarding the camp," Makawee said, leaning forward and placing her hand on Lautiss's arm. "The most important job you have right now is to deliver a healthy baby boy. I will be with you when that happy time comes."

Lautiss stroked her belly and smiled. She repositioned herself to lean against a pole of the crude lodge constructed from limbs and branches.

"The chiefs have a council tonight. The people are saying we will learn where we go next," Lautiss said.

"It will be good to have a direction."

"I heard you will attend."

"I was honored to be invited by Ollokot. Graham will watch our children while I go to the council."

"May I ask a question?

"Yes."

"I do not understand why you left your people. Don't you miss your loved ones?"

Makawee averted her eyes. While she considered the Nez Perce her family, sometimes she dreamed what might have been. Late at night, when everyone was asleep, she would occasionally lie awake and reminisce about her life on the plains of eastern Montana. She missed the rolling hills around the Stillwater River, the sound of the bison calves being born in the spring, the pungent smell of fresh-cut sweetgrass, and the annual ritual of digging for timpsila roots.

She also thought about Long Horse and Fox Woman. How different her life would be if her father had accepted Dakkoótee. It was unfair. Nahkash would not know her grandparents or learn Crow traditions. She resented the narrow-minded chief for refusing to welcome her adopted boy into his family simply because he was a Sioux child.

"Do you miss your family?" Lautiss said again.

The question snapped Makawee from her thoughts.

"Oh! Oh, yes. I do, but I'm happy with my Nez Perce friends."

Lautiss nodded. "And we are glad you're with us."

"*Ta 'c kuleewit,*" ["Good evening"] a man said, interrupting their dialogue. The women were so engrossed in their conversation, neither saw Ollokot approach.

"The chiefs are assembling," he said.

Makawee stood and pointed to the black bag.

"I will return for the medicine kit."

Ollokot and Makawee walked toward a fire at the base of a small hill. When they arrived, Ollokot asked her to wait outside of the circle.

Tribal chiefs and war chiefs sat by the fire, smoking and talking. Makawee was close enough to hear their discussion. A few advocated going west and returning to the Wallowa Valley. Others quickly vetoed this idea. There was no turning back. The government would never allow them to settle in their homeland — not after the army suffered so many losses in White Bird Canyon. The chiefs agreed to travel east through the Bitterroot Mountains.

The council debated what to do after crossing the mountains.

Toohoolhoolzote argued they should turn north, travel through Flathead country, and cross into the British territory called Canada.

"The foolish white men draw borders and expect everyone to stay on one side," he said. "The animals and birds do not know about these man-made divisions. Our ancestors followed the elk herds wherever they went — even when they crossed the imaginary line where the people from two governments are separated. We know soldiers will not cross over this boundary. The line no one can see has magical powers to stop an army. That's why we call it the Medicine Line. Let us use this to our advantage. Go north, cross the Medicine Line, and our people will be safe."

Some nodded in agreement.

"What Toohoolhoolzote has spoken is true," Looking Glass said, rising from his seat around the fire. "I agree the Medicine Line offers a place we can escape the enemy. However, there is another option."

Everyone turned their attention to the spokesman of the Alpowai band. He was not only a tribal chief. He was a war chief with extensive fighting experience.

"We should follow the traditional hunting trails. Ride east through Yellow Stone country and on to the buffalo plains. Travel through friendly Crow territory. We can seek refuge with our allies. Perhaps they will join our fight against the government. If they refuse to assist, then we ride north and cross the Medicine Line to safety."

A half-dozen leaders gestured in agreement. This idea had merit.

"Permission to speak," Ollokot said.

Looking Glass nodded and sat.

"As war chief of the Wallowa band, I support the strategy of Looking Glass. Many of you know Makawee is a guest in the camp of Chief Joseph since the last harvest moon. You may not know her father is the Crow chief, Long Horse."

A low murmur arose from those seated around the fire.

"I invite her to come forward."

He turned and stretched out a hand toward Makawee, palm up.

Makawee was stunned. She wondered why Ollokot invited her to the council. Now it was clear. He wanted her to assure the group the Crow would support the non-treaty Nez Perce!

She stood and entered the center of the circle with Ollokot.

"As the daughter of Chief Long Horse, can you say if the Crow tribe will welcome us?" he asked.

Her jaw tightened. Her breathing became shallow. She peered at the faces illuminated in the dim firelight and saw leaders looking at her with hopeful eyes. She could almost read their minds. If only there was another tribe that would partner with them against the government. That would make this treacherous journey for their families bearable.

These men did not know she was estranged from her father. Their relationship was shattered, if not completely broken. She had no influence on Chief Long Horse. How could she give them hope without lying?

"I have not spoken with my father for almost a year," she began, searching for the right words. "However, I can tell you Long Horse has always respected the Nez Perce. If approached, I'm sure he will listen to you with an open mind."

This was true, she thought.

"Will you invite him to our council when we enter your homeland?" Ollokot asked.

Makawee gulped. Ollokot and Joseph graciously welcomed her family into their camp. What reason could she give for refusing to speak with her father? It was the least she could do, even if she found it unpleasant.

"I will," she heard herself say.

Makawee stepped out of the center of the council. She sat in the darkness behind the men, who were chattering about Looking Glass' proposal to travel through Yellow Stone country before turning north to Canada and seeking asylum. She wished they would accept the original plan by Toohoolhoolzote. If they chose that strategy, they would never enter Crow country — and she would not need to face her father.

Several leaders rose to endorse the route to Yellowstone National Park. The council soon agreed to lead their people through the Land of Burning Ground and into Montana Territory. They chose the most experienced war chief as leader of all the bands. If the Nez Perce were to escape the army, their fate rested with the skills of Looking Glass.

Makawee sat by the dying fire after the council disbanded and considered her future. This would be a bittersweet journey. She would see her homeland. She harbored no ill feelings toward Fox Woman. Perhaps Nahkash could spend time with her grandmother. She would begrudgingly talk with Long Horse about assisting the non-treaty Nez Perce.

As she stood to walk back to her family's tent, Ollokot surprised her by stepping from the darkness.

"Thank you for speaking tonight. Your words helped the council decide to travel through the park. I'm pleased our friends the Crow might offer help."

Makawee nodded, but kept her head down while she walked. She wasn't in the mood for talking.

Ollokot ambled alongside her and shared his thoughts.

"Tomorrow we begin our journey to freedom. We will cross the Bitterroot Mountains through Lolo Pass. Some day we will return."

He considered his words, which changed from hopeful to despondent.

"I fear our people may not see our homeland again."

She looked up at the young war chief. An air of melancholy surrounded him. They shared the same feelings, but for different reasons. Makawee was resentful toward her father. She was going home, but the government forced Ollokot and his people to leave their traditional home — perhaps forever.

For the non-treaty Nez Perce, the Wallowa Valley became *bitter ground*.

Chapter Eight
Traders and Thieves

31 July [146 miles traveled]

The mule balked as Graham's horse entered the Bitterroot River. He tugged on the lead rope of the pack animal and urged it to step into the northward flowing waterway. Because it was the end of July, it was only a few feet deep and easy to ford.

Graham was part of an entourage tasked with acquiring much needed supplies. He, Makawee, and six Nez Perce warriors accompanied two dozen women on an excursion to Stevensville. The group brought along ten mules to carry the goods they hoped to purchase in the small Montana town. As they rode north, Graham considered the events that allowed the Nez Perce to shop in the valley.

Nine days earlier, the Nez Perce refugees followed the centuries-old Lolo Trail through the pass of the same name. They experienced anxious moments in this part of their journey. The territorial governor requested armed volunteers to assemble at the Lolo Trail. The authorities ordered the civilian militia to join thirty soldiers stationed in Missoula and twenty Flathead Indians. This combined force of one hundred men hoped to prevent the Nez Perce from entering the Bitterroot Valley.

The Missoula post commander approached Looking Glass under a flag of truce and demanded the Nez Perce surrender. When the chief refused, soldiers and civilians retreated behind a barricade built across a narrow segment of the Lolo Trail. A fight seemed inevitable.

Instead of confronting the armed men, Looking Glass led the group off the trail, across a ridge, and down the other side. The Nez Perce circumvented the blockade and rode into the Bitterroot Valley without incident. The commanding officer realized he was ill-equipped to fight the enemy with his small force. He ordered the detachment back to Missoula.

The Nez Perce camped in the valley and rested. Other than the soldiers at Lolo Pass, they saw no signs of Howard's army.

It pleased Ollokot and the other war chiefs when several Nez Perce families who were living in the valley joined their Idaho brethren on the trek toward buffalo country.

~ Lean Elk

They especially welcomed a respected hunter named *Wahwookya Wasaaw*, or Lean Elk. He made many trips to the east and knew the terrain well.

Graham hoped this foray into town was not a mistake. The non-treaty bands needed to re-supply. Their sudden exodus at Clearwater meant they left items and prepared foods behind. This visit to the white settlement seemed like a dangerous decision. The homesteaders in the area were on edge. They heard about the renegade Nez Perce. Most residents either volunteered to help the military fight or gathered in a barricaded building until the hostile Indians passed by.

Looking Glass gave explicit instructions to the warrior escorts.

"Do not shoot... unless they shoot first."

The war chief ordered the women to buy or trade for all supplies. There would be no stealing.

Graham glanced at his wife, who was riding beside him. Makawee caught his eye and smiled. Joseph's daughter, Hophop Onmi, was watching Nahkash and Dakkoótee while they made this trip into town. Graham wanted Makawee to stay in camp, but she insisted on accompanying the other women. She reminded him her fluency in English could be useful when they bartered with the shopkeepers.

The Nez Perce crossed narrow irrigation ditches that supplied water to the arid fields planted with potatoes, oats, and wheat. They passed barns and houses. A few miles further, they spotted cattle grazing among the cottonwood trees. Besides farmers, ranchers established homesteads in the valley.

As they approached Stevensville, a collection of false-front frame buildings, the town was eerily quiet. No one was on the dirt street. There were no horses tied to the rails or buggies kicking up dust. The group rode by Campbell's Livery and Miser's Drug Store. Neither business showed signs of activity. Most surprising was the Star Saloon. The proprietor boarded the wooden entrance doors shut and pulled down a dark shade across the front window.

After passing Doctor Kellogg's shuttered office, the group stopped at a freshly-painted building. A hand-lettered sign affixed to the store front identified the business as *Henry Buck & Co. General Mercantile.* Three men stood on the boardwalk in front of the store, whose door was open. They were the only townspeople in sight.

"Kla-how'-ya," the tallest of the three said. "My name is Henry Buck. Does anyone speak English?"

"I do," Makawee said, dismounting.

"What about you, young fella?" Henry asked, ignoring Makawee and nodding to Graham, who remained on his horse.

"Yes, but these women are here to shop. Talk with them."

"Mr. Buck, my name is Makawee. I can interpret if you do not know Chinook Jargon or speak Nez Perce."

"Yes, of course. Begging your pardon. These are my brothers, Amos and Fred. Our store is open. Please come inside."

Makawee turned and interpreted for the group. Everyone dismounted except for three warriors, who stayed outside to tend to the equines and serve as guards while the women walked into the shop.

Amos pulled Henry aside and whispered to his older brother.

"Are you sure this is a good idea? These Indians are being chased by the army. What if they rob us at gunpoint... or worse?"

"Calm down. We will make a nice profit today. Just insist they pay in cash or gold."

Graham followed Makawee into the crowded store. The brothers stocked the shelves with tools, canned foods, boots, hats, blankets, rope, twine, tobacco, coffee, sugar, vegetables, fruits, candy, various articles of clothing, and calico. An iron pot-bellied stove squatted at the back, the door to its firebox hanging open. A line of wolf and fox pelts dangled from a rope strung along a wall.

Fred Buck stood behind a counter at the side of the store while his siblings attended to the women. Makawee interpreted when a storekeeper or a woman asked for help.

The Nez Perce were among the wealthiest tribes in the region because they became proficient at breeding horses and raising cattle. Although they left the camp on the Clearwater hastily, the women took all their money and precious metals. It pleased the Buck brothers when they paid for the items with greenbacks. They also offered gold dust or silver nuggets for the dry goods, which they carried outside and packed onto the mules.

As the store emptied of goods and people, Graham noticed Makawee drifted to the back corner of the shop. She held a two-piece dress of white cotton with a printed blue flower background in front of her. She used one hand to push the skirt against her breastbone and the other to press it to her waist. When she swiveled her hips, the bottom of the ruffled skirt brushed the top of her moccasins and swished along the plank floor.

"You would look even more beautiful wearing that dress," Graham said, smiling.

"Oh! I... I was just passing time while the others paid for everything," she said, blushing.

Makawee hung it on a hook mounted on the wall and stepped back.

"Do you want it?" Graham said.

"Yes!" She paused. "I mean, no. It's not for me. It's for Lautiss. She has gotten so big with child. I remember being pregnant with Nahkash. I could alter it around the waist. It would give her something comfortable to wear on hot summer days like these."

Graham marveled at his wife. She was always thinking of others before herself. It was one of the reasons he loved her so much.

"Well, let's buy it."

She looked at him incredulously.

"Are you sure?"

"You will enjoy seeing Lautiss in that dress."

"But we have little money."

Graham grinned and pulled two bank notes from his jeans pocket.

"Where did you get those?"

"Ollokot gave it to me this morning. He told me to buy something nice for you. He was grateful you agreed to talk with Long Horse about the Crow supporting his people." Graham furrowed his brow. "I didn't know you made that promise. Is this true?"

Makawee dropped her head.

"I agreed to his request. I'm not eager to speak to Long Horse, but I feel obligated because of everything Joseph and Ollokot have done for our family."

Graham lifted her chin with his finger.

"You're doing the right thing. I love you no matter how the conversation with your father goes."

"Excuse me, Miss?" Amos Buck said from across the room. "This lady is confused about the price for these items. Can you help?"

"Go ahead," Graham said. "I'll negotiate with Henry Buck to buy the dress and meet you outside."

She hugged him, then hurried to the front.

Graham surveyed the hand tools stacked in a corner. A short-handled shovel caught his eye. He gripped the well-worn handle. The blade was nicked and slightly bent, but it seemed sturdy. He noted the Nez Perce only packed a few digging tools and decided to buy one for his family. Makawee had to ask to borrow a shovel when she dug for roots. A hatchet and a shovel were handy tools in camp.

"I'll sell that banjo cheap," Henry said. The store owner noticed Graham eyeing up the digging tool.

"Banjo?"

"Yep. That's what the miner I got it from called it. Sold everything so he could buy a stagecoach ticket. He was giving up mining and heading back east."

By the time Graham struck a bargain with Henry and the storekeeper wrapped the dress, the store was quiet. When he stepped outside, Makawee was the only one remaining.

"Where is everyone?"

"The store doesn't carry flour. The group headed to a grist mill next to Fort Owen. We will meet them in camp."

Graham nodded and tucked a brown paper package in his saddlebag. He held up the shovel for her to see.

"We can both use this."

Graham secured the shovel to the mule's load with a length of rope. Makawee grabbed the lead rope of the pack animal loaded with bags of coffee, cones of sugar, and boxes of canned food. She and Graham mounted as Henry Buck stepped onto the front porch.

"Another shipment of goods is coming from Salt Lake City next week," he said. "If you plan on staying in the valley for a while, come see us again."

Graham touched the brim of his hat. He urged his horse forward. Makawee tugged on the rope, and the mule followed.

The couple plodded toward camp, retracing the path the Nez Perce used on their way to town. Graham unbuttoned his buckskin jacket to get some relief from the warm, humid air that settled over the valley. After passing by large vegetable plots, the trail entered a grove of ponderosa pines. A spring gurgled from the ground along a hill and soaked a thick bed of pine needles under the trees.

"Let's stop for a drink," he said.

The pair dismounted. Graham held the horses and mule while Makawee stooped at the spring. She skimmed the needles from the surface of the tiny pool, bent forward, and slurped cool water from her cupped hand.

"How does it taste?"

"Wonderful! Your turn," she said, wiping her mouth with her sleeve.

Graham handed her the reins and kneeled.

Click!

It was the unmistakable sound of a revolver being cocked.

"Hands up, mister. Unless you wanna slug in your back."

Graham's heart pounded. He put his arms in the air.

"Now, stand up and turn around, so's I kin see ya."

Graham did as he was told.

A stocky man with a bushy red beard was pointing a .45 caliber Colt revolver at his chest.

"Tell the squaw to join ya."

"I can speak English," Makawee said defiantly, walking over beside Graham.

"You carryin' any barking irons?"

The Colt Cobra was tucked in his belt. Graham thought about lying for a split second, but he didn't want to put his wife in danger.

"A pistol."

"Fetch it careful and toss it over here."

He obliged. The snub-nosed revolver fell with a thud at the feet of the robber, who picked up the weapon.

"If that don't beat all! You've got half a pistol, fella! Who sawed off the barrel?"

Graham shrugged.

"How 'bout you?" he asked Makawee.

She shook her head.

"Well now, what are y'all packin'?"

Red Beard tucked the Colt Cobra in his coat pocket. Keeping his revolver pointed at Graham and Makawee, he stepped over to the mule. He surveyed the dry goods and whistled.

"Ain't that hunkey dorey! All the fixins and vittles for some mighty good meals!" He lifted bags and boxes to inspect the mule's load. "Got any joy juice?"

Graham furrowed his eyebrows, not understanding. Suddenly, it occurred to him what the man was asking.

"No alcohol."

The robber backed away until he came to Graham's horse. He stroked the neck of the animal and pulled the Spencer carbine from its scabbard.

"Nice horse. I kinda like the gun, too. Sit," he ordered.

Graham and Makawee did as instructed.

"Now look here. I'm a wolfer who's had some hard knocks. Made little on pelts this season. Hardly paid for the poison. I'm thinkin' this winter I'll trap and poison them critters in Yellowstone. I hear tell there's lots of 'em in the park."

Graham seethed. Not only were they being robbed, this thief was a wolfer. Vivid memories came flooding back of poisoned wolves he and Rides Alone discovered near Fort Parker in Montana. Canines who ingested strychnine suffered horrible, painful deaths.

Graham calmed himself and tried to think of an escape from this predicament.

"We can aid you," he said, seeing a potential approach to rid themselves of the thief. "We can give you sugar cones, a bag of coffee, and a box of canned vegetables."

"Hahaha!" Red Beard said with a hearty laugh, tilting his head back to reveal a mouth full of rotten and missing teeth.

"I'll throw in my pistol," Graham added.

"Stop your jawin'," Red Beard said. It's already mine! By the way, what's a white fella doin' with a squaw?" he said, waving at Makawee with the barrel of his gun.

"She's my wife."

"She's a perty little belle," he said, raising his eyebrows.

"If you touch her, I'll..." Graham said, leaning forward with clenched fists.

"Shut your pie hole! You ain't doin' nothin'."

Graham glanced at Makawee. She looked more angry than frightened.

"I ain't as dumb as you think. I followed those Injuns down the holler. They be Nez Purse. The army is chasin' 'em." He scratched the chin under his auburn beard. "I bet there's a nice bounty on yer heads. Prob'ly pays more 'n what I've bin gettin' fer wolf pelts."

Red Beard rubbed the back of his neck and pursed his lips.

"Here's what's gonna happen. I'm takin' the mule and everything that's on her — the whole kit and caboodle. I'm takin' yer horse. You kin keep the other nag."

The thief tied the mule to Graham's horse, then mounted his horse.

"Don't be thinkin' of followin' me. I've killed plenty o' wolves from a hundred yards, and you're a damn sight bigger than those varmints."

Red Beard holstered his pistol. "Much obliged," he said with a grin.

He clenched the lead rope of Graham's horse and left the scene with the stolen mule and horse in tow.

Makawee leaped up and ran to her horse. She grabbed the sheep horn bow hanging from her saddle, snatched two arrows from the quiver, and sprinted down the trail.

It took Graham a moment to realize what was happening.

"Wait!" he shouted, watching in bewilderment as his wife chased after an armed man.

Makawee darted out of the trees. She stepped off the trail to get a clear shot and nocked an arrow. The wolfer turned to see if anyone followed him. An arrow zipped through the air and pierced the hamstring of his left leg.

"Ahh!"

Red Beard let go of the lead rope and grabbed his leg. He slid off his horse and collapsed to the ground. He leaned to one side and clutched the shaft of the arrow.

"Shit, shit!"

He peered behind him and saw an Indian woman approaching with a nocked arrow. The wolfer yanked the revolver from his holster, aimed, and fired.

Crack!

A bullet whizzed by Makawee, who continued unfazed toward her target.

Red Beard raised his pistol again, but the pain caused his arm to shake.

Thwish!

A second arrow punched into his hip. He dropped the gun and fell on his back. His chest heaved as he tried to breathe.

Graham caught up to Makawee and stood beside her as she lowered the bow. They watched the wolfer writhe in pain twenty yards away.

"Wait a few minutes," she said. "Soon he will not move."

Graham looked at his wife. What did she mean? He peered at the squirming wolfer. The shafts below the fletching of both arrows were red.

"Are those poison-tipped arrows?"

Makawee nodded.

It all came together for Graham. He had seen Makawee boiling roots several weeks before the invading army forced them to leave the Wallowa Valley. When he asked if she was making a stew, she replied these roots were for another purpose. She stained half the arrows in her quiver red. Now he knew why.

"What did you use?"

"Water hemlock."

"Eee... ooh..." the wolfer moaned through clenched teeth as he convulsed.

Makawee and Graham walked to the man, whose arms and legs were stiff. Frothy liquid oozed from the corner of his mouth. His pupils were fixed and dilated.

Graham kicked the pistol out of reach and fetched his Colt Cobra from the dying man's coat pocket. He found it ironic that someone who poisoned wolves would die a painful death like his canine victims. It was difficult to have sympathy for someone who inflicted suffering, but it was too gruesome to watch.

"I'll fetch your horse," he said.

When he returned, the wolfer was dead. Makawee was checking on the mule's load to make sure nothing was missing.

"We should bury him," Graham said. "I just bought that shovel."

"He's not worth the effort. Leave him for the coyotes."

"His body could make another creature sick if it feeds on it."

They agreed to cover the thief with rocks to discourage scavengers from eating the flesh.

As they piled the last stones on the body, the Nez Perce entourage came into view. Graham and Makawee gathered their horses, the mule, and the dead wolfer's horse. They rode with the group back to camp.

Graham wondered why no one asked who was under the rocks. Who could blame them? It was an unspoken expectation that more people would die before they reached freedom across the Medicine Line.

Death was coming. That much was certain. No one knew when.

Chapter Nine
Agony and Anger

6 August [221 miles traveled]

G raham pushed his knife blade across the chunk of pine and watched a shaving fall to his feet. He held the carved piece to the firelight and shook his head. This was going to take longer than he expected. He planned to carve a fist-sized bison for Makawee and give it to her on their wedding anniversary. His crude sculpture looked more like a pig than a buffalo. He sighed and tossed the misshapen creature into the fire. Although he spent countless hours assisting his father making rocking chairs, he did not inherit woodworking skills.

He folded the bone-handled Barlow knife, put it in his jeans pocket, and dug into the saddlebag sitting beside him. Loosening the twine, he opened a brown package. White lace bordered the V-shaped neckline of a floral print dress. He bought the second dress at Henry Buck's store after Makawee left. Graham kept this purchase secret. Even if his whittling skills didn't improve, he could still present this beautiful tea gown to his wife on their wedding anniversary. He wrapped the paper around the dress, retied the package, and tucked it back into his saddlebag.

He thought about his family while he leaned against a log and stared at the fire.

Now that the Nez Perce group had re-supplied, they planned to ride south through the Bitterroot Valley. Graham wondered why no one had seen Howard's army for several weeks. The government would not let non-treaty Indians go unpunished. It seemed only a matter of time before soldiers would attack the Nez Perce.

As they were breaking camp, Graham approached Joseph and Ollokot. He proposed to stay behind. If the military appeared in the valley, he would go into town and gather intelligence on the army's plans. As a white man, he could do this without raising suspicion.

Ollokot explained Graham's plan to Looking Glass. The senior war chief dismissed the idea. The Indians always assigned several warriors as a rear guard. If Cut Arm or anyone else attempted to attack the group, they would know it. The white man could do whatever he liked.

Despite a lack of endorsement from the principal war chief, Ollokot thought the idea had merit. Graham told Makawee he would be away from camp for a week. When he asked Yellow Wolf to watch after his family until he returned, the young warrior agreed. After gathering supplies, Graham kissed his family goodbye and watched as the massive entourage of men, women, children, horses, and cattle disappeared from view.

That was four days ago.

Joseph and the others were camped in the first valley on the other side of the Continental Divide. The Nez Perce called this place *Iskumtselalik Pah*. European settlers referred to it as the Big Hole.

Perhaps Looking Glass was right. The army would not follow the non-treaties into Montana Territory. Tomorrow, Graham would ride into Stevensville and talk to the locals. If the enemy was not advancing into the Bitterroot Valley, he would rejoin his friends at the Big Hole.

Lieutenant James Bradley sat at the back of the Star Saloon. He slipped the sharpener over his graphite pencil and twisted it to create a new point, then wrote some notes in the margin of his diary. He read the page again, then pushed his wraparound arm chair away from the table. Interlocking his fingers behind his head, he raised his shoulders and brought his elbows forward to stretch his muscles.

Writing is easy, but editing is hard work, he thought.

~ *James Bradley*

The thirty-three-year-old lieutenant was based at a military post one hundred and seventy miles northwest of Stevensville. General Howard requested forces from Fort Shaw under Colonel John Gibbon intercept Chief Joseph and the non-treaty Nez Perce. Howard was still assembling additional soldiers from the region and gathering the supplies to support a large campaign. He needed to buy time until his army could engage the hostiles again.

Gibbon's column arrived at Stevensville the previous evening. The troops were camped outside town. Bradley's orders were to interview the settlers and find out what they knew about the Nez Perce. After all, the Indians purchased much-needed supplies from the Buck Brothers and flour from the grist mill a few miles away. The locals might provide useful intelligence on the number of hostiles, their weapons, and perhaps where they were headed.

Bradley pulled out his pocket watch. The shops would soon open. He planned to canvass residents as they came into the village. As he stood and walked toward the bar, a man opened the saloon door. Sunlight backlit the bar patron and darkened his face. Something about the tall fellow in the doorway was familiar. When the stranger closed the door behind him, Bradley recognized his friend.

"Davidson!"

The lieutenant walked to the entrance and extended his hand.

Shit, Graham thought. He wanted to remain anonymous. Instead, the first person he met knew him.

He accepted the lieutenant's hand and shook.

"Fancy meeting you here! What are you doing in this part of the country?" Bradley said.

"I'm a hunting guide. Here for supplies. And you?"

"Haven't you heard? The Nez Perce are on a rampage. They're stealing and murdering settlers. Homesteaders reported they raped some women. Colonel Gibbon received orders to find and fight them."

Graham pursed his lips at the rape allegations. He found it astonishing how people transformed rumors into facts and sensationalized events.

"I don't suppose you've come across these Indians in your travels."

"Can't say that I have." Graham made eye contact with the lieutenant as they spoke. He needed Bradley to believe him. He considered the best way to learn Gibbon's strategy.

"Hey, where are my manners?" Bradley asked. "How 'bout we bend an elbow and catch up?"

"Sure. That would be great."

"Bartender, two shots of rye. We don't want *nokum stiff*. Give us the 'A brand'."

Bradley winked at Graham as the man pulled a container from under the bar.

"I got this while in Missoula last week," the barkeep said. He poured whiskey from an unlabeled brown bottle into two glasses. "I had to bring my own bottles. The fella filled it right from the barrel. It's top shelf."

Bradley lifted the glass and sniffed the hard liquor. Graham held his glass up to the light, wondering what had been fermented. Anyone could make, sell, or distribute alcohol in the nineteenth century. Unscrupulous vendors thinned the original distilled product with less expensive alcohols or additives to increase their profit margins.

"You gotta pay extra for the good stuff. That'll be fifty cents each."

Bradley plunked two half-dollar coins on the bar.

"Raise your glass," he said.

Graham imitated the gesture of his host.

"To George Armstrong Custer and those in the Seventh Cavalry who lost their lives at the Little Bighorn last June. May they rest in peace."

Graham silently addended the toast.

To my friend Rides Alone, murdered by a cavalry officer that same day. Shia-nuk [See you later].

They tossed back the whiskey. Bradley licked his lips and set the glass on the bar.

The alcohol burned Graham's throat. He shook his head and coughed. "Could I have some water?" he asked with a squeaky voice and watery eyes.

The bartender grinned and passed a glass to the bearded young man.

"Over here," Bradley said, walking to the table he used as a writing desk.

Graham followed him, tossed his hat on the table, and pulled up a chair.

"Well, now, what have you been up to since we parted ways at the Bighorn River? Are you still with that Crow woman?"

"Yes. We are happily married."

"I'd like to meet her."

"She's with her family."

Makawee was with her Nez Perce family, not her Crow relatives. But he would not divulge that information to the officer.

"And what about you?" Graham asked.

"We've got a little girl and another on the way. My wife is visiting relatives on the east coast. But, I've been quite busy. I've written several articles for newspapers in Bozeman and Helena about the march across Montana last year. I've also given speeches where I talk about seeing Custer and his men. Those remains were a gruesome sight."

"A lot of good men lost their lives that day," Graham said. *Good men from both sides*, he thought.

"Anyway, I'm going to publish my diaries. I'm converting my field notes into a manuscript," Bradley said, laying his hand on a burgundy cloth-bound book.

"That's a splendid idea."

"Thanks. I plan to give this to a publisher in Bozeman when we finish the campaign against the Nez Perce, which could happen within the week."

"You sound optimistic," Graham said, prompting the young officer.

"No reason not to be. We have six companies from Forts Shaw, Ellis, and Missoula. Almost forty civilians volunteered to join us in the fight. The men are well-rested because the infantry have been riding in wagons. We can cover thirty miles a day without tiring." He placed his chin in his hand and stroked his neatly trimmed mustache. "Our march across Montana last summer would have been easier if the boys hadn't had to hoof it the whole way."

"It sounds like you're prepared to fight. Do you have any idea where the enemy is?"

"I'm leading a group of scouts to the Big Hole in advance of the main column. We'll catch 'em by surprise. This campaign could be my next newspaper article — or perhaps even a book. I'm going to write everything in my diary."

Graham gulped. He heard enough. It was time to warn his Nez Perce friends.

"I best be going. I have folks waiting for me," Graham said, donning his hat and standing.

"Ah, the life of a guide. I might do the same when I muster out."

"It was good to see you, Lieutenant."

Bradley pushed the chair away from the table and stood. They shook hands. Graham walked to the saloon entrance, but turned around when Bradley called out.

"Davidson, I hope we meet again."

If you only knew how soon, Graham thought, as he pushed the door open and hurried to his horse.

Graham arrived at the Big Hole on the afternoon of August 8. He paused on a rocky, pine-covered bluff overlooking the valley and gazed at the temporary Indian settlement. One hundred lodges lined the river. The Nez Perce women cut new lodgepoles from the eponymous trees. They rebuilt their tepees and draped the buffalo hides across the structures. Men salted mountain whitefish and arctic grayling filets and placed them in baskets. Boys dragged dead branches into the village and cut them into short lengths for firewood. Young men tended to the massive herd of horses. To the casual onlooker, the scene resembled typical life on the Camas Prairie.

But these Nez Perce were not in their traditional homeland. They were fleeing. Soldiers were in hot pursuit. Yet, these people maintained their lifestyle in spite of the imminent danger.

Graham guided his horse on a narrow trail. It wound down the slopes through the coniferous forest that lined the valley. He rode past lodges until he came to his canvas wall tent and dismounted. Makawee was bent over a fire, stirring a cooking pot.

"I hope you made enough for me," he said.

Makawee turned and ran to hug him. They embraced for a moment and kissed.

"I was hoping you would return soon. I'm making a fish stew."

"Smells wonderful. Where are the children?"

"Playing with Hophop Onmi and Sara. Did you see any soldiers?"

"Yes. I'll share more later. I must speak with Ollokot. Have you seen him?"

"He is with Joseph. Over there," she said, pointing to a tepee nestled under a grove of willows.

Graham strode to the lodge, where the brothers were sitting outside, smoking. "*Kahée.* May I join you?"

Joseph extended his arm and invited him to be seated.

Graham spoke with a mix of Chinook Jargon and *Niimíipuu.*

"I returned from Stevensville in the Bitterroot Valley. I spoke with a *piuapziaunat* [soldier] from Fort Shaw. He was my commanding officer when I served as a Crow scout."

The brothers glanced at one another, but said nothing.

"I learned much. There is a second army chasing us. It is led by another general, not Cut Arm. I estimate they have two hundred soldiers. Those men are marching here. They could arrive soon. We need to break camp and move!"

Graham gauged the reaction of the brothers, who listened intently. He could feel his heartbeat quickening.

Joseph was nonplussed. "I do not doubt your words. Talk to Looking Glass. The leaders elected him war chief."

Graham wondered if it perturbed Joseph that the Alpowai chief was leading the non-treaty Nez Perce. Joseph had the most followers among the five bands. By selecting Looking Glass, the leaders and elders chose war experience over diplomacy skills. If Joseph disagreed with Looking Glass's leadership decisions, he was not revealing it.

Ollokot inverted the bowl of his pipe, banged the lip against a rock, and emptied its charred contents. "Come with me," he said.

Graham and Ollokot followed the river upstream for a hundred yards before stopping in front of Looking Glass's lodge. The elected war chief was chewing boiled beef.

"*Kla-how'-ya*," Ollokot said. "We have news of the enemy."

Looking Glass glanced at the visitors. He waved the chunk of beef in a circle, gesturing for them to speak. He wiped his chin with the sleeve of his tunic before tearing off another piece of meat.

Graham repeated the information he shared earlier at the lodge of Chief Joseph.

Looking Glass swallowed the last bit of beef and washed it down with a cup of water. He crossed his arms over his chest and nodded.

"The white man will leave," he said, looking at Graham. "Ollokot will stay. We will call our council together to discuss."

Graham whispered to Ollokot as he turned to leave. "I'm certain an army is headed this way. Please try to convince the others to move south."

He hurried back to the wall tent, where Nahkash was feeding fish stew to her little brother. Makawee watched as he slurped broth from a wooden bowl.

Graham removed his hat and tossed it on the ground, then sat beside his wife.

"It is ready," she said, handing him a bowl.

"Thanks. I have bad news. Soldiers are coming. I reported this to Looking Glass. I'm not confident he will order us to break camp and move. But that's what we need to do."

Makawee set her bowl down. She lay her head against his arm and put her arm around his waist to comfort him. Husband and wife sat in the low light of the early evening, observing their daughter care for Dakkoótee. Graham tipped the bowl to drink the remaining fish broth, then set it aside.

"We can't wait for the council's decision. I won't allow you and the children to be put in harm's way. We will move our camp to a safer site."

"Graham!" she said, pulling away from him. "We can't go off on our own! This is our Nez Perce family!"

"Makawee, listen to me..."

"I've got to take care of Lautiss. She is due to deliver any day and..."

"Lautiss is Shore Crossing's responsibility! Why are you always trying to save everyone?"

Graham regretted these words as soon as he said them. Makawee stood and defiantly crossed her arms.

"I'm not leaving."

He clambered to his feet and glared at his wife. This decision was non-negotiable. There was no way she was going to talk him out of it.

"I'm not asking you. I'm telling you. We are leaving within the hour."

Makawee unfolded her arms and looked into her husband's eyes. She sensed his steely resolve, but sought a compromise.

"Can we leave the tent assembled and sleep outside tonight? People will ask fewer questions if they see our tent is still in the camp."

Graham admitted this was a good point. He didn't want to incite a panic. He hoped the leaders and elders would make the right decision and urge the residents to pack right away. But he wasn't counting on this.

"Alright. The tent stays. We'll take our horses, the mule, and whatever we need for the night. I'll saddle your horse while you pack."

A short time later, the Davidson family was riding south. The sun set behind the western hills and the sky was turning shades of purple. Dakkoótee sat astraddle the horse in front of Graham, while Nahkash was in a similar position on Makawee's horse. They followed the river for a half mile. Graham chose a grassy knoll as an ideal spot to spread their buffalo hides and blankets. A grove of trees obscured most of the hill from those in camp. After they unsaddled and picketed the horses, Makawee walked to the river to gather driftwood along the banks.

"No fire tonight," Graham said, when she returned with an armload of branches. "I don't want to draw any attention."

She dropped the bundle. "Aren't you taking this too far?"

"No fire."

Makawee shook her head and sat heavily on a buffalo hide. She pulled a blanket over her son and daughter before doing the same. The trio were soon fast asleep.

Graham fetched field glasses from his saddlebag and focused on the camp. Scattered fires flickered among the tepees lining the river. He could discern outlines of men and women sitting in front of their lodges. The neigh of horses drifted from the herd grazing on the far side of the encampment. No one was packing. Women were not dismantling the lodges to prepare for a move. The Nez Perce leaders took the advice of Looking Glass to stay in the Big Hole.

He lowered the binoculars and shook his head. How could they ignore his explicit warning?

Graham peered at his sleeping family. He was glad they were safe, but wondered if he had done enough to convince the war chiefs of the pending danger. He lay back on a buffalo hide and put his hands behind his head. Stars crowded the inky black sky. A waxing crescent moon hung low over the eastern horizon.

He recalled his time as a scout. A clear night sky makes it difficult to move close to the enemy without being spotted. This could be an important advantage for the Nez Perce sentries posted on the perimeter of the camp. With some forewarning, the Indians could defend themselves against a surprise attack.

Graham closed his eyes and recited a prayer.

Lord, let us get through this night without bloodshed.

"Tuelke! Tuelke!" ["Enemy! Enemy!"]

The twelve-year-old boy shouted at the top of his lungs as he sprinted down the pine-covered slope toward the village.

Crack!

A bullet plunged into the young sentry's back, severing his spine.

Crack! Crack! Crack!

Gunfire erupted from the hills in rapid succession, puncturing the gray skies of early morning. Bullets zipped into the canvas lodges. People emerged from the tepees and scurried like ants through camp. Men grabbed rifles and bows. Women frantically searched for the best place to protect children from the deadly hail of bullets.

After the initial volley, the soldiers and volunteers splashed across the river to the lodges on the opposite bank.

The killing was indiscriminate. Anyone that moved was a target. They shot women while running with children in tow. A bullet pierced the skull of a toddler whose mother they killed moments earlier.

There were no safe havens. Children and old people who stayed in a tepee met one of two fates. The soldiers either killed those in lodges with a torrent of bullets or burned them alive by setting the tepee on fire.

Up and down the river, chaos reigned. The army and the civilian volunteers took full advantage of their surprise attack. They poured lead into the Nez Perce with merciless efficiency.

Big Hole Battlefield

Twenty minutes into the battle, the Indians gained their composure. Angered by the ruthless killing of women and children, the warriors fought back. Ollokot rallied the men from his band. Grabbing a repeating rifle, he leaped onto a horse. He rode through camp and implored his men to fight.

"Gather your courage! Shoot the officers first!"

He galloped to the front lines at the river. A soldier shot Ollokot's horse in its forearm, shattering the humerus. The animal collapsed and came to a stop on its side, legs kicking. The war chief let out a whoop as he scrambled from the wounded horse. He kneeled and fired at the enemy.

Yellow Wolf grabbed a dead soldier's weapon and ran toward the heat of battle at the south end of camp. He passed wounded and dying Indians on the way. Others joined him as they sought to repulse the soldiers' advance.

He shot a civilian volunteer who was torching a tepee. The wounded man fell onto the buffalo hide and was engulfed in flames. His cries of anguish mixed with the moans of those trapped inside. The young warrior held one arm in front of his face and used a war club to peel away the burning hide at the entrance. A young girl raised her head from a blanket where she was hiding. He pulled the choking child from the lodge as it collapsed. Scooping the girl under his arm, he dashed toward the far end of camp and handed her to a woman, who was ushering three children away.

Chief Joseph recruited four boys to assist him in gathering the massive herd. He knew the Nez Perce could never survive without plenty of fresh horses.

Joseph's group herded the skittish equines over the eastern hills and away from the battlefield.

Wetatonmi had gone to the tepee of Lautiss to help the pregnant woman. She peeked outside. The warriors appeared to be driving the soldiers towards the river.

"Come quickly," she said.

Lautiss hurried as fast as a heavily pregnant woman could. The two women moved swiftly across the open ground toward a cluster of willow trees.

Pffft! A bullet zipped into the expectant woman's abdomen.

"Ah!" Lautiss cried out, sinking to her knees. Blood gushed from the wound and soaked her cotton dress as she collapsed. "My... my baby!"

Wetatonmi kneeled and tried in vain to staunch the bleeding with her hand. She scooted around and cradled the pregnant woman's head in her lap. Lautiss emitted a wailing sound that trailed off as she took her last breath.

Tears streamed down Wetatonmi's face as she caressed the lifeless woman's cheek. Bullets hummed and zinged in the dirt. Lodgepoles splintered from the hot lead. She closed Lautiss' eyelids and said a brief prayer.

"Lautiss!" Shore Crossing shouted as he skidded on his knees beside his dead wife and unborn child. The warrior gazed at the blood-soaked dress, placed his hands on her abdomen, and hung his head. A moment later, he gave a defiant yell. He charged toward the river with a rifle raised over his head.

The soldiers and volunteers pulled back beyond the waterway and into the hills. Shore Crossing ran pell-mell into the stream, kicking his knees high and churning the waist-deep water. He overtook two soldiers near the opposite bank. He shot one in the back at point blank range. When he fired at the second man, he discovered he was out of ammunition. In a fit of rage, he clubbed the soldier on the side of his head using the butt of his rifle. The wounded man staggered forward and clawed at a willow tree to pull himself from the river.

Shore Crossing grasped the collar of the soldier's coat and yanked him backward. He dropped the empty Winchester, clutched the man's neck, and submerged him. The soldier kicked and thrashed as he fought for air. Adrenaline fueled the grieving husband. He shoved the man's head to the rocky bottom. A few minutes later, the man stopped resisting.

The victorious warrior stood in the river, raised his arms to the sky, and yelled. A bullet zipped into his thigh. Another pierced his throat. The confident young man, whose revenge killings along the Salmon River eight weeks earlier started this war, slumped into the water. As he fell, his legs became entangled with the soldier he drowned. Their bodies floated downstream.

By late morning, the battle became a standoff. The soldiers and civilian volunteers dug rifle pits and fired at the warriors through openings in the trees. The Nez Perce returned fire from across the river and kept their enemy pinned down. Neither side had an advantage they could exploit.

A half mile downstream, Graham lowered his binoculars and handed them to Makawee. She scanned the camp and grimaced at the images in the round lenses. Smoke billowed from dozens of torched lodges. People, horses, and dogs lay scattered among the tepees. Some women wailed over the bodies of loved ones, while others dismantled the lodges that remained intact. On the river bank, thirty warriors exchanged intermittent fire with the enemy.

"We need to help," she said, handing the field glasses to Graham.

He nodded. It didn't seem the soldiers would launch a second attack since the Nez Perce rallied to defend the camp.

"Okay, but first we will take Nahkash and Dakkoótee to stay with the other children who escaped. It looks like the north side was spared."

Graham opted to take a wide detour to avoid the river skirmish as they journeyed downstream. When they reached the area where mothers gathered to await instructions, they saw Springtime, Joseph's second wife, holding her infant daughter.

Makawee was relieved to find Hophop Onmi and Sara among this group. After asking the girls to watch over their children, Graham tied the mule and horses to a cottonwood tree. He pulled the Spencer carbine from its scabbard and escorted Makawee to the camp.

Wetatonmi staggered forward to greet them. Dirt and twigs protruded from her tussled hair. Blood stained her hands.

"We should pack. Ollokot will want us to leave. But I can't find my moccasins," she said, staring absently.

"Let's go over here," Makawee said. She guided the disoriented woman to an oblong rock in the shadow of a western redcedar tree and sat beside her.

Graham grabbed a cooking pot and raced to the stream. He could see the defensive position of the Nez Perce five hundred feet away. They were tucked behind trees and rocks, their weapons pointed at the hillside. Every few minutes, a warrior would fire at the enemy.

He scooped the pot into the river and hurried back to the women. On the way, he stopped and picked up a small blanket lying in a clump of foxtail barley. He wondered who it belonged to and whether its owner survived.

"Here," he said, setting the pot on the ground and wetting a corner of the blanket. "Use this."

Makawee wrung out the excess water and wiped Wetatonmi's ashen face. She wet the blanket again and scrubbed the shocked woman's hands.

"Have you seen Lautiss?"

The question seemed to snap Wetatonmi from her trance.

"Lautiss? Yes. She is sleeping."

"*Kah?*" ["Where?"] Graham asked.

Wetatonmi lifted her arm and pointed toward a stout cottonwood tree.

"Take care of her," Makawee said, jumping up and sprinting in that direction.

Makawee slowed to a walk when she approached the base of the tree. A blanket covered the upper half of someone in a supine position. The legs were exposed up to the knees. She clasped her hand over her mouth when she saw the hem of a white cotton dress with blue flowers. Makawee kneeled beside the slain woman, tears streaming down her cheeks. She pulled the blanket down to reveal what she already knew. Lautiss, wife of Shore Crossing and expectant mother, was dead.

What about the baby? she thought. *Maybe, just maybe...*

Makawee grabbed the edge of the blanket and yanked it off. She gagged at the sight of her friend's bloody stomach, then steeled herself and pressed her ear against the deceased woman's belly, hoping against all odds to hear a heartbeat. She placed her hand over her upward-facing ear to block out the moans of the wounded, the cries of the weeping, and the sporadic gunfire. After a minute, she acknowledged there was nothing audible. The baby died inside his mother.

"*Baaleeták! Baaleeták!*" ["No! No!"]

Makawee wailed. She lifted her face, cried to the heavens, and shook her fist at the spirits. She cursed the bluecoats who shot an innocent woman and her unborn child.

Graham heard Makawee's voice amid the cacophonous chorus of the grieving. He ran to his wife, sat beside her, and grabbed her by the shoulders. He held her head tight against his chest as she shouted and wept. Graham grimaced and closed his eyes when he glanced at the body of Lautiss. *No one should have to experience such a macabre scene, especially of a loved one,* he thought.

He sat with Makawee for a long while. When she stopped sobbing and regained her composure, she told Graham she wanted to make sure her children were okay.

"Go. I'll go check our tent. We need to be ready to move soon."

"Promise we will give Lautiss and her baby a decent burial," she said.

"Yes, of course."

He watched Makawee meander toward the outer edge of camp, then rushed to his wall tent, pitched among rows of tepees. He was relieved to see the soldiers did not burn the lodges in this part of camp.

Crack!

Graham covered his head when a soldier fired another round at the warriors by the river, who responded in kind. He resolved to dismantle the tent and gather their belongings as quickly as possible.

He threw open the flaps and ducked into the tent. He felt his heart drop. Bullets had riddled the rear wall. The back support pole was sheared in half. Twisting around, Graham could see an equal number of holes in the front. The extensive damage reaffirmed his decision to move his family. He trembled at the thought of what would have happened if they stayed here last evening.

Graham pulled up the wooden stakes, removed the poles, and rolled up the damaged canvas.

Returning to the cottonwood tree to retrieve his mule, Graham stumbled over a soldier lying face down in the tall grass. He regained his balance and shifted his gaze to the victim, whose head rested on a patch of ground soaked with blood. A Colt single action revolver lay near the soldier's right hand. He picked up the gun, opened the cylinder, and saw three unfired rounds. He snapped it closed and admired the weapon's seven-and-one-half-inch barrel. It dwarfed his snub-nosed revolver.

"You won't be needing this," Graham said to the dead man. He wedged the toe of his boot under the soldier's chest and flipped him onto his back. The face that stared up at him caused him to gasp.

Someone shot the soldier in the forehead at close range. He was clean shaven except for a mustache. The shoulder knot on his coat showed he was a lieutenant. It was James Bradley.

Graham kneeled and removed the cartridge belt and holster. A palm-sized burgundy book lay partially concealed under Bradley's coat. Graham picked up the diary and leafed through the pages. The lieutenant documented Colonel Gibbon's journey across Montana to the Bighorn Valley. He dated the last entry as June 26, 1876. Bradley was among those who buried the dead and evacuated the wounded from the Battle of the Little Bighorn.

He tucked the book into the deceased man's coat pocket. He felt conflicted about his friend's death. The lieutenant treated Graham fairly when he served as a scout for the army last year. But Bradley and his fellow soldiers murdered innocent women and children. Graham could not forgive a man who committed such atrocities.

After holstering the Colt, Graham draped the cartridge belt over his shoulder. On his way back to find Makawee, he encountered more casualties. A dog limped by, its front leg hanging by a tendon in a grotesque position. Horses were bleeding into the dark soil, their screams of pain echoing against the hillsides. Bodies lay scattered among the bunchgrasses. Some were covered with blankets. Most were not. An elderly man leaned against a tree, his tunic soaked in blood around his waist. Women used wool strips cut from blankets to dress wounds.

Graham observed Makawee as she hurried from person to person with the black medical bag. He joined her in helping the injured.

Ollokot and White Bird rode into the center of the makeshift field hospital in late afternoon. They asked everyone to gather around.

"Our warriors will prevent the bluecoats from crossing the river. Bury the dead. Carry the wounded. Pack your things. Be quick. We leave at sundown," White Bird said. "Lean Elk will be our guide. The leaders have selected him as our new War Chief."

The entire group was aware of why there was a change in leadership. Looking Glass had become complacent. His refusal to acknowledge the possibility of the army catching up to the Nez Perce cost many lives.

"Makawee, we have to bury Lautiss right away. We only have a few hours before the sun sets, and we have to pack our things," Graham said.

"But, there are still people who need our help."

"We will care for them after we take care of Lautiss and our family."

Makawee nodded. She assisted an elderly man who was shot to stand up.

"*Mahsie*," ["Thanks"] the man said, gazing at his bandaged hand.

Makawee walked back to the place where Lautiss's body lay. A few minutes later, Graham appeared holding the short-handled shovel he bought at Henry Buck's store.

"We should place her body in a tree. Her spirit will be trapped if we bury her too soon."

Graham drove the spade into the ground and looked at his wife.

"That's a Crow belief. The Nez Perce don't share that view. You prepare her for burial. I'll dig."

Forty-five minutes later, Graham stood in a grave twenty inches deep, his shirt soaked with sweat. He emerged from the hole and stuck the shovel in the pile of soil and rocks. Makawee gave him a cup of water drawn from a bucket. He gulped it, then wiped his brow with his sleeve.

"We don't have time to dig deeper. It's getting late. This will have to do."

Working together, they slid the corpse wrapped in a blanket over to the grave. Graham jumped into the hole. He lifted the body, then squatted to let it slide over his thighs, past his knees, and onto his boots. He sat on the edge of the grave and swung his legs out.

"I should say something, but I don't know any prayers in Nez Perce," Makawee said. "I know a rhyme in Chinook Jargon."

"The spirits will hear you. It's the sentiment that matters."

Graham removed his hat while Makawee recited the poem.

Nika la-langue halo wa-wa,
Nika tum-tum kopet,
Nika mah-wake ikta tzum;
Pee wake ikta mamook,
Pee pit-tuck me-cika,
Nika wa-wa kla, how-ya, six.

My tongue is mute,
My heart is still,
My hand will nothing write;
Can nothing do,
But think of you,
And bid you, friend, good-night.

"That was lovely," he said.

"Lautiss lost a baby boy, just like me," Makawee said, with a blank expression.

He placed his arm around her shoulder. The same thought crossed his mind, but he was afraid to voice it. Lautiss's murder revived the painful loss of Little Heart, Makawee's unborn son, at the hands of an evil medicine woman. They stared at the dirty blanket that encased a young mother and her baby.

Crack! Crack!

Another exchange of rifle fire at the river shook them from their meditations.

"I'll pack and ready the children while you finish," she said.

Graham felt her slip from his arm. He wiped tears from his eyes and drew a deep breath. They could grieve later. Right now, they needed to escape a ruthless enemy.

He grabbed the shovel and scooped dirt into the grave.

Chapter Ten
Friend or Foe?

11 Aug [293 miles traveled]

General Howard rode through the Indian camp remains, taking in the macabre scene. Ashes from torched lodges smoldered in the early morning mist. The Nez Perce stripped the remaining tepees of their buffalo hides, leaving skeletal frameworks of lodgepoles standing. Blow flies covered horses and dog carcasses. Random mounds of dirt and rocks concealed the bodies of Nez Perce laid in shallow graves.

Unlike Clearwater Creek, the Indians did not leave in haste. They packed essential belongings before fleeing. But they suffered greater losses at the Big Hole. Dried blood painted the grass along their escape route, where makeshift travois dug furrows into the dirt. They were transporting wounded.

A day earlier, a courier delivered an urgent request from Colonel Gibbon for additional forces. Howard and a small contingent rode from Stevensville. Upon arriving at the Big Hole, they discovered the Nez Perce fled the area. Howard decided to tour the battlefield when one of Gibbon's officers reported the colonel was in surgery.

Howard nudged his horse upstream to the south end of the camp and dismounted. His aide, Lieutenant Erskine Wood, held the reins of the general's horse. He watched as the one-armed commander walked to a shallow grave five feet long. Next to this grave, a mound two feet long protruded from the meadow.

"Lieutenant."

"Yes, sir."

"Tell the sergeant I need two men with spades."

Charles Erskine Scott Wood had been appointed an aide-de-camp. The young second lieutenant was only three years removed from West Point. His fortunes improved dramatically with an assignment to work for the general, and he was eager to prove his capabilities. Ten minutes later, he returned with the sergeant and two enlisted men.

"Dig up this body," Howard instructed, pointing to the long grave.

The privates shed their coats and sunk their shovels into the loose dirt. It didn't take long to exhume the body. Someone wrapped the victim in a blanket and placed the body in a grave less than ten inches deep. After the soldiers removed the bulk of the soil, they got onto their knees and wiped dirt from the top of the blanket. Howard motioned for them to peel back the wrapping to reveal the deceased.

Wood gasped when he saw the face of the person lying in the grave. It was a woman in her thirties wearing an elk-hide dress. They shot her through the throat.

"And this one," Howard said, placing his boot on the smaller adjacent mound.

The soldiers unearthed a tiny body encased in a blanket. Howard bent on one knee and pulled the folds of the covering away to reveal a two-year-old girl. One soldier hustled away from the gravesite and vomited.

Howard rested his elbow on his knee. This girl was close in age to his youngest child. He couldn't imagine the pain of losing a child in such a tragic way. Lowering his head on top of a fist, he closed his eyes and prayed. Silently, he asked God to forgive the men who took the lives of innocent women and children. There was no justification for these killings.

After a moment of self-reflection, he owned up to a hard truth. He was culpable. He issued orders to prevent the renegades from slipping away "at any cost." Now, his words came back to haunt him. The ashen faces of the child and her mother reminded him of the price of his orders.

"Sergeant, have your men dig all shallow graves deeper. Three feet minimum. Then re-bury the victims. They deserve better."

The sergeant saluted and nodded to the men, who dragged the bodies from the shallow tombs and began the arduous task of grave-digging.

"Lieutenant, come with me. We're going to visit Colonel Gibbon."

The two men mounted and rode across the river. When they reached the opposite bank, Howard stopped and turned to his aide.

"I'm going to ask the colonel some questions. You will record our conversation. Give me your notes afterwards. What we say to one another is confidential. Understand?"

"Yes, sir."

They rode to the top of the hill, where soldiers erected a hospital tent in a clearing. The moans of injured men seeped from the canvas walls. The surgeon, Jenkins Fitzgerald, emerged from the tent. He wiped his hands on a blood-stained apron before saluting.

"How's the patient?" Howard asked.

The surgeon wiped his forehead with the back of his hand.

"He suffered a nasty wound to his lower leg. Another bullet passed through his arm without causing too much damage. He's luckier than others I've treated."

"How's that?"

"I amputated several limbs. Those boys were mighty upset when I told them they'd be without an arm or a leg."

Howard reached across his body with his left hand. He grabbed the right sleeve of his jacket, which hung by his side. It was an unmistakable reminder he was an amputee.

Fitzgerald realized his *faux pas*. "I apologize, general. I didn't mean to offend you."

"None taken. I know how those men feel. I'll visit the wounded after we talk with Colonel Gibbon. Is he well enough for visitors?"

"He's awake, but I've administered laudanum for pain. His mind may be a little hazy."

Howard nodded. He and his aide ducked into the tent.

A dozen men were lying on stretchers along the outside walls. Blood-soaked dressings concealed bullet and arrow wounds. A soldier carried a bucket of water and a ladle to those who were conscious and offered a drink.

Howard spotted Gibbon at the back of the tent.

~ *John Gibbon*

They had propped him into a sitting position. A dressing encased his left calf. The surgeon tied another bandage above his left elbow.

"Colonel, it's good to see you. Thanks for taking on these hostiles."

Gibbon blinked several times, trying to focus on the officer at his feet. It took a moment to overcome the fog caused by the opium tincture.

"General... General Howard. Welcome, sir."

He attempted to salute, but winced when he raised his right arm.

"No need for formalities, John. You rest. I'm here to get a debrief. This is one of my aides, Lieutenant Wood."

Wood nodded. He pulled a notebook and pencil from his jacket pocket.

The colonel scooted into an upright position.

"Please describe the incident," Howard said.

Gibbon recalled the previous two days. He narrated the substantial harm caused to the enemy during the surprise attack on the camp at dawn. He told of the counterattack that chased his men back across the river, and the sniper fire that kept him from pursuing the Nez Perce as they fled.

"Did you get a casualties report?"

"Twenty-nine men killed. Thirty-six wounded."

"And the enemy?"

"We're not sure. We counted seventy-one Nez Perce graves. Without a doubt, some of the wounded they carried away will not make it."

Howard removed his slouch hat and took a knee beside the stretcher.

"John, I'm sorry for your losses, but there's something I need to ask. I rode through the deserted camp. The Indians buried women and children."

Gibbon tugged on his extended goatee beard.

"You gave orders to hit them hard — to stop them at all costs. Were the boys a little overzealous? Perhaps. But the enemy felt the might of the army. Even though they escaped, there's no way they can last. Not while carrying dead and dying. We did our job."

"Women and children?" Howard asked, pressing his friend.

"Women were shooting at us! When a warrior fell, a woman would pick up a rifle and take his place! Children got caught in the crossfire."

"John, you know we prefer taking non-combatants into custody over killing them."

Gibbon's face turned the color of his blood-stained bandage.

"This is war. People kill each other. We were together at Gettysburg. We didn't want to see those young boys die when Pickett charged. Everyone knew it was them or us." He gathered his thoughts. "This is a different enemy. The Nez Perce women fought as fiercely as the men. We defended ourselves, and I will not apologize."

Howard donned his hat.

"Okay, colonel. What's done is done." He patted Gibbon on the arm and stood. "Get well. Remember to give my best wishes to Fannie when you reach Fort Shaw."

Lieutenant Wood followed the general to the entrance. When they stepped outside, Howard spoke.

"Did you write everything down?"

"Yes, sir."

"Good. I want a legible copy before the end of the day. Dismissed."

Howard clasped his hands behind his back and walked to a rock outcropping that overlooked the Big Hole. Teams of soldiers were busy re-burying the Nez Perce victims, including women, old men, and children. The only way to stop this brutality was to finish the war. The sooner the better. Now that he had a well-equipped and supplied army, he hoped to capture Joseph and his people before they reached Yellowstone.

Graham sat in the firelight and squinted at the section of canvas. He was sewing pieces of elk hide over the bullet holes in the tent's back wall. These were crude but necessary repairs to keep the temporary lodging from leaking. At least he could still erect his tent. Most Nez Perce families were less fortunate. The only lodge poles they took along were the ones fashioned into travois to transport the dead and dying. Each night, the women cut branches upon which they draped the buffalo skins.

He glanced at Makawee sitting next to him. She rocked back and forth, singing tenderly to Nahkash, who had fallen asleep on her lap. He could see crimson lines on his wife's forearms as she stroked her daughter's hair. He winced when he thought of her pain — not the suffering from her self-inflicted wounds, but the heartache of losing Lautiss.

Graham learned the Crow practiced self-mutilation as part of their grieving process. Following the loss of her baby, Makawee gashed her arms and legs. It did not surprise him when she slashed her forearms the first night after their narrow escape from the Big Hole. All he could do was plead with her to limit the number of times she cut herself.

"It's been six days," Graham said.

Makawee stopped singing the lullaby and looked at him. "Six days?"

"Yellow Wolf hasn't spoken to me for that length of time. We haven't talked since we left the Big Hole."

"He's one of the warriors charged with guarding our rear. Those men spend little time in the main camp."

Graham shook his head. "He's deliberately avoiding me."

"He's angry and upset. All of us are."

"I'm willing to listen, but he doesn't want to talk. I'd just like to know why not."

Makawee touched his arm.

"Find him and share your concern."

Graham sighed. She was right. He needed to speak with Yellow Wolf. He lay the bullet-riddled canvas aside and picked up the black medicine bag. After kissing Nahkash on the forehead and peeking into the tent at Dakkoótee, he ambled toward the hodgepodge of shelters along Birch Creek. He made these rounds every evening, offering whatever help he could to the wounded. Perhaps tonight Yellow Wolf would come into camp for something to eat.

Eventually, Graham reached the last fire. An old man lay with his eyes closed and his head resting on a log. Drool ran from the corner of his mouth onto his neck, soaking the top of his cotton shirt. He was mumbling gibberish.

"*Natot imekes komain*," ["My father much pain"] a middle-aged woman said, rubbing her belly. Graham kneeled and set the bag on the ground. He pulled back the blanket covering the man. Someone wrapped his stomach with a torn piece of dress. The bandage was soaked with blood.

Graham reached into the bag and extracted the laudanum. Holding it up to the fire, he could see it was almost empty. He gestured for the woman to assist him in raising her father's head. When she did, he opened his eyes. He pushed the green bottle away and muttered something to his daughter. She nodded and gently placed his head back on the log.

"What did he say?"

"Save *sikiptatas* [medicine] for someone younger."

Tears streamed down her cheeks and landed on the blanket as she wept.

Graham picked up the bag and walked toward his campsite.

"Eagle Bear!" someone spoke from the darkness.

Graham recognized the voice of his friend.

"Yellow Wolf!"

The Nez Perce warrior stepped into the firelight. He was wearing a tunic and leggings. He looked five pounds lighter and ten years older than the last time they were together. Young warriors in these non-treaty bands either grew into fighters or became victims. Yellow Wolf rose to the occasion.

"I heard you were looking for me."

"Yes! We have much to talk about," Graham said, approaching him.

Yellow Wolf pointed a rifle at him.

"Come no closer."

Graham dropped the medicine bag and raised his hands. "What the hell are you doing?"

"That's what I want to know."

"Yellow Wolf, have you gone mad? We're friends!"

"We *were* friends, but not since I learned you are a spy."

Graham's jaw dropped. "A spy? Why would you think that?"

Yellow Wolf took a few steps to his left and leaned against a tree, keeping the rifle pointed at Graham.

"You met with soldiers at Stevensville. The morning after you returned to our camp, they attacked. You let them know we were at the Big Hole."

"No! Not true! I would never betray my friends!"

"Prove you are innocent."

Graham calmed himself by taking a deep breath.

"I shared with Chief Joseph and Ollokot what I discovered about the army's plans. They went to Looking Glass, but he refused to believe we were in danger."

Yellow Wolf cocked his head, trying to process what he heard.

"You knew the enemy was coming and moved from the main camp. Your family did not feel hot lead bullets."

"What could I do?" Graham asked in exasperation. "I don't have any authority with your people. I'm just a *soyapu!*"

"Yes, you are a white man. And you are loyal to your race. You are no different from the citizens that stood with the bluecoats and killed us."

The young warrior pushed away from the tree and walked closer to Graham, who took a step backward.

"Please believe me. Ask Ollokot. He will tell you everything I've said is the truth."

"I intend to speak to him. Regardless, you did nothing to protect our people. A genuine leader would not have easily accepted the war chief's decision."

What about Joseph and Ollokot? They didn't question Looking Glass, Graham thought.

Yellow Wolf leaned his weapon against the tree. He pulled the eagle-bear claw necklace over his head and tossed it at Graham, who caught it.

"I will not adorn myself with the necklace of a traitor."

"Wait! What can I do to earn your trust?"

Yellow Wolf grabbed the rifle. He stepped into the darkness, then turned to face Graham.

"Are you acquainted with the area we refer to as *Smoke from the Ground*?"

"Yes."

"If our people travel through that land without being attacked, I will know you are one of us."

"But... I'm not leading the group! How am I supposed to...?"

Yellow Wolf faded into the night.

Graham was crushed by his friend's accusations and pondered how to convince Yellow Wolf of his loyalty. He rolled the chevron glass beads of the necklace between his fingers and felt the sharp points of the bear claws. Slipping it over his head, he headed back to his family.

Over seven hundred people and a thousand horses had to be guided through the nascent national park to Crow country. To accomplish this, all of them would need the spiritual power embodied in the sacred necklace.

Chapter Eleven
Smoke from the Ground

23 August [522 miles traveled]

Virginia City was on the decline. Half the buildings along Wallace Street were unoccupied, their windows and doors boarded shut. Paint peeled from the frame structures. Nails protruded from the boardwalk, waiting to catch a boot or heel and trip an unsuspecting shopper. Stray cats darted among the establishments, hoping to supplement their rat diet with scraps tossed out by bars and hotels. The community's fortunes had risen and fallen with mining.

The town sprouted overnight after prospectors discovered gold at Alder Gulch in 1863. Two years later, government officials designated it as the territorial capital of Montana. European Americans weren't the only immigrants. Chinese, Mexicans, and African Americans flocked to the area. The town's population grew to ten thousand. Entrepreneurs established saloons, hotels, dry goods stores, banks, clothing stores, laundries, and a livery. Residents pointed with pride to the Wells Fargo Overland Mail and Express Office, which also housed the territory's first Western Union telegraph station, and their own newspaper.

When miners found gold at Last Chance Gulch a few years later, many Virginia City residents moved to Helena, which was named the new territorial capital in 1875. The mining boom town in Alder Gulch was now on life support.

And so, merchants still holding out in Virginia City were excited to see General Howard and his entourage riding down the main street in late August. A well-heeled visitor could invigorate a business, if only for a brief time. This was a military officer who had the deep pockets of the government behind him. If he was here to purchase supplies, it would be great news for the town.

Howard stopped in front of the only brick building. "S.R. Buford & Co" adorned the facade of the grocery and dry goods store with three arched doorways. He dismounted and instructed Lieutenant Wood and the battalion's quartermaster to follow him. Six men waited outside with a pack train of mules and two wagons.

"May I help you, General?" a bearded man in his mid-forties asked. He wore a long sleeve white shirt, tie, and vest.

"I'm looking for the proprietor."

"Simeon Buford, at your service."

Howard removed his hat, tucked it under his arm, and smoothed his rumpled hair.

"This is official government business. We're in need of supplies. My quartermaster, Sergeant O'Malley, has a list. Lieutenant Wood will attend to the accounting and sign for the goods."

"May I see it?"

Buford put on his spectacles and read the catalog of items handed to him. He rubbed the back of his neck.

"We have most of these things in stock, but not in large quantities."

"Any other merchants in town?"

"Most of 'em have closed, but Mr. Merk down the street might help."

"We're interested in working with one person. Negotiate with anyone who can fill our needs."

"Say, we're expecting a shipment from Fort Benton tomorrow. If you wait a day, we should be able to procure most of your supplies."

"Very well. I'll let you get started." Howard turned to exit the building.

"Oh, General Howard!"

"I should mention that Mr. Elling, our mayor, has a nice selection of men's clothing. You might visit his store."

Howard didn't respond. He stepped outside and ordered the captain to find a suitable place to camp. They would stay another day. The general walked next door to the Wells Fargo office. A man stood when he entered.

"Can I help you?"

"Did you receive a telegram for O. O. Howard from General Sherman?"

"Yes, sir," the clerk said. He retrieved an envelope from a pigeonhole atop his desk. "I'm supposed to verify the recipient's identity, but that's unnecessary in this case. We're mighty glad you fellas are chasin' down those murderin' redskins."

He handed the message to Howard.

"Is this the latest newspaper?" Howard asked. A copy of *The Madisonian* lay on the counter.

"Yes, sir. Mr. Deyarmon publishes a weekly edition."

Howard fished in his pocket for coins.

"Oh, no. You can have it. I'll get the newest issue on Saturday."

"Mind if I have a seat?"

The clerk gestured to a chair by the window.

The general set his hat on the floor and placed the newspaper on a table. He gazed at the Western Union envelope holding Sherman's message and thought about their recent correspondence.

Several days earlier, a courier delivered a terse directive from Sherman. The commanding general of the US army demanded to know the size of Howard's force and his plans for capturing the non-treaty Nez Perce. Howard had no good news. In the two weeks since the Battle of the Big Hole, his battalion chased Joseph and the other bands south into Idaho. Each time the army was close enough to strike, the Nez Perce would increase their pace and escape.

The army's latest embarrassment happened three days ago at Camas Meadows. A group of two dozen warriors raided Howard's camp and ran off some horses. They stole most of the mules from the pack train. Not only did the Indians gain valuable supplies, they deprived Howard of much-needed food for his six-hundred-man army. This was the reason he came to Virginia City. His troops had less than a week's rations.

Howard sent a courier ahead to telegraph Sherman. In his note, Howard remarked that the Nez Perce were in Montana, within the boundaries of the Department of Dakota. This area was beyond his regional authority. He recommended Sherman order an eastern force to intercept the renegades, since they were moving toward Crow territory. He reported his soldiers were fatigued — perhaps a fresh set of men and horses would be better suited to pick up the chase.

The one-armed general thumbed open the envelope and extracted the telegram. His face reddened when he read the terse reply.

Pursue Nez Percé to the death, lead where they may. If you are tired, give the command to some young energetic officer, and let him follow them, go where they may…

Sherman rebuked any thought of handing over the campaign to another army. This war was General Howard's responsibility. If he didn't want to accept it, then he should go home alone and allow a junior officer to take his command.

Howard tossed the telegram onto the table and took a deep breath. He needed to think about the best response. His eye caught the lead headline of the newspaper about the Nez Perce War. Picking it up, he read the article about Gibbon's fight at the Big Hole.

The accuracy of the story surprised him. It also reminded him of the sacrifices made by the soldiers under his command. Sherman's telegram and the newspaper account spurred him to renew his efforts in bringing this war to an end.

He pulled a pencil from his jacket and wrote on the back of the envelope. After making a few edits, he walked to the clerk's desk and handed the note to him.

"Send this to General W.T. Sherman at once."

You misunderstood me. We have had a most extraordinary march and the men are weary. But, you need not fear for the campaign. Our scouts are tracking the enemy. We have been resupplied. We will chase the enemy until the end.

Riding through a tree-filled canyon, the Nez Perce caravan passed a forty-foot waterfall pouring over rhyolite rock. The tribes came to a halt in a clear space near the Firehole River shortly after noon. The non-treaty bands were in a familiar, yet rapidly changing region. Ancestors of the Nez Perce traversed the thermal area they call *Smoke from the Ground* for thousands of years to reach the buffalo hunting grounds. Now, they were unwelcome visitors to the nation's first national park.

In the five years since it was officially set aside, Yellowstone became a tourist attraction. The unspoiled wilderness, which some referred to as *Wonderland*, attracted over a thousand visitors each year. Five times that many annual visitors would travel to the park a half-dozen years later when the Northern Pacific Railroad completed a branch line to Cinnabar, three miles north of Gardiner.

Sensing the enormous group of Indians might cross paths with white sightseers, Lean Elk announced they would camp a mile from the Lower Geyser Basin. The location was nearly ideal, with easy access to fresh water and ample forage for the immense herd. Because the river was fishless above Firehole Falls, the Indians slaughtered a cow from their dwindling herd and hunted for food. They planned to water their horses and rest before moving toward Yellowstone Lake in the morning.

Graham led his family south along the Firehole, seeking a suitable site to pitch their wall tent. He glanced back at Nahkash, who was astraddle a molly mule. The docile pack animal was one of those stolen from the army. His five-year-old daughter quickly adapted to riding. She only needed help to get on and off.

"How ya doin'?"

"Good, Daddy. I think she likes me."

Graham grinned. He turned to see Dakkoótee sitting in front of Makawee on her horse. The toddler's long black hair covered his face as he drooped his head. He was sound asleep.

"I'm happy to be back in the Land of Burning Ground," she said.

"Agreed. It seems like home."

After setting up the tent, Graham gathered driftwood and broke off dead branches from the lodgepole stands that stood along the river. As he brought an armload of firewood to their site, he saw Chief Joseph's daughter playing with the children.

"Graham, I'd like to see the great colorful spring. It's a short ride from here. Hophop Onmi will watch Nahkash and Dakkoótee until we return." She pleaded with her eyes.

He dropped the load of wood and looked at his wife.

"Sure, why not? I'd love to see it, too."

The couple rode in silence, following the river upstream to the Midway Geyser Basin. An hour later, they tied their horses to a grove of pines on the western bank of the Firehole and walked across the gray sinter to the edge of Grand Prismatic Spring. The hot spring looked like Graham remembered it when he was with the Hayden Expedition six years earlier. He recalled watching in awe as Thomas Moran sketched the famous thermal feature.

The center of the pool was a deep azure blue. The color transitioned to green closer to the edges, while the shallow parts of the perimeter were shades of yellow and orange. Different species of heat-loving bacteria residing in the water were responsible for the multicolored hues. Reddish-brown channels spread like tentacles from all sides, carrying overflow from the three-hundred-foot-diameter spring.

Graham glanced at Makawee. She tilted her head backward and closed her eyes in a meditative state.

When she finished praying, she clutched Graham's hand.

"Thanks for bringing me here. I needed some time away. We've buried someone almost every day since we left the Big Hole. I thought we would escape death and dying when we departed the Bighorn Valley."

"This is a perfect place to reflect. I feel a spiritual presence here," Graham said, squeezing her hand.

The couple walked down the slope to the massive Excelsior Geyser crater. Steam obscured the surface until a swirling breeze swept the vapors away to reveal a deep blue hot spring. The runoff from the boiling pool cascaded into the river.

"Remember when we bathed in the hot springs along the west side of the lake?" she asked.

"Of course. How could I forget? It's the first time I saw you naked," he said, winking.

"This is an ideal place to bathe and wash our clothes."

"What? No way! The water must be at least one hundred and eighty degrees!"

"I didn't mean we should bathe in the pool. I meant the river. Come on."

Graham followed his wife as she carefully descended the barren sinter slope a few hundred feet downriver from Excelsior Geyser's outflow. When she arrived at the river bank, she slipped off her moccasins and stepped into the water, which came up to her waist.

He removed his hat and jacket, untied his boots, and left them on the river's edge. The cold water caused him to gasp as he stood in the river up to his thighs. Makawee giggled at his reaction.

"It's warm where the boiling water empties into the river," she said, calling over her shoulder as she waded against the current toward the geyser crater's outflow.

Twenty feet from the place where the hot spring's runoff spilled into the Firehole river, the water was six inches deeper and thirty degrees warmer. Four thousand gallons per minute of near boiling water flowed from the dormant geyser into the river. Graham felt like he was standing in a heated swimming pool.

Makawee crossed her arms, grabbed the bottom of her elk-hide dress, and lifted it over her head. She slapped it into the water and swished it around. She was naked except for the obsidian turtle necklace she always wore. Her wet breasts glistened in the afternoon sun as she soaked, then squeezed the water out of the soiled dress.

"I like to watch you do laundry," he said with a smirk.

"What are you waiting for?" she asked.

Graham stripped off his socks, jeans, underwear, and shirt. He draped these over his shoulder. She handed her dress to him, then rinsed each article of his clothing in the warm water. Removing a piece of braided sweetgrass from her hair, she rubbed it into her dress and his shirt. Treating their clothing with the fragrant herb would not only make them smell better, it would repel mosquitoes.

There was something sensual about standing in a thermally heated river, washing clothes in the nude with the woman he loved. Watching her, he became aroused.

"Let's place them in the sun to dry," she said.

Graham nodded and followed her. As they walked downstream, the water became less warm. The cold water did nothing to dampen Graham's desires as he observed Makawee's buttocks flex with each step she took in the river.

"I'll get some blankets," he said, walking to the horses while she spread the wet clothing on rocks.

He returned and laid a blanket atop a cluster of meadow grass. She sat next to him, their wet thighs touching. She smiled when she saw his erection.

"I see you aren't thinking about washing clothes."

"Guilty," he said, placing his arm around her waist.

She reached over and stroked him. Her touch aroused him further. She lay on her back, and he caressed her smooth, wet breasts while kissing her. His fingertips traced her stomach and traveled down to her pelvis. She raised and separated her knees to encourage him. He lightly massaged her before rolling between her legs.

She guided him to her and wrapped her legs around his waist. As he entered her, he gently kissed her breasts. He moved slowly in and out, but she urged him on by clasping his buttocks and pulling him deeper into her. His eagle-bear claw necklace clacked against the obsidian pendant lying between her breasts as they fell into a rhythm.

He wanted this moment to last forever, but he soon felt a burst of pleasure that pulsated through his body. He exhaled, gave Makawee a long, soft kiss, and brushed her hair along the side of her head. As he began to pull out, she grabbed his lower back.

"Please stay in me a while longer."

Graham pushed on his elbows to lessen his weight on her and gazed into her eyes.

"With pleasure, Mrs. Davidson."

A moment later, they heard a low rumbling. Graham reluctantly separated from Makawee. They sat up and looked several hundred feet upstream. Sprays of water leaped into the air, accompanied by hissing and bubbling sounds. Within thirty seconds, broad plumes of water rocketed from the crater. Excelsior Geyser was erupting!

Although the hydrothermal feature is a hot spring in modern day Yellowstone, Excelsior was a sight to behold in the latter part of the nineteenth century. A column of water one hundred feet in diameter shot two hundred feet skyward.

Graham scooted behind Makawee. Straddling her waist and raising his knees, he pulled her back against his chest and cupped her breasts in his hands. A breeze pushed the mist from the geyser in their direction and moistened their skin. They enjoyed the dramatic waterworks for almost ten minutes before the massive water column dissipated and transitioned into a calm, bubbling pool.

"That was amazing," she said.

"It was a spectacular eruption."

He lifted the hair away from the nape of her neck, kissed her soft skin, and became aroused again.

Makawee reached behind and fondled him.

"I wasn't talking about the geyser." She turned her head and whispered in his ear, "Let's do it again."

Chapter Twelve

Hapless

24 August [557 miles traveled]

Eighteen-year-old Henry Meyers hobbled around the campfire. He added a few sticks and watched as the flames licked the dry wood. The rest of the party was still asleep, but they would expect a hearty breakfast of flapjacks and bacon. After tossing a handful of Arbuckle coffee beans into a boiling pot, he sat and reflected on the previous three weeks.

George Cowan hired Henry as a cook and hostler for a trip through the Yellowstone. When George planned the visit, he envisioned a romantic getaway for him and his wife, Emma. However, as word of this adventure spread, more people expressed interest in attending. It seemed everyone with whom they spoke wanted to tour Wonderland. Emma's older brother, Frank Carpenter, and her thirteen-year-old sister, Ida, were eager to see the geysers and hot springs. Frank invited four friends from Helena — Al Oldham, William Dingee, A.J. Arnold, and Charles Mann.

The trip almost didn't happen. George and Frank attended a dinner in July where Philetus Norris was the guest speaker.

~ *Philetus Norris*

The Secretary of the Interior recently appointed Norris as the second superintendent.

He spoke of his vision for improving the roads within the park. He also wanted to prevent vandals and poachers from spoiling the park's resources. Norris fielded questions after his speech. Someone asked about the dangers for tourists from Indians, especially since rumors were rampant that the non-treaty Nez Perce were headed east from Idaho Territory. He reassured the audience.

"Park visitors are quite safe from any hostile Indians. Their fear of geysers and hot springs is well documented," Norris said. "The Nez Perce will not enter Yellowstone."

Nine people left Radersburg, Montana, on August 5. The women and two of the men rode in a double-seated carriage. Henry drove the baggage wagon, and the others rode horses. Eight days later, they crossed the Targhee Pass and followed the Madison River into the park. They established a permanent camp along the Firehole River in the Lower Geyser Basin. Over the past ten days, they toured the geyser basins and made excursions to observe Yellowstone Lake and the Grand Canyon of the Yellowstone.

Henry enjoyed the group's company. Although he was busy making meals and tending the horses, he had time to see the other-worldly sites he heard about as a boy. It would have been a perfect outing had he not suffered a painful injury. Two days earlier, Henry broke through the thin crust surrounding a hot spring. He stepped into scalding water up to his knee. The outer layer of skin peeled off, exposing a pinkish tender epidermis. Emma applied her face cream to the burn, and Henry bathed his leg with cool water several times each day. He was looking forward to seeing a physician who could treat the injury. The group planned to start home today.

"Kla-how'-ya!"

Henry leaped up at the sound. As he looked into the gray pre-dawn light, he made out the silhouettes of three men on horseback. His companions also heard the man's voice and stirred from blankets spread on the ground.

Frank Carpenter spotted the threat and yelled, "Indians!!"

The men clambered to grab a firearm as the trio of strangers halted fifty feet from the camp.

Carpenter stepped forward to greet the visitors.

"Who are you? What tribe?" he asked.

The Indian headman dismounted and walked to the fire.

"I am Yellow Wolf. My leader is Chief Joseph."

"Nez Perce?"

"Yes."

A chill ran up his spine. "Boys, did you hear that?" Carpenter said over his shoulder.

"Sure did," Arnold said, his voice quivering. The others nodded. Superintendent Norris was wrong. These Indians had no fear of geysers, hot springs, or any other thermal feature.

"We are friends of the white man. We only fight soldiers. Have you seen any?" Yellow Wolf said.

Carpenter eyed the Indians and considered whether to fight them. After all, it was seven against three. He wondered if they could shoot the intruders and protect the women if a firefight erupted.

"No, not since we came to the park ten days ago," he said.

His thought of fighting back evaporated when a dozen additional armed tribesmen cantered to the campsite. They strapped full cartridge belts across their waists. The Indians aimed their repeating rifles at the hapless tourists.

"You will surrender your weapons," Yellow Wolf said.

Four warriors strolled into the camp and took the shotguns, pistols, and rifles from the campers. One warrior stroked the neck of a horse tied to the wagon and smiled before returning to the group with the confiscated firearms.

"I'll bet you fellas are hungry," Carpenter said. "How about we give you flour, sugar, and bacon? Then we can be on our way."

"We will take what we need, not what you offer," Yellow Wolf said.

"Hey, wait a minute!" said George Cowan, stepping toward Yellow Wolf, his face reddened with anger. You can't seize all our food! How are we supposed to..."

~ *George Cowan*

Carpenter grabbed Cowan by the arm and held him back.

Yellow Wolf said something to the other warriors, then turned to the campers.

"All of you will come with us."

"Only if I can speak with Chief Joseph," Carpenter said.

The warrior leader did not address the white man's demand. He replied with one word.

"Pack."

The men broke camp and loaded their provisions on the wagon. As they worked, Carpenter spoke in low tones to Oldham, Dingess, Arnold, and Mann.

"Let's not panic. Do as they say. I will negotiate our release when I meet Chief Joseph."

George Cowan comforted his wife, who was crying. "Emma, you have to be strong for Ida."

He talked to Carpenter while they harnessed the teams and hitched the wagons. "These thieving road agents won't get away with this," he said through clenched teeth.

"Stay calm. Don't do anything foolish."

A short time later, the Radersburg tourists were riding north, escorted by fifteen warriors. When they reached the East Fork of the Firehole, they stopped. The immense caravan was on the move. Women and old men were at the front of the line, flanked by a few warriors. Men of fighting age followed. They rode in and out of thousands of horses ten deep, pushing them forward. A trailing group shielded the Indians' procession, regularly turning back to ensure there were no dangers. The great migration stretched for three miles.

As the rear guard passed in front of them, Yellow Wolf instructed his small band to fall in line. The prisoners and their escort only traveled two miles upriver when they encountered dense trees and fallen timber. The Indians ordered the wagons abandoned. Carpenter and the other men unhooked the team horses and fitted them with blankets for riding. While they were doing this, the Nez Perce emptied the supply wagon of the remaining provisions. The warriors used hatchets to snap the spokes from the wheels, then set the carriage and wagon on fire. If the tourists were to return to Montana, they would travel on horses or on foot.

They stopped to eat the noon meal near Mary Mountain. As the Radersburg party sat under a willow tree eating biscuits, Lean Elk came to the rear of the procession.

"You wished to speak with me?"

Frank Carpenter introduced himself. The English language skills of the Nez Perce leader surprised him.

"Are you Chief Joseph?" Carpenter asked.

"He is unavailable. I am Lean Elk, war chief."

"Chief, we are just visiting the park. We are no threat to you. Your warriors have taken our supplies. We request to be set free."

"It is hard to know which white men to trust. Citizens have joined the soldiers in killing our people. You could do the same if given the chance."

Frank Carpenter shook his head. "We only seek our freedom. We will not take up arms against you or your people."

The war chief studied Carpenter's face, as if to discern the veracity of his claim. After a moment, he said, "We will swap ponies. Then we intend to set you free."

Lean Elk said something in *Nimi'ipuu* to a group of men. Warriors removed the saddles from the tourists' horses and led them away. A few minutes later, the Nez Perce returned with nine skinny, sway-backed horses.

"No way!" George Cowan said, jumping to his feet. "You're not trading our horses for those scrawny nags!"

"You can leave on foot or on these ponies," Lean Elk said, shrugging.

"George, we're in no position to negotiate," Carpenter said, pulling his friend aside. "Let's go while we have an opportunity."

The tourists watched the Nez Perce get underway. As the rear guard passed by the willow tree, Lean Elk offered a last word of advice.

"I cannot control all the men. Many lost family members at Big Hole. They want revenge."

The war chief galloped to catch up with the primary group, which had rumbled out of sight.

With George Cowan and Emma in the lead, they started downriver on the weary horses. An air of melancholy surrounded the tourists. Each person was lost in his or her own thoughts. As Emma remembered her looted belongings, she sobbed. Frank Carpenter focused on the group's predicament and decided their best option was to head north to Mammoth Hot Springs. Henry Meyers concentrated on keeping his burned lower leg from rubbing against his horse's bony ribs.

The behavior of the rogue Indians incensed George Cowan. He planned this grand vacation through Wonderland months ago. The previous ten days were marvelous, but hostiles marred the experience of a lifetime by robbing and humiliating him. As he stewed in his indignation, a shout from Al Oldham interrupted his thoughts.

"Indians!"

Nez Perce warriors were trotting in the timber on both sides of the Radersburg group.

"What do we do?" said William Dingee.

"We keep riding. Don't let them know you are afraid. They're trying to intimidate us," Carpenter said.

"They already took everything we own," said A.J. Arnold. "What else do they want?"

Everyone knew the answer. The words of Lean Elk hung in the air. *They want revenge.*

George and Emma reined their horses and stopped. Three Nez Perce warriors on horseback blocked the trail fifty feet ahead. One of them raised his rifle and pulled the trigger.

Crack!

A bullet pierced the left thigh of George Cowan. Another warrior raced from the timber and pointed a pistol at his head.

"George, look out!" Charles Mann shouted.

Cowan slid from his horse and fell to the ground as the warrior fired.

Bang!

The bullet missed, kicking up dirt on the trail.

"Run!" Carpenter yelled.

The tourists jumped from their mounts and dashed in different directions. The trees were so close together, horses could not follow them. Warriors dismounted and chased after those on foot. Everyone except George, Emma, and young Ida ran for their lives.

Emma hurried to aid her husband. A warrior cocked his pistol and aimed it at the wounded man. She threw herself on top of George. A second Indian grabbed her and pulled her away just as the first warrior fired. This time, the bullet found its mark, striking George on the forehead and knocking him unconscious. Blood gushed into his eyes and trickled down his neck.

The warrior kicked his victim. When he did not move, the Indian stuck the pistol back into his belt and nodded. Two Nez Perce dragged Emma away from the scene. She wailed at seeing her husband savagely attacked.

Ida had not moved during the melee. She was in shock. An Indian grabbed her hand and guided her to the place where Emma was sobbing. As the women embraced and consoled one another, a third attacker prodded Frank Carpenter at the point of his gun barrel to join his sisters. They found him hiding in the trees a short distance from the trail.

After thirty minutes, the young Nez Perce assailants gave up searching for the others. They signed the chiefs had changed their minds about setting them free and wanted to see them. Of the nine Radersburg tourists, three siblings remained captive — Emma (Carpenter) Cowan, Ida Carpenter, and Frank Carpenter.

"How terrible!" Makawee said when she heard about the attack.

She and Graham learned of the assault from Ollokot after the Nez Perce set up camp on the shores of Mary Lake. They were traveling with Joseph and the women in front of the caravan since both had knowledge of that part of the park. Because the procession was three miles long, they were oblivious to events in the rear.

Ollokot blew smoke from a pipe. "It was unfortunate, but inevitable."

"Those tourists are innocent."

"As were the families murdered in the Big Hole," Ollokot countered.

Graham looked at his wife. Their friend made a good argument. He tried to imagine how he would feel if someone killed his mother, sister, or child. He would become enraged. How could he fault the warriors for seeking revenge on a race of people that treated them unjustly and murdered their families?

"Thanks for letting us know," Graham said.

"Chief Joseph spoke with the man called Frank Carpenter. My brother apologized to him for the attack, but he has no authority over those from other bands."

What are your plans for the three captives?" Makawee said.

"Lean Elk called a council for tomorrow evening. The leaders will make a decision whether to set them free or kill them."

"Kill them? You would murder two women?"

Ollokot's eyes narrowed as he spoke. "Soldiers and civilians massacred ten women and six children at the Big Hole."

"I know what it's like to lose a child. I'm grieving the deaths of Lautiss and her baby." Makawee pushed the sleeves of her dress over her elbows to reveal the ugly scars where she cut herself. "You are better than our enemy. Please, spare the lives of these women."

Ollokot picked up his rifle and rose from the fire. "It is not my decision. The council will decide."

The Nez Perce broke camp the next morning. They descended from the Central Plateau and entered the Hayden Valley, an expansive subalpine meadow surrounded by rolling hills. Compared to the dense lodgepole stands they encountered after leaving the Lower Geyser Basin, traveling was much easier over the ancient lake bed covered with grass and sedge. While the main body continued on, a group of warriors killed two bison and an elk. After gutting and quartering the animals, they loaded the meat on pack horses, then rejoined their kinsmen on the east side of the Yellowstone River in the late afternoon.

After setting up the patched canvas wall tent, Graham suggested the Davidsons visit *Tó-sál-dàu,* Dragon's Mouth Spring. They forded the river and walked a short distance to a steaming hillside. Makawee held Nahkash's hand while Graham lifted Dakkoótee onto his shoulders.

The visible portion of the hot spring was a small, shallow pool sitting against a hillside. It spewed steam and splashed water against the hidden internal walls of a darkened grotto, generating a roaring noise with each whoosh of boiling water. The sulfurous smell and ominous sounds of the thermal feature were comforting to Graham. It was here that he completed his vision quest. Makawee tossed the placenta of Nahkash into the angry-sounding spring. This was a sacred place to the Kiowa, the Crow, and their family.

"The council is currently meeting to decide the fate of the captives," Graham said.

"I know. I'm going to petition the spirits to guide the leaders to the right decision," she said.

"We'll wait for you."

Graham took Nahkash's hand and led her down the slope to the Mud Volcano. It was a thick, bubbling mud pot.

A violent explosion a half-dozen years earlier destroyed the cone that spawned the name of the thermal feature when it was first observed by the Washburn Expedition. This dramatic change in a thermal feature was a reminder they were standing inside a caldera, created by a supervolcano explosion over six hundred thousand years ago. The geysers, hot springs, and fumaroles in the park were constantly evolving in response to changes in the magma reservoir just beneath the surface.

Makawee joined her family a few minutes later. They sat nearby and watched the mud pot spit mineral-laden blobs a few feet into the air before falling back into the viscous brown pool.

Nahkash picked up a stone and tossed it into the acidic spring. The rock disappeared beneath the churning surface. Dakkoótee giggled as he listened to the gurgling noises of the bubbling mud.

Ploik! Ploik!

"Perhaps someday we can bring our children here when we are not caught up in a war," Graham said. "You can tell them stories of your ancestors."

"Yes... Yes, I would like that very much," she said, pensively.

Graham could tell her thoughts were elsewhere.

"What's wrong?" he asked.

Makawee emerged from her musing. "I'm thinking about the park visitors. The white man brought many awful things to native people. But these women do not deserve to die."

"I agree."

"Let's return to camp and learn what the council decided," she said.

Not long after the couple returned, Ollokot and Lean Elk visited their camping place. Graham invited the men to sit. Makawee held Dakkoótee on her lap. She removed her bead necklace and gave it to him.

Lean Elk spoke first.

"The council discussed what to do with the captives. We will set them free."

Makawee smiled. "Thank you."

"Chief Joseph spoke of their innocence. His argument was convincing."

"That is the right thing."

"Not everyone agreed with this decision. There is much anger over the white man's actions. In the end, we saw no benefit to keeping them."

"We need your help," Ollokot said.

"Oh?" Makawee said.

"We are approaching Crow country. We must establish if the Crow will unite with us in fighting the soldiers. Remember your promise to speak to your father, Long Horse?"

Makawee's heart sank. She knew this day would come. She had no desire to see her bigoted father. Yet, she gave her word. It was time to honor her commitment.

She sighed.

"I remember."

Ollokot leaned forward. "Speak with him. Update us about the alliance status of the Crow."

"I will."

"We are also uncertain about the safest exit from the park. We're eager to know if soldiers are blocking our path to the north."

Graham understood what Ollokot was suggesting.

"You want us to travel to Mammoth Hot Springs on our way to the Crow Agency on the Stillwater River and report if we see any soldiers?"

Ollokot nodded. "And we want you to escort the three captives from the park."

Graham glanced at Makawee, who nodded.

"We will do what you ask," Graham said.

"I will bring the captives to your camp. Leave before nightfall," Lean Elk said.

"Tonight?" Graham said. "Can't we wait until morning?"

"Remember what I said earlier. Not everyone agreed we should release the prisoners. It is best that you start your trip now, before others become aware of their absence."

The war chiefs stood.

"I have a question," Makawee said, staring at Ollokot. She handed Dakkoótee to Graham. "May I rejoin your group, regardless of whether the Crow are allies of the Nez Perce?"

Ollokot hesitated before responding.

"You are Crow. If the Crow are enemies..."

"*Mic'yooxom!*" ["Listen to me!"] Makawee said, interrupting him. "I was born a Crow, but raised by Blackfeet. I married a white man, with whom you are at war. But we share something."

"What is that?"

"Like you, I want the freedom to live my life as I please."

Ollokot looked at Graham, then at Makawee.

"You have been friends of the Nez Perce. You are always welcome in our camp." Makawee was pleased with his answer.

After the men left, Graham looked up at his wife.

"Well, Mrs. Davidson, we should get something to eat and pack. It's a good thing we have clear skies. A waxing gibbous moon will light our path tonight."

"I'll cook buffalo for our journey and make extra for the captives. Nahkash, come with me." They hurried off.

"Your mother is amazing," Graham said to Dakkoótee, who was playing with his adopted mother's glass bead necklace.

Graham's thoughts turned to Makawee's pending conversation with Long Horse. He hoped she would reconcile with her father. They could settle into his camp, at least temporarily. Perhaps Graham could find work in Bozeman. Surely Makawee was as tired as he of running from the army. The group they traveled with was under constant threat. Why should his family be in danger with the non-treaty Nez Perce when they could comfortably assimilate into the Crow community?

His mind shifted back to the present. The frightened and hungry captives would soon arrive. He and Makawee needed to guide them to Mammoth Hot Springs. It would be a long night of riding.

Chapter Thirteen

Nemesis

27 August [589 miles traveled]

G raham removed his hat, stood on the edge of the canyon, and gazed at the idyllic scene. Pastel orange volcanic pinnacles jutted from the edges of a stream like giant alligator teeth. The clear water of Tower Creek cascaded one hundred and thirty-two feet into a narrow gorge guarded by lodgepole pines.

It was easy to see how this setting inspired so many people, among them Thomas Moran. The famous artist painted Tower Fall in his studio after returning from the 1871 Hayden Expedition. His landscape portraits, coupled with the photographs of William Henry Jackson, convinced Congress to set aside Yellowstone as the world's first national park.

Graham walked a short distance from their camp to see the waterfall. He invited others in the group to join him, but no one was interested. He couldn't blame them. The Carpenter siblings — Frank, Emma, and Ida — were physically and emotionally exhausted from the past three days. Emma watched her captors shoot her husband and leave him to die. The incident traumatized her, and she refused to discuss it. Thirteen-year-old Ida, a naturally shy girl, withdrew even further from social interactions. Only Frank maintained an air of confidence and optimism about getting home to Montana.

Graham lied to the Carpenters. He explained the Nez Perce had taken their family captive. Their captors treated them well because Makawee was a Crow Indian. In a gesture of goodwill, Lean Elk freed them along with the other tourists.

The group rode all evening. They skirted Sulphur Mountain, forded Alum Creek, and followed the Yellowstone River downstream until they reached the Upper Falls. Instead of following the river, which flowed northeast through a canyon, Makawee guided the weary travelers through Dunraven Pass. After passing west of Mount Washburn, they followed Carnelian Creek until it emptied into Tower Creek. John Colter took this same route in the early part of the century.

Graham donned his hat and walked back toward the campsite. A rustling noise in the timber startled him. He pulled out his revolver, squatted, and listened. He scanned the dense trees, searching for movement. The only sounds he heard were those of the waterfall and creaking boughs as a light wind pushed through the lodgepoles, causing them to sway.

Kraa! Kraa!

The distinctive throaty croak of a raven pierced the air. Graham strained to identify the distinctive black bird among the trees, but could see nothing.

Tew! Tew! Tew!

A different bird responded to the raven's call from another direction. He didn't recognize this chirp.

Something flashed to his right. He swung the pistol just in time to see a dark figure disappear into the forest. Could it have been a deer? Possibly. Graham sensed whatever or whomever was making the noises, it was watching him. He kept his Colt at the ready as he made his way back to camp.

The tourists were asleep when he returned. Each one was curled under a blanket by the fire. Dakkoótee and Nahkash were chewing pieces of boiled meat and biscuits Makawee made. Graham nodded his head to one side, indicating he wanted to speak with his wife out of earshot of the tourists.

"I think we're being followed," he said, when they were alone.

"Did you see who it was?"

"No. I think they're Indians — most likely scouts. When I worked with the Crow, they used bird calls to communicate. That's what I heard at the waterfall."

"Do you think the army scouts are stalking us?"

"Could be. Or there's another possibility."

"What's that?"

"Nez Perce warriors."

"Why would they shadow us?"

"Perhaps Lean Elk doesn't trust us." Graham paused. "More likely he doesn't trust *me.*"

"I don't believe that."

"All the same, we should keep moving. Let's get these tourists to Mammoth. If we discover soldiers are heading into the park, one of us can ride south and inform Ollokot."

Late in the afternoon, Makawee led her family and the exhausted former captives into a treeless space on a plateau above the Gardner River. The Washburn Range jutted up from the valley floor to the southeast, and the snowcapped mountains of the Absaroka Range painted the horizon in the east. To the north and west lay the Gallatin Range. A strong sulfur smell hung in the air.

Mammoth Hot Springs was created over tens of thousands of years when hot acidic water dissolved limestone rock and bubbled to the surface before re-forming into travertine terraces and pooling as hot springs.

As the party dismounted, a detachment of cavalrymen appeared on the horizon. A supply wagon trailed a dozen troopers. A lanky, clean-shaven man climbed off his horse when the soldiers reached the springs.

Frank Carpenter ran to the officer and shook his hand.

"I'm so glad to see you! I need your help to get my sisters to safety. Those murderin' redskins killed her husband and..."

"Did you say Indians?"

"Sure did. Chief Joseph's renegades held us captive for two days. We're lucky to be alive!"

"Whoa, slow down. You're safe with us. I'm Lieutenant Charles Schofield. Who are you?"

"Carpenter. Frank Carpenter. These are my sisters, Emma and Ida," he said, pointing to the women hugging one another. "We're from Montana."

"And who are these people?" Schofield asked, nodding over Carpenter's shoulder at Graham and his family.

"I'm Graham Davidson. This is my wife, Makawee, and our children."

"Are you tourists?"

Before Graham could spin a lie, Frank Carpenter vouched for him.

"This man and woman are the reason we're here. The Indians held them captive, too. When the Nez Perce freed us, these folks guided us from the Mud Volcano."

"What's your tribe?" Schofield asked Makawee in a skeptical tone.

"Crow. We're headed to the Agency to collect our annuities."

"Sir, we're eager to go home," Carpenter said. "Can you escort us to Fort Ellis?"

"What about George? We need to go back for George!" Emma exclaimed, wiping her nose.

"Emma, darling, I think it best we go home. It's too dangerous. Let the army search for him."

"No! I won't leave without my George!" Emma pounded her fists on Frank's chest. He grabbed her wrists, and she sank to her knees, sobbing.

"Is he the person who died?" Schofield inquired.

Frank nodded. "They shot George twice — once in the thigh and once in the head. You'll find his body along the East Fork of the Madison River."

Schofield pushed up the bill of his kepi with a finger.

"Well, my detail can't fight that many Indians. We're just on a routine patrol. General Howard is on their trail. There's a regiment with more men coming from the north. I'm not sure when they will be here. We've got additional columns blocking possible exit points to the east. I'll telegraph Colonel Gibbon and let him know about your encounter with the Nez Perce."

Graham glanced at Makawee, who caught his eye. Schofield's disclosure about the enemy positions would be very helpful to Lean Elk.

"Will you search for George?" Emma asked, looking up through teary eyes at the lieutenant.

"Ma'am, once we find out where the hostiles are headed, we can send a search party for your husband — unless General Howard finds him before us."

"There were others in our group who escaped. We don't know what happened to them," Frank said.

"Let's focus on getting you home. Give us time to water our horses. We'll start for Fort Ellis directly."

"Lieutenant, more visitors!" a sergeant yelled, pointing to the east.

Six men rode slowly up the slope toward the travertine terraces. One slumped over his horse, grasping its withers.

Someone from the group hollered, "This man is shot!"

Two soldiers helped the wounded man from his horse and sat him on the gray sinter. While the sergeant tended to his wounded hip, one rider introduced himself.

"Name's Andy Weikert."

"Lieutenant Schofield. What happened?"

"Well, sir, ten of us camped near the canyon when we was bushwhacked by the Injuns. Jack Stewart took two bullets," Weikert said, nodding to the man sitting in the dirt. "He's mighty booger'd up. Do ya' think he'll be alright?"

"He's lost a lot of blood and needs a surgeon," the sergeant said.

"Poor Charlie Kenck," Weikert said, shaking his head. "They pumped him full of lead. He's lyin' down by the canyon."

"You said there were ten. What about the other men in your party?" asked Schofield.

"Roberts and Foller hightailed it out of camp when the bullets started flyin'. We ain't seen those shave tails since. Hope they're alright."

Schofield rubbed his chin. The Indians attacked two groups. At least two men were dead — maybe more. He needed to get this information and the injured man to Fort Ellis immediately.

"Get that man on the supply wagon. We're leaving right away," he ordered.

"I'm not leaving. Not until we find those two young men," a pale man with an Eastern European accent said.

"What's your name?" Schofield said.

"Richard Dietrich."

"Staying here is not advisable, Mr. Dietrich, as it's impossible to predict where those Indians are going.

"I'm staying, nonetheless. If they show up, there should be somebody here to help them get home."

"My family plans to stay, too," Graham said. "We're going to rest before riding north."

"Suit yourself," Schofield said, shrugging. He turned to his sergeant. "Have the bugler play 'Boots and Saddles.'"

As they watched the troopers descend the hill toward the river, Graham introduced himself and his family to the young man who chose to stay behind.

~ *Richard Dietrich*

"Where will you stay?" he asked Dietrich.

"At McCartney's hotel, I suppose." He peered at a twenty-five-by-thirty-five-foot log building with a sod roof squatting at the mouth of Clematis Gulch. A storehouse and stable stood behind the spartan log cabin. "I've got enough money for a few nights' stay. How about you?"

Graham pointed to the canvas tent rolled up on the pack horse. "We brought our own shelter. But you're welcome to join us for supper. We've got bison, biscuits, and coffee."

"Much obliged. I'll wash up and join you later."

Later that evening, as they sat by the fire, Dietrich told the story of the attack and his narrow escape. When he finished, he became pensive. He poked a stick in the fire and gazed at the glowing embers.

"So, why are you determined to find the young fellas from your group?" Graham asked.

Dietrich sighed. "I came to America from Prussia to teach music. Joe Roberts is one of my students. When he and his friend, August Foller, learned about our group's venture into Wonderland, they begged to come along. I promised Joe's mother I'd watch after him. And now..."

"The park is enormous, but they can find food and build a shelter," Makawee said in an optimistic tone.

"This place has hot springs that can scald a man and canyons that can swallow him. Not to mention Indians waiting to kill any white man."

Dietrich had second thoughts about his last declaration. He looked at Makawee, who was holding Dakkoótee in her lap.

"Sorry, ma'am. I didn't mean to offend you. Not every Indian is hostile. I can see you'd harm no one."

Unless you threaten her family. Then she's a mama grizzly, Graham thought.

Graham cleared his throat. "What kind of music do you teach?"

"I'm the choir master for St. Peter's Protestant Episcopal Church in Helena, where I play the organ. You can't put one of those on a horse," he said, chuckling at his joke. "But I go nowhere without my mouth organ." He fished a Hohner harmonica from his coat pocket. His disposition brightened.

"Would you like to hear a tune?"

"Love to," Graham said.

"I only know a few songs by heart. Here goes."

The music teacher wet his lips. He slid the mouth organ back and forth over the comb while blowing and drawing air through the holes. Graham recognized the first few songs — "Camptown Races" and "Oh! Susanna."

"Have you ever heard 'New Britain?'" Dietrich asked.

"It doesn't sound familiar. Play it."

Graham recognized the tune with the first few bars. He sang along.

"Amazing grace! How sweet the sound
That saved a wretch like me.
I once was lost, but now am found,
Was blind but now I see."

Dietrich played another verse to the old Christian hymn before lowering the harmonica.

"Strange thing," he said. "The Lord spared me today, but those Indians killed Charlie Kenck. How do you explain that?"

It was a question with no answer.

After a moment of silence, Makawee spoke.

"It's getting late. I need to get the children to sleep. Thank you for the entertainment."

"You're most welcome. I want to turn in as well," he said, standing.

"How long are you planning to stay at McCartney's place?" Graham asked.

"Three, perhaps four days. I can't go back to Helena and tell Joe's mother we lost him."

"We're headed out of the park the day after tomorrow. Be careful. The Nez Perce may send warriors this way looking for food or horses."

Dietrich laughed. "God let me live for a reason. Besides, I'm no threat. I'm just a simple music teacher on vacation."

After Dietrich left, Makawee ushered the children inside the wall tent. A minute later, she sang to them. Graham loved to hear her voice. The lyrics pouring from her throat seemed more like an incantation than the words of an ancient Crow song.

Kraa! Kraa!

He jumped up and peered into the darkness. It sounded like a raven. But it didn't come from a bird. Ravens are diurnal. They are active during the day and sleep at night. This could only mean one thing. Someone was *imitating* a raven. His family was being watched. Since Lieutenant Schofield knew they were at Mammoth, there was no need for army scouts to track their location.

Graham's suspicions were confirmed. A group of Nez Perce scouts were indeed spying on him. It angered Graham he was not deemed trustworthy in their eyes.

As he considered the implications, he changed his mood. There was an advantage to this unwanted surveillance. His family had a twenty-four-hour sentry. No one from the army could surprise them in the middle of the night.

Kraa! Kraa!

A second faux raven croaked.

Graham grinned. *Thanks for the personal security,* he thought. *I'm going to sleep well tonight.*

"I'd better ride ahead and introduce us," Graham said to Makawee, while gazing at the sprawling ranch in the distance. "We wouldn't want someone to shoot at us because they thought you were Nez Perce. I'll signal when it's safe for you and the children to join me."

After saying goodbye to Richard Dietrich, they rode six miles from Mammoth Hot Springs, following the Yellowstone River out of the park. A single-story log cabin on Stephen's Creek served as a general store. Three smaller buildings housed sleeping quarters. The owner, James Henderson, erected a corral beside a barn. Twenty horses milled about the enclosure.

A dark-haired man with a bushy mustache greeted Graham as he approached and dismounted.

"Hello. Graham Davidson. My family is traveling to Fort Ellis. We need a few supplies. Mind if we take a look?"

"Sterling Henderson. I manage the ranch. Come on in."

Graham removed his hat and waved it over his head. Makawee, holding Dakkoótee in front of her, urged the horses forward. Nahkash followed atop a mule. When they arrived, Graham introduced his family to Henderson. The ranch manager was relieved when Graham explained his wife was Crow.

They spent twenty minutes browsing the store, which catered to miners headed to Cooke City. It pleased Henderson when Graham paid for flour and coffee with bank notes.

"Most fellas wanna trade something for goods. Some try to pay with gold or silver nuggets. I can do a stone assay, but I'm never sure of the ore's purity."

Graham thanked Henderson and loaded the provisions on the pack horse. The family rode downstream. They traveled only half a mile when a shout came from behind. Wheeling their horses around, they saw a band of eighteen warriors galloping toward the ranch.

Henderson dashed into the store. A moment later, he rushed outside with another man, carrying rifles and ammunition belts. The two men sprinted toward the river, where three others were fishing. All five men took shelter behind a cluster of boulders along the river.

Half the warriors reined their horses several hundred feet from the ranch. They remained on the trail while the others headed straight for the corral.

"Yellow Wolf!" Makawee said.

"What?" Graham said. "Are you sure?"

"I recognize his beaded leggings."

Graham fetched the field glasses from his saddlebag and focused on the corral. Makawee was right. Yellow Wolf jumped from his horse and opened the gate.

Crack! Crack!

Gunfire erupted from behind the boulders. The ranchers opened fire at the horse thieves. Yellow Wolf and his fellow warriors took cover behind the store and another building. They returned fire. The other Indians hurried to the buildings and joined the gunfight.

"Should we help?" Makawee asked.

Graham lowered the binoculars. "Help who?"

"Yellow Wolf and our friends."

"Friends don't spy on one another," he said, pursing his lips.

"What do you mean?"

"It's clear who was making those bird calls at Tower Falls and Mammoth." Graham pointed his finger at the ranch. "Yellow Wolf and his scouting group have been shadowing us. He doesn't trust me. He believes I will betray him."

"Oh, I see."

"Well, I'm not a traitor. But I will not help them kill innocent people." He tucked the field glasses into his saddlebag. "Let's go."

Graham and his family rode north. The sounds of the firefight faded in the distance. After a few miles, they passed an unusual cliff rock formation on the side of Cinnabar Mountain. The Devil's Slide comprises two parallel vertical walls of rock one hundred and twenty feet high, extending from the base to the summit. The unique geological feature was created from alternate beds of limestone, sandstone, and quartzites that eroded at different rates.

As they stopped to admire the unusual formation, Graham noticed a cloud of dust on the trail ahead. He pulled out the binoculars and focused on a large group of men on horseback. A swallow-tailed guidon fluttered in the wind. It was a cavalry unit, accompanied by civilians and scouts.

"Shit!"

"What's wrong?"

"An army column is headed this way. I have to warn Yellow Wolf."

As Graham turned his horse, Makawee stopped him.

"Wait! I will go."

"Why?"

"If the warriors see another white man approaching in the middle of that fight, they will shoot him."

She had a good point. He didn't like it, but acquiesced.

"I'll try to delay them. We'll wait for you a few miles upriver."

Makawee kissed Dakkoótee on the forehead and handed the toddler to Graham.

"Daddy will take care of you."

She reined her horse upstream and dug her heels into the mare's sides. She galloped away and was soon out of sight.

Graham turned in his saddle to Nahkash, who was seated on the mule beside him.

"Honey, I'm going to talk to these soldiers. There's no need to be scared. We will be fine."

"I'm not scared."

He smiled. She had her mother's chutzpah.

Two Crow scouts riding ahead of the column were the first to reach the bearded man with two children blocking the trail. They halted their horses and were surprised when he greeted them in *Apsaàlooke*.

"*Kahée,*" Graham said, holding up his hand.

"*Kahée.*"

The scouts were taciturn. They eyed Graham suspiciously and waited for the soldiers to arrive.

When the column halted a moment later, a young lieutenant rode forward.

"Can we help you?"

"Yes, sir. I was hoping your farrier might look at this mule's hoofs. She's been favoring her back leg, and I'm not sure if we can make it to the Crow Agency."

"What's the hold up?" a voice said. It came from a rider who made his way to the front.

~ *Gustavus Doane*

When Graham saw the man's face, his heart sank. It was Lieutenant Doane, his nemesis.

Graham clashed with the brash officer while they were members of the 1871 Hayden Expedition. Last year, in the immediate aftermath of the Battle of the Little Bighorn, Doane shot and killed Graham's friend, Rides Alone. He claimed it was a case of mistaken identity, but Graham never forgave him. It wasn't the first time the vainglorious cavalryman killed innocent people. His battalion murdered more than a hundred Piegan Blackfeet, mostly old men, women, and children, on the Marias River in 1870.

"Davidson! We can't seem to avoid each other. What brings you this way?"

"Heading to the Crow Agency for annuities."

"And why, pray tell, are you holding up my column?"

"Our mule is coming up lame. I was hoping your farrier could..."

"The army does not provide blacksmith services to civilians — at least not to those who aren't joining the fight against the Nez Perce. I'm leading a force that includes armed citizens. We're going to track down those savages in the park and punish them."

"Best of luck."

"Care to join us?"

Hell no! Graham thought. "I have to take care of my family."

Doane leaned forward in his saddle and peered at Dakkoótee. "Say, is that the Sioux baby you rescued at the Little Bighorn?"

"Yes."

"We're mopping up any renegade Sioux that didn't follow Sitting Bull to Canada." Doane sat back in his saddle and stroked his mustache. He pointed an accusing finger at the toddler sitting in front of Graham. "That little one should have died on the prairie with the other Sioux."

Graham gritted his teeth and tightened his jaw. He envisioned pulling his Colt from the pommel holster and shooting the arrogant son-of-a-bitch between the eyes. But he told himself to take deep breaths. He had to think about Nahkash and Dakkoótee. Graham itched to get away from Doane.

"We'll be on our way."

"Where's Makawee?"

"She's meeting us on the trail."

"Too bad. It would have been nice to see her. She's a sight for sore eyes for any man who spends a lot of time in a saddle."

He knew Doane was goading him, but Graham was sick of the self-absorbed officer's snide remarks about his family and friends.

"Daddy, why is your face red?" Nahkash said.

His daughter's question prevented Graham from doing something he'd regret.

"Oh, it's a hot day. I think we need to get out of the sun," he said, reaching over and touching Nahkash's shoulder.

"Lieutenant Doane! Look!"

A soldier pointed to a plume of black smoke several miles upriver.

Graham knew the source. Yellow Wolf and the warriors must have set fire to the buildings.

"That's about where Henderson's ranch is located," Doane said. "Lieutenant Scott!"

Second Lieutenant Hugh Lenox Scott, only a year removed from West Point, pressed his horse forward.

"Yes, sir."

"Take two scouts and ten troopers. Find out what's happening up ahead. Send someone back with a message."

The eager junior officer saluted, rode back along the column, and selected the troopers. Within a few minutes, the small force was galloping toward the blaze along the river.

"Duty calls, Davidson. I'm headed back to Yellowstone, the land I discovered seven years ago. I've got to cleanse it of Indians," Doane said, tipping his hat. "Sergeant, move us forward!"

Graham guided his horse, the pack horse, and Nakash's mule to the side of the trail. They watched as a company of soldiers and an equal number of armed volunteers rode by, followed by two supply wagons.

As the last of the column rumbled past and the dust settled, Graham gazed at the rock formation on the face of Cinnabar Mountain. *How ironic to meet a man with satanic traits at Devils' Slide,* he thought.

While he was glad to see Doane leave, Graham hoped he delayed the soldiers long enough for Makawee to warn Yellow Wolf and leave the ranch.

"Come along, Nahkash. Let's find a place to camp and wait for your mother."

The Nez Perce warriors galloped from Henderson's Ranch to Mammoth Hot Springs after Makawee warned them about a column of soldiers approaching. They stole two dozen horses from the corral before setting the main building on fire. Unfortunately, half of the horses had to be left behind because they could not keep pace.

Yellow Wolf instructed the younger fighters to water the horses. They would rest for a few minutes, then push southeast along the Yellowstone River to Baronett's Bridge. He cantered to McCartney's small log cabin at the mouth of Clematis Gulch. Naked-footed Bull and Shooting Thunder joined him. It surprised them when a white man with short, wavy hair and a thin mustache appeared in the open doorway.

"Hello! I mean you no harm!" Dietrich said, raising his arms in front of his body with his palms up.

"What is he saying?" Shooting Thunder said in *Niimiipuu.*

"He says he is unarmed," Yellow Wolf said. He was the only one of the three who understood English.

"I am going to shoot this man," Naked-footed Bull said.

Yellow Wolf turned in his saddle to face the warrior.

"*Ituuezet?*" ["Why?"]

"My three younger brothers were not warriors. They killed them and my sister at Big Hole. This man is just like those that killed my brothers and sister. He will become a soldier sometime and kill us."

"Hey, would you like some coffee?" Dietrich asked. He didn't understand what the warriors were saying, but it was clear from their demeanor they were angry.

"It is true. White men who are not soldiers also kill Nez Perce, but..."

"I am going to shoot this man," Naked-footed Bull repeated.

He raised his rifle.

Crack!

Dietrich clutched his shoulder and yelled in pain.

An instant later, Shooting Thunder fired. The second bullet entered the white man's body just below his left rib cage.

Dietrich crumpled to his knees and fell face forward onto the tiny porch. A harmonica tumbled out of his coat pocket. Blood pooled around the mouth organ and dripped between the wood planks.

The music man's life was spared earlier, only to be taken two days later.

Chapter Fourteen
Burning Bridges

5 September [673 miles traveled]

A scout galloped back to the column and saluted General Howard. "Sir, we've got a problem. They've burned the bridge."

Howard returned the salute.

"How bad is it damaged?"

"Hard to say, but it's definitely not passable."

"How far is it?"

"A couple miles."

"Very well. Dismissed."

Howard turned to his chief of staff, Major Edwin Mason.

"Tell Mr. Baronett to come to the front. He needs to know about this."

As Howard nudged his horse forward, he thought about the events of the past two weeks. After returning from Virginia City with fresh supplies, he picked up the trail of the fleeing Nez Perce in the park.

Most of the men never visited Wonderland. There was something cathartic about seeing geysers erupt. These spectacular phenomena allowed them to forget about their sore feet and aching backs. When scouts discovered George Cowan in the Lower Geyser Basin, the soldiers' blissful mood was shattered.

Cowan detailed his capture and assault as the surgeon tended to him. The Radersburg captive told of being shot three times — in the leg, the hip and the head. The Indians left him for dead. Miraculously, the bullet to his head only grazed his skull and knocked him unconscious. When he woke, he bathed his wounds in the river and crawled several miles back to his camp, where he survived on leftover chunks of bacon and spilled coffee beans.

A courier delivered good news the following day. Emma, Ida, and Frank Carpenter were safe. When Lieutenant Wood relayed this message, George Cowan wept with joy.

General Howard leveraged the Indians' assault on the tourists to motivate his men. He reminded them they were part of a noble cause to punish these savages for attacking innocent people.

Meanwhile, scouts reported the Nez Perce were crossing the Yellowstone River. This meant they would exit the park at its northeast corner. Armed with this information, Howard sent a message to Colonel Samuel Sturgis, commander of the Seventh Cavalry, to post a force on Clark's Fork to block the enemy.

The one-armed general pressed forward with confidence. He was certain to catch the hostiles from behind.

The noose was tightening.

"Guid mornin, General. Ye wanted to see me?"

Howard peered at the balding, middle-aged man who rode up beside him.

"Yes, Mr. Baronett. I'm afraid we've received some bad news."

"Whit's that?" Baronett asked, narrowing his eyes.

"A scout reported the Indians burned your bridge."

"Shite!"

Jack Baronett emigrated from Scotland. He ventured to the Montana Territory in 1864, seeking his fortune in gold. When the precious yellow mineral was discovered near Cooke City, he recognized the popularity of the route through northern Wyoming for prospectors coming from points west. He constructed a bridge across the Yellowstone River in the spring of 1871 and charged travelers a toll.

"We don't know the extent of the damage," Howard said. "I want you to inspect the bridge and see what repairs we need to make. Ride ahead and take a look."

The front of the column reached the river ten minutes later. Howard dismounted and walked with Major Mason to the crossing where Jack Baronett was standing.

A crude wooden bridge spanned the river, where it snaked its way northwest. Flat stones stacked on both banks created a solid foundation for lodgepole logs that served as the main support beams. A box crib sat in the middle of the stream on a rock platform, providing a center pillar for the two-span bridge. A three-foot-high log railing lined both sides of the bridge, which was just wide enough to accommodate a small wagon.

The Indians set fire to the cribbing. The middle section and the railings were burned. Because rain showers extinguished the flames before they spread, the structure was still intact.

Baronett scrambled down the trail and walked cautiously across the weakened span to the middle support. He leaned over the charred railing and scratched at the stubble on his chin. After a moment, he walked back up the slope to the waiting army column.

Baronett's Bridge

"How long will it take to repair?" said Howard.

"Ah dinna ken. Depends on cuttin' trees to make logs."

Howard peered at two one-room cabins squatted on the bank overlooking the river.

"Looks like we have plenty already cut," he said, nodding at the buildings.

"Noo just haud on! Those be mine!"

"I'm requisitioning materials to support this army. The government will compensate you for your losses."

"Yer aff yer heid!"

"We are at war. I'm not asking for permission," Howard said, gazing at the rough-hewn shelters. "Which cabin do we dismantle?"

The Scotsman shook his head. He would earn a substantial profit from all the men, horses, and mules that made it to the other side. He couldn't collect any tolls unless they repaired the bridge for the army to cross. Baronett judged the shrewd business decision was to do anything necessary to make the bridge serviceable.

"The ane on the reit."

"Major, form a work detail. Use the logs from Mr. Baronett's cabin at the top of the hill — the one on the right."

"Yes, sir," Mason said, saluting before heading up the slope.

The general studied the bridge. He looked at the midday sun, then checked his pocket watch. The aim was to have it fixed by mid-afternoon. He needed to make up for lost time. The Nez Perce were getting further from his grasp with every hour that passed.

Baronett cleared his throat.

"Sairy fer me words earlier. Nae problem usin' me timbers. Seein' the burnt bridge made me a wee crabbit."

"We're all in a bit of a bad mood. Things will brighten after we cross this river. We're not far behind Joseph and his people."

"A hafta gang," Baronett said.

He hurried toward the cabin, where soldiers were already hacking away at the outer walls with axes. Even though he had to sacrifice a building to save his bridge, he could at least direct the amateur carpenters to take only what they needed to do the job.

Howard walked back to his horse being held by his aide-de-camp.

"Lieutenant, we're going to be here for no less than three hours. I might as well make use of this time to take care of some correspondence. Fetch my writing table and meet me over there."

Wood returned with a mahogany desk and a camp chair. Howard chose a cottonwood tree that provided an unobstructed view of the damaged bridge. His aide set up the chair and waited until the general fished his reading glasses from his coat pocket and slid them over his ears. The lieutenant opened the hinged lid to reveal a two-piece writing surface covered in red velvet. He laid the desk on the general's lap.

"That's all for now," Howard said.

The general lifted the front compartment and retrieved a lined sheet of paper. As he placed the paper on the desk, he thought about his family. Although he received an occasional letter from his wife in the months since the army left Fort Lapwai, these notes were rare. It was a comfort to have his oldest son, Guy, with him as another aide-de-camp, but he missed his other five children. Bessie, the youngest, would soon turn six. He wondered if she would even recognize him when he returned home.

The sooner we defeat these Nez Perce, the sooner we all can go home to our families, he thought.

He unscrewed the pewter lid on a glass bottle, dipped the steel nib pen into the ink well, and wrote...

Yellowstone Park, Wyoming Territory, Sept 5, 1877

My dearest Lizzie,

"General Howard," Lieutenant Wood said. "A dispatch just arrived."

He handed the sealed envelope to his commanding officer, who pushed it away without looking up. The interruption irritated him.

"Open it," Howard said brusquely. "Let me know if there's anything that demands my immediate attention."

Wood opened the envelope and unfolded the papers. When he finished reading, he grimaced. The general would not be pleased.

"Sir, I think you'd better read this."

Howard dropped his nib pen and snatched the note.

Headquarters Army of the United States

Helena, Montana. August 29, 1877.

General O. O. Howard, Commanding Department of the Columbia in the Field:

I have just received from General Sheridan the dispatch of which the enclosed is a copy. You perceive that he has forces aligned east of the mountains to receive the Nez Perces when they issue from the mountains. Yours, as the pursuing force, requires great patience, but not much chance of a fight.

Tomorrow I start for Missoula and Walla Walla.

There are many things in your department about which I would like to consult you. Really, I see not much reason for your commanding a department after having driven the hostile Indians out of your department across Montana and into General Sheridan's command. I find Lieutenant Colonel Charles C. Gilbert here who has served long in the Territory and is familiar with the Indians and the country in which they have taken refuge.

I don't want to order you back to Oregon, but I do say that you can, with perfect propriety, return to your command, leaving the troops to continue till the Nez Perces have been destroyed or captured. I authorize to you to transfer to him, Lieutenant Colonel Gilbert, your command in the field, and to overtake me en route.

W.T. Sherman

Howard took off his reading glasses and tossed them on the writing desk. Sherman wanted him to give up his command to a lieutenant colonel? After pursuing these hostiles over six hundred miles? A mix of emotions flooded his mind — frustration, embarrassment, and anger. He hurled the desk from his lap. Papers, pens, pencils, and his glasses tumbled onto the rocky soil. The ink well overturned and spattered its contents across the writing surface.

Lieutenant Wood used several pieces of paper to soak up the spilled ink, then reassembled the stained writing desk. He gripped the box and watched as Howard paced under the tree.

The general strode to the top of the slope. Men pried charred planks from the bridge and tossed them into the river. The burned logs disappeared as the swift current carried them downstream.

His reputation and military career were about to be swept away with the stroke of a pen. He massaged the stump of his amputated right arm under his empty coat sleeve. Anytime he was stressed, he felt phantom limb pain.

Howard walked back to the cottonwood tree and slumped into his chair.

"Lieutenant Wood, let me see that dispatch again."

As he read Sherman's letter a second time, his mood shifted. This was not a *direct order*. It was a strong suggestion. His best strategy would be to push ahead toward the Nez Perce. With a bit of luck, his forces could overtake them before Gilbert arrived.

Howard handed the note back.

"Shall I write a response?" Wood asked, opening the writing desk.

"No. Fetch Major Mason."

Sherman's dispatch lit a flame under Howard. He would redouble his efforts to catch the hostiles.

The major appeared a moment later.

"You wanted to see me?" he said.

"I want that bridge repaired within the hour. It doesn't have to be perfect, just safe enough to cross. Understand?

"Yes, sir."

"One more thing. No supply wagons. They slow us down. Pack whatever you can on mules. Leave the rest behind. This army will live on coffee, flour, and salted beef until we resupply on the other side of the mountains."

"Yes, sir."

Howard watched the major hurry away to relay the orders. One factor he could control was the speed of his fighting force, and they would soon be on the move.

Something else was true. He could not be relieved of command *if Gilbert could not find him.*

Yellow Wolf scaled the lodgepole, weaving his way from limb to limb toward the top. The pine jutted from a rock outcropping at the confluence of Sunlight Creek and Clark's Fork of the Yellowstone River. He clung to the trunk of the windswept tree with one arm and pushed a branch down with his foot so he could see the canyon.

An army encampment stretched along the river for a mile. Campfires burned outside wedge and wall tents. Sentries guarded the western edge of the gorge.

He climbed down and shared his observation with the other scouts. The enemy blocked Clark's Fork Canyon.

"I will ride back and tell Lean Elk. We need to find another way to the buffalo plains. Stay here and observe the soldiers. Join us before nightfall."

Yellow Wolf rode upstream five miles before meeting the procession of Nez Perce. Chief Joseph was leading women and children at the front. The Wallowa leader directed the group to pause until the leaders could devise a plan to avoid the soldiers.

Yellow Wolf found Lean Elk and Ollokot riding in the middle of the herd. When he signaled he wished to speak to the leaders, the two-mile-long line of people and horses came to a halt. He reported the soldier camp sighting ahead.

Lean Elk called a council. After the tribal chiefs and leaders were assembled, the war chief invited each person to express his views.

"We should proceed down the main river. We have the element of surprise in our favor," White Bird said. "Let's fight."

"Let our warriors kill the soldiers, so our people can rest. They are tired." said Looking Glass.

Many in the circle nodded.

Toohoolhoolzote stood.

"Why fight? Do you not remember Lapwai? They imprisoned none of you. The white man is ruthless and selfish. They do not care for the Indian." The sixty-year-old prophet sighed. "I have seen my future. I will die in buffalo country under the harvest moon. We need to find a way around the soldiers so I can fulfill my destiny."

"Ollokot, what say you?" said Lean Elk.

"Our scouts report Cut Arm is only twenty miles behind. They could soon overtake us. I fear the army has trapped us."

Lean Elk shook his head.

"We are not trapped. Our warriors cannot fight two armies, but we are more clever than our enemy. We need to make the soldiers believe we are going one way, then go a different direction."

The chief war leader broke off a pine bough and swept clean a flat, muddy area along the river. The tribal leaders and elders gathered around. He placed stones in the dirt, representing the two armies. Using a twig, he drew the Clark's Fork of the Yellowstone and sketched triangles for the mountains to the east.

"There is always another route. We just have to find it."

Lean Elk dug the stick into the moist earth and drew a line over the mountains.

"Our ancestors and other tribes took the easiest route to the east. That is the way the army expects us to travel. We will trick them. We will follow a challenging trail. It is steep. The canyon is narrow. The timber is dense. But, we can get to the buffalo plains without fighting the soldiers. The warriors will mill our ponies by splitting the herd and driving them in several directions, then herding them back together. This will confuse Cut Arm's soldiers."

"What about the army in front? They will see us and change their position," said Ollokot.

"I'm counting on this. We want their scouts to believe we are moving toward Heart Mountain." He drew a line to the southeast. "After the soldiers move in that direction, we will double back and strike the trail along Clark's Fork. We will be on level ground and can move north at a rapid pace."

Lean Elk scanned the faces of the council members. Everyone nodded in agreement.

"A warning. This will be a tiresome journey. Those who are weak — be they horse, man, or woman — will not make it."

Chief Joseph stood. Although his brother, Ollokot, was war chief of the Wallowa band, everyone respected Joseph.

"Some elderly and wounded could die. However, I see no other choice. This is a good plan. It gives us the best chance to escape to the buffalo plains without risking further injuries to our people."

Thirty minutes later, the procession was under way with Lean Elk in the lead. The group rode out of the canyon, making a steep ascent. They crossed a high plateau and headed toward Heart Mountain, ten miles distant. After a brief rest, they turned abruptly northeast.

The Nez Perce scouts that stayed behind to observe the soldiers reported the army broke camp and was marching southeast. The ploy worked. The Indians followed Paint Creek as it flowed into the Clark's Fork branch of the Yellowstone.

Ollokot rode in the back with the rear guard. It was disheartening to see horses too weak to navigate up and down the steep slopes. They left behind dozens of animals that refused to take another step.

A middle-aged man was sitting against a tree as Ollokot passed by. He dismounted and walked over to the warrior, who was holding his stomach.

"You cannot stop here. We will rest in a few hours," Ollokot said as he squatted.

"I am too tired."

He noticed a soldier shot the man in his thigh during the battle of the Big Hole. A foul odor was emanating from the warrior's blackened and swollen leg.

"I can put you on my horse."

"No. I am ready to die."

"Do you have family?"

"They killed my wife and little boy."

Ollokot nodded.

"What would you like me to do?"

Without hesitation, the man looked at Ollokot and begged, "Take my life."

"I refuse to do that. Life is precious and..."

"Put me out of my misery," the man said, grabbing Ollokot's arm. "I do not want the enemy to find me alive."

Ollokot nodded. He pulled a pistol from his waistbelt and placed it in the man's hand.

"I'm not willing to do it, but you can."

"Too weak. Help."

Ollokot wrapped the man's fingers around the handle, positioned his forefinger on the trigger, and raised the man's arm so the barrel was against his temple. He cocked the weapon and held the dying man's arm in place.

"Squeeze."

Bang!

The dying man's body went limp as bits of bone matter and brain exploded from his skull. The gun fell from his hand.

Ollokot threw back his head, lifted his arms, and petitioned the spirits to receive the man's soul. He retrieved the revolver, tucked it into his belt, and stood. Grabbing the dead warrior under his armpits, he dragged the body to the edge of the stream. He stuffed large rocks into the man's trousers and under his shirt, then pulled him into the creek and pushed him under a submerged log. He didn't have time to bury the corpse. The least he could do was prevent the enemy scouts from taking his scalp.

Another Nez Perce died hundreds of miles from his homeland. How many more of us will die before we cross the Medicine Line? he thought, as he mounted his horse.

The non-treaty Nez Perce exited the mountains at sunset. The land transitioned to a broad basin, with the Bighorn Mountains to the northeast. Grasslands extended as far as the eye could see.

They were in Crow country.

The leaders eagerly awaited confirmation their long-time tribal friends would assist them in fighting the government. Their hopes rested with Makawee.

Chapter Fifteen
Pride & Prejudice

10 September [798 miles traveled]

Graham glanced behind him to make sure Makawee was in the tent with the children. He fished a wood sculpture from his saddlebag and sat by the fire. He leaned forward and rotated the partially finished bison in his hand, inspecting it from every angle. The proportions of the animal seemed right. All he needed was to carve some details around the neck and legs.

This was his third attempt at carving a bison from a chunk of lodgepole pine. The first two ended up in the fire because his sculpting skills displeased him. This one was a keeper. He was excited to present it to Makawee as an anniversary gift.

"They are asleep," Makawee said, emerging from the tent.

Graham hid the sculpture under a blanket.

"We've ridden quite a bit the last few days. I'm sure they're tired."

A few hours after Makawee warned Yellow Wolf about the cavalry coming toward Henderson's Ranch, she rejoined Graham. Yellow Wolf and his band of raiders galloped away from the settlement just as the advance group of soldiers approached. Makawee hid behind a knoll on the east side of the river and rode back downstream, undetected by Doane and his militia.

Now, they were camped on the Stillwater River under black cottonwood trees. This location was special to them. They shared many joyous moments at this site when Graham returned to propose marriage five years ago. They made love, talked of their future together, and watched as Nahkash took her first wobbly steps as a toddler.

This grove also witnessed unbearable grief. Makawee's cries were heard by the trees, and the roots absorbed Graham's tears. They gave their baby boy, Small Heart, a tree burial in the towering cottonwood. Graham carved the first letters of his family's first names into the bark, then encircled them with a heart.

"Are you ready to talk to Chief Long Horse at the Agency?" Graham asked.

"I committed to ask if the Crow would help fight the government. I will keep that promise."

"Will you urge Long Horse to accept Dakkoótee into his family?" he said, searching his wife's face for a reaction.

Makawee stood and walked to the tree. She used her index finger to trace each of the initials and the heart carved into the fissured bark.

"When Long Horse accepts Dakkoótee, we will carve a 'D' next to our initials."

"And if he does not accept the Sioux child?"

She dropped her hand and shook her head.

"I don't want to think about that."

Graham stood and hugged his wife from behind.

"I'm the one who asked you to adopt the infant last year. If it is too painful, I can ask Long Horse."

"No! He is my father. I will speak to him."

He could feel her muscles tighten. He massaged her neck and shoulders as they stared at the arborglyph of their family.

"Makawee, whatever happens, remember we're in this together."

"*Diiawachisshik,*" Makawee said, resting the back of her head against his chest.

"I love you, too."

Graham and Makawee reined their horses on a hill and gazed at the Crow Agency along the Stillwater River. A square enclosure three hundred feet on each side guarded eight buildings. Outside the heavy plank wall, contractors built a dozen adobe cabins for Crow residents learning to be farmers. Plots of wheat, oats, and turnips encircled the stockade. Workers dug an irrigation ditch to provide water for crops. Tepees of families who came to the Agency for their annuities dotted the outskirts of the settlement.

"Let's collect the annuities. Then we'll find Long Horse," Graham said.

The Davidsons rode to the palisade and identified themselves to the sentry, who told them to leave the horses outside until they were ready to load their supplies. Makawee kept the children while Graham led their animals to one of the adobe buildings. He asked a young boy to watch the equines, then returned to join his family at the gate.

"The Indian agent's office is over there," the soldier said, pointing to a small log cabin along the southern wall.

Graham's family joined several others queued behind a table. Twenty minutes passed before they reached the front of the line.

"Next!" a thin man with thick, wavy hair and a horseshoe mustache bellowed. "Name?"

"Makawee."

"Mountain Crow or River Crow?"

"Mountain."

He leafed through an oversized ledger, running his fingers down each page. "Don't see your name."

"I married and started my family," she said, looking down at Nahkash and nodding to Dakkoótee, held by Graham.

"Before becoming married, whose lodge did you share?"

"Long Horse."

The agent nodded, flipped toward the front of the register, and located a journal entry.

"Ah-ha! According to our records from last year, Long Horse is married to Fox Woman. The previous agent listed three children. Two sons, both of whom are deceased — Little Wolf and Rides Alone, one daughter, Makawee, and one granddaughter, Nahkash." He looked up. "Is that correct?"

"Yes."

"Your name, sir?" the skinny man asked.

"Davidson."

The agent stroked his mustache and squinted. He sifted through some documents on the table and pulled out a telegram.

"Graham Davidson?"

"That's right."

"In that case, I have some questions. Are you the father of these children?"

"Nahkash is my child. We adopted Dakkoótee," Graham said, rocking the toddler in his arms.

"Do you have the adoption papers?"

"No, but we cared for him since he was a baby."

"Is the child Crow?"

Graham foresaw the path of the interrogation. He wished he lied and told the representative Dakkoótee was his biological son.

"He was abandoned, so we have no knowledge of his parents."

"Is he Sioux?"

"Why does that matter?"

The agent held up his hand. "If he is not Crow, we cannot include him in the census. For annuities, the government only recognizes anyone born or married into the Crow Nation."

"But he is our child," Graham objected.

"I received this telegram from Lieutenant Doane a few days ago," the man said, waving the paper in front of him. "It says you would show up and try to claim a Sioux child as part of your family. Is that what you're trying to do?"

Doane is a pain in the ass even at a distance, Graham thought. He didn't give a damn whether the government, Doane, or Long Horse refused to acknowledge Dakkoótee. He wanted to tell the Indian agent it was none of his business what tribe the child belonged to, but he refrained.

Graham avoided answering the question and asked one of his own.

"What's our family owed?"

"Well, since we aren't counting the bastard child, your family is entitled to annual provisions for two-and-a-half people." He jotted a note on a slip of paper, signed it, and handed it to Graham. "Give this to the man at the warehouse."

Graham snatched the note and glared at the official. Before leaving, he asked, "Has Long Horse received his annuities?"

The agent consulted his ledger.

"Yep. He was here about an hour ago. I imagine he's camped with the others by the river. Next!"

The family walked through the gates. Graham fetched the mule and led it inside. He presented the receipt to the warehouse attendant, then loaded dried beef, flour, coffee, sugar, and salt on the pack animal. He bought a handful of peppermint sticks. When he returned, he presented one to the boy who watched their horses and one each to Nahkash and Dakkoótee.

Makawee stared at a cluster of tepees under a grove of trees a hundred yards away.

"Is that your father's lodge?" he asked.

She nodded, folded her hands together as if she were praying, and rested her forehead on the tips of her index fingers. Graham put his arm around her shoulders, trying to reassure her.

A moment later, she took a deep breath and said, "Let's do this."

Graham and his family walked a short distance to the camp. Fox Woman was bent over a cooking fire, stirring a pot. As the visitors approached, she shielded her eyes from the midday sun and squinted. She dropped a spoon and dashed to meet them.

"Makawee! Makawee!" she shouted, hugging her daughter. Fox Woman stooped and pulled Nahkash close to her breast, then stepped back and marveled at how tall the girl had grown in a year. *"Daásitchikaashe!"* ["I'm so happy!"] she said, tears streaming down her cheeks.

"Mother, don't forget Dakkoótee," Makawee said.

Fox Woman looked at the toddler in Graham's arms and placed a hand to her mouth.

She opened her arms and invited the Sioux child to come to his adopted grandmother. Dakkoótee leaned forward and allowed Fox Woman to grasp him under his arms. She held the child with one arm and playfully touched his nose and ruffled his dark hair with the other hand while he licked the sticky candy.

"He's becoming a beautiful boy," she said a moment later, as she bounced Dakkoótee on her hip. The up-and-down motion made him laugh.

Graham glanced at Makawee, who was smiling. There was no doubt how Fox Woman felt about reuniting with her daughter and grandchildren.

"Where is Long Horse?" Makawee asked.

Fox Woman gestured toward the pole lodge.

As Makawee turned to leave, Fox Woman grabbed her daughter's arm.

"Your father is not feeling well."

"Is he sick? What illness does he have?" Makawee asked.

"I'm sure he will feel better tomorrow."

Her mother's comments bewildered Makawee.

"Thank you," she said, before walking to the lodge.

Graham followed his wife. When they reached the entrance, Makawee turned and said, "Please wait out here. I need to ask about the Crow alliance with the Nez Perce. I'll let you know when you and the children may enter."

Makawee lifted the flap and stepped inside.

Chief Long Horse sat cross-legged in his customary position at the rear of the lodge. His eyes were closed and his head tilted back. With his right hand holding a pipe, he raised his left arm. It shocked Makawee to see a whiskey bottle lying beside him. Her father was in a meditative state, or drunk, or both. She sat and waited.

A few minutes later, Long Horse opened his eyes. It took a moment for him to comprehend the person on the other side of the lodge. He beamed when he recognized his daughter.

"Come!" he said in a slurred voice. "Sit close to your father, the once great and mighty Long Horse."

Makawee obliged. She sat across from him and observed him closely. Loose strands of hair dangled in front of red and glassy eyes. He slumped forward, then jerked back to regain his balance on the buffalo robe. She saw other men drunk, but never her father. It pained her to see this proud man in such a debilitative state.

She held the half-empty whiskey bottle before him.

"Father, what have you done?"

"Rememberin' days gone by."

"You're drunk!"

"*Kooshtattáchii.*" ["a little"]

"Well, I will not talk to you while you're in this condition!" she said, standing.

"Wait!" Long Horse said, grabbing her hand. "Sit. It's been a year since we spoke. Stay."

Makawee hesitated. She dreaded this conversation with a sober Long Horse. His behavior was likely to be worse when inebriated.

"Only if you explain why you did this," she said, holding up the bottle.

Long Horse slapped his cheeks and blinked.

"*Bile?*" ["Water?"] he asked.

She dipped a ladle in a bowl and handed it to her father, who gulped the water. He motioned for a second serving. This time, he dumped it over his head. He tucked the wet hair behind his ears and rubbed his eyes.

Long Horse sighed. "I never touched firewater before."

"I know," she said, sitting. "You always directed us to stay away from it. So, why now?"

"The world of our ancestors has disappeared. They want us to work as farmers — cultivating crops on soil intended for grazing, not planting. White men have killed almost all *bishee*. Our people have to stand in line for food every year."

She could hear the sadness and anger in her father's voice. He spoke the truth. She nodded, but did not respond.

"I am ashamed," he said, looking into his daughter's eyes. "I'm ashamed to be drunk. I feel humiliated for being a farmer. I am a warrior."

Makawee saw an opening in his last statement.

"Father, as you know, we have lived with our friends, the Nez Perce, this past year. We traveled with them from Idaho through the Land of Burning Ground. They are trying to make it across the Medicine Line to freedom."

"I have heard."

"Chief Joseph and his brother, Ollokot, want to know if the Crow will support them in their fight against the military."

Long Horse drew in a deep breath, clasped his hands, and rested them on his lap.

"Many of our young men serve as scouts for the army. They are warriors, not farmers. It gives them a purpose."

"Can we at least allow the Nez Perce to pass through our lands on the way to the British Territories?"

"Our annuities will be forfeited if we help the Nez Perce," Long Horse said after thinking for a moment. "Worse, the government may take more of our land."

"Should I ask any other chiefs these questions?"

"Our people hold Iron Bull and Plenty Coups in high esteem. You are welcome to approach them, but I'm sure they will answer the same."

"I understand. I will let the Nez Perce leaders know."

In reality, she didn't understand her father. Moments earlier, he pined for the life of a warrior. Now, when given the chance to take up arms against the people who deprived them of their centuries-long lifestyle, he made the comfortable choice.

"There is something personal I want to ask of you."

He elevated his open palm. "Speak your mind."

"Before I do, let me bring others into the lodge."

Makawee stood and ducked outside. She nodded to Graham and took Dakkoótee from Fox Woman. "Come with me, Nahkash," she said, taking her daughter by the hand. "We are going to visit with your grandfather."

The Davidsons and Fox Woman stepped into the lodge.

The chief looked tired. His eyelids drooped. Instead of a straight posture, he slouched forward. His loosened tunic revealed his rib cage. He lost at least twenty pounds since the last time they met.

"Father, you remember Nahkash," she said, placing her hands on the girl's shoulders.

Makawee leaned down and whispered into her daughter's ear. "Give your grandfather a hug."

Nahkash stepped forward. Long Horse sat erect and took the girl. She encircled his neck with her arms.

The chief's countenance changed. A smile creased his face as he embraced his granddaughter. As he squeezed the young girl, a tear trickled down his cheek. He placed her on his lap, lifted her chin, and said, "*Káahke* [Grandfather] is so happy to see you!"

"And this is your grandson, Dakkoótee," Makawee said, looking at the toddler perched on her hip.

Long Horse's eyes narrowed, and his jaw tightened.

"You dare to bring a child of my enemy into this lodge?"

"He is our adopted son. That makes him your grandson. Why can't you accept this?"

"Why? His people murdered my sons and your brothers, Rides Alone and Little Wolf. That's why!"

"Sioux warriors killed your sons, not this baby!" Makawee retorted.

"I will never welcome Dakkoótee into my family!"

"*Káahke*, why are you angry?" Nahkash asked, tilting her head and touching her grandfather's face.

Long Horse took a deep breath and clasped the girl's hand. "I'm not angry at you. I am upset with your mother."

"Nahkash, come," Makawee said, motioning for her to leave Long Horse.

The little girl kissed her grandfather on the cheek and slid from his lap to join her mother.

"Eagle Bear, Nahkash, and you are welcome in my lodge — but not the Sioux child," the chief said.

"You don't mean that!" Fox Woman said. "It's the alcohol talking. That boy is our grandchild!"

"I meant every word," he said defiantly.

Fox Woman covered her face with her hands. The joy she experienced from her family's reunion dissipated like the smoke from a cooking fire. She sat and wept.

Makawee handed Dakkoótee to Graham.

"Take the children. I will join you in a minute," she said to her husband.

Graham started to say something, but nodded instead. This heated argument was between a father and a daughter. He ushered Nahkash toward the opening of the tepee and stepped into the midday sun.

"Dakkoótee deserves a community where everyone loves him. That place is elsewhere," Makawee said, staring at the Crow chief.

"I agree," Long Horse said, folding his arms.

Makawee picked up the whiskey bottle and threw it at Long Horse, missing his head by inches. It thumped against the rear wall of the tepee. Her bravado crumbled. She burst into tears and wiped her eyes with the back of her hand. After a moment, she regained her composure.

"*Shia-nuk*, ["See you later"] Mother."

Fox Woman did not look up.

As Makawee ducked out of the lodge, her mother's sobbing grew louder. The doleful sound heightened her anguish.

I don't need my Crow family. I'll start a new life in the white man's world with Graham, she thought.

Deep in her heart, a part of her died today.

They spoke no words that night as they sat around the fire. Graham tried to console his wife earlier, but she said she wanted to be alone, and he respected her wishes. He took the children with him to go fishing in the Stillwater. Dakkoótee was too young to comprehend this family turmoil or the animosity his adoptive grandfather had toward him. Nahkash, on the other hand, was affected by the day's events. Even catching a trout did not improve her somber mood.

Now, as Graham pushed the fish around in the frying pan, he struggled with words of consolation. After losing her brothers several years earlier, today his wife severed ties with her parents.

"My father is *akbaalúupia* [a prejudiced man]," Makawee said, breaking the silence. "But we agree on something."

"Oh? What's that?"

"Dakkoótee should grow up in a place where everyone welcomes him. A Sioux village should raise the boy."

"He has a loving home with us."

"Of course he does. We love this boy, but you are *baashchiile* — a white man, and I am Crow. We cannot teach him the traditions of the Lakota people. He has a Sioux name and Sioux blood, but he will always feel like something is missing when he is older."

Makawee's argument was based on personal experience. Her parents died from smallpox when she was an infant. She lived with Blackfeet and a white man before Long Horse and Fox Woman welcomed her into their lodge as a teen. If anyone could imagine what it would be like growing up in a foreign culture, it would be her.

"What are you saying?"

"Our son..." She paused, as if the words choked her. "The greatest love we can give Dakkoótee is to place him with a Sioux family."

Graham knew she was right. They planned to do this for a while. That time came too soon. They were less than three-hundred-and-fifty miles from the Canadian border. Sitting Bull and his followers successfully escaped from the army and were now camping north of the Medicine Line.

"Are you telling me you want to rejoin the Nez Perce on their journey?"

"Yes."

Graham stroked his beard and grimaced.

"Makawee, we can no longer put our family in danger. Let's make the trip to the British Territories ourselves rather than with the Nez Perce. An army is chasing them!"

"Can you guide us through Assiniboine country?" she said.

She had a point. There would be as much risk traveling as a family as with hundreds of non-treaty Nez Perce.

"Well... I've never been to northern Montana."

"Neither have I. We committed to reporting to Ollokot and Chief Joseph. They need to know the Crow will not support their fight against the government. They are our friends — and the only tribe where our entire family is welcome."

Graham could see her pleading eyes.

"*Kahee!*"

A familiar woman's voice called from the darkness. Fox Woman approached the fire. She hugged Makawee and Graham, and they invited her to sit.

"I didn't expect to see you again," Makawee said.

"You are my daughter, and those are my grandchildren," she said, nodding at the open wall tent where they were sleeping. "I don't want to lose you — or them."

"If you came to convince me to stay, I will not. I made my decision."

"Your father is a fool. His words were selfish and hurtful," Fox Woman said. She placed her hand on top of Makawee's. "I don't fault you for being angry with him."

"I never meant to hurt you."

Fox Woman nodded. "Our reservation land is enormous. Why not search for a place to settle your family miles from the lodge of Long Horse?"

"Graham and I will venture across the Medicine Line and find an adoptive Sioux family for Dakkoótee."

Fox Woman pulled a shawl around her shoulders. She picked up a stick and poked at the fire for a moment before speaking.

"When are you planning to depart?"

"Tomorrow," Graham said, looking at his wife.

"You will travel with the Nez Perce?"

"Yes," they said in unison.

He saw a look of approval from Makawee.

"Are you intending to return to America?"

"Yes, but not to Crow Land," Makawee said. "We plan to settle somewhere else in Montana Territory."

Fox Woman's eyes lit up.

"Let Nahkash stay with me. There is no need for her to make that arduous journey. Until you return, I will look after her."

Makawee looked at Graham, who shrugged. "It's alright with me. I would feel better if Nahkash stayed here."

"Me too, but..."

"I know. You'll miss her. So will I. This will be a wonderful opportunity for Nahkash to get to know her grandmother."

"Okay, mother. Please come back in the morning to take her with you."

Fox Woman jumped up and hugged Makawee, then did the same to Graham.

"Would you like me to escort you to your lodge?" he asked.

"Unnecessary. It is *áhpaaitche* [a beautiful evening]." Fox Woman turned toward the dimly lit tepees in the distance and sang as she faded into the night.

"You made your mother very happy," Graham said, putting his arm around her waist.

"It's the only positive thing that happened today."

"I have something to cheer you up," he said. "Wait here."

He returned to the fire a moment later.

"Our anniversary is next month. I thought this would be an ideal time to give you one of my presents."

He handed her a crumpled brown package.

Makawee sat and placed the gift on her lap. She loosened the twine and unfolded the paper. She put her hand to her mouth, then lifted a floral print dress with white lace trim from the packaging.

"Where did you get this?" she asked, her eyes gleaming.

"Remember when we went shopping for supplies at Henry Buck's store in Stevensville?"

"Yes. That's where I bought a dress for Lautiss."

They sat in silence, recalling the tragic death of the expectant mother. Graham made a sign of the cross, while Makawee mouthed a silent prayer.

Graham cleared his throat.

"Well, I bought it at the general store. Is it to your liking?"

"It's beautiful!"

"Sorry, it's wrinkled and soiled. It's been in my saddlebag for six weeks and six hundred miles."

"I'd like to try it on."

"I was hoping you would say that," he said, grinning.

When Makawee returned from behind the tent wearing the tea gown, Graham gasped. The light-colored dress contrasted with her smooth dark skin and jet black hair. The color of her obsidian turtle necklace matched the floral design. She was stunning.

He stood, tossed his hat on the ground, and extended his arm, palm up.

"Mrs. Davidson, may I have this dance?"

She stepped in to meet him. He clasped her right hand with his left and rested her other hand on his shoulder. Then he placed his right hand on the small of her back.

"Graham, I don't know how to dance."

"Neither do I. It doesn't matter. Let's just hold each other. Think of something beautiful, because that's what you are."

He leaned down and met her lips. They swayed to and fro in rhythm, shuffling their feet on the dew-covered bunchgrass. He pulled her closer, placing her head under his chin until her breasts pressed against his stomach.

Graham wanted to hold on forever. He wished he could squeeze the pain from Makawee. Today she shared an angst similar to that of Chief Joseph and his people. Both had been rejected from their land — the non-treaty tribes by the government and Makawee by her own father. Just as the Wallowa Valley was bitter ground for the Nez Perce, the Stillwater River Valley became bitter ground for Makawee.

By dancing with his wife, Graham hoped to provide a haven from the turmoil swirling around her. For one night, he wanted her to focus only on the present moment. Not tomorrow, when she would leave her daughter behind. Not the next few days, when they would rejoin a people harassed and threatened by a military focused on punishing them. Not in a few months, when they would give up their only son to another family.

Graham's mind drifted to a song he heard on the radio as a teen. It was the high-pitched voice of David Gates of Bread singing "Make it with you." One line of the lyrics stuck in his head — *life can be short or long.*

He didn't know what the next few months would bring, or where his life would lead. One thing was certain. He would make it with Makawee.

Chapter Sixteen

Canyon Creek

13 September [942 miles traveled]

A cloud of dust rose from the plains north of the Yellowstone River. Forty miles per hour gusts whipped the tasseled stalks of cordgrass and bluebunch wheatgrass. Thousands of horses and hundreds of refugees trekked across the dry prairie, inching toward a place they imagined would be their new home.

Graham lowered his field glasses and handed them to Makawee. She looked through the eyepieces, nodded, and returned the binoculars. They found the trail of the Nez Perce.

He tugged on the lead rope of the pack mule and urged his mount forward, choosing a route that would allow him to meet the front of the entourage several miles distant. Makawee, with Dakkoótee sitting astraddle her horse, followed.

Warriors intercepted the family, but let them pass when they recognized Graham. He wove his horse among the assemblage of women and children. The Nez Perce plodded forward on malnourished horses, many of which were pulling travois loaded with household items. As he observed the beleaguered bands of Indians, he felt guilty for having a full belly. While his family resupplied at the Crow Agency, their friends subsisted on whatever the raiding parties of young warriors could find at ranches scattered along Clark's Fork.

Graham spotted Chief Joseph at the head of the column. He signaled his desire to talk with the leader, who reined his horse off the trail.

"*Ta'c meeywi,*" ["Good morning"] Joseph said, raising his hand in greeting as the procession pressed forward without him.

"*Kla-how'-ya,*" Makawee said.

"I am glad you have returned. Did you meet with your father?"

"Yes. I would like to share what I learned. Can we speak with Ollokot and Lean Elk?"

"They should be coming soon. We will wait here."

A few minutes later, the rear of the column appeared. Joseph waved at his brother and Lean Elk. The two men veered from the rear guard and rode to meet them.

After initial greetings, Makawee delivered the bad news.

"I met with my father, Chief Long Horse. The Crow are unwilling to assist the Nez Perce, for fear of retribution by the government."

Joseph and Ollokot were visibly disheartened. The brothers were optimistic the Crow would align with the non-treaty Nez Perce against the military.

The world had changed in the last few years. Friends were enemies, and enemies were friends. Not long ago, it would have been unthinkable for the Nez Perce to find refuge with the Sioux. Now, Sitting Bull's people were the only ones to accept them — if for no other reason than they shared a common enemy in the US government.

Lean Elk nodded. "I am not surprised. Enemy scouts have been following us the past few days. We could not get close enough to see their faces, but we suspect they are Crow."

"I can confirm your suspicions. Some Crow warriors are scouting for the army. I'm sorry our people will not help," Makawee said.

"You tried. That's all we could ask," Ollokot said.

"Where is your daughter?" Joseph said.

Makawee dropped her head and swallowed hard.

She struggled to leave Nahkash yesterday. The three generations of women said their emotional goodbyes. Makawee explained to her daughter that Daddy and Mommy were going on a long trip, and they would be back in the spring.

As she mounted her pony in the gray of dawn, Makawee told Nahkash, "I will return. Mind your grandmother."

More than once, she reined her horse west, telling Graham she couldn't endure leaving her daughter behind. Each time, he stopped her. He reminded Makawee she was doing the right thing.

Now, Joseph's question caused her to regret the decision again.

When Graham saw she was having difficulty speaking, he responded on her behalf.

"We thought it best to leave Nahkash with her grandmother."

Everyone knew what Graham implied with this statement. This was a dangerous journey. At the Big Hole, it was proven that indiscriminate killing was the norm for a ruthless army. Women and children were as vulnerable as warriors.

Another pang of guilt washed over Graham. He could provide a safe place for his child, but the Nez Perce did not have that option.

"A wise choice," Lean Elk said. "I would do the same."

"Can we stop to rest? Let's wait until the winds die down." Ollokot said. "The dust is choking everyone."

"Not yet. The scouts have seen us. The army is not far off. Let's get to the other side of that canyon," Lean Elk said, pointing to a narrow gorge five miles ahead.

"Makawee, ride with the women and children," Graham said.

"Where will you be?"

"With the warriors."

She tightened her grip on Dakkoótee and galloped with Joseph toward the front of the caravan. Ollokot and Lean Elk fell in at the tail end of the procession.

"*Kla-how'-ya*, Eagle Bear," a voice called out from the rear guard.

Yellow Wolf's long hair flowed over his shoulders as he trotted to Graham. The Nez Perce warrior's skin was darker than he remembered. Sun and wind weathered his face.

Graham wondered if his own appearance was altered by constant exposure to the weather these past three months.

"*Kla-how'-ya.*"

It surprised Graham that the young warrior approached him. They had not spoken for a month — not since the night after the Big Hole battle, when Yellow Wolf accused him of being a traitor.

"Let us ride while we talk," Yellow Wolf said.

They traveled silently for a moment before the warrior spoke.

"*Kaiziyeuyeu!*" ["Thanks!"]

Graham glanced at the man riding beside him. "For what?"

"Makawee alerted us about the soldiers approaching the ranch. We were able to escape because of her... and you."

Graham nodded. "That's what friends do."

Another minute passed before anyone spoke.

"You have returned. Why?"

"Makawee and I have the same destination as you — the camp of Sitting Bull north of the Medicine Line. We will take our baby boy back to his people."

This comment surprised Yellow Wolf. He reined his horse and turned to face his friend.

"You would do this?"

Graham sighed. "It will not be easy. But it's best for the child. He needs to be raised by his kin."

These words moved Yellow Wolf. He extended his right arm. Graham clasped the warrior's arm just below his elbow.

"I'm no longer a spy or a traitor?"

Yellow Wolf shook his head.

"*Taz lautua*." ["Good friend"]

The battalion of four hundred soldiers under Colonel Samuel Sturgis took a much-needed rest along the Yellowstone River. Traveling up to fifty miles every day for a week exhausted the men.

After the Nez Perce slipped past Sturgis' forces and escaped the national park, General Howard ordered the colonel to take the freshest horses and ride day and night. His orders were to overtake the fleeing Indians, engage them, and hold them in place until the rest of Howard's command arrived.

~ *Col. Nelson Miles*

The general sent a courier to Colonel Nelson Miles, commander of the Tongue River Cantonment.

He urged Miles to advance toward the Canadian border and head off the Indians. If the Nez Perce crossed into the British territories, they could join forces with Sitting Bull and renew their attacks. Howard emphasized the critical nature of the mission and pressed the colonel to "make every effort in your power to prevent the escape of this hostile band."

General Howard rebuked Colonel Sturgis about the debacle at Clark's Fork. Major Merrill, his senior officer, assured Sturgis the general unfairly chastised him because Howard was under a lot of pressure from his commanding officer. Rumors circulated among the officers General Sheridan was eager to replace Howard. This news didn't sit well with the one-armed general. Howard had been chasing the non-treaty Nez Perce for three months and had nothing to show for his efforts except a victory at the Big Hole by Colonel Gibbon.

"I'm not sure what other options we had," Sturgis said to Major Merrill. "Those Indians are smarter than most officers I served under during the war."

"I agree. We just need to catch these red devils and engage in a fight. Trouble is, they never stay in one place long enough to taste the lead from our cannon and rifles. Those tactics would frustrate any military man."

A man galloped into camp and dismounted before his horse came to a halt. Stanton Fisher, a volunteer who was chief of scouts, handed the reins to a soldier and strode to Sturgis' tent.

"Colonel, we spotted them. They're five miles north of our position."

Sturgis jumped up from his chair.

"You're sure?"

"No doubt. Hundreds of women, children, and men. Thousands of horses. They're kickin' up enough dust to choke a pack of mules. It's them alright."

Colonel Sturgis rubbed his hands together. *At last*, he thought. *We're in open country. They can't hide in a forest or behind a mountain. With a little luck, I can end this war today.*

"Tell Captain Benteen. Have the men saddle up, Major."

A bugler sounded "To Horse."

Thirty minutes later, the officers watched the Nez Perce from a bluff overlooking Canyon Creek. The Nez Perce caravan advanced toward the canyon, whose ochre rimrock walls towered four hundred feet above the stream. The wind howled along the ridgeline, making it difficult to hear.

"Captain, take Company F and Company L," Sturgis shouted. "Follow the ridge and cut off the Indians before they can escape. Major Merrill and I will lead three other companies and attack them. Hurry!"

"Yes, sir."

Sturgis watched as Benteen rallied his troops and raced along the ridge toward the exit of the canyon.

The colonel ordered his battalion to charge the Indians. A few minutes into their advance, the Nez Perce fired at the pursuing troopers.

"Companies, halt! Dismount!" Sturgis barked. "Battle line!"

One-hundred-and-fifty cavalrymen slid from their horses. Every fourth soldier held the reins of his horse and those of three others. The men advanced toward the enemy, firing as they walked.

The warriors of the rear guard returned fire from their mounts. Their strategy, similar to the one used at White Bird Canyon, was to kill as many officers as they could. Any soldier with bars, a gold leaf, or an eagle on his uniform was a prime target.

Both sides fired hundreds of rounds, with few finding their marks because of the fierce crosswind. It was challenging to hit a moving target; it was impossible to be accurate when also accounting for the powerful air currents. The blustery weather gave a distinct advantage to the Nez Perce. They stayed mounted and rode in circles at the rear of the caravan, taking turns firing at their pursuers on foot.

With each passing minute, the distance between Sturgis' troops and the Indians grew.

Meanwhile, warriors scrambled to the ridge ahead of Captain Benteen and pinned them down, buying precious time that allowed the women, children, and most of the herd to escape from the canyon and head onto the treeless plains.

The combatants exchanged gunfire for hours, fighting to a standstill. By late afternoon, it was clear the Nez Perce staved off the attack.

"Dammit! They're getting away again!" Sturgis said as he looked through his field glasses.

"Let's mount and chase them," Merrill said. "They have women and children, for God's sake. There's no way they can outrun us."

Samuel Sturgis lowered the binoculars and considered this suggestion. Should he send his troops into the canyon? Or was this a clever trap to lure them into the narrow gorge and ambush them on the other side? He concluded it was not prudent to chase the enemy.

"Tell Captain Benteen to withdraw from his position."

Merrill shook his head, but followed orders. He sent a runner with this message to Benteen. The captain reported in some time later.

"How many casualties, men?" Sturgis asked, tearing a piece of tobacco from a twist and stuffing it into his mouth.

"Two killed and eight wounded in my battalion," Benteen said.

"One killed and three wounded," Merrill replied.

"And how much of their herd did we capture?"

"The Crow scouts retrieved three hundred ponies," Fisher said.

Sturgis spit a stream of tobacco juice and used his thumb to wipe his lip.

"We've done enough for today. We'll wait until dawn and catch them tomorrow."

Major Merrill glanced at Captain Benteen, who shrugged. *They were so close to victory. Why not finish the fight?*

"But colonel, General Howard gave orders to..." the major said.

"We've lost daylight, and the men are fatigued," he said with a steely glare. "We will pick up the pursuit tomorrow."

"Yes, sir."

Merrill walked with Benteen toward the waiting troops. When they were out of earshot of the colonel, Merrill turned to Benteen, a veteran who fought under Custer.

"If we charged the Indians, this war could have ended," he lamented.

Benteen stopped, removed his hat, and wiped dirt from his forehead with his coat sleeve. He looked at Merrill.

"Do you have a son?"

"Yes."

"Has your boy been to war?"

"No."

"Last June, Custer attacked the Sioux's flank at the Little Bighorn. He believed he could kill or capture them with two hundred men. He paid for that mistake with his life and the lives of everyone who rode with him, including James Sturgis, the colonel's son. I'm certain that influenced his thinking."

"Oh, I see."

Every cavalry officer knew about the massacre. It embarrassed Merrill he was ignorant about his commanding officer's personal loss. Benteen's comments put the colonel's decision in a whole new light.

"May I offer an opinion, one officer to another?" Benteen said, donning his hat.

"Sure."

"There's a fine line between bravery and recklessness. Don't confuse them."

Chapter Seventeen

Bonanza

23 September [1129 miles traveled]

Yellow Wolf stepped out of the shadows and into the glow cast by a fire. He waited for Graham to emerge from the canvas wall tent.

"*Kla-how'-ya*. I didn't know you were here," Graham said. "Makawee made biscuits and coffee. Would you like some?"

Yellow Wolf shook his head.

Graham noticed a pained expression on the young man's face.

"What's bothering you?"

"I cannot believe the Crow helped the soldiers. Do they not remember how some of our tribe fought with them against the Sioux several winters ago? This is why Chief Looking Glass advised us to take the path through buffalo country. He assumed the Crow would provide assistance."

"Yes. It's disappointing. I don't know what else Makawee could do."

"I am not blaming her. She is a good woman." He paused before looking at his *soyapu* friend. "I am tired."

Graham sat beside him and nodded. "Everyone is exhausted."

In the days since the skirmish at Canyon Creek, Lean Elk pushed the caravan hard. The group covered twenty or thirty miles every day, pausing only for brief breaks and skipping noon meals.

The unrelenting pace allowed them to pull away from their pursuers. Rear scouts reported no sign of the army for the past three days, but the long marches exacted a toll.

Each day, the ranks of the weak or sick swelled. Families carried elderly relatives on travois. They provided meager provisions and water to those too frail to continue the journey, said tearful goodbyes, and left them along the trail. If they were lucky, a soldier would find them before an Indian. Although the army was merciless in punishing hostiles, they offered prisoners food and shelter. If Bannock, Shoshone, or Crow scouts encountered an adversary, they killed and scalped them.

The Nez Perce assemblage forded the Missouri River a few hours earlier near a place the whites called Cow Island. Water levels were too low in autumn for steamboats to navigate farther upstream. Contractors erected a half dozen tents on the north bank of the river, then dug drainage ditches around the temporary shelters. Cow Island Landing served as an important location for unloading cargo. Wagons and pack mules transported goods to points west, including Fort Benton.

They were in the heart of buffalo country, but there were no signs of the beasts that numbered in the millions a decade earlier. The war leaders anticipated encountering abundant bison to hunt. The non-treaty bands were not only exhausted, but also hungry.

"I'm arranging a party to collect food. Would you like to come with me?" Yellow Wolf said to Graham.

"Right now?"

"Yes."

Graham fetched his carbine from the tent, where Makawee was singing Dakkoótee to sleep. He kissed her and whispered he'd return in a couple of hours.

He joined eight warriors and a dozen women. Each woman led several pack mules stolen from the army weeks earlier. Yellow Wolf guided the party along the river for three miles before stopping.

"The supply camp is just around the bend. I scouted it earlier today," he said. "I approached the landing and asked for food. A man gave me a bag of hard biscuits, but he would not offer anything more. I counted twelve men."

"What's the plan?" said Graham.

"Attack the storage place. Keep the shooters busy. Women gather food and pack mules."

Yellow Wolf told the women to wait. He would let them know when it was safe to gather supplies. The warriors climbed a low ridge overlooking the landing and surveyed the layout of the facility.

Three steamboats chugged up the river within the last few days and disgorged their contents at the supply depot. With the tents mainly used for sleeping, there was limited space available for storage. They stacked much of the cargo outside. Laborers piled boxes and sacks of dry goods near the dock, several hundred feet from the canvas shelters. A lone watchman stationed himself with his back against a tent pole, smoking a cigar.

Yellow Wolf signaled for the warriors to spread out along the tree-lined hillside to enable different firing angles. The hill above the depot had a shallow, rock-strewn ravine that provided perfect cover for the raiders. When everyone was in place, he propped his Springfield on a boulder and squeezed the trigger.

Crack!

A bullet zipped into the sentry's boot. The man howled and dropped his cigar. He grabbed his rifle and limped inside the tent. Within seconds, men scrambled outside. Warriors peppered the tents as soldiers and civilians dove for cover into the irrigation ditches which served as breastworks.

The men at the depot returned fire, but they were severely disadvantaged. Yellow Wolf's warriors held the high ground. They could maneuver among trees and rocks in the dark and shoot from various positions. The soldiers lay behind the crude rifle pits and fired blindly into the darkness.

Yellow Wolf motioned for Graham to join him behind the rock.

"We will keep them pinned down. Tell the women to load the mules. Guard them while they work."

Graham nodded. He crouched and darted from tree to tree along the slope, working his way down to the river. He trotted back upstream to where the women were waiting and waved them forward.

The cache of goods stored on the riverbank was impressive. It was a veritable outdoor warehouse. Roustabouts piled burlap sacks of coffee, sugar, beans, rice, flour, and bacon on planks. Crates filled with pots, cups, buckets, knives, hard candy, leaf tobacco, and cigars sat next to cartridge boxes.

The women set to work loading sacks and boxes onto the mules and fastening them with ropes. The army exposed the mules to rifle and cannon fire over the years. The pack animals didn't spook, despite the sound of bullets echoing against the hill a short distance away.

Graham was astonished at the calm demeanor of the women. With each passing minute, Graham grew more jittery. A soldier could escape from the firefight and check on the unguarded supplies. Yet, the Nez Perce women packed the mules as if this was just a routine day to strike camp and move.

It occurred to him that, like the mules, these women were numb to the sounds of fighting. Their families were under attack for three months. Providing food and shelter under fire evolved into a way of life.

The women led the pack train back to the Nez Perce camp after securing the final load. Graham breathed a sigh of relief as the last mule disappeared into the night.

Sporadic gunfire erupted as he climbed the slope at an angle. Warriors fired every thirty seconds or so, keeping the soldiers hunkered down in the irrigation ditch. He found Yellow Wolf concealed on the far side of a stout willow tree.

"The women loaded the mules with as much as they can carry and are heading to camp."

Yellow Wolf smiled.

"We have one more thing to do before our work is complete."

"What's that?"

"We cannot allow the army to have the remaining supplies."

Yellow Wolf put his hands to his mouth and imitated a bird call. A moment later, a warrior appeared. Teeto Hoonnod proved himself an excellent marksman at Canyon Creek.

"Teeto, your bullets are more accurate than all others. We need to keep those men behind the low earth wall. Are you running low on ammo?"

"Yes, I'm almost out."

"Find a favorable shooting position and ask others for more cartridges. Keep a constant fire on the soldiers while I burn those supplies," he said, pointing to immense stacks of bacon, flour, and coffee stacked a short distance from the breastworks.

Yellow Wolf creeped down to the stockpile. Teeto and his fellow warriors increased their firing rate. Bullets zipped and zinged into the embankments, kicking up dirt and splintering rocks.

A moment later, a small flame flickered in the corner of a storage tent. It mushroomed into a blaze as Yellow Wolf raced to the landing and torched the remaining supplies. When the bullets stopped flying, soldiers and dock hands dashed from the makeshift rifle pit. They scooped buckets into the river and tried in vain to douse the flames.

The raiding party scampered away, pausing briefly to admire the inferno, which lit up the darkness.

Graham stopped a half mile from the landing and looked back. The giant bonfire crackled and popped as it consumed the dry goods. A light breeze carried the smell of the burning supplies upriver. The pleasant aroma of coffee mixed with bacon filled his nostrils.

It would be daylight in a few hours. The Nez Perce would have a hearty meal for the first time in weeks.

Colonel Nelson Miles sat outside his tent on the bank of the Missouri River and watched as a sergeant barked orders. Men loaded horses, mules, and supplies onto the steamer *Fontenelle*. A day earlier, the colonel sent a regiment ahead of his main column to halt any boat and hold it there for the army's use. The captain of the St. Louis-bound vessel was not pleased, but complied with Miles's request to ferry his fighting force to the north side.

When Miles got a telegram from General Howard asking him to stop the Nez Perce before they crossed the British line, he prepared for a two-hundred-and fifty mile march. He departed Tongue River Cantonment with four-hundred-and-fifty men, including cavalry and mounted infantry, on September 17. The troops had two pieces of artillery with them — a Hotchkiss gun and a Napoleon cannon. Three dozen wagons and a string of pack mules carried tons of supplies and thousands of rounds of ammunition.

The work of loading, ferrying, and unloading started in the late afternoon. By ten o'clock, they moved less than half of the equipment and material across the river. The task would take most of the night.

Miles turned his attention to the dispatches he received. Colonel Sturgis reported his encounter with the Nez Perce at Canyon Creek, where he claimed to have inflicted heavy damage on the enemy. Howard's message provided insight into the general's latest strategy.

```
The moment we check pursuit, they stop thirty or forty miles
ahead and rest until their scouts detect our forward movement.
Therefore, we shall not hasten our pursuit in order to give you
time to get into position between them and Sitting Bull.
```

The colonel smirked when he read his former commanding officer's note. The two men knew each other well. Nelson Miles was Howard's aide-de-camp early in the Civil War. He imagined the general's mindset after a three-month pursuit of an elusive quarry. Self-doubt would creep into his consciousness.

Was the goal of Howard's "intentional lagging" strategy not to chase the Indians across the border? Or was he exhausted and willing to concede defeat?

O. O. Howard might give up, but Nelson Miles never would. Because he was not a West Point graduate, Miles felt he always needed to prove himself. He earned several accolades and brevets during the Civil War. Senior officers acknowledged him as an effective field commander.

He saw defeating the Nez Perce as a chance to climb the ranks in the military.

Miles picked up his folding chair and toted it inside his tent. He unfolded a map, smoothed it out under a lantern on a table, and stroked the edge of his thick mustache with his thumb and forefinger.

"Lieutenant Baldwin!"

The colonel's aide-de-camp poked his head inside the tent. "You wanted to see me, sir?"

"I'm plotting a course to the Bears Paw Mountains. The mounted troops should be organized to move out by four o'clock. We will leave our wagons and the Napoleon here. They can catch up with the main column. Speed is of utmost importance. Tell the captains to plan accordingly."

"Yes, sir."

Miles pulled a bent billiard pipe from his coat pocket, packed the bowl with tobacco, and lit it. After a few quick puffs, he took a long pull. Outside, men grunted as they hoisted heavy boxes of ammunition and stacked them on the deck of the steamship. Pack mules clambered up the gangway onto the boat. They would soon ferry another load across the mighty Missouri.

Chief Joseph might outrun Howard, he thought, *but he will not escape me.*

Miles pictured himself with a brigadier general silver star on his shoulder, which he would earn by capturing or killing the hostile Nez Perce leader.

Lean Elk continued to push the pace after the night raid at Cow Island. The long marches didn't please everyone in the caravan. Some warriors and a few chiefs openly complained the people and horses needed to rest. Looking Glass called for a council the evening of September 25.

"I asked everyone to come, so we can talk," Looking Glass said, after the leaders gathered. "Other than a few soldiers at the river, we have seen no one. Cut Arm and his army are at least two days behind us. Our people are weary. Our horses are weak. The stolen provisions will only last a few more days. We are now in buffalo country. We can hunt, eat, rest, and regain our strength before crossing the Medicine Line."

White Bird stood. "The leader of the Alpowai band has spoken true words. My people are ailing. What good will it serve if we rush to the Medicine Line but lose more of our injured and elderly? Just like you, I want to travel beyond the reach of the soldiers. We must do this thoughtfully."

"We are inviting the earth to receive more of our dead if we make our people walk on weak legs," Toohoolhoolzote said in agreement.

Husishusis Kute spoke next. "We are the smallest group, but there are half as many of us today compared to when we left our land. I implore you to rest for a short while."

Other leaders and elders joined in. The majority desired a slower pace to the British Territories.

Ollokot, war leader of the Wallowa band, rose to speak. His face flushed with anger.

"Now is not the time to rest. We can soak our feet and care for our people when we cross the Medicine Line in five days. We do not know where the enemy is. The government can always send fresh soldiers after us. I beg you — carry the elderly, help the wounded, and keep moving!"

A murmur of disapproval rose from the council members.

"Chief Joseph, what do you say?" asked Looking Glass.

"My brother speaks for the Wallowa band. He is our war leader."

"All who wish to travel more slowly to care for the health of our loved ones, please stand," Looking Glass said.

Ollokot, Joseph, and Lean Elk remained seated.

Lean Elk stood and moved to the center of the circle. He studied the faces of the men whom he guided since the debacle at the Big Hole.

"My brothers, many more of us will die from bullets than from weary bones. I shall lead you no farther."

Lean Elk returned and sat with the brothers of the Wallowa band.

Looking Glass took his place.

"It would honor me to be your principle war chief," he said.

A chorus of approving whoops and yells erupted from the standing council members. The men scattered to their respective camps, comforted in knowing the dawn would yield short rides and long breaks.

They didn't know Lean Elk's prediction would be deadly accurate.

Chapter Eighteen
Edge of Freedom

30 September [1170 miles traveled]

Forty miles, as the crow flies. That was the distance separating Joseph's people from the country where Sitting Bull's followers had taken refuge.

After leaving the Missouri River, Looking Glass led the group on a course east of the Bears Paw Mountains. The caravan reached Snake Creek at the end of September. The fatigued Nez Perce embraced a period of routine amidst the disorder that dominated their lives since mid-June. With every day of no army sightings, the refugees became more confident the government would leave them in peace.

Hunters roamed the expansive grasslands. They hadn't seen any bison since entering buffalo country weeks earlier, so discovering a small herd was a blessing. The warriors thanked the Great Spirit for providing the animals before killing a half dozen. Women skinned and butchered the massive bovids. The meat cooked over flames was nourishing and warming.

The temperatures were increasingly colder in mid-autumn. Ice formed on pans of water overnight. Heavy frosts blanketed the plains.

Women and children gathered dried buffalo chips to burn. Indeed, the site where they camped was fittingly named *Tsanim Alikos Pah,* roughly translated as "The Place of the Manure Fires."

Graham tightened the ropes on the mule and pushed against the load to make sure it was secure. His plan was to depart camp soon after breakfast. Clouds obscured the distant peaks of the mountains. He learned to read the skies for changes in weather. Today looked and felt like snow.

He walked to the cooking pot where Makawee prepared a stew. He dipped a ladle into the kettle and held the dipper to his nose. The meat dish emitted a mouthwatering aroma. He blew on the bison broth to cool it, then slurped.

"Wow, that tastes wonderful!" he said, chewing on the softened meat while placing the serving spoon on a flat rock.

"Better than dried beef," Makawee said, with Dakkoótee perched on her hip. "It's almost ready."

"Put him down. Let's see if he can walk yet."

The Sioux child took his first tentative steps a week earlier. They laughed as he stumbled across the uneven ground and fell forward. He struggled to his feet, brushed the grass and dirt from his hands, and wobbled before falling again.

"I hope he figures it out soon," Graham said, chuckling at his adopted son's walking skills.

"Compared to girls, most boys are slow learners. Of course, the same thing is true when comparing women to men," she said, with a twinkle in her eye.

"Is that so? Are you saying...?"

Makawee held up her hand, then pointed to a bluff on the south side of the camp.

"Look!"

Graham turned to see what his wife noticed.

A scout galloped his horse in a circle. He waved a blanket overhead and shouted.

"What is he communicating?" Graham asked.

Makawee's lips tightened, and her eyes grew wide.

"He's signaling an attack!"

"Shit!" Graham said. "Follow me!"

He grabbed Dakkoótee and dashed to his mare with Makawee on his heels.

"Mount!" he yelled. She got on the horse, and he gave her the boy. Graham withdrew the Colt from his belt and slipped it into the pommel holster. "Shoot anyone in uniform. Ride north as fast as you can. I'll catch up later. Go!"

The horse didn't move.

"What are you waiting for? Go!"

Makawee slid from the horse and helped Dakkoótee down.

"We're a family. I'm not leaving without you," she said.

"Dammit, Makawee! Don't argue with me!"

Dakkoótee cried at the sound of his father's angry voice.

"I'll protect our son with my life, but I'm not going anywhere," she said, soothing the boy by holding him against her chest and rotating her torso back and forth.

Graham clenched his fists. She was so stubborn! He knew he could not change her mind, so he scanned the camp for a place they could take shelter. Where would his family least likely face harm? It was hard to know.

The alarm spread throughout the camp. One word was on everyone's lips - a word that provoked fear.

"*Piuapziaunat!*" ["Soldiers!"]

People scattered in every direction. Bullets rained from mounted troopers.

Chief Joseph splashed across the stream and ran toward the pony herd. His eldest wife, Heyoom Yoyikt, and their daughter, Hophop Onmi, were loading the ponies.

"*Aakinnaak aalée! Ihkammíssee!*" ["Ride away!" Hurry!] he shouted.

The mother and daughter climbed onto their horses. They joined others fleeing the camp just as a cavalry regiment appeared on a plateau. A bugler sounded an order, and three dozen soldiers rushed in the direction of the herd, intent on separating the horses from their owners.

Fifteen warriors followed Joseph across the creek. While some herded a cluster of frightened horses toward camp, others mounted and rode to meet the enemy's charge.

The largest band of Nez Perce grabbed weapons and raced to the top of the ravines that drained into Snake Creek. They fanned out and formed defensive lines facing south, where the army launched its strongest attack.

Graham scanned the deep fissures that emptied into the creek bed on the east side. The coulees offered the only sanctuary within miles. *That's where my family belongs,* he thought.

Bears Paw Battlefield

He snatched his revolver from the pommel holster and handed it to Makawee.

"Go to the bottom of the deepest ravine," he said. "I'll bring my horse and our mule. Run!"

Makawee nodded. She dashed toward the mouth of a chasm where other women and children were converging. Dakkoótee jostled and bounced against his mother as she ran, his cries growing louder with each step.

Graham sprinted to fetch the mule, which was wide-eyed and skittish. The pack animal tugged on the picket line he fashioned by looping the lead rope around a heavy rock. He freed the animal, gripped his carbine, and led the mule to the ravine guarded by a cluster of warriors.

Makawee huddled among other women and children. He handed her the rope, squeezed her arm, then scrambled up the slope to join the fight.

Graham stumbled over a corpse halfway up the steep incline. He rolled the man onto his back. Blood soaked the front of Lean Elk's shirt. A bullet had pierced his throat. Graham closed the dead man's eyes, made the sign of the cross, and continued to the top of the ravine.

A deep rumbling sound cascaded across the grassland as Graham flopped below the edge of the embankment and trained his carbine on the horizon. A thousand yards away, a cavalry unit galloped toward the bluffs. The hot breaths of horses filled the air with vapor. Hooves pounded the sod as the cavalrymen raced toward the Nez Perce, who were concealed in the ravines.

The warriors showed great discipline. Holding fire until the last possible moment, they unleashed a torrent of bullets. Horses squealed and crumpled, throwing their riders. Warriors cocked and fired again, with devastating effect.

Fourteen soldiers, including two officers and a bugler, fell from their mounts. The troopers halted at the precipice to the ravine before reining their horses and retreating. The soldiers dismounted and formed a skirmish line in a shallow gully several hundred yards from the Nez Perce's defensive position.

By early evening, the fighting abated. The Nez Perce carried the bodies of their dead into the ravines.

Graham, Makawee, and Wetatonmi sat together with their children in the fading light. Graham retrieved two blankets from the mule. He handed one to Wetatonmi and wrapped the other around his wife and son to shield them from the bitter cold. No one spoke. They were in shock, assessing the disastrous events of the day.

While Graham slurped water, two men dragged a body to where the families huddled. They laid the fallen warrior at Wetatonmi's feet, bowed, and hurried to fetch other victims in the dark. The Nez Perce woman glanced at the dead man, screamed, and threw herself across his chest. Sara buried her face in her mother's back and sobbed.

Ollokot — war chief, brother of Joseph, father of Sara, and husband of Wetatonmi, was dead.

Makawee scooted next to her friend and put an arm over her shoulder. Dakkoótee was asleep in his mother's arms. The toddler cried so hard and for so long, he was exhausted.

Graham stood, stretched his cramped legs, and walked into the darkness. He needed a moment alone, but there was nowhere he could go to silence the sounds of pain and grieving.

"Eagle Bear," someone said from behind.

The man's voice startled Graham. He turned to see Yellow Wolf approaching. His friend was bare-chested, and he carried a Winchester.

"Aren't you freezing?"

"I stripped for battle. My *wey-ya-kin* protected me. You were shielded from harm as well," he said, pointing to Graham's chest.

Graham felt the eagle-bear claw pendant under his buckskin jacket.

"Some warriors didn't have a spiritual guardian today."

"Or it was their fate to die," Yellow Wolf said laconically. "Toohoolhoolzote met his destiny. They killed him in the area of our pony herd. Chief Joseph, Looking Glass, Husishusis Kute, and White Bird are alive."

"How many warriors died?"

"At least twenty. More are missing."

"Did you hear about Lean Elk and Ollokot?"

"No."

"They both lost their lives," Graham said. He found it ironic the two leaders who urged the caravan to keep marching were among the first to die.

"The soldiers lost many men as well," Yellow Wolf said. "I need to dig a rifle pit. I suggest you do the same." He turned and disappeared into the night.

The moans of wounded and dying troopers lying between the battle lines drifted toward the ravines and intermingled with the wails of the Nez Perce mourners. So much suffering by so many people. Graham wondered how long the non-treaty bands could hold out against such a powerful army.

He walked back to the ravine and found Makawee leaning against a boulder with Dakkoótee on her chest. Both were sleeping. Wetatonmi was sobbing. She wiped tears from her cheeks, then tucked Ollokot's braids behind his ears.

"Joseph visited while you were away," she said with a blank expression. "He will bury his brother in the morning."

"Is Joseph's immediate family safe?"

"Heyoom Yoyikt and Hophop Onmi escaped with the others at the beginning of the battle. Springtime and her baby girl are unharmed."

Graham squinted in the dark at the steep slope leading up to the bluff. He tugged on his beard, considering the best way to construct a shelter.

"Wetatoni, I know this is a difficult time, but would you mind asking Sara to watch Dakkoótee? The three of us need to dig a trench."

"Yes. Of course," she said, wiping her nose.

He woke Makawee and explained their task. He untied the short-handled shovel from the mule's pack. The tool he bought at Henry Buck's store months ago would be especially handy tonight. Reaching into the supply pack, he fished out cups, bowls, and spoons.

"Grab something and start digging," he said to the women, tossing the utensils on the ground. He picked up the shovel and plunged it into the hillside.

As they scooped, the frozen top layer of soil became sandy and loose. Sounds of metal sinking into the ground permeated the frigid night air as hundreds of people of all ages dug shelter pits. The deepened trenches served two purposes. They protected the occupants from the biting winds that whipped snow across the prairie, and they concealed the Nez Perce families from the army's bullets.

As the night progressed, the builders became creative with their crude designs. They stretched pieces of canvas and buffalo hide across the openings to trap body heat and keep out snow. Women moved belongings from the village into the subterranean rooms. Families connected their individual shelters via underground tunnels. There was something comforting about knowing you were not isolated in your fight for survival.

A few hundred yards to the south, the soldiers were also digging rifle pits and trying to stay warm. Their temporary shelters on the plateau were more shallow and less protective than those of the Nez Perce in the ravines.

Before midnight, Nelson Miles ordered the Hotchkiss gun repositioned to a bluff overlooking the ravines. He vowed to use the artillery piece against the entrenched Indians if necessary. In his mind, there were only two outcomes. Either the Indians surrendered, or the rapid-fire mountain cannon would lob explosive shells into their bunkers.

Both sides spent a miserable night trying to stay warm. Officers reminded the soldiers the best way to prevent frostbite was to move. They would forget about their chilled bones once they started firing on the enemy.

As one captain put it, "The colonel is going to give 'em hell this morning. Be ready to shoot if they start scramblin' outta their holes."

"Lieutenant, is your artillery squad set?" Nelson Miles said as he trained his field glasses on the rifle pits built by the warriors at the top of the bluffs.

"Yes, sir."

"Okay. Let's wake them up, shall we?"

The thunderous boom of a cannon shattered the silence of a gloomy dawn. A mortar round whistled through the air and exploded over the heads of the besieged Indians. Less than a minute later, another shell burst over the ravines where families spent a sleepless night. The gun commander adjusted the sights and ordered a fresh round loaded. He stood to the side before yanking a lanyard and firing the next shell.

Screams erupted from the entrenchments as loose soil cascaded down the slopes. People grabbed pots and scooped out the debris that threatened to fill the fragile holes where they cowered from the blasts. Babies cried. Children huddled close to their mothers.

Warriors positioned at the edge of the bluffs seethed with anger at an enemy that dared shoot unarmed women and children with such a weapon. But they could do nothing to silence the artillery, as it was beyond the reach of a rifle.

Twenty minutes later, Miles ordered the firing to cease. Smoke drifted across the snow-covered ground. Five inches had fallen, and now it was turning to sleet.

"That should give them something to think about," the colonel said, lowering his binoculars. "I suspect they may be open to talking. Lieutenant Baldwin, I understand you know Chinook Jargon?"

"I am able to have a basic conversation in that language, sir."

"Good. Fasten a white cloth on your rifle and hold it aloft. Ride close to their lines so you are within sight and sound. Announce that I'd like a meeting with Chief Joseph."

The colonel's aide-de-camp saluted and hurried to his horse. The officer rode onto the plateau and waved the flag of peace. He yelled something toward the bluffs, repeated the phrase several more times, and waited. A moment later, two men emerged from the shadow of the bluff and walked to the lieutenant.

"My name is Tom Hill. I will interpret for Chief Joseph."

Hill joined the non-treaty Nez Perce as part of Lean Elk's band in the Bitterroot Valley. The interpreter was still mourning his leader's death, but welcomed this opportunity to end the fighting.

Baldwin dismounted. He led his horse and the men toward his commanding officer's tent. They passed the Hotchkiss gun on the way. Chief Joseph and Hill could view up close the source of the terrible noise and destruction. Empty shells lay behind the breech-loading cannon. The hot casings melted the snow on the ground where they were ejected.

The aide-de-camp held open the flap of the tent and ushered the two men inside.

It surprised Joseph to see a broad-shouldered man with a bushy mustache. He was not General Howard.

"I am Nelson Miles, the army commander," he said, noting the chief's puzzled look. "And you are Joseph?"

The chief nodded.

"Would you like a hot meal?"

When Hill interpreted this question, Joseph shook his head. He refused to accept anything he couldn't give to all his people.

"Chief Joseph, the war is over. We have almost all your ponies. You have nowhere to go. Your tribes are suffering from cold and injuries. There is no need for anyone else to die. I'm asking you to bring all of your arms and lay them right here," Miles said, pointing to his feet.

"Half for you. Half to keep for hunting," Joseph said in response.

"I need *every* weapon you have today. You will get them back once you return to your reservation. Go tell your people to stop fighting."

The chief shook his head.

"Mr. Hill, please go back to the camp and repeat the terms of surrender. Chief Joseph will remain here as my prisoner until everyone hands in their rifle."

When Tom Hill reached the ravines and skidded down the wet slope, he saw a cavalry lieutenant being held by two warriors. He was being questioned by White Bird and Looking Glass. Graham acted as an interpreter.

"What did the army commander say?" Graham asked.

"His name is Colonel Miles. We have to relinquish all weapons and surrender. He has taken Chief Joseph prisoner and will not release him up unless we comply."

"Well, isn't that interesting? This is Lieutenant Lovell Jerome. He was curious about our camp and decided to visit. He's a spy," Graham said.

"What should we do with him?" Hill said in *Niimíipuu*.

"Kill him!" White Bird said, pulling a knife from his tunic and pointing it at Jerome's neck.

The lieutenant's eyes grew wide and his lips tightened. He arched his back to avoid the blade hovering at his throat.

"Wait!" Graham said, pushing White Bird's forearm down. "He's worth more alive than dead."

"That's right," Looking Glass said. "Pass the word to the commander. We have one of their men. If they release Joseph, they can have this man back. If not…"

Early the next morning, the Nez Perce suffered another leadership casualty. Looking Glass assured everyone Sitting Bull would hear about their plight and come to save them. Several times during the night, the war chief imagined hundreds of hooves thundering toward their besieged camp. Each time, he scaled the slope of the ravine and poked his head above the edge of the bluff, expecting to see a powerful Sioux contingent.

As the late autumn sun peaked over the horizon, the Alpowai band leader scanned the plateau for horsemen yet again. This time a sniper sent a bullet through his skull.

Warriors placed the war leader's body in a grave next to those of Ollokot, Lean Elk, and Toohoolhoolzote.

Of the seven principal Nez Perce leaders, only Joseph, Husishusis Kute, and White Bird remained alive.

At midmorning, Miles dispatched a messenger waving a flag of truce toward the Nez Perce defenses. The colonel informed the Indians of a prisoner exchange. Thirty minutes later, Yellow Wolf and Tom Hill accompanied Lieutenant Jerome. Two soldiers escorted Chief Joseph. The parties met in the middle of the battlefield, and the prisoners walked back to their respective sides.

The events of the past day incensed Joseph. He told the others soldiers bound his hands and feet, then rolled him in a blanket "like you would a papoose on a cradle board." They placed him with the mules for the night.

This was not the reason he was angry. Rather, it was the army commander's deceitful use of a flag of truce. Miles was not to be trusted. The chief was leaning toward surrendering before they took him captive. After last night, his view changed.

Joseph's jaw clenched and his eyes narrowed. "Go back to your trenches. We must fight more."

While Joseph lay bound among the mules the previous evening, army supply wagons arrived from the Missouri River. The soldiers gave a hearty cheer when the train pulled into their camp. They eagerly helped unload the cargo, knowing what the wagons brought — the men could sleep in tents and eat something other than hard tack and bacon.

A second, heavy artillery piece also arrived with the supply train. A wooden carriage supported the twelve-pounder. They needed six mules to haul the cannon, which was much more powerful than the Hotchkiss. As soon as the weapon arrived, Colonel Miles ordered it to be set up.

Lieutenant Jerome provided valuable intelligence based on the night he spent in captivity. He informed his commanding officer about the number of warriors, their weapons, and the location of the entrenchments.

At noon on day three of the siege, Miles unleashed the Napoleon cannon. The noise from the explosive shells was deafening. The ground shook with each impact, loosening the soil and collapsing many of the trench walls. After an hour of pounding the enemy, the artillery crew ceased fire, not knowing whether they killed anyone.

The Nez Perce lost two people in the assault. An elderly woman and her granddaughter were buried alive when tons of gravel and soil filled the pit where they had taken refuge.

As the smoke from the latest barrage cleared, Colonel Nelson Miles smiled. Although he could not see their faces, he imagined the terror the Napoleon wrought on those hunkered in the shelter pits.

The goal of using artillery wasn't to inflict as many casualties as possible. It was to weaken the will of Joseph and his people to fight. The army captured most of their herd. They were running low on food and ammunition. Without a fire, frigid temperatures made life miserable for anyone huddled in a crude trench.

"Joseph will surrender," the army commander said to his aide-de-camp. "It's not *if*, but *how soon*."

"I agree, sir."

"Please prepare a hot cup of tea and bring my writing desk. I need to pen a note to General Howard and inform him of our imminent success."

Chapter Nineteen
Fight No More Forever

5 October, 1877

General Howard stood outside his tent and sipped a steaming cup of coffee. He peered through the foggy, gray dawn at the bluffs in the distance and wondered what the day would bring.

Howard and a tiny contingent from his battalion arrived in the camp of Colonel Miles late the previous evening. After receiving word of a skirmish near Bears Paw Mountains, the group raced north. The general chased Chief Joseph and his people twelve hundred miles. He came close to capturing the non-treaty Nez Perce, but they always slipped away. He didn't want to miss an opportunity to take part in the battle that would end the war.

Nelson Miles briefed Howard on the events that took place over the last six days. The colonel recounted the initial attack on the Nez Perce camp, the army's success in taking most of the Indians' ponies, the failed negotiations, a prisoner exchange, the use of artillery to terrorize the opponent, and the current siege. Miles was confident a surrender was forthcoming, but the stubbornness of the enemy to concede frustrated him.

"We can starve them out," Miles concluded last evening. "But the longer they hold out, the more likely Sitting Bull will do something foolish — like rallying his tribe and attacking from Canada. It's in everyone's best interest to end this soon."

Howard suggested a different tactic. He brought two men with him from Lapwai, who served as his scouts. Jokais and Meopkowit had a personal stake in bringing a peaceful conclusion to this bloody conflict. Both had grown daughters whose husbands were among the non-treaty warriors. They wanted to find and bring them home. The general planned to send these scouts to Joseph's camp in the morning with another offer to surrender.

He raised the collar of his greatcoat to protect the bottom of his ears from the breeze. The stump of his right arm ached from the wintry air. *Montana Territory is beautiful country,* he thought. *But it seems like the wind always blows here.*

"More coffee, sir?"

The question snapped Howard back to the present. He pivoted towards his aide-de-camp, Lieutenant Erskine Wood, who was holding a tin coffee pot.

The general proffered his cup and allowed Wood to fill it.

"I wonder if Joseph is ready to go home," Howard said, slurping the steaming liquid.

"Well, sir, I don't believe he has a choice."

"People *always* have choices. Some have more favorable outcomes than others," Howard said. "I only hope he chooses wisely for his people."

"More fighting at this point makes no sense," Wood said.

The general focused his gaze on the ravines where the enemy was hiding. He tried to imagine the Indians cloistered there with little food, no warmth, and weakened bodies. Surely, they would welcome peace. What if they continued to fight? More deaths. More suffering. And no difference in the ultimate outcome. He gulped the remaining coffee and handed the cup to his aide.

"Have you sent my dispatch?"

"Yes, sir. The rest of your command should be here by tomorrow."

"Excellent. Are the scouts ready?"

"Yes, sir. They await your orders."

"Ask Colonel Miles to come and see me."

Howard ducked into his tent and fetched his Bible. In times of uncertainty, he often found comfort by reading the scriptures and letting God speak to him. He would sometimes try to find inspiration from a favorite verse. Other times, he used the holy book to provide a divine oracle.

He laid the Bible on a table, closed his eyes, flipped it open, and jabbed at a page with his left hand. Opening his eyes, he noticed it was the Gospel of Matthew. He read the verse under his index finger.

Take therefore no thought for the morrow: for the morrow shall take thought for the things of itself. Sufficient unto the day is the evil thereof.

The verse reminded the general to stop worrying about what might happen. Focus on what's happening in the moment. Right now, the aim was to get Joseph and his people to lay down their weapons.

He lifted his head and looked at the roof of the tent.

"Thank you, Lord," he said.

"Colonel Miles to see you," Wood said from outside.

Howard snapped the Bible shut and ducked out of the tent.

"Another chilly day," Miles said, cupping his hands over his mouth and blowing into them. "I've been thinking about your plan. If we pound their position for a few hours, we can encourage them to make the right decision. I'll light up the Napoleon and..."

"No more cannon!" Howard said. "I know Chief Joseph better than you. He cares about his people. Let the Nez Perce scouts appeal to his sense of duty."

"Of course. As you say."

"Colonel Miles, let's be clear on something. Although I outrank you, I will not assume field command. You cornered the enemy. You will have the honor of finishing the battle by accepting Joseph's surrender."

Howard remembered his anger and embarrassment at Gettysburg in '63 when Winfield Hancock took over as battlefield commander. He vowed to himself he would never grab another officer's rightful authority in the field.

"Thank you, general."

Miles envisioned the accolades and his subsequent promotion after the world learned of his victory over the notorious Nez Perce leader, Joseph.

A moment later, Jokais and Meopkowit strolled across the frozen ground. Jokais waved a white flag of truce on a stick.

General Howard and Colonel Miles stood behind the soldiers' rifle pits and focused their field glasses on the two Nez Perce mediators. The men soon disappeared into the ravines and clambered down the slopes toward Snake Creek. Every officer and enlisted man was thinking the same thing.

If the Indians surrender, we can go home.

"*Ta 'c meeywi,*" ["Good morning"] the envoys shouted as they headed toward the ravines. They were both dressed in white men's clothes and had short hair. Jokais wore a slouch hat adorned with turkey feathers.

Warriors posted at the south entrance to the camp recognized the visitors. One led them to Chief Joseph, who summoned White Bird, Husishusis Kute, and Yellow Wolf to hear what the men had to say.

"It's heartwarming to see so many of our neighbors and friends," Jokais said.

"Are you with the one-armed general?" Chief Joseph said.

"Yes. We traveled all the way from Lapwai with him. We were asked by Howard to talk with our brothers. He wants peace between our people."

White Bird leaped at the messenger's throat and shoved him to the ground. He jumped on Jokais, drew a knife from his tunic belt, and raised his arm. Yellow Wolf and Husishusis Kute grabbed the chief and pulled him off the terrified man.

"Enough!" Joseph said.

White Bird pushed his elbows outward and struggled against the men restraining him.

"Let go of me!"

Joseph nodded, and the men released their grips on White Bird. Jokais got to his feet and straightened the buttoned white shirt under his coat.

"Did you not hear what Jokais said?" White Bird shouted. The veins in his neck were visible as he spoke through clenched teeth. "They followed us for months. These men are traitors!"

"Please listen," Meopkowit said. "We are seeking our daughters to bring them home."

Joseph leaned in and whispered in White Bird's ear, his hand resting on the war chief's shoulder. These words abated White Bird's rage. He took a deep breath and sat on a boulder, arms crossed.

"Your daughters are alive and well," Joseph said to the visitors.

"Oh, what joyous news!" Meopkowit said.

"Hallelujah!" Jokais exclaimed. "When can we see them?"

"Later. What does Howard want?"

"The general wants you to know additional soldiers will be here tomorrow. Your people should not be afraid. The army will treat everyone well. They will be given blankets and plenty of food, and...," Jokais said, pausing for a moment to think. "Oh, and if you surrender, no one will be executed."

"Tell them where they will go," Meopkowit said, prompting his fellow emissary.

"Yes, of course," Jokais said. "General Howard and Colonel Miles say they will send you to the reservation at Lapwai."

"Lies! All lies!" White Bird said from his seat on the rock.

Chief Joseph glared at the angry chief, then turned to address the messengers.

"We will hold a council. Return to the soldiers' camp."

"Can we see our daughters?" Meopkowit said.

"That depends upon what we decide. Go."

The envoys scrambled up the steep slope of the ravine. Jokais poked the stick with the white cloth into the air, and the two men walked across the snow-covered ground toward the officers' tents.

Joseph sent word for all tribal elders to meet in council with the chiefs to discuss the latest terms of surrender from the army. The circle was smaller at Bears Paw Mountain compared to the first council meeting of the Nez Perce non-treaty leaders.

Graham and Makawee joined the other tribal members standing outside the circle. They struggled to listen to the arguments for and against surrendering to the bluecoats. This was no ordinary council meeting. The decision of these leaders would have a significant impact on their lives.

Joseph repeated the surrender terms, then solicited each man for his opinion. Husishusis Kute spoke first.

"In the spring we were wealthy. We had many horses. Now, they have stolen our ponies and our land. We are poor. Let's demand that the white men return our land, or pay us for what they have taken."

A few elders in the circle nodded to support the Palouse River band chief.

"What you say is true," Joseph said. "However, we have nothing with which to negotiate. We have little ammunition and not much food. We are living like ground squirrels, praying a cannon shell will not bury us."

Other tribal leaders stood and professed they were tired of fighting. They wanted to escape the cloud of constant fear. If they were allowed to return to Lapwai, at least it was a familiar land. They could start over and rebuild their lives.

White Bird spoke last.

"The generals are liars. Do you believe them? Will we be allowed to go back to our homeland unpunished? No, my brothers. If you surrender, you and your families will be slaves. Go if you wish. I am going to the British possessions, where I can live free. I welcome anyone who wants to join me."

"How will you escape?" an elder asked.

"We found a weakness in the soldiers' defense. Last night, two warriors from my band slipped through the enemy lines. They corralled a small herd of horses the soldiers chased away on the first day of fighting and tied them up. We depart tonight, before more soldiers arrive. We will cross the Medicine Line in less than two days."

The spectators chattered among themselves at this news. White Bird offered a path to freedom for the courageous.

All eyes turned to Chief Joseph as he rose.

"Winter is coming and the soldiers have trapped us. My heart breaks to see so many people suffering. Our wounded need care. Our children need food. Everyone needs rest. It is time."

"You do not speak for everyone," White Bird said.

"Every family has to make their own decision. Whether you surrender or attempt to escape to a new land, both have uncertainty. As chief of the Wallowa band, I will give myself up in two hours."

The council dispersed. Each family retreated to their shelters to discuss the options. Chief Joseph conversed with those who lingered, then approached Yellow Wolf and asked to speak with him.

"Nephew, I have a favor to ask."

Yellow Wolf nodded.

"I am worried about my eldest wife, my daughter, and your mother. They are out there somewhere," Joseph said, sweeping his hand to the north. "It would ease my mind if they made it to Sitting Bull's camp. Would you find out and send word to me?"

"Are you asking me to escape with White Bird?"

"Yes."

"Who will watch over you?"

A thin smile creased Joseph's face.

"Do not concern yourself about me. Wetatonmi also told me she wished to go to the British territory with Sara. After Ollokot's death, she has no reason to stay with our band. It would please me if you would escort her family. Will you do this?"

"I am honored."

"You are a fearless warrior. I am grateful for everything you have done for our people."

Joseph walked toward his shelter and prepared to dress for the somber occasion. If he was going to surrender, he planned to do so with his pride intact.

"General, he's coming!" Lieutenant Wood said, peering through his binoculars.

All the officers' eyes turned to look at the enemy line.

Joseph sat tall in his saddle and held his chin up, but his posture belied his state of mind. The spiritual leader of the non-treaty Nez Perce had a melancholy look. Dark circles were noticeable below his eyes. Thick braids hung on either side of his face, and a bullet mark creased his forehead. He wore buckskin leggings and a cotton shirt. A gray blanket pocked with bullet holes draped across his right shoulder and extended across his left arm.

Four warriors, plus the interpreter Tom Hill, accompanied Chief Joseph on foot. The Nez Perce proceeded to the midway point between the adversaries and waited. General Howard, Colonel Miles, and their aides rode to the meeting point while soldiers trained their sights on the Indians.

The officers and the chief slid from their horses. Joseph approached the general and held out his Winchester "Yellow Boy" 1866 carbine. Howard motioned the chief should offer his weapon to the colonel, who accepted the rifle.

Chief Joseph took a few steps back, raised his arms, and spoke.

"I am tired of fighting. Our chiefs are killed. Looking Glass is dead. Toohoolhoolzote is dead. Lean Elk is dead. My brother is dead. The old men are all dead. It is the young men who say yes or no. It is cold and we have no blankets. The little children are freezing to death. My people, some of them, have run away to the hills, and have no blankets, no food; no one knows where they are—perhaps freezing to death. I want to have time to see how many of them I can find. Maybe I shall find them among the dead.

Hear me, my chiefs. I am tired; my heart is sick and sad. From where the sun now stands I will fight no more forever."

The Nez Perce war ended just past two o'clock on Friday, October 5.

After shaking the hands of the officers, the chief mounted his horse. General Howard and Colonel Miles did the same and escorted him into the army camp. Lieutenant Wood offered hot tea to the Nez Perce leader, who sat and waited for others to surrender.

Survivors slowly emerged from the ravines. People of all ages made their way across the battlefield toward the army camp over the next five hours. Howard and Miles assigned their respective aides to coordinate receiving and tallying the prisoners as they arrived.

The physical condition of the Indians appalled the young officers. The Indians' brightly colored clothes were dirty and ragged. Grass and leaves protruded from their braided hair. Old men and the wounded hobbled on walking sticks. Babies and children cried and clung to their mothers. The fighting-age men of each surviving family emulated Joseph's symbolic gesture by handing their rifles to an officer.

Nelson Miles pulled a watch from his pocket and tilted it toward the fire outside his tent. It was nine o'clock. He finished writing a dispatch to General

Alfred Terry reporting on Chief Joseph's surrender. The colonel was in high spirits. All that remained was to verify no Nez Perce were hiding in the ravines. He ambled to the table where his aide was recording the names of the survivors.

"Lieutenant Baldwin, how long has it been since the last Indian reported?"

"No one has surrendered since dusk, sir."

"And how many prisoners do we have in custody?"

Baldwin ran his finger to the most recent entry in the ledger.

"Three hundred and eighty-seven, sir."

"Hmm," Miles said, pursing his lips. "I expected more. Post someone here in the event others show up during the night, then get some rest."

The colonel consulted with General Howard. They agreed to wait until dawn. If no other Indians surrendered, they would send troops into the ravines and look for anyone hoping to escape capture.

Early the next morning, Miles sent a battalion to the ravines. Rifles at the ready, the soldiers searched every rifle pit and shelter. They discovered torn blankets, pieces of clothing, rotting meat, battered pans, and saddles — but no people.

When word reached Miles and Howard the camp was vacant, it incensed them. General Howard summoned Tom Hill and stormed into the tent where Joseph was sleeping and confronted the chief.

"Less than a day after we agreed to surrender terms, and your people have already violated our accord."

The interpreter repeated Howard's accusation.

"I do not speak for all Nez Perce, only those from the Wallowa Valley. All who wished to surrender have done so."

"I looked at the list of those who turned themselves in. One prominent name is missing — White Bird."

"He chose a different path," Joseph said, shrugging.

Exasperated, Howard ducked out of the tent and reported this conversation to Miles.

"How could they get past your perimeter? Did your pickets fall asleep?"

Colonel Miles's face flushed.

"Sir, please do not lecture me on the discipline of my troops. These Indians eluded you for over four months. I'm the one who caught them and forced their surrender."

Howard clenched his teeth, but said nothing. He told himself to focus on the victory, not a minor setback.

"The warriors under White Bird won't strengthen Sitting Bull's followers. They might not reach the Sioux leader's camp because they are poorly clothed, wounded, and the weather is turning colder," the general said. "Still, we should stop as many of them as possible from crossing the border."

Nelson Miles stroked his chin.

"Why not enlist our Indian friends to help us?"

"What do you have in mind?" Howard said.

"I could send word to the Assiniboine that a group of Nez Perce are crossing their land. We could encourage that tribe to kill the non-treaties. They can keep any ponies or weapons."

"What about White Bird? He's the one we really want."

"I'll post a five hundred dollar reward for the chief. Dead or alive."

"Excellent. Make it happen," Howard said. "Now, let's work on the logistics of transporting these prisoners to your fort before the heavy winter snows."

General Howard ordered Lieutenant Wood to look after Chief Joseph. The chief was valuable to the army as part of a public relations campaign. Newspaper reporters would seek interviews with the famous Nez Perce leader. If Joseph made comments about his fair treatment, it could burnish the general's reputation as someone who was tough, but reasonable.

This assignment delighted the young officer. He spent hours talking with Joseph through the interpreter Tom Hill. The lieutenant quickly became impressed with the man's strength and dignity, even in defeat.

As the late afternoon transitioned to evening, Chief Joseph's head bobbed, and his eyes grew heavy. It had been an exhausting day for the Nez Perce leader.

"I must go, and you need rest," Wood said, as he and Tom Hill stood to leave. "I enjoyed our time together and look forward to more conversation. We have a long journey to the Tongue River Cantonment. Colonel Miles will take you and your people to the Lapwai Reservation in the spring."

The chief nodded. Over two hundred Nez Perce died during their journey from White Bird Canyon to the Bears Paw Mountains. Perhaps those who survived could go home and start new lives. He raised his arms skyward and asked the Great Spirit to grant his desire to see his homeland again. He lay on a blanket, drifted to sleep, and dreamed of visiting his beloved Wallowa Valley.

Chief Joseph's dreams would never come true.

Chapter Twenty
Medicine Line

6 October, 1877

White Bird led thirty-seven Nez Perce along Snake Creek under a waxing crescent moon after midnight. The war chief instructed everyone to move in silence. The escapees needed to avoid detection by sentries guarding the northern boundary of the camp. They brought only essentials, leaving behind pans, pots, or anything that might make noise and communicated with sign language. Men tied strips of clothing and blankets around the feet of the horses and mules to soften the sounds of the animals' hooves on the rocky soil.

The war chief sent scouts ahead to assure their path beside the stream was unguarded. He gave instructions to kill soldiers by slitting their throats or shooting them with arrows. Gunfire would give away their position and result in them being captured.

Graham led a mule with his wife and adopted son aboard. The pack animal was stronger than his horse, which became frail from lack of forage. He transferred his saddlebags from the equine to the mule, hoping to find a stronger mount among the animals that escaped the initial onslaught by the army.

He worried if Dakkoótee fussed while they were within earshot of the enemy, the crying child would put entire group at risk. A short time before they left camp, Graham pulled a bottle of whiskey from the medicine bag and explained his plan for keeping the boy quiet.

The act of giving their son liquor offended Makawee. She saw how alcohol destroyed lives, and her father's drunken state a month earlier was fresh in her mind. Makawee relented after Graham argued this decision was necessary to ensure everyone's security. She gave a thimble-sized portion to the toddler, who fell into a deep sleep.

The dull *thump-a-thump* of horses and mules plodding along the snow-covered creek bottom amplified in the ears of those trying to remain undetected. Every snort or nicker increased the anxiety among the disheveled travelers.

Their confidence in escaping grew with each mile they put between themselves and the soldiers.

White Bird stopped the procession after an hour. The scouts retrieved the stray ponies they corralled two nights earlier and herded them to the group. Most of those walking could now ride, albeit bareback, since there were no extra saddles.

A short time later, the refugee column moved ahead.

Yellow Wolf waited for Graham's family, then fell in line. The Nez Perce warrior was escorting Wetatonmi, Ollokot's widow, and her daughter Sara. Graham nodded and flashed a thin smile at his friend.

White Bird allowed conversing in hushed voices, but no one uttered a word. Perhaps they were afraid they might alert the soldiers, even though they were many miles away. Maybe speaking required more effort than they wanted to expend. Most likely, the reason for their silence was that this was the final leg of a sorrowful journey.

Everyone in the forlorn group lost a loved one. Some family members died in June. The soldiers killed others as recently as yesterday. Over two hundred of their family and friends perished. To the people wrapped in thin blankets and riding on empty stomachs, they were not escaping to a new home. They were part of a funeral procession.

The caravan followed the Milk River east at a steady pace and halted for breakfast at sunrise. White Bird proclaimed a two-hour break, then ordered everyone back on the trail. He sat on his horse and watched the group pass by, encouraging his fellow travelers to keep moving and promising a longer rest at sunset. Although the pace was exhausting, no one argued. The army caught the Nez Perce because Looking Glass chose a leisurely tempo. White Bird would not make the same mistake.

Late in the afternoon, the weary party camped on the north bank of the Milk River. The sight of bison dotting the grasslands buoyed the spirits of the travelers. Hunters killed two of the massive bovids, which the women butchered and prepared. They filled their bellies with lean meat and rested by fires on another frigid October evening.

Wetatonmi and Makawee built a fire to share between their respective families. White Bird visited after dinner.

"Tomorrow, we turn north. We should cross the Medicine Line before sunset," he said to Yellow Wolf and Graham.

"It looks like our people will make it to safety," Yellow Wolf said.

"We are still in danger."

"From the troops?" Graham said, wrinkles creasing his forehead. "Do you think they are on our trail?"

"My biggest concern is not the soldiers, but the Assiniboine. We are in their territory."

"What should we do?" Yellow Wolf asked.

"Use scouts and post a rear guard," White Bird said. "I plan to travel in back with four other warriors. Will you and Graham move to the front?"

"Yes," the two replied.

"How will we know when we reach the Medicine Line?" Yellow Wolf said.

"They say there is a marker at the boundary," White Bird said. "I have not seen it."

The group broke camp before dawn and headed north.

Graham hung field glasses around his neck and tucked the Colt into his belt. He gave the Spencer carbine to Makawee. He was not at ease holding it on his lap while riding an unfamiliar horse. Yellow Wolf offered Graham his riding gear, which the white man declined.

The warrior said he was accustomed to riding bareback. He insisted Graham take the saddle so he could "focus on what lies ahead, not what's missing under your butt."

Secretly, Graham was relieved. His inner thighs felt sore after twelve hours of bareback travel.

The friends rode several miles in front of the small procession, scanning the treeless landscape for signs of Assiniboine warriors. The snow-covered ground made it easy to stay on course. Others on horseback had taken the same route within the past few days. They followed the tracks of Nez Perce who escaped the Bears Paw battle.

As the sun crept toward the western horizon, the friends crested a knoll and reined their horses. A conical earth mound ten feet high and twenty feet in diameter at the base jutted from the prairie. A trench encircled the geometrical shape, and a large stone crowned its apex.

Graham dismounted and handed the reins of his horse to Yellow Wolf. He raised the field glasses and panned west. A similar structure protruded on a plateau several miles away.

They had reached the Medicine Line.

He let the binoculars dangle from his neck and walked to the base of the mound. He took a few strides to the south of the cone, turned to Yellow Wolf, and said, "Montana territory."

After walking a half dozen paces to the northern side of the earthen marker, he said, "British territory."

Yellow Wolf nodded. He slid off his horse, gave the reins of both animals to Graham, and retraced his friend's footsteps.

Standing on the southern edge of the conical structure, he said, "Oppression." Walking north, the warrior planted his feet shoulder-width apart, crossed his arms over his chest, and declared, "Freedom."

Yellow Wolf and Graham embraced and savored the moment.

Eventually, White Bird's group approached the Medicine Line, but no one stopped. The Nez Perce rode past the earth mound on both sides. No joy, no brief celebration of accomplishment. Just people who wanted to find a place where they could sleep without fear of bullets piercing their lodge or cannon balls exploding overhead.

Makawee, holding Dakkoótee in front of her, reined her mule out of the procession to rejoin Graham. He reached over and pulled the toddler to his horse.

"He can ride with me," Graham said. "You need a break."

White Bird paused as the last of the refugees passed into Canada. He considered the boundary marker for a few seconds before speaking.

"We are safe from the bluecoats. But we have a long ride to find Sitting Bull's camp. I told everyone we would rest for the night at the next stream."

Just before sunset, White Bird halted the column. The bone-weary exiles camped on the banks of Whitewater Creek ten kilometers inside the boundary line separating the United States and Canada. The Indians were relieved the US government could no longer threaten them.

Just before nightfall, the sound of approaching horses startled the group. Warriors stationed as pickets whistled a warning for the camp residents to seek shelter. Families scrambled to find somewhere to hide. Women scooped up children and dove into shallow ravines. Their habitual drill of trying to protect their loved ones from an enemy was front and center again.

The horses stopped. Voices called out. These words were not English. They were *Niimíipuu!*

A moment later, the Nez Perce warrior Two Moons led two dozen people into camp. These men were among those who fled during the first day of the battle at Bears Paw. Shrieks of joy erupted as the people in White Bird's group recognized relatives — brothers, sons, and fathers. Everyone gathered around to celebrate their arrival.

A chaotic scene unfolded as those who escaped with White Bird questioned the Nez Perce men about their loved ones. Have you seen them? Are they safe? Was anyone wounded?

Heyoom Yoyikt, Hophop Onmi, Springtime, and Joseph's infant daughter were among those reported alive.

After the initial excitement abated, Two Moons introduced seven warriors from Sitting Bull's camp who accompanied the Nez Perce. He explained the Sioux took them in when they arrived five days earlier. Two Moons asked for fresh horses, as he wanted to return to rescue the families trapped by the army at Snake Creek. Upon hearing of their plight and seeing the malnourished and weakened people who entered his camp, the Hunkpapa chief was more than glad to help. He gave them horses and provided an escort to the border.

White Bird told of Chief Joseph's surrender and his group's escape. He thanked the Sioux for their support and expressed his eagerness to meet the famous chief.

The visitors stayed in camp that evening. While the Sioux and a few Nez Perce planned to accompany the recent refugees to Sitting Bull's settlement, a dozen Nez Perce men would ride to Snake Creek in the morning. Their aim was not to fight the soldiers. For this mission, the most important tool they carried was a spade.

They were returning to bury their dead.

The last group of refugees under White Bird rode into the Canadian Nez Perce camp on the afternoon of October 8. Their friends and relatives who preceded them were grateful to see people whom they thought were captured or killed. The new residents unpacked their animals and made temporary shelters using hide and canvas. They were filled with a mix of happiness and melancholy.

As Graham set up the wall tent, he noticed additional tears and rips in the canvas. The fabric of the tent weakened because of exposure to the sun and wind, along with being folded and packed hundreds of times. He ran his hand along the corners and noted the seams were pulling apart. The army tent would be serviceable for a while, but they would need a more sturdy shelter for the winter.

"We made it, Makawee," Graham said as he dropped a load of dead balsam fir branches by the fire and sat beside her. Dakkoótee fell asleep on her lap. Graham stroked the boy's cheeks with the back of his hand, then leaned over and kissed her.

"No more soldiers. No more bullets. I may sleep until the sun is high in the sky tomorrow," she said.

Makawee turned a chunk of bison meat on a spit. The flames popped as the juice dripped into the fire pit.

"We need something better than a thin tent to be comfortable in cold weather," he said.

"Wetatonmi and I will work together to build a lodge for both families. There are plenty of buffalo. If you cut poles, we will tan hides and sew them together for the covering."

Graham marveled at his wife's industrious nature. She worked harder than most women he met.

"That's wonderful, but..." He paused, choosing his words carefully. "I hoped you and I would build a shelter of our own."

"One tepee is large enough for five people — you, me, Dakkoótee, Wetatonmi, and Sara."

"True, but there won't be much privacy."

Makawee scooted next to Graham until their hips touched. Dakkoótee stirred momentarily, then drifted back to sleep. She stroked Graham's beard.

"Do you miss me?" she said.

He leaned down and met her lips, then kissed her neck.

"I miss our intimacy."

He couldn't remember the last time they made love. Could it have been on the banks of the Firehole River? The constant threat of a ruthless enemy on their heels crowded out any romantic thoughts.

"I miss our tender moments, too," she whispered in his ear. "After we build a lodge, I will replace the canvas on our tent with buffalo hides. That will be a place for just you and me."

Graham smiled and kissed her again.

"I like that plan."

The six-man detail of the North West Mounted Police reined their horses on a knoll near Pinto Horse Butte and looked at the settlement below. Hundreds of pole lodges straddled both banks of the Mud River. The only difference they noticed when they revisited Sitting Bull's camp was a group of makeshift animal hide shelters on the western edge.

Major James Morrow Walsh, superintendent of the Mounties in the Cypress Hills region, spent most of his time as a negotiator and peace broker.

~ James Walsh

After the Battle of the Little Bighorn, bands of Sioux crossed the Medicine Line to find sanctuary from the American government. Late in 1876, Four Horns brought nearly sixty lodges across the border. In May 1877, Sitting Bull led thousands of his followers to the same location. Small bands of Sans Arc and Minneconjou Sioux found their way north to the refuge.

The police commander visited the leaders of every group and outlined the conditions for them to remain. Now, another group of exiles arrived. Sitting Bull informed Walsh about the arrival of the latest group, so when he noticed additional fires near the Hunkpapa chief's camp, he wasn't surprised.

"Looks like the Nez Perce have joined the party," Walsh said.

"Really?" asked Sergeant McCutcheon. "We received word Chief Joseph surrendered to the Americans."

"Not everyone agreed to give up their weapons. These are the ones who escaped. Did you send word for their leader to meet us at the lodge of Sitting Bull?"

"Yes, sir. His name is White Bird."

"Where is Pierre?"

"*Ici,*" ["Here"] a voice said from the rear. A man dressed in buckskins and wearing an otter-skin cap rode up to join the major.

The NWMP employed Pierre Leveille as an interpreter. The former fur trader was biracial. A growing number of residents in western Canada identified as Métis, which means "mixed" in French. They were children of a European (usually Scot) and an indigenous person (often Cree, Blackfeet, or Assiniboine).

"Pierre, we need to talk to the Nez Perce leader, White Bird. You have strong language skills. Can you communicate with the Nez Perce?"

"I used to barter with them when they came to my trading post. I can fall back on Chinook jargon or sign language if necessary."

"Good. Let's go see our friend Sitting Bull and remind our latest visitors how we expect them to behave."

Walsh urged his horse down the slope. The Mounties rode through the camp until they arrived at a lodge guarded by two warriors. The major ordered the other officers to remain on their horses. He dismounted and straightened his scarlet jacket. Leveille followed him to the tepee. Sitting Bull and two other Indians Walsh did not recognize exited the lodge just as the police officer and his interpreter arrived.

~ *Sitting Bull*

The forty-something Sioux chief was just under six feet tall. He had a barrel chest and walked with a limp. His broad, pockmarked face featured a prominent hooked nose. Two braids hung over his shoulders.

After shaking hands, Walsh addressed Sitting Bull.

"I've come for two reasons. First, I understand Nez Perce refugees settled in your camp. I would like to speak to their leader, White Bird."

"I am Two Moons," a stranger said. "I will interpret for White Bird," nodding at the Nez Perce chief standing beside him.

"Oh, splendid. I am Major James Walsh, commander of the fort in the Cypress Hills. This is Pierre Leveille, my interpreter. As you speak English, it seems we won't require the services of Mr. Leveille today."

The men exchanged handshakes.

"I speak only a little of the Lakota tongue," Two Moons said. "Another interpreter will be helpful for everyone to understand one another."

Sitting Bull opened the flap of the tepee and motioned for the guests to enter. A warrior entered the lodge with a pipe after everyone was seated. The Sioux chief lit the tobacco mixture, drew air through the bowl, and exhaled the smoke before passing it to White Bird, who did the same. The pipe circulated among everyone. When it returned to its starting point, Sitting Bull spoke. Leveille translated.

"The chief says he has given refuge to White Bird and his people. He shared food and lodges with them until they have the strength to care for themselves."

White Bird listened as Two Moons interpreted. The Nez Perce leader expressed his gratitude again for the hospitality shown by their former enemies.

For the next thirty minutes, the men in the lodge communicated in short sentences, then waited for an interpreter to translate. Although the conversation took longer than normal, the dialogue was cogent. Everyone who spoke was keenly aware of using an economy of words.

Major Walsh talked to White Bird and repeated something he told all tribal leaders who left the US for British territories. He paused after each sentence of his talk about "the basic rules of honorable conduct."

"You left the land of the White Father, President Hayes. You now live in a land governed by Queen Victoria. I must tell you about the White Mother's laws. Everyone, white men and red men alike, must obey these. You must not make war against other tribes. No one will steal anything, especially horses. You must not kill or injure any other person. You must not use the White Mother's country as a refuge to strike the American soldiers. If you break any of these laws, I will send you back across the Medicine Line."

White Bird listened. When Walsh finished, the Nez Perce leader assured the major that his people would respect the White Mother's laws.

"Thank you," Walsh said. "Now, I would like to speak privately with Sitting Bull."

Two Moons translated. He and White Bird rose and exited the lodge. The Nez Perce leader was eager to share the news with the others. They were welcome to stay in the White Mother's land.

"There is a second reason for my visit," Walsh said, after the Nez Perce men departed. "I need to ask a favor."

Sitting Bull held his fingers to his lips and extended his arm while opening his palm. He wanted the major to speak his mind.

"General Alfred Terry wants you and your people to return to the United States. He will be at Fort Walsh on October 17. That is one week from today. Will you meet with him?"

The Sioux chief's eyes narrowed, and his lips tightened. Terry was the same general who spearheaded the multi-pronged attack on his people that culminated in the Battle of the Little Bighorn. Sitting Bull may have considered attending a council with someone else, but not this man. After seeing the pitiful Nez Perce stumble into his camp with only rifles and a few skinny horses, his heart hardened against the US government.

"No."

"Please listen," Walsh said, raising both hands. "My commander, Commissioner Macleod, is also traveling to Fort Walsh. If you do not attend, he might replace me with another officer. That person may not allow you to stay here."

Sitting Bull crossed his arms and looked at the smoke hole of the lodge. He considered the consequences of refusing to meet with the American general. Walsh was tough, but fair. The chief respected the young police officer and considered him a friend. As distasteful as it seemed, attending the meeting at Fort Walsh was the right decision.

"I will go under one condition."

"What's that?"

"Your men will protect us from the bluecoats."

"Agreed."

Sitting Bull and a dozen other Lakota chiefs arrived at Fort Walsh late on the afternoon of Wednesday, October 17. Before leading his entourage through the front gates of the palisade, the Sioux holy man approached White Bird and Two Moons, whom he invited as guests.

"This meeting with the bluecoats is between the Lakota and the US government. Just like us, your people experienced American oppression. What we decide today will determine if you can remain in our camp. Stay outside the fort. We will talk after the council."

Two Moons translated and White Bird nodded. They dismounted and led their horses to a grove of white spruce to wait.

The Sioux contingent passed through the gates and rode into the compound. A series of rectangular, whitewashed buildings made from lodgepole pine were arranged along the outer walls of the stockade. A cluster of single-story structures near the center served as officers' quarters, a carpentry workshop, a blacksmith shop, and a commissary. Along the east wall of the fort, the NWMP established stables for their horses.

A half dozen blue-uniformed soldiers gathered outside a large building with pane-glass windows. Oil lamps illuminated the interior. Smoke from a cast-iron stove drifted skyward from a pipe that protruded from the roof. Sitting Bull recognized an officer with a full V-shaped beard as Alfred Terry. The sight of the American general caused a chill to run up his spine, but outwardly, he maintained his composure.

The participants crowded into the log building. General Terry sat in a ladder-back chair by the stove, with his escort standing behind. Sitting Bull and the other chiefs declined an offer for seats. They stood on the opposite side of the room. The tension was palpable.

Commissioner Macleod cleared his throat and made some introductory comments. He explained the US government asked to meet with the Sioux about returning to their homeland. He requested everyone to talk slowly and give the translator time to do his job. Macleod invited General Terry to speak first.

"I am here on behalf of President Hayes," Terry said, rising from his chair. "The president desires a lasting peace. In the spirit of achieving this, we will grant amnesty to all Sioux. We will care for your people, provide annual allotments, and give you a large piece of land where you can live a full life."

"We are living in this land the way we have for thousands of years," Sitting Bull said.

"Well, that may be true, but we cannot expect the British government to keep you indefinitely. You are American Indians."

"We are Indians."

General Terry raised his eyebrows. This was not going well. He sweetened the deal.

"We will give you a large herd of cattle, which you can raise to feed your families."

"*Tatonka* plentiful in the land of the White Mother. You killed all of them on our original hunting grounds."

Terry looked over his shoulder and whispered to his adjutant, "Any other ideas to encourage them to return?"

"Perhaps we could allow them to keep some of their rifles," the junior officer suggested.

The general bristled at this comment. He glared at the aide, who stepped back against the wall.

"Let's get to the heart of the matter," Terry said, turning to face the chiefs. "We offer all these things if you surrender your rifles and horses and return to the United States. You can live in peace — and go home."

Sitting Bull turned his back to the general and caucused with the other Sioux leaders. After a brief discussion, he faced his adversary.

"Did you offer the same conditions to the Nez Perce?"

"Every tribe's situation is unique."

"One thing is the same. You never keep a promise. You lie to everyone."

To support Sitting Bull's accusation, many of the Indians stamped the plank floor. The thuds of dozens of moccasin-clad feet echoed in the room.

General Terry raised his voice to regain control of the conversation.

"Let's focus on your people, shall we? You have a generous offer. What do you say?"

Sitting Bull crossed his arms over his chest and took a few steps toward the general. He looked into the American officer's eyes as he spoke.

"For sixty-four years, you have kept and treated my people bad. What have we done that caused us to depart from our country? We could go nowhere, so we have taken refuge here. We did not give you our country, you took it from us. See how I live with these people? Look at these eyes and ears. You think me a fool, but you are a greater fool than I am. This is a Medicine House. You come to tell us stories, and we do not want to hear them. I will not say any more. I shake hands with these people. That part of the country we came from belonged to us. Now, we live here."

The Sioux holy man walked past the general and shook the hand of James Walsh, Commissioner Macleod, and men in the room clad in scarlet. Following his example, the other chiefs shook hands with the NWMP officers and ignored the bluecoats. The Indians exited the room, mounted their horses, and rode toward the gates.

The meeting was over in less than twenty minutes.

As the Sioux exited the stockade, White Bird and Two Moons joined the group. Sitting Bull said nothing for the first few miles. He hoped one day to return to his homeland, but under his terms. As long as the redcoats treated them with respect and there were bison to hunt, the land in the Cypress Hills would be their home.

Sitting Bull reined his horse and waited for the Nez Perce chief and his interpreter to ride alongside.

"No agreement with the general?" White Bird asked, and Two Moons interpreted.

The Sioux chief shook his head.

"They are full of lies and unfulfilled promises."

White Bird nodded. "That is why I am here. I fear the bluecoats lied to Joseph to convince him to surrender."

"We see the world the same way," Sitting Bull said. "Joseph's journey from your distant land inspired me. That is why I welcomed you into our camp, despite being long-time enemies. You may remain with us through the flowering moon."

"We appreciate your generosity. As soon as we regain our strength, we will establish a village among these hills. Our plan is to live here, above the Medicine Line."

Neither man imagined their camps would be temporary. In less than four years, the bison in southern Saskatchewan would be gone. The Canadian government would refuse to provide for the American Indians on their soil, and officials would remove James Walsh from his post.

When Sitting Bull surrendered in 1881, government authorities consigned the Hunkpapa Lakota holy man to the Standing Rock Reservation.

As White Bird and Sitting Bull were speaking, Chief Joseph was on his way to Fort Leavenworth, Kansas. The following summer, the army transferred the Nez Perce leader to Indian Territory in present-day Oklahoma.

Joseph would never see his beloved Wallowa Valley again.

Chapter Twenty-One
Honor and Heartache

25 December, 1877

The wind whistled between the lodges, causing the buffalo hides to flap against the wooden support poles. The air was filled with swirling snow crystals that formed drifts against the north edge of the tepees. The temperature was hovering near zero.

Wetatonmi and Sara lay sleeping. The mother and daughter were both wrapped in a buffalo robe.

Makawee swaddled Dakkoótee in a thick blanket and placed him close to the fire. Graham rested on his back under an animal hide with his wife snuggled under his arm. He felt at ease despite being naked on this cold evening. He thought about the canvas wall tent adjacent to the lodge. His family would be miserable trying to sleep in that shelter on a night like this.

Perhaps he was comfortable because of the clever design of the tepee, which allowed occupants to build fires inside for heating and cooking. He glanced at their fire, which funneled smoke up and out of the apex. A thick layer of dried grass on the lodge floor insulated them from the frozen ground. Heavy buffalo hides beneath and on top of them trapped their body heat.

Makawee's smooth black hair brushed against his chin as she leaned her head on his shoulder. He could feel her breasts pressing against his ribs. She rested her arm on his chest while her leg draped over his thigh. His ankle supported her foot.

He covered their heads with a blanket to keep their faces and ears warm.

"Are you asleep?" Graham whispered.

"No," Makawee said. "Just thinking."

"Wanna talk?"

"Sure."

They made love earlier. Graham thought it was odd to have sex while others were in the same lodge. Makawee convinced him there was no cause for shame. Intimacy was expected. Others sharing the same shelter ignored what was happening a few feet away. If Ollokot were still alive, he would be in this tepee.

Graham would have learned to roll over and look the other way while Wetatonmi and her husband had sex.

Making love in complete silence had a sensual quality to it. The meaning behind the touches seemed deeper. Stroking was more deliberate. The kisses were more passionate and lasted longer. One thing didn't change. Graham lost all his inhibitions and moaned pleasurably after climaxing. During that moment of ecstasy, Makawee and he were the only ones in the lodge.

"You know what today is?" he said.

"It's Christmas in the white man's world."

"The two of us haven't celebrated this occasion together yet."

"My Crow family celebrates Winter Solstice. They say prayers and thank the Great Spirit for returning the sun. I can imagine people in my village performing their Winter Dance a few days ago."

"Christians observe this day as the birth of Jesus. Exchanging gifts is one of our traditions. I have a surprise for you!"

Makawee lifted her head and looked at him.

"Oh?"

Removing the blanket from their heads, Graham twisted his body and extended his arm to the tepee wall. He plucked something out of his saddlebag, scooted beside Makawee, and handed it to her.

"Merry Christmas and Happy Anniversary!"

Makawee grasped the carved bison. She held the wood sculpture close to the fire to admire it.

"Oh, Graham! This is beautiful!"

"I crafted a small buffalo replica because I know how crucial the animal is to your people."

"How thoughtful!" she said. "You mentioned something about our anniversary?"

"Yes! It's been two years since we got married. It doesn't matter what the Territory of Montana says in their records. We committed to each other five years ago. So, this is our fifth anniversary."

After leaning in to kiss him, she lay back down and snuggled next to him. She turned the carving in her hand, admiring the details of the oversized head, sharp horns, and beard under the animal's chin.

"I will treasure it." She wrinkled her forehead. "But I didn't get you a gift."

"Oh, yes, you did."

She looked at him, tilted her chin, and lifted her eyebrows.

"What was that?"

"You've given me a lovely daughter."

Makawee set the figurine on the hide and placed her head back on his shoulder. A moment later, tears dripped onto his chest.

"Hey, why so sad?" Graham said.

"I... I miss Nahkash," she said, wiping her nose with her thumb.

Graham shifted to his side and faced her. He grabbed his shirt and used it to wipe tears from her cheeks. He lifted the obsidian turtle-shaped pendant hanging on an elk-hide cord lying on her chest.

"Your necklace keeps her close to your heart."

Makawee forced a thin smile. They chose to name their daughter Nahkash because it translates as 'turtle' in Apsáalooke.

"Graham?"

"Yes?"

"I'm ready to go home."

Graham lifted her chin.

"I am, too. We can head south at the first sign of spring."

She nodded and rested on her back. He lay next to her, their hips touching. He grasped her hand and interlocked their fingers.

"We must take care of something before we cross the Medicine Line."

"I know. We need to find a home for our little boy."

Graham glanced at the swaddled child sleeping by the fire. His mouth opened in an oval, and he was snoring. A lump formed in Graham's throat. The way Makawee said *our little boy* made him uneasy. The thought of giving up Dakkoótee was distressing.

"Are you sure about this? We provide him with a loving home. You are a wonderful mother and..."

"We came to Canada for two reasons," she said. "To escape the soldiers and to find a new family for Dakkoótee."

"Why not take him back to your father's village? Your mother would love to have a grandson."

Makawee reached over and put her finger on Graham's lips.

"Don't make this harder than it already is. I am committed to making sure this boy learns the customs of his people. I'm keeping that promise."

Graham knew she was right. Long Horse would never allow Makawee in his lodge if she cared for a Sioux child.

"We will visit Sitting Bull after this storm passes and seek his advice on finding a couple to adopt Dakkoótee," he said.

Makawee rolled on her side and propped on an elbow. She ran her fingers across his chest.

"Graham, will you make me a promise?"

"Anything. Well, *almost* anything," he added, with a smirk.

"Our culture is disappearing with the buffalo. I aspire for our daughter to learn the ways of the Crow, just as one day Dakkoótee will be proud of his Sioux heritage."

"Of course."

"We need to ensure Nahkash receives an education. She should know about the world around her."

"I agree with everything you've said."

"Nahkash is biracial, like the Métis here in Canada. Crow should be her primary identity, not white."

Graham paused. He wondered where she was leading him with this conversation.

"That's something she can decide later."

"The more time she spends in your culture, the less she will remember her mother's roots."

"What are you asking?" Graham said, as wrinkles creased his forehead.

Makawee lifted her head and looked into his eyes.

"Promise she can stay with the Crow until she can make her own choices."

What about my future? Graham thought. He envisioned moving his family to Bozeman or Denver — maybe even Salt Lake City. Living on the reservation would limit his opportunities.

"Are you asking this for our daughter, or for yourself?"

"Both. We saw many lands during this journey with the Nez Perce. Some were spectacular. But, I miss the Stillwater River Valley. That's where my people are. My heart lies in that place. It's home."

Graham closed his eyes and pursed his lips. Her words were tough to hear. For the first time since they were married, their future was cloudy. A fork in the road loomed on the horizon, and he did not know which path to take.

"Graham?"

"Huh?"

"Do you pledge Nahkash will be raised in a Crow village?"

"Sure," Graham heard himself say.

"Thank you," she said, then kissed him.

She repositioned herself with her back turned to him. "Hold me," she said over her shoulder.

Graham moved close and wrapped his arm around her waist. Soon she was in a deep sleep, her rib cage rising and falling in rhythm.

His unsettled mind traveled in a dozen directions, most of which led to a dark destination. How could a night that began romantically end with his stomach twisted in knots?

He lay awake, listening to the storm. Snow-laden evergreen branches creaked as gusts of wind whipped through the camp. Weakened limbs tumbled from the trees.

It was going to be a long, cold winter.

Graham waited outside the tepee with Makawee, who was balancing Dakkoótee on her hip. She covered the toddler's head with a blanket to shield his face from the biting wind. The new-fallen snow glittered under a bright January sun.

White Bird and Two Moons entered Sitting Bull's lodge earlier. The Nez Perce leader consented to arrange an introduction to the Sioux chief and request an audience.

Two Moons poked his head out of the entrance and gestured for them to step inside.

Sitting Bull was positioned at the back of the lodge, with family members situated around the perimeter. A fire crackled in the center.

Makawee and Graham stepped forward, and the chief motioned for them to sit. They were presented by Two Moons, with the explanation that they were not Nez Perce but traveled with the exiles from Lapwai.

Sitting Bull named the people in his lodge, starting with his wife, Red Woman, who sat on his left.

"The chief has agreed to listen. I will interpret," Two Moons said. "It is customary for the man to speak first."

Graham nodded. He practiced his words earlier, but his throat tightened when he spoke. Taking a deep breath and exhaling, he recounted the story of discovering the Sioux child orphaned after the Little Bighorn battle. To avoid arousing the Hunkpapa chief's suspicion of white men, he left out crucial information.

After the translation of Two Moons, Sitting Bull clasped his hands and leaned forward.

"Iyunge."

"The chief has questions," the translator said.

"You say you have never been a soldier. What were you doing at Greasy Grass?"

"I was a civilian scout."

"You scouted with the Crow?"

This was the delicate part. The Crow and Sioux were blood enemies. Graham thought it better to tell the truth than to make up a story.

"Yes."

The response caused murmurs among those in the room.

"You killed some of our people that day?"

"No." This was true. He fired his Spencer carbine while he was with Reno's battalion, but he never hit a target.

Upon hearing the exchange, White Bird defended Graham.

"Eagle Bear is a friend of the Nez Perce. He fought against the bluecoats," he said.

Graham glanced at White Bird and nodded. He was grateful for the war chief's support.

"Why bother saving a Sioux when the soldiers killed so many that day?" Sitting Bull asked.

"No child deserves to die," Graham said. He could tell he gained credibility with this reply.

"Who is the woman?"

"This is my wife, Makawee. She is Crow."

A rustle of uneasiness erupted in the lodge. A white man and a Crow woman were in their midst. The Lakota Sioux held these people in the highest contempt.

Sitting Bull raised his arms to silence the crowd.

"Makawee, speak."

"Great chief," she said, "We are seeking to return this lost child. When my husband, Eagle Bear, brought him to me, I raised him as my son. We traveled with Joseph and the Nez Perce to your settlement because we believe this boy should be with his people. That is why we are speaking with you today."

"*Aku La.*" ["Show us the little one"]

Makawee kneeled down and pulled the blanket away from the boy's head, turning towards the chief and Red Woman so they could see his face.

"I named him Dakkoótee."

This pronouncement elicited a chorus of "ahs" from those in the lodge. The boy was named after the tribe that was considered an enemy by her own people. Graham could sense the atmosphere changing from skepticism to respect.

Makawee offered the child to Red Woman, who hesitated, then took him into her arms. The chief lifted the boy's chin with a calloused hand. A faint smile creased his face.

"What do you want in exchange for this child?"

"The only thing we ask is that you give him to a deserving couple who will provide a loving home."

Sitting Bull tilted his head and crossed his arms over his chest.

"Why do you give away this boy?"

Makawee told her story. When she was born, running face sickness took the lives of her parents. Blackfeet stole her and raised her. Later, they sold her to a trading post operator. She gained her freedom at eighteen years old.

The people in the lodge whispered to one another as they listened to the Crow woman's story.

"I felt lost until I was able to live with my people. I don't want this child to feel like he is among strangers as he grows up. He was born Sioux and should be raised that way."

Graham put his arm around his wife. Her life story reignited his admiration for his wife. She suffered so much, yet was loving. She was gracious enough to surrender a child she looked after for eighteen months.

Sitting Bull's eyes became glassy. The Crow woman's unselfish act touched him. He leaned over and whispered to Red Woman, then turned to a warrior on his right. The two men spoke in a low tone.

"Please wait outside, as my family needs to talk."

Graham, Makawee, White Bird, and Two Moons stepped out into the bright winter sun. They walked to a fire and warmed their hands while awaiting the chief's decision.

"I did not know your story," Two Moons said. "You are a remarkable woman."

"She is," Graham said, putting his arm around her shoulders and kissing her forehead.

The host invited them back into the lodge a few minutes later.

Red Woman supported Dakkoótee with one arm under his bottom. The child giggled when she playfully gummed his fingers when he placed his hand on her mouth.

"My nephew, White Bull, and his wife, Holy Lodge, are childless. They will raise this boy as their own. White Bull is the son of Makes Room, a respected Minniconjou chief. White Bull is a fearless warrior. He proved this at Greasy Grass by killing five soldiers, including Yellow Hair. Holy Lodge is a strong and caring woman. They will teach the boy the ways of his people."

Graham noted the chief's reference to Yellow Hair, the name most Sioux called Custer. He glanced at Makawee, who was looking at her moccasins. When she didn't reply to Sitting Bull, he spoke.

"We need to spend time with Dakkoótee before we give him up," he said.

"Of course. I will send the new parents to your lodge tomorrow so they may become acquainted with their son."

Red Woman got up and walked towards Makawee.

"*Lila pilamayaye,*" ["Thank you very much"] she said, giving her the boy.

Makawee hugged the toddler tightly and gave him a kiss on the cheek. She turned to leave, tears streaming down her face.

Sitting Bull spoke, and Two Moons translated.

"Makawee, you are doing an honorable thing."

Following a winding path up the knoll, Graham and Makawee arrived at an exposed lignite deposit. The absence of trees at the hill's crest allowed for a fantastic view of the vast Sioux and Nez Perce settlements along the Mud River. The couple claimed this as their special place to get away from the crowded, sometimes noisy village.

There were still traces of snow in the shadows of the conifers. Although it was a frosty morning in mid-April, the temperature topped fifty degrees earlier in the week. A cloudless azure sky suggested another warm day. After a harsh winter, it seemed spring was here to stay.

They sat on the brown sedimentary rock ledge and surveyed the scene below. Graham slurped coffee from a tin cup, as his wife sipped on fireweed and wild mint tea. She placed a blanket over her shoulders to protect herself from the chilly morning breeze.

They adjusted to life without Dakkoótee. Life was simpler. They only had to take care of themselves. They slept peacefully without worrying about a crying or fussing child in the middle of the night. No need to worry whether older children might knock him down as they raced between the lodges. No need to soften his food before feeding him. With the adoption of the boy, White Bull and Holy Lodge took on all these parental responsibilities, and many more.

Sitting Bull's nephew and wife came to Makawee's lodge after the January meeting. The Sioux couple quickly grew attached to the boy. Dakkoótee was his typical innocent and outgoing self. He enjoyed having someone new play with him. Over the next few weeks, Dakkoótee spent more time with his new parents. By February, Graham and Makawee visited only once each week. Graham convinced his wife to let go when March arrived. The visitations were over. The little Sioux boy was in his new home.

Makawee cried herself to sleep that night. She didn't know it, but Graham wept at the same time. They lay on the buffalo hide, backs to each other, and grieved the loss of their son.

That was six weeks ago. They had not spoken about it since. They refrained from mentioning it, as it could rekindle their heartbreak. The healing process was best left undisturbed.

"We can make the journey home whenever you are ready," Graham said, breaking the silence.

Makawee set the cup beside her and pulled up her legs, clasping her hands around her knees. Closing her eyes, she turned towards the east and absorbed the warmth of the sun.

Graham studied his wife's face. Fine lines were noticeable at the corners of her eyes. Underneath her coal black hair, a few strands of gray were visible. Although she was only twenty-eight, she looked ten years older. The stress from the past two years was visible. Graham imagined a reflection of himself would likewise reveal signs of premature aging.

"Are we prepared for the journey?" she said.

The winter gave Graham time to plan this trip.

"I believe so. You did a great job repairing the tent. We have a cache of dried buffalo meat and flour. There are plenty of places to catch fish along the way. We have two sturdy horses and a mule."

"How long will it take to reach my father's camp in the Bighorn Valley?" she asked, still facing the sun with closed eyes.

"I'm guessing about two weeks. We can cover more distance daily without Dakkoótee."

Makawee turned toward Graham. He could see the forlorn look in her eyes.

Shit! Graham thought. He had no intention of including their son in the discussion.

"I can be ready in two days," she said, turning away. "I wish to say goodbye to our friends."

"Alright. Yellow Wolf mentioned he would travel part way with us. He wants to find Chief Joseph and let him know his family is safe."

Makawee rose and paced in a circle. The corners of her blanket dragged on the ground. She returned after a few minutes and stood behind Graham.

"I will see my son before we depart," she said in a defiant voice. She wasn't seeking his approval. She was declaring her intentions.

"I'm sure White Bull and Holy Lodge will welcome us."

That evening, Graham sat by the fire. He suggested giving Dakkoótee a farewell present. Would she mind giving up the bison sculpture?

Makawee was delighted with this idea. While she prepared the evening meal, he carved an additional feature into the wooden bison. He etched "G + M" into the belly of the beast.

After dinner, he showed his handiwork to Makawee.

"When Dakkoótee is older, White Bull can share the story of his early years. He can talk about the day when Yellow Hair and the bluecoats attacked their village. He can proudly narrate how he defended the village by killing the invaders and how Dakkoótee lost his mother in the attack. White Bull and Holy Lodge can present this bison and show him our initials. Two loving people named Graham and Makawee raised him before returning him to live as he was born — a Sioux."

Makawee grabbed the miniature bison and pressed it close to her chest, then lifted her chin and raised her arms. She said a prayer to the Great Spirit, asking for blessings on the statue and protection for its owner.

Graham and Makawee spent the next morning packing. They said goodbye to Wetatonmi, Sara, Heyoom Yoyikt, and Hophop Onmi. Graham thanked White Bird for guiding them across the Medicine Line. He told the chief that any Nez Perce were welcome to use their lodge, as they would use the canvas soldier tent for shelter.

Yellow Wolf tended to the equines as Graham and Makawee walked to the center of the Sioux camp at midday. White Bull greeted them in front of his tepee. He stuck his head in the entrance and asked his wife to come outside.

Holy Lodge appeared with Dakkoótee, causing Makawee to gasp. The boy seemed bigger since the last time she saw him six weeks earlier. He held onto Holy Lodge's leg and sucked his thumb, uncertain of the strangers' identity.

After Graham gave the bison to White Bull, Makawee used a mix of Sioux and sign language to explain its importance. She informed the couple they were leaving the camp and would not be returning.

She kneeled and stretched out her arms, inviting Dakkoótee to come to her. He briefly hesitated before stepping towards Makawee and accepting her hug.

Graham reached down and tussled the boy's hair. Tears welled in his eyes.

Makawee kissed Dakkoótee, then stood. The boy ran back to his new mother. Holy Lodge embraced the Crow woman and signed, "thank you."

Makawee wiped her cheeks with the sleeve of her dress. She sighed and grabbed her husband's hand.

The couple heard a mourning dove's call coming from a nearby lodgepole pine as they walked to their waiting horses.

Coo-ah, coo, coo, coo.

The presence of the small gray bird in southern Canada was a harbinger of spring — a time of rebirth and new beginnings. White Bull's Sioux family would link the unique sound of the dove with a joyous event. They welcomed a child into their home.

The Crow family interpreted the mourning dove's call differently. Graham and Makawee would always associate the bird's sorrowful sound with a profound personal loss.

Coo-ah, coo, coo, coo.

Chapter Twenty-Two

Homecoming

April, 1878

T he horses plodded through the rolling hills at a steady pace beneath a cloudless night sky. The moonlit terrain seemed like an unending sequence of swales and ravines.

Yellow Wolf, Graham, and Makawee slept during the day and rode at night to avoid the Assiniboine.

On the morning of the fourth day, the trio arrived at the Missouri River. Snowmelt swelled the river. The volume of water was much greater than last September when the Nez Perce caravan crossed at Cow Island. Yellow Wolf instructed the others to wait as he rode west along the northern bank. He returned a short time later and said he found an acceptable place to ford. They rode a half-mile upstream to a sweeping bend where the river widened.

"The water is moving slower in this area. Stay here. I will cross."

The Nez Perce warrior nudged his horse into the frigid waters. At the midway point, the water was up to his knees, and the horse struggled to maintain its footing. Yellow Wolf emerged on the opposite bank, then recrossed the river.

"I will lead the mule. You follow."

Graham breathed a sigh of relief when they reached the south bank. There were a few harrowing moments when his horse panicked as the water lifted it from its feet. But he calmed the animal when the river became more shallow at a sandbar. Makawee was unfazed. She crossed first and grinned when she saw the distressed look on his face.

"Why do white men struggle to cross rivers?" she said.

She had a point. Most soldiers lacked the skill to guide a horse across a deep waterway. Graham observed this when he rode with the Montana Column on their march to the Little Bighorn. General Howard's battalions were dreadfully inept at following the Nez Perce through a river.

"We will camp here and dry out," Yellow Wolf said.

Graham set up the tent. Within an hour, the travelers sat beside a crackling fire, warming their hands and feet. Graham stripped, wrapped a blanket around himself, and hung his soaked jeans in front of the flames. He suggested Makawee change out of her damp elk-hide dress, but she rejected the idea, explaining it would dry as she sat by the fire.

"I will rest for a few hours before heading west," Yellow Wolf said. "We are no longer in Assiniboine territory. It is safe to travel in the daylight."

"Are you going to Lapwai?" Makawee said.

"Yes. I need to speak with Chief Joseph. The bluecoats said they would take him to Fort Lapwai. He should know his family is safe in Sitting Bull's camp."

Yellow Wolf was unaware his uncle and four hundred other Nez Perce were on their way to a reservation in Oklahoma. They would remain there for seven years before being transported by train to the Colville Reservation in Washington.

Just before noon, Yellow Wolf packed his horse and readied to leave.

"Will you be alright traveling alone?" Graham said.

"I can take care of myself."

After seeing Yellow Wolf fight last summer, Graham had no doubts about his friend's survival skills.

"You have a powerful *wey-ya-kin* to guide you," Graham said.

"*Qe'ci'yew'yew,*" ["Thank you"] Makawee said to Yellow Wolf. "You are a loyal friend."

Graham was unsure how to say goodbye to a man with whom he had become close.

"I hope we meet again someday."

Graham and Yellow Wolf shared an embrace.

"If it is meant to be, it will be," he said, mounting his horse. "*Qo'c 'ee hexnu, Wéeptes Xáxaac* [See you later, Eagle Bear]."

As Yellow Wolf rode away, Makawee and Graham put an arm around each other's waist. She shivered as they walked back and sat by the fire. Sitting next to her, he covered them both with a blanket.

"We should be home in ten days," he said, poking at the fire with a stick.

"I'm eager to see Nahkash," she said, laying her head on his shoulder.

"So am I."

The weather in April was fickle. It was sunny for the first few days. Inevitably, a cold front pushed through the region, bringing storms across the prairie. They rode through heavy rain. With the temperatures plummeting into the upper thirties, the travelers were grateful to set up camp and change out of their wet clothes. Inside the tent, they huddled together and waited for the inclement weather to pass.

Graham set a goal to ride thirty miles each day, but Makawee tired quickly. By the end of the fourth day, they had ridden only one hundred miles.

Makawee complained of chest pain, and she started coughing.

"It's miserable weather. The best thing we can do is keep warm and dry," Graham said, assuring his wife.

"Will you boil water? I'm going to make tea."

While Graham heated a pot of water in the pouring rain, Makawee sat in the tent wrapped in a blanket. She sprinkled dried chokecherry leaves and twigs into a bowl, used a rock to grind the plant material into fine pieces, and emptied the contents into a tin cup. Graham ducked inside the tent and poured the hot water into her cup.

"Our people use *malupwa* tea for many ailments," she said, watching the water slowly darken. "If I drink this every day, I will feel better."

Despite attempting to rest after dinner, her persistent cough kept her awake through the night.

The sun broke through the low-hanging clouds the next morning. Graham told Makawee to rest while he packed the mule, then helped his wife onto her horse.

Graham took on additional camp responsibilities, urging Makawee to rest and recover her health. She was getting weaker every day, and he could see it. By the time they reached Yellowstone River, Makawee was coughing uncontrollably.

"Look!" he said, pointing to a massive sandstone butte squatting on the south bank.

The unique formation jutted one-hundred-and-twenty feet into the sky. It attracted indigenous people for thousands of years, as evidenced by the petroglyphs and inscriptions on its sides. Captain William Clark, who co-led the Corps of Discovery Expedition with Meriwether Lewis, visited the outcropping during his return trip in 1806. He named the isolated sandstone hill Pompeys Pillar.

"Are you strong enough to cross the river?" he said.

She nodded while holding a hand to her chest.

"We'll set up camp on the other side."

Graham rode close to his wife. He leaned over and grabbed a fold of her dress around the waist to keep her upright as they splashed across the river. Thankfully, the water level was low enough for the horses to wade through, despite the recent rain.

He unsaddled the horses and started a fire using driftwood that washed onto the bank. Makawee sat next to the fire and wrapped her arms around herself. He noticed she was shaking as he draped a blanket over her.

"Graham?"

"Yes?"

"I have *baaanneeïtchissee* [a bad illness]."

He touched her forehead with the back of his hand. She had a fever. Had she contracted a virus? Her immune system appeared to be reacting to something, as evidenced by her chills and high body temperature.

"I'll get some water."

He grabbed an otter skin bag from the mule and dashed to the river. When he returned, she covered her mouth and coughed into her hand. A mass of greenish-yellow phlegm flecked with blood filled her palm.

"It hurts when I breathe," she said, looking up at him with glassy eyes. "What's wrong with me?"

Graham sat beside his wife and gave her the water bag. Despite not being a physician, he felt sure she had pneumonia. It was irrelevant whether it was bacterial or viral. He had no medicine.

"You have a sickness in your lungs. Drink plenty of water and rest. We'll stay here until you feel better."

Graham propped her against a saddle. He passed the cup of meat broth when it was ready, but she couldn't drink it because her coughing was so violent. She drifted asleep for a few minutes, then jolted awake with another coughing fit.

"Oh, Graham!" she said, after an hour of brief naps interrupted by coughing. "My chest feels like it's being stabbed!"

He moved closer and listened to her breathing. It was both labored and shallow.

"I'll get the medicine bag," he said, standing up.

"Wait," she said, reaching for him.

"Yes?"

"This might be my time," she said, tears in her eyes.

"Time for what?"

"My journey to the next world."

"Nonsense!"

"When I go, will you place my body next to Small Heart and Rides Alone?"

"Makawee, stop talking like that!"

She leaned forward, coughed, and expelled another mass of bloody phlegm between her legs. Graham held the water bag to her lips and helped her drink.

"Will you do as I ask?"

Graham tried to suppress his anxiety. His wife's critical illness left him feeling helpless.

"Yes! Yes! Now get some rest."

"How can I rest... when I cannot... sleep?"

Graham sprinted to the mule and retrieved the medicine bag. He carried the kit back to the fire and debated whether to use the mercury thermometer to take her temperature, but decided against it. He already knew she had a high fever. What's the point of measuring it if he can't bring it down? The one thing he needed was absent. Penicillin would not become widely available until the next century.

He pulled out the bottle of laudanum and held it up to the fire. A tiny amount of the opium tincture was visible through the green glass.

"Graham, please, will that help me sleep?"

He hesitated. Makawee winced and clutched her chest each time she coughed. Laudanum would likely suppress her cough, but would it do more harm than good?

He uncorked the container, held it to her lips, and tilted the bottle. She swallowed the remaining liquid, leaned back, and rested her head on the saddle. Within a short time, her coughing lessened, then ceased.

"*Diiawachisshik*," she said, as she struggled to keep her eyes open.

"I love you, Makawee."

When she fell asleep, he retrieved a second blanket and covered her.

Graham stood. He walked to the horses and the mule, untied them from a willow, and led them to the river. A full moon cast a long trail of shimmering light onto the rippling surface of the Yellowstone River. He envisioned cuddling with Makawee under a buffalo hide by the river discussing their future. Now, she was too sick to enjoy tonight's moonlit scene.

They were only three days from Long Horse's camp. Someone might come down the river tomorrow or the next day, and he could send for help. He resolved to stay here until she was well enough to ride.

Graham led the horses and mule to his camp after they finished drinking. He made his way to the fire and noticed that Makawee was still sleeping. It was a clear night, so he decided not to disturb her. They would sleep under the stars.

He set his saddle down, unfurled a blanket, and lay beside her. The only sounds breaking the silence of the night were the rippling water and the crackling fire.

Graham glanced at Makawee, who lay perfectly still. Too still.

Something didn't seem right. The darkness made it hard to see her face, so he got on his knees and leaned over her. When he didn't see her chest move up and down, he laid his ear by her nostrils. No breath.

He grabbed her wrist. She had no pulse.

No! Please God, no!

Graham flipped over the medicine bag. The contents spilled onto the ground. His hands trembled as he assembled the monaural stethoscope by screwing the two wooden pieces together. He placed the trumpet-shaped end of the instrument on Makawee's chest before placing the other end to his ear. He heard nothing.

He grasped her shoulders and shook them.

"Makawee! Makawee! Wake up!"

Her head flopped to the side.

Graham held her tightly against him, hugging her limp body. His heart pounded. Tears streamed down his cheeks.

"No! It can't be!" he cried, rocking back and forth on his knees as he clutched his wife's body.

Time seemed to stand still.

It wasn't until a cramp tightened his thigh that he realized he had been kneeling for a long time. He laid her head gently against the saddle and struggled to his feet. He rubbed his legs and walked in a circle around the fire.

His grief morphed into rage. He needed someone or something to blame for his wife's death. Graham clenched his fists, threw back his head, and emitted a scream that echoed against the rock face of Pompeys Pillar.

One thing was obvious. Her god and his god were merciless. Why take the life of a young mother who was days from reuniting with her only child? What divine being behaves that way?

Graham collapsed to the ground and put his head in his hands. Tears wetted his palms and ran down his wrists. His reason for living was dead.

He breathed deeply and tried to clear his mind. *What would Makawee want me to do?*

Graham looked at his wife's peaceful face. She was so beautiful, even in death. He needed to honor her wishes and give her a proper burial.

He lifted her necklace over her head and placed it around his neck. The turtle pendant clacked against the bear claws of his necklace.

Leaning back, he reached into his front jeans pocket and fetched a pocketknife. He unfolded it and cut two inches from the ends of her braids. He retrieved the sutures lying by the empty medicine bag and tied off the ends so the hair would not unravel, then placed both braids in his pocket.

Graham spread a blanket beside Makawee, then rolled her body onto it. He folded it over her torso, but stopped as he held the edges of the blanket at her head. Her lips were blue. The color drained from her face. He leaned over and kissed her before covering her head.

He cut a side wall from the tent and wrapped her in the canvas, then secured it with rope. Physically and mentally exhausted, Graham gulped water from the otter skin bag. He pulled a blanket over himself and placed a hand on his wife's encased body. As he gazed at the stars, he wondered why God had forsaken him.

Graham always said a silent prayer each evening. Not tonight. The Great Spirit or the Holy Spirit, or whatever spiritual entity existed, did not deserve his time or attention. In his hour of grief, bitterness supplanted faith.

The mourning husband only slept a few hours. Graham woke early. After packing, he draped the canvas cocoon over Makawee's horse and tied it to the saddle. He fastened the lead rope of the mule to her horse, then led the animals to the base of Pompeys Pillar.

He tied the equines to a cottonwood tree, then hiked to the base. As he approached the northeast side of the massive rock formation, he noticed hundreds of inscriptions and petroglyphs. A shallow carving beneath an overhang caught his eye. It was inscribed by W. Clark in 1806.

Graham searched through the scree until he discovered a sharp rock. Walking along the face, he located a smooth surface on the sandstone ten feet from Clark's writing. Pushing the point of the rock into the soft sandstone, he carved,

Makawee, 1878

When he returned to the horses, he spoke to his wife as if she were alive.

"One hundred years from now, our great grandchildren will visit this butte. They will see your name and remember you."

He wiped his eyes with the sleeve of his buckskin jacket, then put his hand on the fabric wrap that held his beloved Makawee.

"Let's go home."

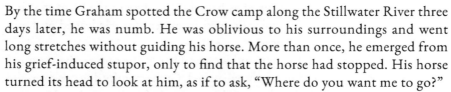

By the time Graham spotted the Crow camp along the Stillwater River three days later, he was numb. He was oblivious to his surroundings and went long stretches without guiding his horse. More than once, he emerged from his grief-induced stupor, only to find that the horse had stopped. His horse turned its head to look at him, as if to ask, "Where do you want me to go?"

Now, as he scanned the cluster of lodges nestled along the river, he thought about the heartbreak Long Horse and his kin were about to experience. How do you tell parents their child died? True, they adopted Makawee when she was a teen. She wasn't a blood relative. But she was their only daughter — and their only living child.

Graham took a swig of water, looped the bag around the pommel, and nudged his horse.

"Let's go tell your family you've come home," he said to Makawee.

Two Crow warriors galloped to meet the stranger. They approached Graham cautiously while cradling rifles.

"*Kahée!*" Graham said, raising his hand to show he was unarmed. He explained he was the son-in-law of Chief Long Horse.

The men nodded and let him pass. Graham overheard them talking. They were curious about who was wrapped in the buffalo hide. He ignored them. They would learn soon enough with the rest of the village about his personal tragedy.

One warrior rode ahead to announce a visitor. As Graham rode through the camp, people stopped what they were doing and pointed to the encased body.

Long Horse and Fox Woman stood at the front of their tepee as Graham dismounted. He practiced the first thing he would say to Makawee's parents. But in this moment, as they anxiously peered over his shoulder at the horse carrying a body, he blurted out the harsh truth.

"*Kalakóolassaa-k.*" ["She died"]

Fox Woman ran and hugged the canvas wrap. She wailed, threw her arms into the air, and collapsed next to the horse.

Word spread quickly that Makawee's body was in the cocoon. Within minutes, villagers gathered. They released the corpse from the horse and set it down on the ground. The women formed a circle around the deceased and sang songs of anguish.

Graham looked at Long Horse, who stood motionless. He wanted to tell his father-in-law so many things, starting with the sorrow in his heart at losing the love of his life. But this was not the time. The chief ducked inside the lodge.

Long Horse's reaction appalled him. Was Makawee's father unable to reconcile with his daughter, even after her death?

A moment later, the chief exited his lodge with Nahkash. The noise confused and frightened the girl.

Graham squatted, held out his arms, and called to her.

"Daddy!" the little girl shouted as she ran to his embrace.

"Oh, honey, Daddy missed you so much!" He hugged the girl tightly and planted a kiss on her cheek.

"Where is *Naha?*" [Mommy]

Graham pushed Nahkash away while holding onto her arms. He looked into her eyes and swallowed hard.

"Mommy got a terrible sickness and... and she died."

Nahkash screamed and ran to Fox Woman, who was lying on the burial wrap and weeping. The other women in the village chanted and danced in a circle of mourning. The little girl tried to comfort her grandmother and grieve her mother's death at the same time.

Graham couldn't listen to the screaming and wailing. He felt sick to his stomach, and he thought he might vomit.

Leaving the horses and the mule, he meandered through the camp, then along the river. The sounds of despair were too much for him to bear. He needed to find a place where he could escape.

Eventually, he tossed his hat on the ground and slumped beside a cluster of willows to collect his thoughts. Makawee's family would take care of the funeral preparations, and they would give his wife a traditional Crow service. He was adamant about burying her in the same place as Rides Alone and Small Heart, their son who was born prematurely.

He knelt by the river and cupped his hands. He slurped the cool water, then splashed his face and rubbed his eyes.

You've got a little girl who needs you, he thought. He would get through the next few days if he focused on her. He donned his hat and trudged back to camp, where the wailing continued unabated into the night.

Graham led two dozen people up the Stillwater River in the late morning. Nahkash rode with her father, who led the horse that carried Makawee's body. Long Horse and Fox Woman were next in line, and everyone else followed. Lamentations and sounds of anguish were replaced with a somber procession. Only two sounds broke the silence - leaves rustling in the trees and an occasional snorting horse.

While they rode, Graham recalled his conversation with the chief the previous evening. He and Fox Woman wanted to bury their daughter close to the village. When Graham explained his wife's wish to be laid to rest by her brother and unborn child, they agreed. Rather than place Makawee's body in a tree, the chief said they would bury her remains. Since it had been three days since she died, her spirit already ascended to the heavens.

The funeral party arrived at a grove of black cottonwood trees. Graham slid off his horse and helped Nahkash down. He grabbed a spade and walked with his daughter to the large tree where he carved their initials of their family years earlier. A heart encircled the initials G, M, and N. He was comforted to see the carving in the rough bark was still legible.

"Wait here," he said to Nahkash.

He stood at the base of the majestic tree and took three steps from the trunk. He sunk the spade into the soft earth, then nodded. A group of men with shovels came forward and began digging the grave.

While the men worked, Graham sat with Nahkash under the tree and cherished the memories he shared with Makawee on this riverbank. They made love here. They planned their wedding and dreamed dreams.

This place witnessed great sadness as well. The villagers buried Rides Alone a short distance away. Graham and Makawee buried Small Heart's remains on the other side of the tree.

After finishing their work, the men untied the burial wrap from the horse and laid it beside the grave. Fox Woman took Nahkash's hand. Together they placed a bouquet of yellow arrow leaf balsamroot flowers on the canvas.

Graham removed a bear claw from his necklace last evening. He kneeled and tucked it under a flap of the canvas. He brought his hand to his mouth, then placed his fingers on the wrap.

"*Shia-nuk*," ["See you later"] he said, wishing it were true.

The grave digging crew filled the hole after lowering the body into the tomb. A woman started chanting, and others joined in. Graham leaned against the tree with Nahkash standing between his legs. He gently squeezed her shoulders.

When the last shovel of dirt was tossed on the mound, the villagers silently mounted their horses and rode toward camp. Makawee's immediate family stayed behind.

Graham reached into his jeans pocket and extracted a braid of Makawee's hair. He walked to Fox Woman and held out his hand, palm up.

"Here's something you can keep as a memory."

Tears streamed down her cheeks as she plucked the braid from his hand and held it tightly to her chest. She opened her arms and embraced him.

"Daddy?"

"Yes?"

"How will I remember *Naha*?"

Graham removed the obsidian necklace from around his neck and placed it over his daughter's head.

"Do you know what your name means?"

"Turtle."

"That's right."

He held up the green turtle pendant for her to see.

"Your mother wore this every day. You were always with her. Now, she will always be with you."

Chapter Twenty-Three

Guide My Path

June, 1878

The tip of the knife turned blue as Graham held it over the flame. He rested his left arm on his knee with his palm facing up. Holding the handle of the Bowie knife between his thumb and forefinger, he took a deep breath and etched a one-inch gash on the underside of his forearm. Clenching his teeth, he cut three additional lines to form the letter *M*.

The self-inflicted wounds were painful. He applied a water-soaked cloth to the lacerations to stop the bleeding and leaned against the willow backrest outside his tent. He gained a new appreciation of the pain Makawee endured when she cut herself after losing Small Heart. The crude tattoo was his way of keeping her memory alive.

Two months passed since they buried Makawee. He felt her absence keenly. It was a blessing to spend time with Nahkash, but seeing her only seemed to amplify his grief. As he looked at his daughter's eyes, images of her mother flashed before him.

Graham thought about his conversations with Fox Woman and Long Horse after the funeral. Makawee's mother was gracious, even amid her sorrow. She harbored no ill feelings toward him or what happened to her daughter. She adored Nahkash and was pleased to be raising the child.

Much to Graham's surprise, Long Horse was contrite. The chief was scarred by his daughter's death. He expressed to Graham his remorse for pushing Makawee away because of her adoption of a Sioux baby. Long Horse felt relieved when Graham assured him that a Sioux family adopted the child and would love and care for him.

Fox Woman and Long Horse invited him to stay in their village as long as he liked. Graham wondered if they extended this invitation because he might take Nahkash when he left. He told them he needed time to think.

Graham lifted the cloth and gazed at the red and swollen wounds. He hoped the flame sanitized the blade so they would not become infected. He planned to get a traditional tattoo in the future.

Seeing the *M* on his arm, he recalled the promise he made to his wife last Christmas.

"Do you pledge Nahkash will be raised in a Crow village?" she asked.

He made a commitment, and he intended to keep it, even though it would have significant consequences. He pictured himself living on the reservation and realized he wouldn't be content. Reluctantly, he decided his daughter would stay, and he would leave. Nahkash was in the loving home of her grandparents. She would learn the ways of the Crow people, and he would fulfill the pledge to his late wife.

His only remaining question — where would he go? The answer became apparent after many sleepless nights and careful thought. He would go home. For Graham, that was not a place, it was a time. He belonged in the latter half of the twentieth century. There was no longer anything keeping him here. His entire future relied on a life with Makawee, but she was gone.

Tomorrow, he would say goodbye to Nahkash, ride to the Bighorn Mountains, and ascend to the Medicine Wheel. Graham touched the bear claws suspended on his necklace. He had a ticket home.

All he needed was a full moon and a benevolent spirit to grant his request.

Graham stood outside the lodge, hat in hand. He gripped the brim, silently practicing what he would say to his daughter. His decision made sense. Makawee was a Crow, and he was a *baashchiile*. Nahkash's mother insisted their daughter be raised in the Crow culture. By allowing Nahakash to stay with her grandparents, he was fulfilling his obligation. It was better for everyone to part ways — at least, that's what he told himself.

Nahkash dashed from the lodge and ran towards her father.

"Daddy! What are we going to do today? Will you take me fishing?"

Fox Woman and Long Horse followed their granddaughter out of the tepee. Graham informed them earlier of his plans. He kept his destination a secret and only mentioned he would travel east and not return. They had mixed emotions about his decision. While they hoped Nahkash's father would be there for her, it elated them to raise her in the village.

Graham squatted, dropped his hat, and grasped the girl's hands.

"Nahkash, do you love your grandparents?"

"Oh, yes!" she said, turning and smiling at them. "I'm learning so much. I can cook, and I can almost get on a horse by myself."

"They care for you deeply. As much as your mother."

Nahkash looked down and clutched the turtle pendant hanging from her neck. "I miss *Naha*."

"I miss her, too. Your mother wanted you to live among the Crow people, and you are happy here. I want that, too, but..." Graham felt a lump form in his throat. "But I am a white man."

Nahkash shrugged her shoulders, as if to say, "What difference does that make?"

Graham reflected on his daughter's innocence. *Why do we readily accept others as children, but reject those who are not like us as adults?*

"Just like you are happy living with your grandparents, I wish to live among my people."

Her brow creased.

"Are you going away?"

"Yes."

The girl paused before inquiring, "When will you return?"

Tears welled in Graham's eyes. He dreaded this question. Should he lie and give her hope about seeing her father again, or should he tell her the truth?

"I am traveling to a distant land and... I will not be back."

Nahkash leaped forward and hugged him by throwing her arms around his neck.

"No! Don't leave, Daddy!"

He felt her tears wet his shoulder as she clung onto him.

Graham stood. Nahkash threw her legs around his waist and pressed her cheek against his beard. He walked in a circle, using soothing tones to comfort the girl and repeatedly whispering "I love you" into her ear.

He settled her down, gave her to Fox Woman, and picked up his hat.

"Nahkash, I will never forget you. You will always be my little girl."

Graham kissed her on the cheek and climbed onto his mare. He wiped his eyes with the sleeve of his coat and cast a last glance at Nahkash, who was crying on her grandmother's shoulder.

"Shia-nuk," he said to his family, as he urged his horse into a trot.

His choice of words suggested they might meet again, but he knew better.

This was a final goodbye.

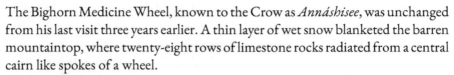

The Bighorn Medicine Wheel, known to the Crow as *Annáshisee*, was unchanged from his last visit three years earlier. A thin layer of wet snow blanketed the barren mountaintop, where twenty-eight rows of limestone rocks radiated from a central cairn like spokes of a wheel.

Graham dismounted, then removed the saddle and bridle from his horse. He grabbed a sack of dried beef and biscuits, looped a water bottle over his head, and tucked a blanket under his arm. Carrying the Spencer carbine and the cloth bag, he walked to the cairn.

As Graham waited for the sun to set and a full moon to rise, he removed his hat, placed it on the cairn, and sat down, resting his head against the rock wall behind him. He set the butt of the rifle on the ground and lay the barrel against his shoulder. He checked the cylinder of his Colt to ensure it was loaded and placed it on his lap.

It was a four-day ride from the northern banks of the Stillwater River. Graham considered the range of emotions he experienced on his way to this sacred place.

He wept the first night. The sounds of Nahkash crying as he departed from Long Horse's camp lingered in his head. His heart ached all over again. He lost Makawee and voluntarily surrendered his daughter. How much could a man bear in such a short time? While he sat by the fire that night grieving his losses, a band of coyotes howled, amplifying his melancholy mood.

Graham second-guessed his decision. Was this the right thing to do? Or was he being selfish?

His thoughts alternated between embracing his future in the next century and staying in the present with a daughter he adored. Upon reaching the Bighorn Mountains, Graham knew he crossed the Rubicon. The draw of the time portal was irresistible, as it offered him the opportunity to return home. The potential of a fresh start helped suppress the bitter feelings of losing his Crow family.

Now, Graham pulled the eagle-bear claw necklace from under his coat. He rubbed the smooth edges of the pendant, and touched the sharp points of the grizzly bear claws. The only thing he needed was to have the spirits grant his petition to return to his rightful time.

"Kahée!" a man's voice called out from the perimeter of the stone circle.

Graham snatched the revolver and aimed it in the voice's direction.

"Who's there?" he asked in Apsáalooke. He scrambled to his feet and held the pistol in a firing position.

A shadowy figure emerged from the tree line and walked out into the open. Graham could see he was unarmed. As the man drew closer, Graham lowered his weapon. The stranger was an elderly Indian dressed in a tunic and leggings.

"You have returned," the old man said, stopping ten feet from the cairn.

Graham tucked the pistol into his belt. He recognized Wind at Night, the shaman who appeared the evening Graham petitioned the spirits to return home after Long Horse promised Black Hawk he could marry Makawee.

"Is Eagle Bear here to connect with the spirits?"

"Yes. Are they active tonight?" Graham asked, trying to assess his chances of success.

"They are here," the enigmatic Indian said. It wasn't the full-throated endorsement Graham hoped to hear.

"I have my sacred necklace," Graham said, clutching the eagle pendant and bear claws under his buckskin jacket.

"Where do you seek to go?"

"Home."

It was the truth, even though it may not have been what the old man wanted to hear.

"If that is your destiny, your petition will be granted."

What's that supposed to mean? he thought.

"I'm not supposed to be here," Graham said, with an edginess to his voice.

"You are in the wrong state of mind."

Graham pursed his lips. He reminded himself to stay calm.

"In what way?"

"The spirits will not heed demands, only requests."

Wind at Night admonished him for the same fault the last time they spoke.

"I will *ask* the spirits to guide me," said Graham, attempting to conceal his annoyance.

Wind at Night stepped closer. Graham could discern the wrinkles lining the old man's face and his deep-set brown eyes.

"Consider what you have left undone, and take the path presented to you."

Graham's brow furrowed.

"What's left to do?"

Wind at Night shrugged.

"The path to a man's destiny is never a straight line."

That may be true, but right now I want a one-way ticket home, Graham thought. He grew tired of the shaman's cryptic statements.

He walked to the other side of the cairn and stared at the moon shining on the Bighorn Basin. The conditions were perfect for a vision quest. He just needed to set his mind straight. Perhaps Wind at Night could advise him on the ideal words to use.

When he turned back to ask the old man for guidance, he was gone.

Graham was alone on the mountaintop, but hoped a spiritual presence would soon join him.

He prepared for the ritual by placing the carbine, the revolver, and his sack of food next to the cairn. He stood at the southeast face of the rock tower. A full moon peeked above the horizon. Graham pulled the eagle-bear claw necklace from beneath his shirt and placed it on the front of his jacket.

Closing his eyes, he said, "Holy Spirit, hear my prayer. Thank you for the blessings of the earth. Open my eyes. Open my ears. Open my heart. Guide my path!"

Initially, the movements of the heavenly bodies were imperceptible. The full moon moved slowly from left to right in an arc toward the western horizon. When it disappeared, it was replaced on the opposite horizon by the sun, which raced across the sky in a brief but brilliant flash of light. The moon rose after the sun disappeared, creating a night sky that lasted a few seconds before the sun rose again. The pattern of day and night repeated until the sky was a blur of light and dark.

Graham felt dizzy. He sat with his back against the cairn. The heavens slowed and eventually stopped. A morning sun appeared stationary in the eastern sky. He remained conscious throughout the mystical event that lasted less than a minute.

Graham stood and scanned the mountaintop, expecting to see a post-and-rope fence encircling the Medicine Wheel. If he were in the twentieth century, visitors would have adorned the rope with an array of items such as tobacco bundles, feathers, dream catchers, and prayer flags. There was no enclosure around the ancient wheel.

Dammit! Graham thought. *I didn't travel forward in time. I must have imagined it.*

"Thanks for nothing!" he yelled, shaking his fist at the sky. "You took away everyone I care about, and now you deny my request to go home?"

He shook his head. It would be another twenty-eight days before he could attempt to travel home again. He had no choice but to find a place to camp in the valley until the next full moon. He picked up the blanket, carbine, and sack, then trudged to the perimeter to fetch his horse.

The mare was gone. He called and whistled, but there was no response. When he searched the area, he noticed the saddle and bridle were missing. It was as if he never set foot on this mountain.

Graham brought his hand to his mouth. His eyes grew wide. Could this mean he traveled back in time? He wracked his brain, trying to visualize the rotation of the sky during his brief visioning experience. No, the heavens moved in the usual pattern. He was propelled into the future, but which year?

He dropped his belongings and sat on the rocky soil. What now? He knew *where* he was, but not *when*. With no horse and few options, he decided to hike down the rocky ridge to the Bighorn River. If he followed the stream, he would eventually reach a camp or settlement.

Graham packed by rolling the blanket, tying a knot in the food sack, and tossing both over his shoulder. After taking a final look at the Medicine Wheel, he picked up his carbine, and trudged down the mountain.

The round boat lay upside-down in a willow thicket by the river. Someone placed a broad-bladed paddle against the base of the shrubs. He strained to see if the owner was nearby, peering upstream and downstream. He could see no one.

Graham observed the Nez Perce use bull boats like this one. Indians and fur traders made them by covering a cottonwood pole framework with raw buffalo hide, hair facing outward. The lightweight boats were useful for fishing and crossing rivers. Someone concealed this one to use later.

He dragged the boat to the riverbank, tossed his belongings and the paddle into the circular watercraft, and set it afloat. After confirming it was watertight, he shoved off from the shore and got in. It took a few minutes for Graham to figure out how to balance the flat-bottomed boat while perched on his knees. Once he got the hang of it, he dipped the oar into the water and steered toward the center of the river.

He didn't have to do much work. The current carried him downstream. He used the paddle as a rudder to keep the boat in the middle of the river and made minor course corrections as needed. He welcomed the opportunity to travel by water and give his fatigued legs a rest.

Graham hiked along the Bighorn River for almost fifty miles. So far, he had not observed any signs of a camp but knew this could change at any moment.

He needed to be vigilant, as he did not know if those he encountered would be friendly or hostile.

The bull boat bobbed along the river, which deepened and widened as it flowed north. He came ashore in the evening. Using sticks to prop up the upturned boat, he converted it into a temporary shelter.

After paddling for an hour the next morning, Graham spotted a campfire in the distance. Erring on the side of caution, he paddled toward the bank and disembarked. Peering from behind a rock, he observed a man cooking outside a tent. A dozen canine pelts were suspended from a rope tied between two trees.

Wolfer, Graham thought. *I have no desire to talk to him.*

He portaged this section, staying hidden among the trees on the opposite bank, before returning to the river.

He floated around a bend on his fourth day and saw something that caught him off guard. A bridge spanned the Bighorn River just south of where it emptied into the Yellowstone River. Graham steered the tiny vessel toward the bank and pulled it ashore. Gathering his things, he hiked up the slope.

This structure wasn't made for wagons and horses. It was a railroad bridge! The Northern Pacific Railroad had not advanced their line this far west in 1878. This could only mean one thing.

I moved forward in time, he thought.

A small structure and several whitewashed, clapboard buildings lined the tracks to the east. He followed the rails to a covered platform. A sign suspended by chains swung in the hot summer breeze, announcing the stop: "Welcome to Big Horn City, Montana Territory."

Another clue. Montana was still a territory. It had not yet been admitted to the Union.

Advertisers plastered the center wall on the platform with papers. Eager to read the notices, Graham dropped the blanket and sack at his feet. Doctors, midwives, and attorneys advertised their services. Banks offered loans. A stagecoach line promoted service from the Cinnabar Station into Yellowstone National Park. By examining a train schedule with arrival and departure times, he discovered it was 1884.

Taking up most of the wall space was a poster of Buffalo Bill's Wild West exhibition, measuring two feet by three feet. The placard advertised a host of attractions, including cow-boys, bronco busting, roping, Indian chiefs, Mexican vaqueros, buffalos, mountain elk, Texas steers, and other wild animals. Annie Oakley was one of the featured acts. The list of performers didn't include Sitting Bull, even though he traveled with the show for a season.

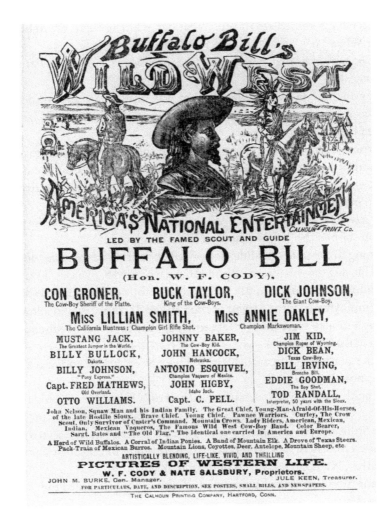

He was reading about the showman's tour when a gust of wind passed over the platform. A newspaper clipping tore loose from the wall and fluttered along the planks. He used his boot to trap it, then picked it up.

HELP WANTED. Stage Hands, Animal Handlers, and Teamsters. Hard Work, Long Hours, Extensive Travel. Be a part of Buffalo Bill's Wild West exhibition! Applications accepted by Mr. John M. Burke, General Manager.

Graham looked at the flyer and gazed at the employment ad in his hand. Did these omens foretell his immediate future? What did Wind at Night say to him at the Medicine Wheel?

"Take the path presented to you, even if it is unexpected. Consider what you have left undone."

There was only one way to learn what was unfinished. He would pursue working as a laborer with the exhibition — something he would have never considered before his vision quest.

The promoters listed the show's itinerary for the year. He ran his finger down the column of locations and dates. The exhibition appeared in the northeast earlier. It would tour towns along the Ohio River in the fall. The troupe was booked to perform in Cairo, Illinois in late November.

That's where I'll meet the traveling show and submit my application, he thought.

Graham stashed the 'help wanted' ad in his back pocket.

Returning to the train schedule, he noticed an eastbound train was due within the hour. He dug into his jeans and pulled out a wrinkled bank note. There was no ticket window, so he hoped to pay the conductor for a one-way fare to Bismarck. Finding employment in the capital of the Dakota Territory would allow him to save enough money for a steamer fare to Cairo, the town at the junction of the Ohio and Mississippi Rivers.

Graham squatted and sat against a post. He removed his hat and rested his head on the support column.

When he closed his eyes, his mind wandered to Nahkash. She would be twelve years old in 1884. What was life like on the reservation? He was tempted to visit her in the Stillwater River Valley by taking the train west, but he rejected the idea. He promised Makawee they would raise their daughter in the Crow culture. Just like her father, Nahkash needed to find her own path.

A distant rumbling woke him from his slumber. He scrambled to his feet and donned his hat.

The forlorn sound of a train whistle pierced the afternoon air. The steam locomotive's brakes hissed as it stopped beside the platform. Two minutes later, the whistle blew, the couplings between the cars clanked, and the train chugged from Big Horn City with one additional passenger.

A young man was headed east to join the Wild West.

About the Series

The Story Behind the *Frontier Traveler Series*

My debut novel, *Burning Ground,* was published in July 2021. It is part autobiography, part historical, and part fiction. It garnered numerous awards, including:

- Wyoming State Historical Society, First Place - Publications Category.

- Best Multicultural Fiction Book of 2021 by American Book Fest.

- Category Finalist for the 2022 Eric Hoffer Book Award.

- 2022 IPPY Award Bronze Medal Winner for Best Regional Fiction.

Two seminal events in my life inspired the book. I met Redfield, a Crow Indian, as a teenager. He lived a simple life but had a profound effect on the way I saw the world. As a young man, I spent a summer in Yellowstone National Park giving guided tours on Yellowstone Lake. The cultural and geological history of the park fascinated me. When I was not working, I spent my days exploring all corners of that magnificent land, often in the backcountry.

The following stories are part of the *Frontier Traveler series*.

- *Burning Ground* (Book 1)

Graham Davidson travels back in time and joins the 1871 Hayden Expedition as it explores the future Yellowstone National Park, facing the perils of an uncharted wilderness while falling in love with a Crow woman, Makawee.

- *Fatal Ground* (Book 2)

Graham thought his most difficult test was earning the right to marry Makawee. But nothing compared to his anxiety as he rode into the Little Bighorn Valley in 1876 as a scout for Custer.

- *Bitter Ground* (Book 3)

Graham and his family join the Nez Perce in their flight from the US army in 1877. The caravan treks through Idaho, Yellowstone National Park, and Montana. The exiled people hope to reach Canada, where Lakota Chief Sitting Bull and his followers have taken refuge.

(If you enjoyed this story, please consider leaving a review on Amazon or Goodreads. Thank you!)

<u>Future Release</u>

- *Sacred Ground* (Book 4)

Graham joins Buffalo Bill Cody's Wild West show in 1884 as it tours America and Europe. When Graham learns his adopted son Dakkoótee is living with a Sioux tribe near Wounded Knee, he races to save him from the impending massacre.

About the Author

David Allan Galloway grew up in rural Pennsylvania near Gettysburg. After a long career in manufacturing and writing a bestselling nonfiction book, *Safety WALK Safety TALK*, he launched a second career as a novelist.

He enjoys reading about adventurers and explorers, traveling internationally, riding a recumbent tandem bike, and spending time with his four grandchildren. David lives in Springboro, Ohio, with his wife, Leesa.

If you would like to read about news or history related to Yellowstone or our national parks, or be notified when the next novel in the Frontier Traveler series will be released, subscribe to David's free newsletter on his website:

dagalloway.com

Acknowledgments

Bitter Ground is centered on the flight of the Nez Perce from the army in 1877. Although it is a work of fiction, the dates, events, and people in this story are historically inspired. I kept the important elements of this tragic tale intact while imagining how Graham and his family would interact with the principal characters during their epic fight for survival.

I encourage those who want to read a more complete account of the non-treaty Nez Perce to consider the many nonfiction books and references about this historical event, including the ones listed below.

Period photographs augment the reader's experience. You can find more information about these people and images on the "Notes" pages.

Among the many sources I used for writing this novel, the following are noteworthy.

- The reference I most relied upon when writing the story was Daniel Sharfstein's *Thunder in the Mountains: Chief Joseph, Oliver Otis Howard, and the Nez Perce War*. Sharfstein's research was invaluable as I imagined actions and dialogue among the military and Native American leaders.

- It was a blessing to consult L.V. McWhorter's version of the Nez Perce experience as told to him by a young man who was actually there. *Yellow Wolf: His Own Story* provided keen insight on the events from the perspective of Chief Joseph's nephew. It helped me bring this warrior to life in my novel.

- Historian and scholar Elliott West's *The Last Indian War: The Nez Perce Story (Pivotal Moments in American History)* contains many references that helped complete the picture of this epic journey.

- Jerome Greene consulted government and military records, newspaper reports, and other documents in his book, *Nez Perce Summer, 1877: The U.S. Army and the Nee-Me-Poos Crisis.*

- Most accounts of the Nez Perce flight end with Chief Joseph's surrender in northern Montana. I envisioned Graham and his family escaping north of the "Medicine Line" with a group that escaped capture. Detailed accounts of the non-treaty bands' life in Canada are well documented by Jerome Greene in *Beyond Bear's Paw: The Nez Perce Indians in Canada.*

I am grateful to those who read some or all of the manuscript and provided feedback or advice.

Thanks to Heidi Archer, Laurie Baker, Brenda Barrett, Lee Bendtsen, Yvonne Bennett, Dean Benjamin, Wes Bolyard, Monica Bond, Dave Bonistall, Lisa Briem, Cindy Carlson, Daniel Clark, Kathy Collins, Cherie Davis, Cindy DiMaggio, Vicki Dismuke, Christina Duddy, Glenn Elms, Janelle Erwin, Lori Fahrbach, Deb Fisher, David Fitz-Gerald, Jill Frego, Ann Furlough, Gail Gardner, Nancy Hart, Daphne Harver, Becky Havey, Elaine Henry, Tamsen Hert, Kathleen Howard, William Igoe, Adele Jacobson, Marie Johns, Deb Keller, Christiana Kettelkamp, Kay Kinney, Katie LaSalle-Lowry, Carol LeCrone, Rich Leever, Dan MacDuff, Greg Marchand, Bill Markley, Arnold Marsden, William Martin, Marilyn Mcleod, Sherrill Medley, Bob Newton, William Platt, Joleen Ramirez, Robyn Rofkar, Mickey Rup, Connie Sauerbrei, Hans Schmellencamp, Jamie Seagroves, Polly Scoville, Launi Shellard, Yvonne Siemer, Adam Simpson, David Sinkhorn, Dan Small, Bill Smith, Diane Sperber, Jim Steele, Betsy Steele, Mark Swenson, Renee Swickard, Kent Taylor, Dawn Thomas, Wanda Titman, Deborah Turman, James Tyrone, Joette Van Ness, Linda Waits, Melanie Wallace, Frank Wallis, Richard Warner, and Florence Woods.

A special thanks to Brian R. Smith, a firearms historian who generously advised me on weapons and other story elements. His attention to detail and feedback strengthened the historical accuracy of the novel.

The cover of this book is a painting by Kristin Llamas of Nashville, Tennessee. Armed with only the title and a description of the book, she channeled her creative talents. The poignant illustration that emerged from her blank canvas perfectly captures the essence of the story. (She is also the artist behind the cover for *Fatal Ground*). Thank you, Kristin!

An enormous thank-you to my bride of forty-four years, Leesa. She is my first-line editor. Leesa made invaluable suggestions that enhanced and clarified the manuscript. Her love and encouragement kept me going.

Notes

Foreward

Map: The flight of the Nez Perce and key battle sites. *United States Department of Agriculture-Forest Service - https://commons.wikimedia.org/w/index.php?curid=18177945*

Prologue

General Winfield Scott Hancock (1824 – 1886) served in the Army for four decades, including service in the Mexican–American War and as a Union general in the American Civil War. Known to his Army colleagues as "Hancock the Superb," he was noted in particular for his personal leadership at the Battle of Gettysburg in 1863. Hancock's reputation as a war hero, combined with his status as a Unionist and supporter of states' rights, made him a potential presidential candidate. When the Democrats nominated him for President in 1880, he ran a strong campaign, but was narrowly defeated by Republican James A. Garfield. Hancock's last public service involved the oversight of President Ulysses S. Grant's funeral procession in 1885.

General Oliver Otis Howard (1830 – 1909) was a career United States Army officer and a Union general in the Civil War. As a brigade commander in the Army of the Potomac, Howard lost his right arm while leading his men against Confederate forces at the Battle of Fair Oaks in 1862, an action which later earned him the Medal of Honor. As a corps commander, he suffered two major defeats at Chancellorsville and Gettysburg in May and July 1863. Howard commanded troops in the West, conducting a famous campaign against the

Nez Perce tribe, led by Chief Joseph. Known as the "Christian General" because he tried to base his policy decisions on his deep, evangelical piety, he was given charge of the Freedmen's Bureau in mid-1865, with the mission of integrating the former slaves into Southern society and politics during the second phase of the Reconstruction Era. Howard was a leader in promoting higher education for freedmen, most notably in founding Howard University in Washington and serving as its president 1867–73; and aided in the charter of Clark Atlanta University in 1867.

Lewis Addison Armistead (1817 – 1863) was a United States Army officer who became a brigadier general in the Confederate States Army during the American Civil War. On July 3, 1863, as part of Pickett's Charge during the Battle of Gettysburg, Armistead led his brigade to the farthest point reached by Confederate forces during the charge, a point now referred to as the high-water mark of the Confederacy. However, he and his men were overwhelmed, and he was wounded and captured by Union troops. He died in a field hospital two days later.

The Soldier's Prayer Book. Arranged from The Book of Common Prayer with Additional Collections and Hymns. Protestant Episcopal Book Society. 1224 Chestnut Street, Philadelphia. June, 1863.

Adolph von Steinwehr was born in Blankenburg, in the Duchy of Brunswick, Germany, the son of a military family. At the start of the Civil War, Steinwehr raised a regiment, consisting primarily of German immigrants. These volunteers largely made up the XI Corps. One brigade within the corps was the victim of the surprise flanking attack by Stonewall Jackson at Chancellorsville on May 2, 1863. The men rapidly withdrew from the enemy, causing outside observers to label the volunteers as cowards. During the Battle of Gettysburg, confederate troops forced the XI corps to retreat through the town to Cemetery Hill. These two defeats seriously degraded the combat effectiveness of the corps and humiliated many of the German immigrant soldiers.

Battle Hymn of the Republic also known as "Mine Eyes Have Seen the Glory" or "Glory, Glory Hallelujah" outside of the United States, is a popular American patriotic song written by the abolitionist writer Julia Ward Howe. She adapted her song from the popular soldiers' song "John Brown's Body" in November

1861, and first published it in The Atlantic Monthly in February 1862. In contrast to the lyrics of the soldiers' song, her version links the Union cause with God's vengeance at the Day of Judgment (through allusions to biblical passages such as Isaiah 63:1–6 and Revelation 14:14–19).

Photo: O'Sullivan, Timothy H, photographer. Battlefield of Gettysburg. Bodies of dead Federal soldiers on the field of the first day's battle. Pennsylvania United States Gettysburg, None. [Photographed 1863 July, printed between 1880 and 1889] Photograph. https://www.loc.gov/item/2012647835/.

Tuekakas (Old Chief Joseph) (c. 1785-1871) was leader of the Wallowa Band of the Nez Perce. Old Joseph was one of the first Nez Percé converts to Christianity and a vigorous advocate of the tribe's early peace with whites. In 1855 he aided Washington's territorial governor and set up a Nez Percé reservation that expanded from Oregon into Idaho. The Nez Perce agreed to give up a section of their tribal lands in return for an assurance whites would not intrude upon the sacred Wallowa Valley. Nevertheless, in 1863, following a gold rush in Nez Percé territory, the federal government took back approximately 6 million acres (24,000 km2) of this land. That confined the Nez Percé to a 750,000-acre (3,000 km2) reservation in Idaho, which was only one tenth its previous size.

Hallalhotsoot (Chief Lawyer) (c. 1797–1876) was a leader of the Nez Perce. He was the son of Twisted Hair, who welcomed and befriended the exhausted Lewis and Clark Expedition in 1805. His mother was a Flathead woman. Lawyer learned the languages of his parents and knew some English. After a group of missionaries arrived at Whitman Mission Station in Waiilatpu in 1838, Lawyer taught Asa Bowen Smith the Nez Perce language, from which Smith developed a grammar and dictionary entitled Grammar of the Language of the Nez Perces Indians. In 1855, he took part in the Walla Walla Council and signed the Treaty of Stevens. This obtained for him a reservation to the greater part of his territory, between the Clearwater and Salmon rivers. After gold was discovered in Pierce in 1860, Lawyer agreed to new cessions of land in the Treaty of 1863, in 1868, which Old Joseph did not accept and considered it a betrayal. Therefore, in 1872, Hallalhotsoot was displaced by Chief Joseph as the head of the tribe.

Henry Harmon Spalding (1803–1874) and his wife Eliza Hart Spalding (1807–1851) were prominent Presbyterian missionaries and educators working primarily with the Nez Perce in the U.S. Pacific Northwest. The Spaldings and their fellow missionaries were among the earliest Americans to travel across the western plains, through the Rocky Mountains and into the lands of the Pacific Northwest to their religious missions in what would become the states of Idaho and Washington. Their missionary party of five, including Marcus Whitman and his wife Narcissa and William H. Gray, joined with a group of fur traders to create the first wagon train along the Oregon Trail.

Treaty between the United States of America and the Nez Perce Tribe of Indians. Concluded June 9, 1863; Ratification advised April 17, 1867; Proclaimed April 20, 1867.

Calvin Henry Hale (1818 – 1887) was an American settler in the Washington Territory who became involved in territorial government. In 1862 he was appointed Superintendent of Indian Affairs in the territory which included Washington and Idaho.

Chapter Two (Volatile Valley)

Photo: *Chief Joseph_1877* by Orlando S Goff. (public domain).

Photo: *Ollokot, war chief for the Nez Perce*, Washington State, May 1877. Ellensburg Heritage. Kittitas Valley Crossroads Collection. (public domain).

Letter from Indian Agent John Monteith. "Report of the Commissioner of Indian Affairs," pp. 505-879. In U.S. House. 44th Congress, 1st Session. *Report of the Secretary of the Interior, 1875* (H.Ex.Doc.1, Pt. 5, Vol. 1). Washington: Government Printing Office, 1876. (*Serial Set* 1680).

Photo: *Oliver Otis Howard.* Cleaveland, N. and A. S. Packard. History of Bowdoin College: with biographical sketches of its graduates from 1806 to 1879, inclusive. J.R. Osgood & Co., Boston. 1882. (public domain).

Photo: *Spalding Mission*, Nez Perce Encampment, Northwest Museum of Arts and Culture, circa 1880 (public domain).

An Indian's View of Indian Affairs. Introduction by William H. Hare. by Chief Joseph. North American Review 128 (April 1879): 412–33.

Chapter Three (Ultimatum)

Yellow Wolf (aka, Himiin Maqsmaqs, Five Times Looking Through, and White Thunder) was born in 1856 in the Wallowa Valley. He had a prominent role in the Nez Perce War of 1877, taking part in every battle during the campaign. He chose not to surrender with Young Joseph at Bears Paw, but escaped to Sitting Bull's camp of exiled Hunkpapa Sioux in Canada. He eventually returned to Idaho, where he was arrested and sent to Indian Territory in Oklahoma. Yellow Wolf was relocated permanently to the Colville Reservation in 1885. He died on August 21, 1935 at Nespelem, Washington.

Photo of *Yellow Wolf*, unknown date. University of Idaho (public domain).

The creek and the town of *Asotin* would eventually take their name from a mispronunciation of Hesuutin, a Nez Perce word that means "place of the eels."

Drawing: Fort Lapwai, Idaho by Vincent Colyer. 1877.

Photo: *Looking Glass*, a Nez Perce' chief, on horseback in front of a tepee, 1877 - NARA - 530914.tif. (public domain).

Chapter Four (Retribution)

Photo: The Steamer *Spokane*. Historic Photographs Subject File https://libraries.wsu.edu/masc/finders/pc2.htm at Washington State University Libraries' Manuscripts, Archives, and Special Collections (MASC) https://libraries.wsu.edu/masc (public domain).

Chapter Five (Chaotic Canyon)

Photo: Battle of White Bird Canyon Site, Nez Perce National Historical Park, White Bird, Idaho, CC BY-SA 2.0, https://commons.wikimedia.org/w/index.php?curid=99515364. Ken Lund from Reno, Nevada, USA

Chapter Six (Raining Bullets)

Photo: Clearwater Battlefield site. NPS. *General Management Plan Nez Perce National Historical Park and Big Hole National Battlefield.* Department of the Interior. September 1997 (public domain).

Chapter Eight (Traders and Thieves)

Lean Elk (18?? - 1877) went by several monikers, including *Poker Joe*. Half French Canadian and half Nez Perce, his birth name was *Joe Hale*.

Chapter Nine (Agony and Anger)

James H. Bradley was born in Ohio in 1844. At the outbreak of the Civil War he joined a volunteer Ohio regiment and served primarily in the Western Theater. After his discharge at the end of the war, Bradley joined the Eighteenth U.S. Infantry Regiment as a second lieutenant. He was promoted to first lieutenant in July 1866, and was stationed in what is now Wyoming. While stationed at Fort Benton, Montana Territory, Bradley, inspired by his association with men who participated in the early fur trade, began the study of Montana and Northwestern history. Bradley served as a chronicler of military activities and of the history of the Indian tribes his regiment encountered. Bradley was assigned to Colonel John Gibbon's "Montana Column" in 1876. He participated in the events leading to the Battle of the Little Big Horn. Bradley served under Gibbon the following year in his pursuit of the Nez Perce Tribe. James H. Bradley was killed at the Battle of the Big Hole, on August 9, 1877.

Photo: James H. Bradley, 1st Lt. 7th U.S. Infantry [no date] Montana Historical Society. Photo Archives # 941-317.

Photo: Big Hole Battlefield. NPS (public domain).

The poem *Makawee* recites at the burial of *Lautiss* was written in 1910 by Charles Hallock (1834-1917).

Chapter Ten (Friend or Foe?)

John Oliver Gibbon was born on April 20, 1827. On graduating from West Point he received the commission of brevet second lieutenant. During the Civil War, he served the United States Army. He was injured at Fredericksburg and at Gettysburg during Pickett's Charge. In 1866, Colonel Gibbon was ordered west to take command of the post at Fort Kearny, Nebraska, beginning a career in the West that would last until his retirement. In 1876, his command rescued the survivors and buried the dead of George Armstrong Custer's 7th Cavalry after the Battle of the Little Big Horn. On the night of August 9, 1877, Colonel John Gibbon led a mixed command of soldiers and civilians against the Nez Perce Indians camped at the Big Hole River. This battle would actually be a tactical defeat for Gibbon's small force, but the losses inflicted on the Nez Perce had a profound effect on the final outcome of the events of 1877.

Charles Erskine Scott Wood was born on February 20, 1852 in Erie, Pennsylvania. He graduated from West Point in 1874 and served as aide-de-camp to General O.O. Howard. Wood was present at the surrender of Chief Joseph of the Nez Perce. He transcribed (and potentially embellished) Joseph's surrender speech, which ended with, "My heart is sick and sad. From where the sun now stands, I will fight no more forever." Scott and Wood became close friends. At the time of his death in 1944, Wood was West Point's oldest living graduate.

Chapter Eleven (Smoke from the Ground)

www.mtmemory.org/nodes/view/103817 Attribution 4.0 International (CC).

Image: Montananewspapers.com. 1877-08-18 (public domain).

Photo of *Excelsior Geyser* by F.J. Haynes, 1886. Rijksmuseum, CC0, via Wikimedia Commons (public domain).

The first reference to Yellowstone as "Wonderland" in print was in a series of articles in the *New North West* newspaper in 1871 and 1872. *A ride to the Infernal regions: Yellowstone's first Tourists.* Calvin C. Clawson. Lee Silliman, editor. Helena, MT: Riverbend Publishing, 2003. (Book Review by Tamsen Emerson Hert. *Yellowstone Science.* 2007.

Chapter Twelve (Hapless)

Philetus W. Norris (1821 – 1885) was the second superintendent of Yellowstone National Park and was the first person to be paid for that position. When the Civil War began, Norris joined the Union troops, eventually rising to the rank of Colonel. He served as a spy behind Confederate Lines and Captain of the West Virginia Mountain Scouts. While fighting near Laurel Mountain, West Virginia, Norris's horse was shot out from underneath him, severely injuring his shoulder and spinal cord. In 1870, Norris again traveled west, entering the Yellowstone Park area; he returned again in 1875. During this time, Norris wrote a series of articles on "The Great West" which were published in the Norris, Michigan Suburban. In 1877, Norris became the second superintendent of Yellowstone National Park, a position he held until 1882. In June 1878, however, that Congress finally approved a salary of $10,000 a year for the park's superintendent, as well as minimal funds "to protect, preserve, and improve the Park." Norris hired Harry Yount to control poaching and vandalism in the park, leading Yount to be considered the first National Park ranger. When Norris arrived there were approximately 32 miles of roads and 108 miles of trails. By the time he left in 1882, there were five times as many roads and twice as many trails. The roads were crude and many described them as only "fair" wagon trails. Still, they provided access to "the land of wonders."

Photo: *Philetus Walter Norris* Public domain, via Wikimedia Commons. Taken before 1885. Public domain.

Al Oldham and *Henry Meyers* were rescued by Howard's column thirty-six hours after the attack.

Charles Mann walked back to the Lower Basin camp, where army scouts found him the next day.

A.J. Arnold and *William Dingee* abandoned their horses and eventually reached the Gibbon River, where they were rescued.

George Cowan was left for dead. When he regained consciousness, he tried to stand upright, but was shot in the hip by another warrior. He remained still, then pulled himself along the ground by his elbows. He alternately crawled and rested. Over the next four days, he covered twelve miles. Reaching the camp site at Lower Geyser Basin, he found chunks of bacon and loose coffee beans. Howard's scouts rescued Cowan on August 29 near the mouth of the East Fork of the Firehole River. They gave him the good news that his wife and sister-in-law had been released unharmed.

Photo: George Cowan, lawyer of Radersburg and Boulder, MT, and husband of Emma J. Cowan. Taken at City Photograph Gallery in Helena, Montana, by Edgar H. Train, between 1868-1876. Montana Historical Society Photo Archives # 941-613.

Chapter Thirteen (Nemesis)

Painting: *Tower Fall* by Thomas Moran. Watercolor, 1872. 02.1457. 1872. Tulsa: Gilcrease Museum, https://collections.gilcrease.org/object/021457 (03/21/2019).

Richard Dietrich was born in Breslau, Prussia. Dietrich immigrated to Helena, Montana in the 1870's. He was the organist and choir master for St. Peter's Protestant Episcopal Church. He led the Gesang Verein Harmonia choir and the Helena Silver Cornet Band. [Photo of Richard Dietrich: Likely taken at Bundy and Train studio in Helena, Montana between 1876 and 1877.

Photo: *Richard Dietrich*. Montana Historical Society. Photo Archives # 941-952.

Camptown Races (1850) and *Oh! Susanna* (1848) by Stephen Collins Foster.

Amazing Grace. Lyrics 1772. Published 1779. By English Anglican clergyman and poet John Newton.

Photo: *Lt. Gustavus C. Doane.* Unknown photographer. 1875. (public domain).

Chapter Fourteen (Burning Bridges)

Jack Baronett emigrated from Scotland and served as a scout for the Confederacy during the Civil War. He ventured to the Montana Territory in 1864 seeking his fortune in gold. When the precious yellow mineral was discovered near Cooke City, Baronett recognized the popularity of the route through northern Wyoming for prospectors coming from points west. He constructed the bridge in the spring of 1871 and charged travelers a toll.

Photo: Baronett's Bridge by William Henry Jackson, 1871. NPS.

Letter from W.T. Sherman to O.O. Howard courtesy of the George J. Mitchell Department of Special Collections & Archives, Bowdoin College Library, Brunswick, Maine. (edited for clarity).

Chapter Sixteen (Canyon Creek)

Samuel D. Sturgis (1822 – 1889) was breveted brigadier general and major general, Regular Army, in March 1865 and mustered out of the volunteer service in August. He reverted to his regular rank of lieutenant colonel of the 6th U.S. Cavalry. On May 6, 1869, he became colonel and commander of the 7th U.S. Cavalry and his lieutenant colonel was George Armstrong Custer. Sturgis was on detached duty as the Superintendent of Mounted Recruiting Service and in command of the Cavalry Depot in St. Louis, Missouri, when parts of the 7th Cavalry were destroyed at the Battle of Little Big Horn (one of Sturgis's sons, Second Lieutenant James G. Sturgis, was also an officer with the 7th and was killed in that battle.) Samuel Sturgis then took personal command of the regiment and led the 7th Cavalry in the campaign against the Nez Percé in 1877. Sturgis and his soldiers headed off the Nez Percé and waited to attack them once they emerged from their passage through the wilderness of Yellowstone Park. The Indians deceived Sturgis with a feint and eluded him, continuing their flight northward toward Canada. Sturgis soon caught up with the Nez Percé but at the Battle of Canyon Creek, the Indians, although outnumbered two to one, again escaped from his grasp.

Nelson Appleton Miles (1839 – 1925) entered the Civil War as a lieutenant of volunteers, without having attended West Point. He was involved in almost every major battle of the Civil War and was awarded the Congressional Medal of Honor. During the Indian Wars he commanded the Fifth U.S. Infantry regiment and took part in nearly all the major campaigns the army waged against the Plains Indians. He defeated the Kiowa, Comanche, and Southern Cheyenne in the Red River War (1874-1875), intercepted Chief Joseph and the Nez Percé (1877), and captured Geronimo (1886). In the 1890s he put down the Pullman Strikes and served in Cuba and Puerto Rico during the Spanish American War. He reached the rank of lieutenant general in 1900 becoming the last commanding general in the U.S. Army, the position being changed to the army chief of staff upon his retirement in 1903. He died May 25, 1925.

Photo: *Nelson Miles* by Stanley J. Morrow Studios. Yankton, Dakota Territories. circa 1875 – 1880 (public domain).

In the fall of 1876, Colonel Nelson A. Miles and his Fifth Infantry established *Cantonment on Tongue River* (later renamed Fort Keogh) from which he operated throughout the winter of 1876–77 against any hostiles he could find. In January 1877, he fought Crazy Horse and many other bands at the Battle of Wolf Mountain. In the months that followed, his troops fought the Lakota at Clear Creek, Spring Creek and Ash Creek. Miles' continuous campaigning pushed a number of the Northern Cheyenne and Lakota to either surrender or slip across the border into Canada.

Major Lewis Merrill (1834 – 1896) Fought in the Civil War and the Indian Wars. In 1851, he entered the US Military Academy. Appointed Captain, 1st Cavalry, on 3 Aug 1861. Promoted to Colonel, 2nd US Missouri Volunteer Cavalry, and fought in numerous battles in northern Missouri, Arkansas, and Georgia. Brevetted to Brigadier General, on 13 March 1865 for service. Mustered out on 14 Dec 1865, he reverted to his regular army rank of Captain. Promoted to Major, 7th US Cavalry, 1868. In South Carolina from March 1871 to June

1873, suppressing Ku Klux Klan activities. At Shreveport, LA, from late 1874 to 1876, when he was detailed to Chief of the Military Staff to the President, for the 1876 Centennial celebrations, thus missing the Battle of the Little Big Horn in which most of his regiment was killed. On frontier duty at Fort Abraham Lincoln in May 1877, when he commanded a battalion of the 7th US Cavalry departing for the Nez Perce campaign. Engaged in the Canyon Creek fight.

Stanton G. Fisher (1840 - 1915) was a civilian scout for the United States Army during the Nez Perce War of 1877. Fisher was known as Howard's chief scout. He organized and led a company of civilian scouts across Idaho and Montana in pursuit of the Nez Perce. The US Army relied heavily upon him and his men to track down the Nez Perce as they fled violence and were forced to leave their ancestral homeland. Fisher, while a post trader for the Bannacks operating out of Fort Hall, Idaho became well acquainted with the Bannacks and spoke their tongue fluently. His knowledge of both the Bannacks and Nez Perce and the region made him an obvious choice for Howard as a chief scout.

Frederick Benteen (1834 – 1898) was a military officer who first fought during the American Civil War. He was appointed to commanding ranks during the Indian Campaigns and Great Sioux War against the Lakota and Northern Cheyenne. Benteen is best known for being in command of a battalion (Companies D, H,& K) of the 7th U. S. Cavalry at the Battle of the Little Bighorn in late June, 1876. Benteen participated in the Nez Perce campaign in 1877. He was brevetted brigadier general on February 27, 1890, for his actions in that campaign at the Battle of Canyon Creek, as well as for his earlier actions at the Little Bighorn.

Chapter Seventeen (Bonanza)

Lieutenant Frank D. Baldwin (1842 – 1923) is one of only 19 servicemen to receive the Medal of Honor twice. Baldwin received his first award for his actions during the Atlanta Campaign where he led his company in battle at Peachtree Creek and captured two commissioned officers in the American Civil War. He received his second for conspicuous bravery in 1874 during the Indian Wars. He served under General Nelson A. Miles as chief of scouts during campaigns against Sitting Bull and Crazy Horse. Baldwin holds the distinction of being a recipient of the Medal of Honor in different conflicts.

He also fought in the Philippines during the Spanish–American War and rose to the rank of major general before retiring.

Chapter Eighteen (Edge of Freedom)

Photo: Bears Paw Battlefield. NPS (public domain).

Chapter Nineteen (Fight No More Forever)

The bible verse is Matthew 6:34. (King James version).

Chief Joseph's surrender speech is taken from *Harper's Weekly,* November 17, 1877. It has been slightly edited. At least four other versions were published.

The Nez Perce were never returned to Lapwai, as promised. Instead, the army sent them to a reservation in Indian Territory (present day Oklahoma). Many of the people died from sickness, including Joseph's infant daughter born at the start of the war. In 1885, Chief Joseph and some of his followers were allowed to return to the Colville Reservation in North Central Washington, 150 miles from the Wallowa Valley. He died on September 21, 1904, in Nespelem, Washington. Numerous landmarks and features bear his name: Chief Joseph Dam on the Columbia River, Chief Joseph Pass in Montana, Chief Joseph Scenic Byway in Wyoming, as well as Joseph Creek, Joseph Canyon and the town of Joseph, Oregon, in the Wallowa Valley.

Chapter Twenty (Medicine Line)

In 1818, Canada and the United States agreed that from Lake of the Woods to the Pacific Ocean the border between the two countries would be drawn along the 49th parallel. On June 15, 1846, the United States and Great Britain signed the Oregon Treaty, which made the 49th parallel the boundary between the United States and British North America (it would not become known as "Canada" until 1867 -- and British Columbia would not join the new country until 1871) from Point Roberts east to the crest of the Rocky Mountains in what is today northwestern Montana. In 1872, the British and American governments appointed the North American Boundary Commission to survey and mark the boundary. The teams identified the stations by cutting a path through the forest (where necessary) 40 feet wide along the border, 20 feet on either side. Where possible iron posts were set in the ground to mark the exact point of the border, and depending on the condition of the ground, the posts were placed anywhere from a few hundred feet to two miles apart. In some places the posts were covered with pyramid-shaped earth or stone cairns, six to eight feet high, to mark the border. The Canada–United States border is the longest international border in the world.

Photo: "No. 154 Boundary Marker - Pyramid Creek" [1872-1876] Archives of Manitoba. Manitoba.ca

James Morrow Walsh (1840 – 1905) was appointed a Superintendent of the North-West Mounted Police in 1873. He recruited, trained and led part of the new police force and held commands at Fort Walsh, which he founded in 1875, and later at Qu'Appelle. Until his resignation in 1883, he vigorously enforced the law in the North West and is best known for his part in persuading Sitting Bull and his Sioux to return to the United States. In 1897 he was appointed Commissioner of the Yukon Provisional District, a post he held until his retirement in September 1898. Photo courtesy of *Galt Museum. North-West Mounted Police – A Tradition in Scarlett.*

Sitting Bull (ca. 1837 – 1890) was a Hunkpapa Lakota leader who led his people during years of resistance against United States government policies. Before the Battle of the Little Bighorn, Sitting Bull had a vision in which he saw many soldiers, "as thick as grasshoppers", falling upside down into the Lakota camp, which his people took as a foreshadowing of a major victory in which many soldiers would be killed. About three weeks later, the confederated Lakota tribes with the Northern Cheyenne defeated the 7th Cavalry under Lt. Col. George Armstrong Custer on June 25, 1876, annihilating Custer's battalion and seeming to fulfill Sitting Bull's prophetic vision. Sitting Bull's leadership inspired his people to a major victory. In response, the U.S. government sent thousands more soldiers to the area, forcing many of the Lakota to surrender over the next year. Sitting Bull refused to surrender, and in May 1877, he led his band north to Wood Mountain, North-West Territories.
Sitting Bull and his people stayed in Canada for four years. Due to the smaller size of the buffalo herds in Canada, Sitting Bull and his men found it difficult to find enough food to feed their starving people. Sitting Bull's presence in the country led to increased tensions between the Canadian and the United

States governments. Hunger and desperation eventually forced Sitting Bull and several hundred of his family and followers to return to the United States and surrender on July 19, 1881. When authorities feared he would join the Ghost Dance movement, he was killed by Indian agency police on December 15, 1890 at the Standing Rock Indian Reservation during an attempt to arrest him.

Photo of *Sitting Bull* by David Francis Barry, Public domain, via Wikimedia Commons.

Chapter Twenty-One (Honor and Heartache)

White Bull (1849 – 1947) was born in the Black Hills in South Dakota. As a boy he was known as Bull-Standing-with-Cow. His father and grandfather before him were chiefs of the Minneconjou Lakota, and his mother, Good Feather, was Sitting Bull's sister. Some historians say White Bull killed Lt. Col. George Armstrong Custer at the Little Bighorn. Others close to White Bull claim he never took credit for shooting Custer, but admitted to struggling with the leader of the Seventh Cavalry. After the battle, White Bull joined his uncle, Hunkpapa Sioux leader Sitting Bull, in fleeing to Canada.

He eventually returned to Cheyenne River Agency along the Missouri River in present day South Dakota and became a chief, replacing his father Chief Makes Room upon his death. He acted as a judge of the Court of Indian Offenses, and was a proponent of Lakota land claims in the Black Hills.

In 1932, White Bull narrated his story as a warrior in his youth to historian Stanley Vestal. It is among the most complete accounts of a northern Plains Indian warrior's life.

Chapter Twenty-Two (Homecoming)

Pompeys Pillar is a sandstone butte that overlooks the Yellowstone River about 25 miles east of Billings, Montana. The pillar itself stands 150 feet above the Yellowstone River. The base of the pillar is approximately 1 acre. It features an abundance of Native American petroglyphs, as well as the signature of William Clark, co-leader of the Lewis and Clark Expedition. Clark's inscription, made on July 25, 1806, is the only remaining physical evidence found along the route that was followed by the expedition. Clark wrote he climbed the sandstone pillar and "had a most extensive view in every direction on the Northerly Side of the river". He named the outcropping after Jean Baptiste Charbonneau—the son of expedition member Sacagawea—whom he nicknamed "Pompey". His original name for it was "Pompey's Tower"; it was changed to the current title in 1814.

Signature of William Clark on 1806-07-25 at Pompeys Pillar National Monument, Montana. Bureau of Land Management. Public domain via Wikimedia Commons.

Chapter Twenty-Three (Guide My Path)

Poster of Buffalo Bill's Wild West Show. Originally produced by Calhoun Printing Company, Hartford, CT. ca. 1885. Circus World Museum.